ELUSIVE TREASURE

A STEELE OPS NOVEL

BOOK FIVE

ERIN MOIRA O'HARA

O'HARA PUBLISHING

ALSO BY ERIN MOIRA O'HARA

STEEL OPS SERIES

The Kalista Diamond

Precious Gems

Jewel of the Kimberley

The Amethyst Code

Elusive Treasure

Steele Justice - coming soon

BINDARRA CREEK

Tempting Fate

Date with Destiny

A Twist of Fate

Protecting their Destiny

Mistletoe Magic

SANTINI/DEROSA FAMILY

Conspiracy in Emilia Romagna

DEADLY FORCES

Beat of the Jungle

FANTASY

The Knight of Castle Kildare

Romance Intrigue Suspense

Erin Moira O'Hara

DEDICATION

To my wicked sisters. Maureen, Louise & Michelle. You wanted to come on a fact finding mission with me to Magnetic Island. Research, interviews, cocktails and riding horses in the ocean. A trip we all remember fondly.

PROLOGUE

Twelve years ago - Currawong Island, East of Australia's Great Barrier Reef

"I dare you to go first." Ryan grinned at his best friend.

Zane lifted his chin. "No way. We'll do it together. Like always."

"You idiots," yelled Tommy. "Don't expect me to tell your parents you're splattered at the bottom of Morcago Ledge. You can tell them yourselves."

Ryan and Zane fell into each other laughing.

"How? As ghosts?" spluttered Zane.

"Ignore them, Tommy." Cammy rolled her eyes at Ryan and Zane. "If you get caught by the elders, you'll be in *so* much trouble. Morcago Ledge is off limits."

"Which is why no one has found the treasure." Ryan frowned at her. Camilla used to be up for anything, but lately she put a downer on anything exciting. All she wanted to do was hold hands and make out.

"Yeah," called Zane. "That's why we joined Townsville's abseiling club. We've been training all year for this. Go home, Cammy, and if Tommy's too *chicken* to be our watcher, he can go with you."

"We're not supposed to be here." Tommy crossed his arms and glared at Zane.

"If you weren't in love with *Ryan's* girlfriend, you wouldn't act like a turd." Zane threw a disgusted look at Ryan. "Why does she have to tag along? Tommy's useless with her around."

Camilla huffed. "I have as much right to be here as you, Zane."

"You're an annoying girl."

"Well get used to it, because in four years, when I'm nineteen, me and Ryan are getting married and leaving this stupid place."

"No, we're not." Ryan shuddered. "That's too young to get married, and I'm never leaving this island. When we find the treasure, I'll build my own house, then me and the boys will go fishing and scuba diving whenever we want."

"No way." Camilla pushed out her lower lip. "We're moving to the Gold Coast. I want to live in one of them fancy penthouses at Surfer's Paradise. I'm going to open a classy café on the boardwalk and call it Camilla's."

"Forget it." Horror filled Ryan. "I'm not living in a skyscraper. I plan to die on this island."

"Same here," called Zane.

Camilla heaved a heavy sigh. "What ya gonna live off, Ryan? Air?"

"Course not." He looked out over the island's hinterland, his gaze skimming the native bushland between them and Kingfisher lookout. Turning slowly, his gaze swept over Rocky Point and Palm Beach, then the treacherous reefs to the south-east of the island. Finally, Ryan dropped his gaze to Shark Bite Bay and the boulders below Morcago Ledge.

"We're gonna find pirate treasure then buy a sea plane to transport rich tourists to Curra. We'll even have a huge catamaran to take them out whale-watching."

"In your dreams, Ryan. You've been searching for treasure every holiday since you were twelve years old. Time to think about the future. I'm gonna run a café, *on the Gold Coast.*"

"She's right. We need proper jobs." Tommy grinned at Camilla. "I'll train as a waiter, so I can work in your café."

Zane gave Ryan a what-the-hell look, before scowling at Tommy. "Do whatever yanks your chain, Tommy. Me and Ryan will work on

Barnacle Bill's fishing boat till we find the treasure. Then you'll be sorry."

Camilla threw up her hands. "There's *no* treasure, Zane. If there was, the elders would know about it."

"Our great-grandfather knew," insisted Zane. "Me and Tommy heard stories years ago round a campfire. You're a girl. Elders don't talk about important things around girls."

"That's not true." Camilla crossed her arms and glared at Zane. "I know things."

"I wish they'd told *me*," grumbled Ryan. "I don't understand why I can't be part of the storytelling."

"Just the way it is." Zane grinned. "We're the descendants of the traditional custodians of the island, so we get to hear all the stories."

Ryan sighed. "You belong here in a way I can only dream of. My ancestors arrived on Currawong Island in 1870. It's not quite the same, is it?"

"I tell you stuff," called Zane as he peered over Morcago Ledge. "I told you about the cave drawings, didn't I?"

Camilla huffed her impatience. "If there were drawings, the elders woulda found them years ago. You won't find them by jumping off Morcago Ledge. It's a sheer cliff."

"We're looking for a secret cave, Cammy," soothed Ryan. It wouldn't do to have her walk off in a temper and dob on them. "We've crisscrossed the whole island. All that's left is Morcago rockface. There's a hidden entrance."

"You've already scrambled over the boulders below and found nothing. Give it up already."

Zane scowled at Ryan. "This is why I didn't want her along."

"Leave off, Zane." Tommy called. He put his arm around Camilla's shoulders. "Cammy, last night us guys were hanging out on Heron Peak. We saw hundreds of bats fly out of Morcago's cliff face. There's an opening we couldn't see from below or in the daylight. Ryan reckons it might lead down to a cave and the pirate's stash."

She huffed. "No pirates scaled this cliff with heavy chests of treasure."

"No, but four hundred years ago, there might have been a cave at its base and the entrance was blocked by all those boulders. If we find a treasure, you can open your café."

"That's true."

Ryan met Zane's gaze and gave his head a slight shake to keep quiet. He glanced across at Camilla as Tommy whispered in her ear, making her giggle. Their flirty friendship grated on Ryan. Camilla was *his* girlfriend. Lately she'd been pushing to take their relationship to the next level, which both excited and scared him. If they got caught, there'd be hell to pay. Discovering she wanted to get married so young and leave the island added to his dilemma. It was hard enough attending school on the mainland. No way could he live on the Gold Coast. It would kill his spirit.

Camilla giggled again. "No, I haven't told Ryan, and anyway she's wrong."

"Told me what?"

She shrugged. "Aunty Frankie reckons you're the only one who will leave Curra. It's all crap. I'm going with you, and I don't care if we never come back."

"I told you I'm not leaving." Ryan shrugged off the shiver that ran down his spine. Francine Ellis' predictions always came true. He looked from Camilla to Zane. "I know your grandmother is a respected elder, and I'm privileged to call her aunty, but she's way off this time."

Zane huffed. "She must mean you leave to get your pilot's license. That'll be it."

Ryan sure hoped so. He drew a deep breath. "I've double-checked everything. The ropes and carabiners are brand new, and these trees are solid. We gonna do this or what?"

"You bet." Zane strapped on his helmet then pulled on his gloves. "If we don't find the cave this way, we'll borrow some scuba gear from Barnacle Bill and search Shark Bite Bay."

"Shark Bite Bay?" A chill ran through Ryan as he checked his Prusik loop. There were good reasons this bay was off limits to swimmers and divers. The name said it all, but he wouldn't admit his fear in front of Camilla, or his mates. He was their leader after all. "First things first. On the count of three. One … two … three."

They both edged over the lip, balancing their boots carefully as they leaned back, well apart. "Don't look down," called Zane, his voice wobbling.

Holding his breath, Ryan scraped his right foot down several inches. More afraid than he was willing to admit, his heart pounded as he met Camilla's terrified eyes. She was clutching Tommy's arm, and he was loving it.

Ryan and Zane slowly lowered themselves down the cliff face to the midway point, searching for an entrance. Ryan's arms ached from the strain.

"Where is it," called Zane. "I'm positive this is the area."

Ryan looked up to see Camilla high above, still watching. "We must have missed it," he shouted. "Let's swing over further my way and go back up." His muscles were beginning to cramp. This was nothing like climbing an indoor rock wall or the tame outdoor stuff they'd tackled before. It was scary as hell, heart-stopping and hot. The jagged rocks below glistened in the sun as the outgoing wash retreated. Ascending was harder than descending. His arms were on fire.

They'd climbed a few more feet when Zane yelled, "There! What's that?"

"A crevice." Ryan scrambled closer, placing the tips of his boots on a thin ledge so he could pull himself into the cliff face and examine a vertical gap. "Wait up." He stuck his arm through the foot-wide gap, almost as tall as his shoulder. "I think we can squeeze through."

"Ryan's found something." Zane yelled. "We're going to check it out."

It took a bit of maneuvering, but eventually Ryan wriggled in far enough to unhook his safety gear then he squeezed through the gap sideways. It was a tight fit. Sharp rocks scraped his helmet and chest.

"What's that foul smell?" He flicked on his flashlight then screamed as hundreds of flapping wings beat above his head. He dropped to the ground curling into a ball. "Bats."

Once the fluttering stopped, Ryan glanced at the entrance, where the vertical gap gave him a view of ocean and a slice of Australia's coastline in the far distance. No wonder no one had discovered the cave. He was probably the first human to enter this way.

Zane shuffled closer on his hands and knees. "Raise your beam slowly so we don't set the bats off again."

"Wow." Ryan stared at a wall of primitive drawings. A ship with sails, lying sideways in the water. Stick figures standing on rocks and a what looked to be a whale breaching the water.

"Look!" Zane crawled forward then pointed.

Mouth wide open, Ryan stared at more stick figures standing at the foot of a cliff in front of a cave. "We've found the drawings."

"Yeah." Zane laughed. "Now we gotta keep it a secret till we find the treasure."

Lowering his flashlight, Ryan hunched and crept closer to the drawings. "There *was* a cave at the bottom of the cliff and a small beach."

"You were right. A massive rock fall covered everything."

"Come on." Ryan shuffled to the back of the cave. "I see a tunnel. I bet that's how your ancestors got up here to paint those pictures."

His beam found three foreign words, roughly scrawled across the rock face. "*Cueva de los Murciélagos.* What do you think it means?"

Zane scuffled closer. "*Murciélagos* is sort of like Morcago."

"Yeah." Ryan's beam picked up a small round disc a foot into the tunnel. "What's that?" He picked it up and rubbed it against his shirt. "Far out, Zane. It's a gold sovereign, just like the one Barnacle Bill gave me four years ago. This has to mean the treasure is here."

"I can't believe it." Zane's voice cracked. "We'll leave our gear up top and come back tomorrow without Tommy and Camilla."

Ryan groaned. "We should tell Tommy and swear him to secrecy."

"It's time you got your head out of your ass. Those two are like this." Zane crossed his fingers. "Let's meet at the foot of Morcago trail at ten o'clock."

"Done." Ryan punched the air. "Whoopee, I'm *never* leaving this island."

CHAPTER ONE

Ryan adjusted his bowtie. The damn thing kept twisting and poking into his neck. As for his close-fitting Armani suit … if something went down tonight, he'd likely rip the seams, which meant he'd have to buy the bloody thing. At least it kept him warmer than the designer-clad women on this cool May evening.

As far as fundraisers went, this one had drawn the cream of Australia's wealthiest movers and shakers, media moguls, celebrities, politicians, and bejeweled socialites. The bank of French doors on the north side had been flung open to reveal the shimmering lights reflected in Sydney Harbour.

Avoiding a determined-looking socialite, he strolled among the items for auction. Gold-plated watches, a jewel-encrusted tiara, over-the-top diamond necklaces, dazzling sapphire, ruby, diamond, and emerald rings — all displayed under locked, glass domes.

He raised an eyebrow at the more impressive items. A penthouse on Sydney Harbour, a luxurious holiday for two through Europe, and a racehorse. What couldn't be carried into the ballroom had been showcased in glossy posters on easels. Millions of dollars in prizes. He almost ran his fingers over the red Ferrari that took center stage. Now *that* was nice.

An orchestra played jazz music from the other end of the ballroom, hidden by glamorous couples dancing under twinkling chandeliers. Sculptured urns stuffed with long-stemmed red roses edged the walls, tall and stately in pewter. Colorful bouquets decorated the center of the dinner tables set out around the room. The flowers alone would pay the average person's mortgage for a number of years, but then the average person couldn't afford two thousand dollars to sit at one of the round tables.

Ryan chuckled. There was so much cutlery, he wouldn't know what to use when.

His gaze settled on Jarred Steele. The Colonel had relaxed somewhat since leaving the SAS to run his grandfather's security firm. With the addition of a Special Ops branch, Jarred hadn't needed to expend much effort to persuade Ryan and the boys to leave their elite SAS unit. Working for Steele Security had been a good decision.

So much had changed over the last seven months, especially for his team. They'd each been hit by Cupid's arrow and were now in happy relationships.

Ryan's lips twitched. Jarred spoke to a woman in red, her hair caught up in a fancy tumble of auburn curls. If his body language was anything to go by, the Colonel was enjoying her company. He looked comfortable in his surroundings, and why not? He'd been raised in a wealthy family. A family who trusted and looked up to him with pride. Ryan had never had that from anyone except his sister, and great-uncle in recent years.

Pushing away unpleasant memories, his gaze shifted to Sam, Talos and Nick who chatted together near a potted palm, looking as bored as he felt.

For the last hour, they'd been stone-walling glamorous guests whose flashy engagement rings and wedding bands didn't appear to mean much. No way would the boys be tempted away from their own lady waiting for them at home. As for Simon — manning the cameras in their high-tech surveillance van, and the latest victim to fall under Cupid's sharp arrow — he could barely keep his mind on the job.

In Ryan's case, he was still waiting for that one special woman, and he wouldn't find her here. He'd turned down a chatty actress who'd desired a discreet rendezvous in her suite upstairs. Not happening. One … he took his job seriously. Two … a quick fuck didn't do it for him anymore. He wanted someone he could talk to, someone down-to-earth and easy to get along with, someone who would stand by him as he would stand by her.

He let his gaze wander the room, amused to find the woman in red now chatting to Sam and Nick. Surprisingly, they appeared relaxed too. She stretched up to whisper in Nick's ear. Whatever she said made him laugh.

Ryan couldn't see her face, but there was something familiar about her.

"Oh, happy days. Madeline Shaw has arrived." The dry comment came through Ryan's earpiece, drawing his attention back to Jarred. The colonel's gaze was riveted on a stunning blonde who had a habit of sticking her nose in where it wasn't wanted. She was also under their protection tonight, which meant mics on and time to be extra vigilant.

The investigative journalist looked a million dollars in a fitted dark-blue sheath of silky fabric caught up on one shoulder. Matching gems sparkled from her earlobes. She stood with a classy older couple. The man had an arrogant bearing and appeared to be looking down his nose at Madeline. The woman's bone structure and posture resembled Madeline too much to be anyone but her mother. Unfortunately, her scowl — also directed at Madeline — marred her elegant beauty.

Ryan's breath caught as the woman in red turned to wave at Madeline. Recognition hit with a rapid punch to his gut. "What the devil is Safiya doing here?"

"Madeline invited her." Jarred didn't sound amused. "Keep your distance, Ryan. She's here with her brother and parents."

"Great, if I so much as look her way, I can expect the Sheikh to use his jeweled dagger to cut off my balls."

"You're kidding?" Simon's shock summoned a round of chuckles.

"I might have embellished a little, but Senior Inspector Gibbs has made it clear. He and his father don't want me anywhere near Safiya."

"That's what you get for flirting with the Sheikh's daughter at my wedding." Nick's taunt wouldn't normally bother Ryan. Tonight, it chafed.

"What's the difference between a millionaire and a billionaire?" Simon didn't wait for an answer. "The size of their yachts. Sheikh Farid has a luxurious super yacht with its own helipad, swimming pool and open-air cinema. Think he'd lend it to us for a weekend?"

"In your dreams, mate." Ryan chuckled. "At least Safiya's mother likes me."

"Don't bet on it," came Sam's amused voice. "She's been in the diplomatic service for years. Protect your assets and give the lady a wide berth. I hear the Sheikh has taken on six ex-special force soldiers as crew. Five Seals and a Night Stalker."

"Where'd you hear that," asked Jarred. "It's supposed to be top secret."

"Gibbs mentioned it. The Sheikh intends to surprise his wife and daughter by taking them on a world cruise." Sam chuckled. "The Sheikh's not the only one who might gut you, Ryan."

"Funny man." It hadn't occurred to Ryan that Safiya might attend this event. An invisible band tightened around his chest. How was a man to focus on the job with the flirty, dark-eyed beauty in the same room?

Her gaze skimmed the crowd, halting abruptly when she recognized him. A provocative smile played across her lush lips. Only a blind man would be immune to her beauty. Her wealth was obvious in the diamonds adorning her neck and earlobes. The ruby red, ankle-length dress screamed designer label. Yep, way out of his league.

"Ryan, your scowl's worse than the Colonel's," mused Sam. "You'll scare the socialites."

Dragging his attention from the sultry woman, Ryan shifted his attention to his boss. Jarred did indeed wear a heavy scowl as he cut a direct line through the crowd toward Madeline Shaw. She was the only person in the world who could provoke Jarred into losing his rigid control, as their last three missions attested.

"Without her husband?" Ryan did a quick perusal of the huge ball-room, spotting Elliott Shaw at the bar. "Amazing … Shaw *is* here."

"A miracle." Nick's sarcasm came through loud and clear. "Fifty bucks says he leaves early. Without Madeline. Do I have any takers?"

Sam laughed. "No way, mate. Since that mission in Vietnam, where he as good as dropped her in our lap to protect, he's barely spent five minutes with her. He'll never get husband of the year, that's for sure. Say hello to Madeline for us, Colonel."

Jarred shook his head. "There's a lot of things I'd like to say to Madeline Shaw. *Hello* isn't one of them."

Ryan's gaze shifted back to Safiya, only to find her gliding toward him, the red dress swishing about her legs. He cleared his throat. "Good evening, Safiya-Ameerah. I didn't expect to see you here."

"Hello, Ryan. Madeline told me Steele Security were safeguarding the prizes tonight. It's nice to see you again."

"I noticed your brother is here."

Safiya rolled her eyes. "Zac insisted on chaperoning me, then my parents flew in and decided to attend." She pointed at a stylish blonde woman on the arm of a distinguished olive-skinned man. Sheikh Tariq Zakour Farid. An extremely private man who watched over his daughter like an eagle, now that the world knew of her existence.

Safiya beamed. "Would you like to dance?"

"I'm working, Safiya, and your brother is on his way over here to threaten my manhood."

"I didn't take you for a scaredy-cat." Her eyelids lowered. "After what we did at Nick's wedding, I thought you'd enjoy repeating the experience."

Jarred's gaze swiveled Ryan's way, as did Nick's and Sam's. Talos was out of sight, yet his distinct baritone came through the earpiece. "Who's been a naughty boy?"

"Dancing barefoot in the moonlight, while drunk isn't a good idea tonight," he said aloud for the boys' benefit.

"We were tipsy and didn't just dance. We also sat by the harbor and talked for hours. Are you saying you don't remember our conversation?"

"I remember, but as I said, I'm working tonight." He checked the crowd; surprised Zachary Gibbs hadn't descended on them. He found him deep in conversation with Elliott Shaw. The two men had been friends from school according to Simon's research.

As if sensing his regard, Gibbs' focus locked onto Ryan. The message clear from the scowl on his face and the intent glare in his dark eyes. *Move away from my sister.*

Safiya stepped closer, her delicate fragrance wafting about Ryan like a cloud of seductive poison, casting a spell over every sense he possessed, blocking out everything else. Her long hair had been twisted up in a sophisticated-looking knot with a thick ringlet of auburn curls falling around her neck. She gave him a tentative smile. "This type of event isn't my thing. I'm not into rubbing noses with the rich and famous."

"Really?" He found that hard to believe.

"It's true. I don't fit in. Never have. Any chance you can get a week off work?"

"Why?"

She stepped closer, stretching up as if to whisper in his ear. Instead, she nipped his earlobe. "We could run away to that island of yours … get to know each other."

If she only knew. Ignoring his flare of lust and the chuckles in his ear, Ryan stepped back. "Safiya-Ameerah, I'm not running away anywhere with you. I'm working."

She sighed. "Fine, I'll let you *work* if you dance with me later?"

More chuckles sounded in his ear as he sensed a presence behind him.

"Miss Farid." A solid, dark-eyed man moved Ryan aside with a nudge to the shoulder. "A few minutes in private, if you please."

"Jamal." Safiya's chin rose. "It would not please my father if I were to be alone with you. He is over there should you wish to speak to him." Safiya pointed across the room before ducking around the man to latch onto Ryan's arm.

"Why are you alone with this man then?" Jamal's arrogant gaze could have stripped shreds off Ryan's rented suit.

"Mr. Dutch is on our security detail tonight and he was just about to escort me outside for some fresh air."

Jamal glared at Ryan. "I am Jamal Al-Saad. I am a guest at Sheik Farid's table this evening. I will escort Miss Farid outside."

"I beg your pardon?" Sparks ignited in Safiya's eyes.

Ryan stilled her with a hand at her waist. "Ryan Dutch." He held out his right hand.

Jamal ignored it. "Come, Safiya. You need to learn your place."

Ryan stepped forward to shield Safiya from the man's hand seeking her arm. "I am responsible for Miss Farid's safety tonight. Rest assured, she will be returned her father's table unharmed." With a hard look, he dared the man to make a scene.

Jamal looked around the room. They'd attracted attention. "Once we are married, Safiya, you will do as I say." He gave a curt nod and stepped back. His stance suggested he wasn't done yet.

Stunned, Ryan steered Safiya away from Jamal. Surely, she had more brains than to marry a domineering jerk like that. Did she realize what her life would be like? She'd have no rights. No say in anything. Her life wouldn't be her own. Her bright, outgoing personality would be crushed.

Ryan looked at her. "You're engaged?"

Fury sparked in her honey-brown eyes. Her fingernails bit into his arm. "No. I am not."

"Care to explain what that was about then?"

"Jamal approached my father with a marriage proposal, and now he thinks it's a *fait accompli*. It isn't. We haven't even been on a date. Not that we ever will. The man is a pompous social climber after a rich wife with connections."

Ryan glared over his shoulder at Jamal. "He's got to be close to forty."

"Thirty-eight and a widower with three sons. He assures me he has no need of more children. I, of course, wouldn't have a say in the matter." She screwed up her nose. "Can you imagine what my life would be like married to that moron?"

Yes, he could. "What about what you want?" Ryan waved her through a French door onto the cobbled courtyard.

"Ooh, now there's a novel idea." She laughed, the soft tinkle stirring something deep inside Ryan. "My parents would prefer me to marry a sensible man with strong family values and a head for business. Someone mature." She huffed. "Jamal thinks he's the perfect candidate."

"Do you want to marry?" He didn't even understand why he was asking. It wasn't like he could afford to keep her in the lifestyle she was accustomed to living. Or wanted to.

"Yes, but first I need to fall in love with a man who appreciates and adores me." She gave a deep sigh. "I want children to cuddle and mother. I want a house with a big enough garden for a dog and cubby house. I don't think it's too much to ask."

He frowned. It sounded fine to Ryan, yet he doubted his idea of the perfect house and garden wouldn't be anything like hers. He glanced back into the ballroom to check Gibb's position. Still talking to Shaw. A rather serious conversation by the looks of things.

Safiya wandered over to the fountain and traipsed her fingers through the water. "My father is being overwhelmed with marriage proposals for me. Not because the men love me, or want to get to know me, but because I'm a desirable asset. It's offensive. There is so much more to me than being the daughter of a rich sheikh. Why can't anyone *see* me? And another thing ... nobody is going to stop me dancing in the moonlight."

He followed, stopping beside her. "You are incredibly good at dancing barefoot in the moonlight. Just saying."

"You are too. Just saying." She gently nudged his shoulder. "I am working on my future, but it means vanishing for a while. I could use your help."

What the hell? He should march her over to her brother, leave her there and be done with it. Years of training kept all expression off Ryan's face. This was out of his field.

"Fuck." Nick's oath almost made Ryan smile. "Get rid of her, mate."

"No!" Jarred's sharp command came as a surprise. "Discover her plan, then we inform Gibbs."

There was no way she could hear what was being said, but she was smart enough to realize he'd be on comms and his team just heard her request. He met the flare of anger in Safiya's eyes. Excellent. Great way to piss off the beautiful woman who wanted to know him a whole lot better. Their barefoot dance in the moonlight had been an impulsive thing, which he'd enjoyed more than he'd admit, but Safiya-Ameerah was impulsive, and too damn sexy for his ongoing health.

Her gaze swept over the crowd before returning to his face. Her disappointment almost palpable. "Your team can hear us, can't they? Let me guess. You've been advised to stay away from me?"

This was no time for a conscience. She was trouble and not his responsibility. He'd find out her plan then be rid of her. "My mic is off. How can I be of service?"

Her face lit up, transforming her from beautiful to breathtaking in a heartbeat. "I need a place to lay low, where I'm unlikely to be recognized. Like Currawong Island."

It took a couple of seconds for her words to compute. "Say again?"

Safiya's eyes sparkled. "You could introduce me to your parents as Fia Gibbs."

Never. Ryan cleared his throat. "As what, Safiya, the love of my life?"

"Don't sound so enthusiastic. It might go to my head. We pretend we're … good friends, which makes it easier for me to fit in when you return to Sydney."

Choked laughter echoed in his earpiece and from further down the room.

"Are you serious?" Ryan clasped Safiya's elbow firmly before guiding her back towards the French doors. "Bored, over-indulged, rich girls don't hang out with security guards." A timely reminder she wasn't for him. He should be grateful, yet frustration consumed him. He wanted the impossible. Safiya would never settle for anything but the best. "Out of the question."

"You know nothing about me." Safiya jerked her elbow out of his hand. "I'm of legal age. No one can arrest you for taking me to meet your family."

"Dream on, honey. Your brother will string me up by my balls." Ryan found a secluded spot between two Roman statues and trapped her firmly against the wall, crossing his arms. "You have one *hell* of a hide asking such a thing of me, Safiya. Have you *no* thought for the worry your disappearance would bring your family? *Or* what it would do to the good reputation I've spent *years* building —" His scathing dressing-down ended abruptly as her eyes welled with tears.

"I am trying to build a life of my own. To be like any other normal twenty-three-year-old. You wouldn't understand." She placed a hand on his chest. "I guess this is goodbye." She stepped into him, wrapped her arms around his neck and touched her pillow soft lips to his.

Not what he was expecting, but she certainly had tantalizing curves in all the right places. Ryan reluctantly eased his mouth from hers to cradle her head against his shoulder. Kissing her with his friends listening would be bad form. With a soothing hand on her spine, he tried to remind himself why holding her was a bad idea, until his fingers brushed her ass. Her very *nice* ass that fit perfectly in his hand. She pressed closer, a soft moan slipping from her lips, distracting him.

"Release Miss Farid immediately!"

Ryan snapped out of his brain freeze to look over his shoulder. The guy who'd shouldered him out of the way earlier hovered a couple of feet away like a foul smell. Clenching his jaw, Ryan gave the jerk the once over then met his gaze. "Safiya-Ameerah was upset. I am comforting her. Nothing improper is happening."

"I insist Miss Farid return inside with me this instant."

She gasped. "How dare you —?"

"Easy." Ryan drew her against his side, clamping his fingers around her trim waist before meeting Jamal's glare. "Why do you assume you have the right to direct Safiya anywhere?"

"Our families have mutual business interests, as such it makes sense to negotiate a closer alliance. As you have been out here quite a while, I assume Miss Farid has told you of my interest?"

"Sorry, your name didn't come up in our ... conversation." He raised a suggestive eyebrow, letting the moron use his imagination to guess what had come up — or would have if they'd kissed for much longer.

Judging by Jamal's clenched fists, his imagination had gone into overdrive. He sneered at Ryan. "You are a security guard. How could you possibly afford to support Miss Farid? To fill her wardrobes with beautiful garments and shoes? To take her anywhere she wishes. To buy her a suitable engagement ring?"

Ryan glanced at Safiya, noticing the fury in her eyes. He took her hand and drew her into his arms. "Expensive trinkets, labels and holidays may be how you show your affection, Jamal. I prefer the hands-on approach, doing things that give us both pleasure and enjoyment."

That took the sneer off the dickwad's face.

"Stop this." Safiya glared at Jamal. "I don't need material things or to be kept in a gilded cage. I need a man who values my opinion, respects me, and treats me as an equal. A man who loves *me*, not what I represent."

Jarred swore in Ryan's earpiece. "Wind this up and get back to work."

Safiya trembled in Ryan's arms. She turned her fury on Jamal. "You are looking for a stay-at-home bride to raise your sons. I wouldn't do at all. I'm far too independent to let any man direct my life. There's also my career to consider, which I'm not willing to give up at this point, or the extreme sports I regularly pursue. Plus, I'm about to embark on an environmental volunteer project. I would not make *you* a suitable wife."

"You are correct. Please excuse me." He strode off, his face a mottled shade of beetroot.

"That's telling him." Ryan squeezed her waist reassuringly. "Although the career and volunteer work might be stretching it a bit far."

"Said like a man who doesn't know me." A soft blush covered her cheeks.

"I'd believe you're into extreme sports. Your enthusiasm and energy are contagious."

Her face broke into a stunning smile, causing his breath to hitch. She leaned into Ryan, her lashes fluttering, a flirtatious pout on her lips. "To be honest, I'm the biggest scaredy cat around." She smoothed her hands over her hips. "It took all my courage to wear this dress, but my mother insisted. Do you like it?"

His gaze drifted over her shapely breasts, sheathed by red lace, before drifting down the sheer fabric to her red stilettoes.

"Very much, but then you would look spectacular in a sack." He winked at her.

Her delighted laugh had an infectious effect, drawing his own chuckles. "Have you had enough fresh air?"

"Yes." She strolled beside him through the French doors. "I intend to visit Currawong Island. It would be nice to meet your family."

Ryan froze. *When Hell freezes over.*

Safiya continued, oblivious to his souring mood. "I read it's just outside the Great Barrier Reef, in the Coral Sea. Surrounded by treacherous reefs and rumored shipwrecks. You said your sister runs dolphin- and whale-watching cruises."

"Did I?" On the night of Nick's wedding, Safiya had quizzed him about the island he'd spent his childhood on. He definitely hadn't mentioned shipwrecks. Safiya must have done a little research.

"So how long have your family lived on Currawong Island?"

"In the late 1800's a European ancestor staked a claim and we've been there ever since."

He needed to distract her. The dance floor had filled with couples. *Perfect.* Ryan swept Safiya onto the dance floor, aware most of the boys hadn't said a word during the last ten minutes. He glanced around the room, noting Jamal tight-lipped at the table where Sheikh Farid chatted with his wife and son. They all watched Ryan and Safiya.

"Okay, Safiya, why me?"

"Because I trust you."

The music slowed and she rested her head against his shoulder. After a minute she looked up. "My father believes fortune hunters and the tabloids will take advantage of me. The private life I've fought so hard for is being threatened. He intends to surround me with body-guards, which will end any chance of living a normal life. That's why I need to act fast."

Ryan frowned. "Safiya, can you live a normal life? Do you even know how to cook?"

"I'm not going to answer that, except to say, anyone can learn to cook basic meals."

"Sure." He accepted her reprimand with a guilty nod. Basic meals were his forte. "I'm sorry, Safiya, but Jamal is right. A man on my salary couldn't afford to keep you in the lifestyle you're accustomed to. No one would believe you're my girlfriend, especially my family, and I would prefer you stay away from Currawong Island."

She stepped away, her eyes losing their bright sparkle. "I see. Thanks for the dance." Without another word, she turned on her high heels and stalked away, chin up and shoulders back, like an Amazon Warrior preparing for battle.

CHAPTER TWO

Hell, Ryan, was that necessary? Talos' words from two hours ago wouldn't leave Ryan's thoughts, but what choice did he have?

Safiya spent her teenage years running away from boarding schools. She'd dropped out of university. She couldn't hold down a job. Safiya thought him callous, but she needed to face reality.

As for returning to Currawong Island … Hell would freeze over before he willingly stepped foot on the golden sand or forgave the people who turned their backs on him twelve years ago. It would be bad enough having to view the island from his great-uncle's boat in two weeks. Yet he couldn't disappoint the boys. They'd been looking forward to this fishing trip for months, and as usual they'd stay on Magnetic Island. The boys understood and respected his reasons for avoiding his childhood home and family. They might not be bound by blood, yet they were brothers. Bound by trust, friendship, and honor.

Ryan rolled his shoulders, irritated as all hell. The night might almost be over, but he'd spent two hours observing guests as they consumed a five-course meal, along with copious amounts of wine and spirits. The noise level rising each time the auctioneer worked the crowd, raising mind-boggling amounts.

The boys and Ryan had stayed out of sight, beyond the dais

curtains, eating gourmet meals as they watched monitors. The only hiccup had been caused by Jamal Al-Saad, who wanted his twenty-thousand-dollar diamond earrings immediately. To everyone's astonishment he presented them to Safiya, as a token of his esteem. Apparently, he'd had a change of heart. Probably motivated by the connections his family sought.

Mortified, she'd refused the earrings. Jamal had laughed it off, although Ryan noticed the man's gaze rarely strayed from Safiya. He left alone, after Senior Inspector Gibbs spoke to him. It seemed Safiya's brother wasn't a fan of Jamal's either. Strangely, neither Gibbs nor the Sheikh approached Ryan, yet he'd caught them watching him throughout the evening.

The next hours dragged like a slow Sunday, as Ryan strolled the ballroom, monitoring the crowd; trying, and failing to keep his attention off Safiya. Not surprisingly, Jarred consigned him to the private courtyard to get his head together. When a drunk socialite ignored his plummeting mood and propositioned him, she almost ended up in the lily pond, before registering his intention and hightailing it inside.

As predicted, Elliott Shaw departed after dinner. He paid Steele Security a ridiculous amount of money to provide protection for Madeline, a necessity after she'd written a string of damning articles, uncovering people smuggling, slave labor, drug running and any number of human rights infringements. In Ryan's opinion, she deserved a medal. At least she'd enjoyed tonight, moving from table to table, speaking with other guests, and dancing.

Mingling with these people appeared second nature to the beautiful journalist. The orchestra had finished at eleven and now a DJ entertained the dwindling crowd.

It was no hardship watching over Madeline and her latest dance partner, as it gave Ryan a reason to observe Safiya without his friends giving him a hard time.

With ten minutes to go before the clock struck one, most of the guests had departed. Sam and Nick had also left, taking expensive prizes to be stored in the Steele Security vault until they could be delivered. Simon had driven the Ferrari to Jarred's residence, where it would stay until the owner arranged collection.

The last table of guests rose from their seats, red-faced, eyes glazed, and slurring as they wove past the empty tables. Ten or so die-hards were out on the dance floor, most so drunk they staggered about without any coordination. Madeline and Safiya were tipsy and laughing as they bumped hips to the DJ's beat. Their respective parents had left around twelve, leaving them under the watchful guard of Steele Security and Zachary Gibbs.

Safiya had ignored Ryan since leaving him on the dance floor. It was for the best.

His cell phone vibrated against his chest. Reaching inside his suit, he checked the ID, then raised his phone to his ear. "Bill?"

"Hello, lad. I realize it's late — or early — but can you talk?"

"Of course." His great-uncle was one of only two people from the island he spoke to.

"I wouldn't bother you if your parents were here, but they've gone to Melbourne, along with your grandparents, for a coach trip through Victoria."

Ryan had a lot of time for his great-uncle. Of late, Bill had taken to calling Ryan a couple of times a month for a chat or technical issue he needed help with. Never this late though. "What's the problem?"

"Treasure hunters. They arrived a week ago in two yachts with flashy equipment."

"Nothing new there. What's got you worried?"

"I don't like the way they're pestering your sister."

Ryan's gut spasmed. "How are they pestering Zoe?"

"Hanging around the Surf Shack every afternoon. Showing off and big-noting themselves. Zoe's taken to closing early."

"Has she spoken to the cops?"

"Yeah, but unless these fellas do something illegal, Pete Hawthorne's hands are tied. I want you to come home, lad. It's time."

"Bill, I'll be up that way in two weeks. Simon's birthday bash is in three days."

"Oh, that's right. Wish him well for me."

"I will." Barnacle Bill knew the boys from several fishing trips over the last five years. They'd even slept on his fishing boat one trip. Mostly Bill stayed with Ryan and the boys on Magnetic Island, telling yarns well into the night. Magnetic Island and Townsville were where Ryan usually caught up with Bill and Zoe.

Ryan rubbed his jaw. Zoe had a naïve streak, having attended a private girls' school on the mainland, before returning to the island. She hadn't been exposed to opportunistic guys or a lot of stuff most girls her age dealt with. Hell, she was probably still a virgin. Now that she'd reached the ripe old age of twenty-two, her surfer girl looks and buoyant personality would attract a bunch of randy guys.

"Bill, tell Zoe I'll ring her later today."

"Thanks, lad. You're welcome to stay in the boatshed. We can keep it quiet like."

"Thanks. Gotta go." Ryan slipped the phone into the pocket of his suit jacket, unsurprised when Jarred strolled over. He would have heard most of the conversation through his earpiece.

"I can send Adam Garcia to check on Zoe if you wish. In the meantime, Zachary Gibbs asked me to put a tail on his sister. He doesn't trust Jamal Al-Saad. In fact, he asked Simon to do a discreet background check on the man."

"Really? I assume Gibbs would prefer it wasn't me tailing Safiya?"

"That goes without saying." Jarred frowned. "I informed Gibbs you have no interest in his sister, which pacified him. He's hoping your presence has deterred Jamal Al-Saad."

"I doubt it." Ryan checked the dance floor, surprised to see it empty. "Where —"

"Jarred!" Madeline's screech had Ryan and Jarred reaching for their guns as they sprinted for a set of open French doors.

Ryan cursed his lapse in concentration. In the past five months there had been six attempts to kill or kidnap Madeline, and although Steele Security had dealt with the criminals behind the first four attempts, the last two had them baffled.

They burst through the doorway, shoulder to shoulder into the empty courtyard. A blue stiletto and a red stiletto lay between the lily pond and a marble statue of some goddess.

"Madeline," Jarred roared, taking off toward a clanging metal gate.

"They've taken Safiya too." Ryan's heart thundered under his ribs. *Fuck.*

"Talos! Madeline and Safiya have been snatched." Ryan yelled into his mic. "Cut off the lane behind the hotel."

"What the fuck?" Talos' booming voice almost deafened Ryan, yet it was a relief to know the big guy was still tuned in.

Jarred reached the gate first and kicked it hard, taking it off its hinges with a monstrous crash. They clambered over it and ran toward a black sedan at the end of the lane. Two men in suits lumbered ahead, each carrying a screeching woman over their shoulder. Safiya struggled frantically, thumping her fists into the man's back. Madeline screamed retribution.

"Stop." Jarred fired a warning shot into the wall.

Both men whirled, drawing their own weapons as they backed toward the sedan, using the women as shields.

"Shit!" Ryan dived for a large metal skip bin as shots filled the lane. It was like being in the narrow alleys of an Afghani village, without the stifling desert heat bouncing off the ground and buildings. He yelled into his mic. "Two males, black sedan. Clear the area, they're armed and firing at us."

Jarred leaned out of a doorway. "Release your hostages or you won't live to see another fucking day."

Ryan winced. Jarred was rattled. One man got the rear door open, except Madeline lifted her bare feet and pushed against the frame. Her captor let out a bellow, probably because she was attempting to rip his ears off. *Go girl.*

Relying on years of training, Ryan rolled into the center of the lane, sighted the sedan's rear window, and fired, praying the other asshole didn't cross his line of fire. The paperwork would be hell. The window shattered, exposing a driver's profile.

Jarred fired a barrage of shots into the rear of the sedan as he ran forward. It was enough to panic both men. They tossed Madeline and

Safiya aside then jumped into the car. It screeched out of the lane, leaving skid marks on the concrete and a plume of stinking fumes from burning rubber. Talos ran past the lane's entrance, chasing the sedan.

Falling to his knees, Ryan scooped Safiya into his arms. "It's okay. I've got you."

"Ryan." She clutched his jacket, burying her face against his neck, shaking uncontrollably. Jarred had Madeline in his arms and was striding back toward the courtyard.

Ryan followed at a run. At least the ballroom had emptied. He carried Safiya to a chair, setting her down gently on the velvet cushion. Jarred paced back and forth, updating Gibbs over his phone.

"Hey." Ryan crouched in front of Safiya and clasped her shaking hands between his. He looked to Madeline who sat on the next chair. "Do you know those men?"

"No," Madeline replied, "but they spoke English with heavy accents."

"German." Tears rolled down Safiya's face. "They reverted to their native language when they panicked."

Ryan supposed it was possible. Simon's background check stated Safiya had spent the first twelve years of her life in Switzerland, where German was commonly spoken. It made sense she'd recognize a language from that part of the world.

"What happened?" Jarred stood with his arms crossed, his jaw set as he stared down at Madeline. "I can't comprehend what made you go outside."

"I didn't." Madeline glared back at him. "One of those men came up to me on the dance floor. He said *you* had been hit by a car and were in a serious condition." She huffed in disgust. "I should know it would take more than a car to kill you, but I didn't stop to think. I told Safiya to find Talos or Ryan."

Safiya let out a shaky breath. "I didn't like the way the man was sweating, and when I saw the other one waiting at the French doors, I followed them into the courtyard."

She sniffed. "One man was holding the gate open. The other had his arm around Madeline and a hand over her mouth, so I jumped on his back. Next thing I know, I'm being abducted too."

Madeline's look of disgust didn't surprise Ryan. She'd been through some close calls over the last six months. To fall for a stunt like this was foolish. On the other hand, it said a lot about whoever the kidnappers were working for. They knew enough to use Jarred as bait to trick Madeline. If it hadn't been for Safiya, they would have succeeded.

A ripple of unease shivered through Ryan. He stepped away and lowered his voice so only Jarred and Talos would hear. "As usual Elliot Shaw has an airtight alibi."

"Safiya!" Gibbs burst into the ballroom, the relief on his face palpable as his gaze roved over her. He ran forward, a bunch of cops behind him.

Gibbs pulled his sister into his arms. "Are you hurt?"

"Only bruised. Ryan rescued me."

He looked at Ryan. "They got away, but I have officers accessing street cameras. With luck, we'll identify the vehicle's plates."

"Good." Ryan turned to Jarred. "I assume you'll see Madeline home?"

"Of course." Jarred motioned a police officer forward. "Mrs. Shaw's husband is on his way to Vietnam, so once you take her statement, I will escort her home."

How convenient. It troubled Ryan that Elliott was never present when attacks were made on Madeline. By the steel in Jarred's voice, it bothered him even more. Leaving Jarred to deal with the cop, Ryan glanced at Safiya, standing several inches shorter without her stilettoes. "I didn't mean to hurt your feelings earlier."

She lifted her chin. "I'm tougher than I look." She turned to walk away.

"Safiya."

She swung around, a new coolness filling her beautiful dark eyes. "Yes, Mr. Dutch?"

Yep, she was pissed off. "I'm not the big bad wolf you think I am."

"Just a guy, flirting his way through life. You can't be bothered to

26

get to know me, because you believe I'm an irresponsible airhead with a rich daddy."

"What I know came from background research, Safiya."

She blinked several times. "I should be used to this, but I hoped you were different." Her breath hitched. "Goodbye, Mr. Dutch. I wish you well."

Damn. He watched her limp over to the officer waiting to take her statement, shoulders stiff, chin up and hands fisted. Maybe she had been into him, yet a romance between them was out of the question. They might be attracted to each other, but they had nothing in common and he valued his balls.

Gibbs held out his hand. "Thank you for rescuing Safiya. My parents and I owe you an enormous debt."

Ryan shook his hand. What else could he do? Safiya had walked out of his life and didn't want a bar of him. It niggled that Simon's background check into Safiya might contain misinformation or half-truths. Unlikely, but possible.

Once Gibbs and Safiya left the ballroom, Jarred rolled his shoulders. "You did the right thing, Major. That young lady would run you ragged."

"What rot." Madeline sprang to her feet, placing her hands on her hips to glare at Jarred. "You don't know a thing about Safiya."

"And you do?" Jarred's sarcastic drawl had Madeline bristling.

"Thanks to you, Colonel Steele Feather, I spent six weeks on Sheikh Farid's Fijian Island. Safiya being my only companion for four of those weeks. So, yes, I know a great deal about her, which is why I enjoy her friendship. We have much in common, one of which is intelligence."

Jarred raised an eyebrow. "You can add impulsive, reckless and insensitive to the worry you both cause your families."

Madeline ignored him completely and focused on Ryan. "Unfortunately, there are parents who fail to provide a loving environment for their children. Either because of neglect or abuse. A lot of parents put far too much pressure on their children, or in Safiya's case, keep them hidden and employ others to raise them."

She drew in a shaky breath, her eyes sparking with fury. "It hasn't helped that people have betrayed Safiya, or lied for their own gain, spreading vicious rumors. Safiya may be impulsive, but she has a kind heart, and a keen mind." She lifted her chin. "I dare you to get to know her. You will thank me. I guarantee it."

The vehemence in Madeline's voice took Ryan by surprise. A quick glance at Jarred showed him to be just as astonished.

"It might be too late for that, Madeline."

"It's never too late, Ryan." Her gaze shifted to Jarred. "You just need the right incentive."

CHAPTER THREE

With calm resolve, Safiya dug deep for courage to stand up to her father. She placed her fine bone china teacup and saucer on the French inlaid parquetry table, which far exceeded the value of her maternal grandparents' furniture, now residing in a storage unit. How she yearned for a normal, close-knit family. The rigid protocols her parents maintained — even on this yacht — drove her batty. She had to make them truly listen and understand.

"Baba, nobody on the island has any idea who I am." Safiya stood and paced the plush carpet of the yacht's largest saloon. "I don't need a passport to get there and it's out in the middle of the ocean. I couldn't be safer."

"What is the name of this island, Safiya? Who is offering you work?" Her father leaned back in the leather armchair; his gaze locked on her.

"I prefer not to say, as you will send spies to watch me."

Her mother gasped from the sofa, spilling her tea. "Safiya, we do *not* spy on you."

"Let me rephrase that … I don't want a posse of bodyguards watching my every move to report back to you." She tilted her head toward two of the intimidating men her father had recently hired.

They were washing down the sundeck outside the saloon. Three more were somewhere on the yacht attending to other chores. She couldn't even have an early morning kayak around Rozelle Bay without two of them following her.

Although scary, she had to admit the Americans were extremely fit and good looking, however, they held no attraction for her. Even after Ryan's decision not to help her, she'd still dreamed of his blue eyes, fair curls, broad shoulders, and wicked smile over the last two nights. It was beyond annoying.

Not that she wouldn't trust any of her father's new security guys to protect her. After sneaking a peek at their files, she'd concluded anyone silly enough to slip onto the yacht uninvited would regret it. They wouldn't risk their lucrative paychecks to keep her from harm.

As for the pretty chopper pilot, Rose Blackett had taken to assisting in the galley with gusto. Her jubilant outlook on life making it a fun place for Safiya to hang out and practice her cooking skills under Chef Micaela's guidance.

"Habibti, my crew are here to keep us safe." Her father held his hands wide. "You are our beloved daughter. We don't want any harm to come to you."

"It won't." She sipped her tea. "I plan to make friends and live a normal life. It's all I've ever wished for. I have my grandparent's legacy, so I don't need you to support me. I will work part-time and do voluntary work on the island."

Her mother dabbed at the tea stain on her white pants then threw the linen napkin on the coffee table. "Safiya, your father is a wealthy sheikh. The world now knows of you and your brother. You can't expect us to agree to this."

"You have no choice. I *will* marry a man of my choosing and when we have children, I'll raise them myself and tuck them into bed each night."

Her father's nose flared, a sure sign he was losing patience. "You cannot be serious about moving to some little island in the middle of nowhere without a security team!"

"Why not? Do you expect me to stay here, bow to Jamal and do as I'm told instead?"

"Forget Jamal. He is unworthy of you." Her father flicked his hand as if swatting away an insect. "Will Ryan Dutch be on this island?"

"No … He thinks I'm spoilt and reckless. That my life is one big round of parties and shallow relationships. He asked me if I even knew how to cook a basic meal."

"Do you?" Her father's question made her flinch.

"Yes, Baba, I do. If you'd taken the time to sit down and talk to me for more than five minutes, you would know I'm an accomplished cook." She crossed her arms. "Enough of this. If you promise to leave me alone, I will tell you where I'm going. If you betray my trust, I will change my name and live my life far away from you. Sound familiar?"

"Safiya." Her mother's cup and saucer rattled as she placed them on the coffee table. "We had no choice."

"There is always a choice. You chose the wrong one. You left me with an *au pair* and tutors in Switzerland. At least I was happy there, but then you sent me to those boarding schools, where you expected me to hide my identity, so you could be together."

"That was not the reason, Safiya. We did it to protect you," insisted her mother.

"I was bullied and ignored. If I told the truth, I was labelled a liar. All so you could keep your marriage a secret and remain working together. Why have children if you didn't want to be with us?"

"There is much you do not understand, Habibti." Her father stood and moved to sit on the sofa, reaching for her mother's hand. "Even though I brought untold wealth to the family, when my mother and uncles heard of my marriage to a western woman, they demanded I take another wife or abdicate as head of the family."

Safiya gasped. "I thought you wanted to abdicate."

"No. Your grandmother wants nothing to do with your mother whatsoever. She will accept you and your brother if I agree to a marriage between you and Jamal Al-Saad, and your brother to Jamal's youngest sister, who I believe is seventeen."

"You're kidding?"

"I refused and have stepped away completely. My brother is floundering. He does not have a head for business. He also loves his wife and three daughters, so is refusing to take a second wife to gain a son, which is causing major disharmony within the family." He sighed. "In hindsight, perhaps we could have done things differently. However, the past cannot be undone. We have only ever wanted you and your brother safe."

Safiya shrugged. "I've gone to great lengths to find an island where I'm not known. The person I'm working for is highly regarded in her conservation work on the outer reefs. I've volunteered to help and will have my own cabin close to her house."

Her mother wiped away a tear. "We will grant your wish, darling, as long as you promise to phone us once a week."

Her father almost choked on an olive. "Dana?"

"Deal." Safiya sank to her knees in the plush carpet, taking one of their hands in each of hers. "The lady I'm working for is sweet. Her family live on the island as well. For obvious reasons I won't be using my real name."

Her mother squeezed Safiya's hand. "Darling, what work will you do?"

"Zoe has a business, hiring out snorkels, scuba gear, canoes, kayaks, and paddle boards. I'll be serving holiday makers while she teaches them to paddle board. She also runs dolphin and whale-watching cruises, and owns three other holiday cabins, which I will clean."

"Serve people and clean?" Her father stared at her in horror.

"Yes. In our spare time, Zoe and I will remove a coral pest called Crown of Thorns."

Her father raised an eyebrow. "This is what you want?"

"Very much, Baba. The island is within range of the Great Barrier Reef. To get there I fly from Sydney to Townsville then take a ferry to the island."

"For my peace of mind, will you allow us to take you to this island?"

"No, Baba. I doubt there's ever been a yacht this size anywhere near the island. It will draw attention I don't want."

"What if we cruise to Townsville, stay a few days to enjoy the warm climate then you can make your way to this island. Once you are safely on the island, your mother and I will cruise on to New Zealand and the Cook Islands."

"Thank you, but no. I've booked a flight tomorrow, so I can have the weekend to explore the island before I start work Monday."

"Will you at least dine on the yacht with your family tonight? Your brother is joining us."

"That would be lovely, Baba. I need to finish packing." Safiya almost skipped out of the saloon and down the spiral staircase to her state room. She snatched up her phone then flopped on the enormous bed to make a call that would hopefully give her the freedom she craved. Her father had given in much too easily, which worried her, yet if he knew one fact about his daughter, it had to be that she never threatened anything she wouldn't carry through if pushed.

"Hello, Zoe speaking."

"Zoe, it's Sa– Fia Gibbs. I arrive on Friday's ferry."

"Fia, that's fantastic. I can't wait to meet you face to face. We've had a little trouble with some men staying on the island, but it's nothing to worry about. My brother works for a security firm and his boss sent up a guy to keep an eye on things."

"What guy?" Safiya's stomach churned. This couldn't be happening. Not now.

"His name is Adam Garcia. He's recuperating from broken ribs and a dislocated shoulder. I would have preferred my brother, but we don't always get what we want, do we?"

"No, we don't." Safiya chewed her lower lip. "Is Adam Garcia a friend of your brother's?

"More an acquaintance. Adam is American."

Thank goodness.

Zoe's sigh overrode Safiya's relief. "It will make a nice change having you here, Fia. There aren't any single girls our age on the island. They move to the mainland first chance they get. There's not much in the way of a social life to keep them here, and work is pretty scarce."

Safiya smiled. "Sounds like my kind of place. I'm looking forward to helping you with the dolphin cruises and ridding the reef of those horrible crown of thorn things."

"I appreciate that, Fia. We also have three nests of unhatched sea turtles due any day that we need to keep an eye on. They normally hatch further up the beach in summer months."

"So, they're late hatching?"

"Yes, their mothers migrated back here late this year."

"I can't wait. I've never seen turtles hatching before." Safiya settled in for a nice long chat, her body tingling with anticipation, feeling like the luckiest person in the world.

Currawong Island was the perfect place to learn more skills, make friends and be herself. Maybe, one day, Ryan would come home and realize she was worth knowing. Why she yearned for his respect and admiration, she couldn't fathom. He wasn't the only pebble on the beach, but for some reason he was the only pebble she wanted.

DANA FARID PACED across the thick carpet of the yacht's master stateroom. Back and forth, as her handsome husband watched her with one eyebrow raised, his lips quirked.

"This is not funny, Tariq. I was playing for time." She spoke Arabic to be safe. "We can't leave Safiya on an island unprotected? What if she's taken advantage of by another fortune hunter? It could destroy her. What if Jamal Al-Saad finds her? He might kidnap Safiya and force her to marry him."

"I won't allow that to happen. I had hoped she'd join us as we cruised around New Zealand and the Cook Islands."

"What if she elopes with the security guard?"

"It wouldn't be the worst thing in the world, my love. Ryan Dutch is not your average security guard. According to Zakour, he flew Black Hawks in the Australian Army before joining an elite unit within their Special Forces. He has commendations for bravery and admirable service. He has the respect of his commander and every soldier within that unit."

"You've already had him investigated?"

"Zakour enlightened me. Ryan Dutch has an apartment close to Sydney Harbour. As part of Jarred Steele's Special Operations team, he continues to serve Australia with honor and bravery when required. Zakour told me Jarred Steele and his Special Unit still belong to the army as reservists and maintain their previous ranks. Ryan Dutch is a Major."

"That may be so, Tarik, but Safiya is such a restless spirit. I'm not surprised Ryan Dutch is attracted by her beauty. What happens when he tires of her?"

"Time will tell, my love. He did rescue her after the Gala last night. It remains to be seen whether he is the right person to handle Safiya's rebellious streak. We gave her our word. We can't send a posse of bodyguards to an island. However, there is an alternative."

She narrowed her eyes. "Tariq Farid, what are you up to?"

"Ah, my wife, you know me too well." He prowled toward her. "Come, I will tell you how clever I am, then you may thank me anyway you like."

Dana allowed him to guide her to the bed. He sat down and drew her onto his lap, into the circle of his arms. "Who are you thinking of sending?"

"*I'm* not sending anyone. Our son will ask Jarred Steele to return a favor. I kept the female journalist safe on our island, as well as hosted two of his men's weddings. Plus, Zakour loaned the Steele Ops Team my jet so they could go to the aid of their friend in Western Australia. I should think an ex-Special Force soldier, who is trained in covert operations, might enjoy an all-expenses paid holiday on an island in the Great Barrier Reef."

"What if Jarred Steele sends Ryan Dutch? He might think Safiya spoilt and shallow, but he watched her closely most of the night."

Tariq frowned. "A good thing or she would have been taken from us."

"Yes, but do you think he has genuine feeling for Safiya?"

"I shall test him, my love. Money speaks louder than words. In the meantime, Zakour will ask Jarred Steele to send his best man to protect our daughter, which is our first hurdle. Colonel Steele doesn't do anything he doesn't approve of. He is not a man to be taken lightly."

Dana shook her head. "He can't send a man Safiya will recognize."

"They are ex-Special Forces. If the man doesn't want her to see him, she won't. Safiya will return to us once she realizes living frugally and cleaning cabins isn't fun."

"I lived frugally before you whisked me away to your opulent lair, Tariq."

"Yes, darling, but would you wish to return to that damp attic in a building with no lifts, or sleep on a lumpy mattress that folds out of the wall."

"I thought you loved my Parisian attic."

"I loved making love to you in your Parisian attic, darling. I did not enjoy climbing the hundred and twenty-three steps, or the draft that blew in through the gap above your window. How would you like a nice slow cruise up the coast of Australia before we head to New Zealand? We could spend a night or two on the Great Barrier Reef, just in case Safiya changes her mind."

"That's an excellent idea, my love."

"I know. Now, what of my reward for being so clever?"

"It is yet to be seen if you are clever, Tariq. Things may not go as you plan."

"Nonsense." He fell back, taking her with him. "Everything always goes as I plan."

CHAPTER FOUR

A rush of nostalgia hit Ryan as he gazed across the beach he hadn't set foot on in twelve years. To hear the gentle lapping of the tide, feel the sea breeze ruffling his hair as it took the heat out of the midday sun. To hear the currawongs chattering in the tall gum trees along the road, as if they couldn't wait to spread word of his return.

His heart beat a rapid tattoo. He'd been all over the world to amazing, exotic, and beautiful places, yet not one claimed his heart and soul like this small oasis. Currawong Island might seem isolated to many people, but to the island's residents and custodians, it was paradise.

Ryan had explored every cove, bay, cave, lookout, and reef. He loved every inch of this island. Once upon a time, he'd known all two hundred residents. According to Barnacle Bill, that number had almost doubled in the twelve years since he'd last been here.

Paradise surrounded him. While he'd experienced the horrors of the war-torn regions and hostile territories of his army career, he'd pined for his peaceful island home.

He strode along the jetty, his baseball cap pulled low, his duffle bag slung over one shoulder, keen to slide in under the radar and take a cool shower. May in the Queensland tropics was always balmy. It beat the cooler weather in Sydney, that was for sure.

Holding his runners in his hand, Ryan jumped off the low jetty, sinking his toes into the golden sand. He let out a deep sigh, his connection with the island flowing up through his feet, through his veins to his heart, like an essential lifeline. So much had happened since he'd left. So many opportunities he never would have experienced if he'd stayed. Lifelong bonds formed in harsh environments.

Leaving the SASR had been a tough decision, although made easier when the other boys had taken the leap too. He had a great job, friends, all his limbs and a healthy bank balance. Yet, he yearned to go back in time, to that wretched day when he'd lost everything.

Raising a hand to block the sun, Ryan watched the seaplane soar into the air then fly back toward the mainland. It had been a real buzz taking over the controls to fly here. As a teenager, it had been his dream to form the Currawong Island Seaplane and Catamaran Service. Now he had his chopper, seaplane, and boat licenses. Only one obstacle remained. To gain the Island council's approval. Except they'd never give it, which hardly mattered as he'd never return as a resident.

"It's good to have you home, lad."

Ryan grinned as his great-uncle stepped out from the shade of a palm tree. Barnacle Bill, at seventy-two, stood tall and proud, his blue eyes somewhat faded with age, but as alert as ever.

"Hey, Bill, you're looking well. I take it no one else is here to meet me?"

"Your parents and grandparents will be in Melbourne for a couple of weeks."

"That's probably for the best."

"They don't know about the treasure hunters, or that you've come home."

"We'll talk about that in a minute. Has anyone asked about Adam Garcia?"

"Sergeant Hawthorne. The American stands out like a broody gorilla. Once I let slip he's an ex-Navy Seal, Pete relaxed."

Ryan laughed. "When Garcia's recovered, he might join our Special Ops Team."

"So, you're not planning to give up that dangerous work anytime soon?"

"It's nothing compared to what I did overseas." Ryan shuddered. "The scariest thing now is Cupid's arrow. It's struck four of the boys in the last seven months."

Bill clapped Ryan's shoulder. "Can we hope you might be next, lad? What of that lass you met in Fiji?"

"It's complicated." Ryan glanced out over his family's private beach, trying to ignore the memory of Safiya's seductive dark eyes and teasing smile that were never far from his mind. Everything about Safiya-Ameerah was enthralling, yet she wasn't for him.

"When I find a lady willing to take me on, I promise to send you an invitation to our wedding." He turned his attention back to his great-uncle. "I hear Camilla had another baby."

"That's right. She's got four boys now, and Tommy's a National Park ranger."

Ryan shrugged. He'd got over Camilla and Tommy's betrayal years ago. Shit happened. What tormented him was the way they'd ditched him, along with so many others he'd cared about or loved.

"You okay, lad?" Bill touched his arm. "It was a long time ago."

"Yeah." Ryan looked along Dutchies Beach to the steps leading up to the family compound, which held center place on the headland. "I can't imagine what it would be like to have four kids." He could have been their father. Time to change the subject and deal with the reason he'd been called home. "Tell me what's been happening."

Bill sat on the edge of the jetty; his worn runners planted well apart on the sand. "We've had a couple of break-ins."

"Can't the police handle them?"

"Pete Hawthorne's doing his best. He spoke to the elders, and held a community meeting, but I don't believe our local kids are behind these break-ins. I think it's treasure hunters. One group party hard every night and have no respect. I want you and your special ops friends to locate the thieves and send them packing."

Stunned, Ryan took a moment to process the request. "Bill, bringing in an elite force of ex-soldiers to deal with a couple of break-ins isn't viable." He could imagine the boys rolling around, laughing their asses off if he suggested such a thing. "The council couldn't afford to pay for our services, and they wouldn't want me here."

"Lad, you and your mates are highly equipped to take care of this, without drawing attention from the mainland."

Ryan rubbed his chin. "Except for you and Zoe, no one knows I belonged to a special unit within the SASR."

"That's not quite true." Bill ran a wrinkled, aged, and trembling hand through his white hair, alerting Ryan to his anxiety. "I discussed your team with Sergeant Hawthorne. He mentioned it to the council members. I'm sorry, lad, but they know you're trained in anti-counter surveillance and reconnaissance. They've … requested your help."

"What?" Ryan blinked, unable to believe his ears. "I owe them nothing." He ground his teeth as resentment snaked through his body. "Jarred Steele did me a favor by sending Adam Garcia to keep an eye on Zoe. I'm only here to check things out. There's no way Jarred would take a job like that."

Bill straightened; his hands fisted. "The thieves broke into the museum last week. Stole some artifacts and raided our historic filing cabinet. It held stories and files on the first settlers, and our early collaborations with the traditional custodians. Steve Thomas spotted a light, so went to investigate. He got hit over the head and needed six stitches."

"Hell." Ryan took a seat beside Bill on the jetty. Steve was one of the island's historians and volunteered at the museum along with Barnacle Bill. Steve had driven the only bus on the island for years, doing the school run and then a regular circuit of the island every day. He had to be in his sixties now. "Why didn't you tell me this when you rang?"

"It's island business. I wanted to wait until you came home."

Home? That was a joke. "Unless things have changed drastically, no local kids would attack Steve. He's too well liked."

"That's a contentious point and it's dividing the community. The attack and thefts have upset everyone."

Ryan stared at his feet, almost hidden under the golden grains of sand. "Doesn't my grandfather have copies of the historic files?"

"He does indeed. So did I, but the boatshed was ransacked three days ago, while I was out fishing. The thieves took the files, my great-grandfather's diary, and the ornate saber that the traditional owners gave William Dutch after he settled here in the 1800's. As you know, my great-grandfather believed it came from that fabled treasure you were always searching for."

"Damn, I'm sorry, Bill." The saber and diary were precious to Bill. "I'll do my best to get them back, but it still doesn't prove the treasure hunters are behind the robberies, mate."

Bill wiped a tear away. "No, but whoever it is, they're looking for something specific. The diary does refer to a hidden treasure and we do have that saber and some sovereigns that possibly came from a ship that sank close to the island." He sighed. "Zoe has been on her own at night until Adam Garcia turned up. When he heard about the robberies, he decided to sleep in your parent's sunroom. We're worried the thieves could hit there next."

"That's wise." Ryan glanced up at the headland. He'd been thinking the same thing. The Dutch House was an historical home and landmark on the island. It had been modernized over the years, and a major extension added thirty years ago, when his father had brought his bride to the island. Ryan's grandparents lived in one wing, and his parents' and sister in the other. The house was secluded. Thankfully, Garcia was a light sleeper.

"Treasure hunters wouldn't keep coming if you and Steve Thomas stopped telling sunken shipwreck stories to tourists."

Bill chuckled. "We do it to drum up business for the museum and the island's economy. There hasn't been animosity like this for …" Color flushed Bill's cheeks.

Ryan clenched his fists, digging his toes into the sand. "Twelve years." He looked out over the ocean so he wouldn't see the pity in the old man's eyes. "I'll drop by the police station and talk to the new sergeant, but first we'll check my grandfather's files are still in the study. I'd like to do a little spear fishing before it gets too late. Fancy a nice bream or perch for dinner?"

"Sounds grand." Bill smiled. "Zoe's at the Surf Shack if you want to say hello?"

"I can't. I need to keep my presence secret for now."

"The big American sticks to her like glue, and it's working. The treasure hunters have stopped bothering her."

"That's good to hear." Adam Garcia's cold eyes could freeze the balls of any guy unwise enough to approach Zoe. "You really didn't mention my arrival to her?"

"Nope. She's so excited about your upcoming fishing trip, she's employed a Swiss lass to help. Zoe will be over the moon when she finds out you're back."

"Business must be good if Zoe's taking on staff?"

"Got her cheap by offering free accommodation. Starts Monday. Zoe showed me a picture of the lass. Adam Garcia will need to keep her safe as well. She's got amazing dark eyes and a stunning smile."

Amazing dark eyes and a stunning smile. Ryan rolled his shoulders. It seemed he couldn't even have a conversation without thinking of Safiya. His gaze drifted out over the calm ocean again. It had always soothed him. "How many men are we talking about?"

"Six fellas are camping at Rocky Point. They've got a yacht anchored in Palm Beach. Then there's two brothers, who sleep on their yacht in Dugong Marina. The two groups don't appear to be together as they go off in different directions to dive among the reefs. It's the large group that worry me."

"I see." Ryan kicked the sand. He didn't like the sound of the larger group either, especially now Zoe had an attractive employee arriving. "I assume this girl arrives on the ferry tomorrow?"

"Yes. She'll stay at the main house until it's safe to move to a cabin."

"That would be best."

Bill placed a shaky hand on Ryan's shoulder. "Will you ask your team to help us?"

The crackle in Bill's normally gruff voice sliced into Ryan's heart but hiring a special ops team was out of the question.

"Let me do some reconnaissance, Bill, and keep your boatshed locked. If there's trouble brewing Jarred might agree to bring our fishing trip forward, if we don't have any important jobs booked in." Having the boys on the island would certainly scare off treasure hunters and save the council a fortune.

"Thank you, lad. I knew I could count on you to fix this."

That was yet to be determined. He'd use darkness to scope out the island and the latest batch of treasure hunters. At least it would keep his mind off Safiya-Ameerah.

TWO HOURS LATER, Ryan surfaced, pleased with his catch. Bill was in for a treat tonight. Perch and bream grilled over a fire pit of lemon-scented gum woodchips would have the old guy drooling. Corn cobs and sweet potato thrown on the grill would round the meal up nicely.

Barnacle Bill had run his fishing trawler and charter boat since retiring from the army. If Bill hadn't arranged for Ryan to live with a mate in Western Australia, Ryan never would have finished school, or joined the army, or met Nick Flanagan.

Two eighteen-year-olds without a family, running from their past. They'd formed a bond, become Blackhawk pilots, and gained a cowboy reputation for going into enemy territory to retrieve soldiers who'd otherwise be imprisoned or massacred. Then Jarred Steele had selected them to join his elite team within the SASR. Those men became their brothers, friends, family. They'd be there for Ryan, no matter the circumstances. They'd have his back.

A throbbing engine drew Ryan's attention north of the island where a large yacht was coming straight at him. Several shirtless men stood on the bow, holding up bottles of beer and cheering. Ryan waved his speargun to alert them to his presence. They kept coming.

"Hey," he yelled.

He was met with raucous laughter. One guy gave him the bird. "This is our bay, Miguel. Can't say we didn't warn you."

"What the hell?" Ryan dived, kicking hard to avoid the yacht's underbelly. *Fuck. They tried to run me over.*

43

Dumbfounded, he surfaced, expecting to see the yacht heading toward Sanctuary Cove. To his dismay it circled then made another run at him.

"You've got to be kidding." If they hit him, it would kill or injure him badly. There'd be blood, which would attract sharks. Unlike the Great Barrier Reef, the Coral Sea ran extremely deep outside the scattered reefs. Thank fuck he wasn't in Shark Bite Bay. Attracting White Tips, Tiger, Bull, even Bronze Whaler Sharks was a high possibility over there. If there were any Great Whites in the area, they'd also come to investigate. Even this water in Palm Beach was deep enough to attract sharks with blood floating around.

Two of the men emptied what looked like fish guts into the water.

Whipping out his fishing knife, Ryan slashed the line holding his fabulous catch of fish to his belt, sending them sinking to the ocean floor. He had bigger things to worry about than dinner.

The yacht kept circling then made another run at him as the drunken fools jeered. He had no choice but to dive deep again then try to make it to his runabout. There was going to be one hell of a reckoning when he caught up with these fucking idiots. Common sense cautioned Ryan to wait for backup. He needed proof these men were behind the robberies and assault. He'd put them under twenty-four-hour covert surveillance, starting tonight.

Surfacing again, he let fly a string of curses. The bastards had caught the anchor rope of his runabout and were towing it toward Rocky Point, leaving him no alternative but to swim for the beach, where Zoe had her Surf Shack, which meant there'd be a good chance she'd recognize him.

Ryan fastened the speargun's strap to his ankle. Once his team heard about this, they'd be more than willing to lend their assistance. During his six years in the SASR, the boys had used the Great Barrier Reef for down time. They'd been warmly welcomed aboard Barnacle Bill's fishing boat for deep-sea fishing trips. Zoe had taken time off to scuba dive and hike with them on Magnetic Island. She'd stayed several days each time, bringing Ryan up to date on Curra news. No one else had ever reached out to him.

After the gruesome action the boys had seen overseas, they more than appreciated Barnacle Bill's outrageous stories, Zoe's happy nature and Magnetic Island hospitality. They would have loved exploring Currawong Island too if Ryan hadn't vetoed the idea.

Irritation flared as he thought of the twelve-kilometer, barefoot hike home. He'd been in far worse situations; except this was personal. A new energy surged as Ryan ploughed toward the sandbar. Another ten meters and he'd be safe from sharks. He almost sighed with relief.

A gray fin surfaced to Ryan's left. "Fuck."

The shark circled; its cold black eye fixed on him. A Bull shark.

"Double fuck." Ryan pulled out his knife then faced the shark, roaring like a madman.

It darted away.

Kicking hard and praying he'd reach the sandbar before the shark came back, Ryan ploughed through the water; his thoughts erratic as memories flashed through his mind. Hanging out with Zane and Tommy as they explored every inch of Curra. Teaching Zoe to bait a hook. Flying Blackhawks with Nick. Retrieving his mates from hostile insurgents. Relaxing with the boys. Safiya in her red dress.

His fingers scraped through a sandbar. With a huge sigh of relief Ryan pushed to his feet and viewed the beach. A family stood at the Surf Shack's open window, snorkels and flippers dangling from their fingers. A huge guy in board shorts and an arm in a sling stood by the shack staring toward Ryan. Garcia. With luck Zoe had too many customers to notice her brother walking out of the ocean.

A hefty splash then solid weight against his calf, sent Ryan plunging over the sandbar, fearing jagged teeth would latch on any second. He rolled, ready to kick the motherfucker in the face. His ferocious attacker waddled onto the sandbar, dropping Ryan's catch of fish at his feet. Another hefty splash further out signaled another long-lost friend.

"Fuck." Ryan staggered to his feet, drawing deep breaths, as his racing heart calmed.

The seal barked, then dived back into the water. "Bloody hell,

Pong, you scared the bejesus out of me." The seal rocketed away like a mini torpedo. A very happy torpedo.

Ryan yanked off his flippers, grabbed his fish then waved Garcia toward the northern end of the beach. He needed to make the big fella aware just how dangerous those idiots were. Zoe's new employee would have to be waylaid and sent home on the return ferry until the danger could be dealt with, but Ryan could take care of that. This was the last place an attractive woman should be right now, which of course swamped him with thoughts of Safiya-Ameerah in her red dress. *At least she's safely out of the way.*

CHAPTER FIVE

A beady-eyed seagull hovered above the tall wheelhouse, its wings spread wide, allowing it to drift on an updraft. Not a single cloud blemished the powder blue sky all the way to the horizon. Safiya breathed in deeply, raising her face to the morning sun, basking in an amazing serenity she hadn't experienced since ... forever.

The cool breeze stirred the loose strands of hair around her face and sent goosebumps skating along her bare arms, yet she was loathe to find a seat inside, or rummage through her bulging suitcase for a jacket. Nor did she wish to retrace her steps between the loaded trucks and delivery vans to fetch her suitcase from the high luggage rack, her aim being to avoid recognition.

Most drivers had chosen to go inside for sustenance and company. Several stood at the other end of the ferry smoking. Some remained in their vehicles, the sun warming them as they dosed. The only other women to board were both indigenous; an elderly Aboriginal lady and a young mother pushing a pram.

Safiya twisted her grandmother's ring on her left hand. Waving it about had discouraged two young guys from striking up a conversation with her. It hadn't deterred them from watching her, which was why she'd sought refuge port side at the front of the ferry, using a large truck to shield her. The straw hat and sunglasses hid her identity, but she wasn't taking any chances. At least she hadn't spotted any of her father's security personnel.

She flinched at a sudden squawk then laughed at the seagull balancing on the rail, watching her keenly. "I don't have food and you're disturbing my peace."

"So-wee."

Safiya spun around, blinking at her tiny, brown-eyed interloper. He couldn't be more than three. "Hello." She crouched down and smiled. "I didn't mean you, sweetie. I was talking to the seagull." She nodded at the offender, strutting back and forth along the top rail.

"That's good, cause you not s'posed to feed them."

"Is that right?"

"Yep, it teaches 'em to be lazy. What's your name?"

"My name is Fia. What's your name?"

"Robbie. It's my birfday tomowo. I'll be free."

"Three! Congratulations. Where's your mommy, Robbie?"

"She's feeding Caden inside. He's a baby. I like tigers and trucks."

"I like dolphins and dancing."

He screwed up his nose at that. "My big bruvver likes football and Joel does too."

"Who's Joel?"

"My aver bruvver, a course. He's five. Don't you know anyfing?"

"I'm new to Currawong Island." She stood and held out her hand. "Would you walk with me? I'd like to meet your mommy."

"Sure fing." His pudgy, sticky little fingers gripped hers. "Wait." He stopped momentarily to stroke the truck's tire, which was taller than him. "Isn't it lovey?"

"I suppose." Safiya drew him away from the filthy tire. "Does your mommy know you're out here, Robbie?"

"She finks I'm asleep under her chair."

"Oh, dear. Won't she be scared when she can't find you?"

"I know where I am."

"Yes, but what if a big gust of wind blew you off this ferry. No one would know you fell in the water, would they?"

"Nah." He screwed up his nose then gave her a bashful grin. "I can't swim eva."

"Then you should stay with your mommy. Come on, let's get you back inside before she discovers you're missing." Safiya lead him through the vehicles then pushed against the heavy metal door, amazed the little boy had managed to get out without jamming his fingers.

As they stepped into the passenger cabin everyone looked at them.

"Robbie?" The young mother covered her mouth as she jumped to her feet, her dark eyes wide with horror. "I thought he was asleep." She laid the baby in the pram then hurried over. "Where was he?"

"Looking at a truck."

The woman paled. "That'd be right." Robbie's mother gripped his free hand then dragged him onto a chair. "You silly boy. Haven't I told you over and over not to leave my side?"

"Yes, Mommy. So-wee." His chin and lower lip drooped. "I forgot."

"No, you didn't, Robbie. You sneaked out on purpose. I should cancel your birthday."

"No, Mommy." Tears poured down the little guy's cheeks as his tiny shoulders quaked with grief. Safiya's heart went out to him, but Robbie's mother was right. Anything could have happened.

"Thank you for bringing him to me." She drew in a shaky breath. "I'm Camilla Curran. You must be Fia?"

"I am. How—?"

"It's a small island. News travels fast, especially after Barnacle Bill told Steve, the island's bus driver, you were coming to work for Zoe. Now everyone knows. I've been in Townsville, so Robbie could see a specialist. He's got a hernia."

"Oh, I'm sorry to hear that. So, you live on the island, Camilla?"

"Yeah. I planned to leave years ago. Wanted to own my own bistro on the Gold Coast, live in a fancy apartment overlooking the ocean, but four kids later, I'm still here."

"You look too young to have four children."

"I'm twenty-seven, been here all my life."

"So, you would have grown up with Ryan Dutch."

Camilla reared back, her face paling even further. "How do you know Ryan?"

"I ... um ... he's ..." Safiya stepped back, startled by the bitterness in Camilla's voice, annoyed with herself for making such a blunder. "He's ... Zoe's brother."

"Yeah, but Ryan left Curra when he was sixteen." She almost spat the words out. "He hasn't been back since and doesn't have anything to do with his family. I'm surprised Zoe mentioned him to an *outsider*."

Okay, that's putting me in my place. Except she's wrong. "Zoe clearly loves her brother and is extremely proud of his achievements." Safiya crossed her arms. "Being a Blackhawk pilot would keep him away during overseas missions."

"Blackhawk pilot?"

"Yes, and paramedic. He must be in contact with Zoe. How else would she know so much about him?"

"Maybe through Barnacle Bill. You can bet your last dollar Ryan won't step foot on Curra. He hates the island, and everyone on it."

"That's nonsense." Safiya stiffened with indignation. "Anyone listening to Ryan describe Currawong Island, can tell he loves the place. It's why I chose to come here."

Camilla visibly stiffened. "You *do* know him?"

Damn, me and my big mouth. "Our paths have crossed." Safiya unfolded her arms to twist her ring back and forth. She didn't want this woman's curiosity messing things up, or Zoe finding out.

"We met briefly."

"You're engaged?" Camilla's gaze locked on the ring.

"No, this was my grandmother's ring." She didn't want to begin her life on the island with a lie. Once they were off the ferry, she would swap it to her other hand. Safiya smiled at Robbie, who was yawning, obviously bored with their conversation. "It's nice to meet you. Maybe I'll see you around the island."

"You will." Camilla hesitated, as if pondering something, then shrugged. "If you're not doing anything tonight, there's a Spanish thing on at the pub. Tapas and music. It should be a good night. Zoe will be there."

"I'd like that. Thank you, Camilla."

"No worries. Is anyone picking you up?"

"I'm not sure. I did tell Zoe I'd be on the ferry. Is her place far from the dock?"

"It is with a suitcase as big as yours. I saw you struggling to get it onto the luggage rack." Camilla wiped Robbie's nose. "There's one taxicab on the island and a minibus, but it can be a bit hit and miss. Except for emergency vehicles, we don't have traffic on Curra. These trucks and vans unload then return on the afternoon ferry. If Zoe's not there to pick you up, ask for Shirley Thomas' number. She owns the taxicab."

"Okay, thank you."

Claw-like fingers gripped Safiya's wrist, startling a gasp from her. Twisting, Safiya discovered the elderly lady holding on to her firmly. For a moment they stared at each other. Close up the woman's dark eyes shone with curiosity. Fine, white hair curled about a compassionate, aged-lined face. She had a serene aura that enfolded Safiya like angel wings, protecting her from all evil.

"Aunty Frankie, this is Fia, the girl come to work for Zoe." Camilla touched the woman's shoulder, breaking their strange connection, although she didn't release Safiya's wrist or gaze.

"I'm Frankie Ellis, an elder of the Bindal People on Currawong." She tilted her head. "You don't look like a Fia. What's it short for?"

"Er …" Safiya blinked, her face warming with discomfort, yet something warned her this woman would see through a lie. "It is a shortened version of my name, but most people don't pronounce it properly, so it's easier to use Fia. It's nice to meet you, Frankie."

The elderly lady's lips twitched. "You're a keeper of secrets, I see. Interesting, but not unexpected. I've been expecting a storm. It looks like you've finally arrived."

Camilla gasped. "Did you just call Fia a storm, Aunty Frankie?

"A big storm, I expect." Frankie nodded, as if agreeing with herself. She slowly released Safiya's wrist. "You might want to head back outside for your first glimpse of Currawong. We're about twenty minutes out. If you're lucky, you'll see a humpback whale. They're here for the winter, to mate and give birth."

"I will. Thank you."

Mystified by Frankie's behavior and excited to spot a whale, Safiya waved to Robbie then opened the metal door. As she stepped through, she glanced back to find Frankie watching her and Camilla staring at the floor, her shoulders bowed. Did the younger woman dislike island life that much or was it something else?

Why would Camilla think Ryan hated Currawong and its people?

What had happened twelve years ago?

A squawk startled her. The same pesky seagull stood on the hood of a truck, watching her keenly. At least it looked like the same seagull. She shut the door and stepped closer.

"Robbie said I can't feed you."

With an indignant shriek, the seagull flew off over the deep blue ocean toward an island with three peaks. Safiya ran between vans and trucks to grasp the rail, searching the calm ocean surface for any disturbance. She'd read that between May and August, thirty-five thousand whales were expected to migrate from their feeding grounds in Antarctic waters. They'd travel up the east coast of Australia to the sub-tropical waters, where they'd mate and then the pregnant females would give birth. To see them up close would be amazing. Unfortunately, today wasn't the day.

Looking out over the side rail, Safiya's heart soared. The sea water surrounding the island ranged from cobalt blue to cool shades of aqua, so clear she could see a school of striped black and yellow fish darting about a small reef. Her heart soared as the ferry passed a turtle the size of a car tire.

There was so much to see. Two golden beaches, fringed by coconut palms and pine trees stretched away to either side of an opening in the headland. A sandstone home surrounded by hibiscus trees rested peacefully on a bluff to the far right. Below it, she could make out a tiny cove and beach, with a jetty extending out into the sea.

As the ferry drew closer, she noticed masts and then a small marina to the right of the opening, protected by a granite wall. Behind the wall on the point was a large Balinese style hut, a large sign with sketches of fish surrounded the words, *Anglers' Point Café*.

Up on the left bank of the small harbor she noticed a helipad and long single-story building. Bright red signage on the brick caught her attention. *Emergency Services, Ambulance and Medical Center.*

A fishing trawler was moored in the Marina alongside small sailing boats and a Marine Rescue craft. A walkway ran along either side of the cute harbor, lined with cocos palms, hibiscus, and park benches, the effect serene and inviting. Safiya couldn't help but be charmed.

A splash below drew her attention to the rippling surface, although she couldn't see anything, then a dolphin shot out from under the ferry, barely breaking the water's surface before diving again. To Safiya's delight it kept resurfacing and diving as it led the way into the harbor.

"Oh, my goodness. This is magic."

"Her name's Ping," called a teenage deckhand. "Her mate, Pong, will pop up any second now. They're best mates."

"Ping and Pong." Safiya giggled then searched the water for another dolphin.

A seal popped up and barked at her then dived and sped away after the dolphin.

The sea life here amazed her. She glanced at the deckhand. "I see a seal?"

"That's Pong. Years ago, a kid rescued her from a fishing net after a young dolphin towed her into the shallows, or so the story goes. The kid nursed the baby seal back to health then released her, but she stayed and so did the dolphin. The kid named her Pong because her farts stank. Rumor has it he used to swim with them." The deckhand shrugged. "Could be one of Barnacle Bill's stories. He's full of them."

"Barnacle Bill?"

"Yeah, he's a tough old guy who owns that fishing trawler and a charter boat called *Francine*. It's moored in the next cove. Doesn't go out much himself anymore, but he's a good boss to work for. I gotta go, we're about to dock."

"Okay, thanks for the story."

The engine slowed to a low rumble as the captain lined up with the slipway. Safiya glanced up at the mountain towering over the island, like a mighty guardian. No vehicles were queued up for the return trip, which didn't surprise her, as the ferry wouldn't be leaving for several hours. Enough time for the van and truck drivers to unload their goods and have lunch before the return trip.

Ahead of the slipway, she could see a roundabout. In its center, surrounded by flowers, stood a monument of a soldier. Safiya's thoughts instantly flew to Ryan. Thankfully, he'd survived his time in the army. As for working for Steele Security, he might claim to be a security guard, but she knew better. Eavesdropping on her brother and father had been extremely interesting. She could only hope they caught Madeline's abductors.

The ferry jolted then the huge steel ramp lowered. The deckhand ran to connect the ferry to a heavy-duty chain. Another older deckhand stepped in front of a van with its engine running. He held the handle of Safiya's suitcase and signaled her forward with his other hand.

"Enjoy your stay, Miss."

"Thank you, I will." Safiya accepted her suitcase then towed it over the steel ramp and up the slight incline, her gaze darting about, trying to take everything in at once. Across the road to the left stood a grocery store. Beside it she could see two shop fronts. *"Michelle's Ladies Wear* and *Jody's Hair, Beauty and Nails."* A pub with a wide deck stood on the other side of the monument. To Safiya's right was a tiny park with a bus stop, and a loading lane for the ferry.

"Hmm, where's Zoe?"

A battered silver taxicab rolled to a stop in front of her and a frizzy, red-headed woman jumped out. "Hello, luv. I'm Shirl Thomas. Give us ya suitcase and jump in."

"Thank you, but Zoe Dutch is meeting me."

"Nah, she got caught up with a family who want to go paddle

boarding. Came in yesterday on that blue and white yacht. I'm to drop you off at the Dutch House. Zoe said to tell you to settle in and she'll be home for lunch."

"Oh, thank you, Shirl."

"No worries, luv. You reckon this suitcase is big enough?" Shirl cackled as Safiya helped her lift it into the boot.

"I plan to stay a while." Safiya laughed. "I brought my favorite things."

"With all the trouble brewing, I can't help thinking you might be better getting back on the ferry. Let's hope it's only a storm in a teacup."

Another storm analogy. Safiya shivered, as the strangest feeling slithered over her. She glanced over her shoulder to see Frankie Ellis watching her from the small park. The elderly lady gave a wave then turned away.

CHAPTER SIX

After his close brush with the drunks on the yacht yesterday, Ryan wasn't in a good mood. He'd never forget facing that bull shark, armed with nothing but a six-inch knife and spear gun. Thankfully roaring like a madman had startled the shark, giving him time to reach the sandbar. The walk back to the boatshed hadn't improved his mood.

In collaboration with Garcia and Sergeant Hawthorne, he'd kept his arrival under wraps, and the treasure hunters under constant surveillance, at least while they were on the island. He'd yet to eyeball the two men moored in Dugong Marina, as they dived all day among the surrounding reef, returning late in the afternoon. According to Garcia, the men were brothers and spoke English, although Garcia swore it wasn't their first language. He'd seen them in the grocery store yesterday, stocking up on supplies.

A persistent, one-legged seagull squawked at Ryan's bare feet, demanding a share of his egg and bacon roll. "Scram." He waved the obstinate gull away. "Go catch your own lunch."

Ryan finished his roll, his gaze riveted on the still waters of Coral Cove. Not a board or motor craft to be seen, and only one snorkeler. His sister's new employee, who had arrived on the morning ferry.

She'd disembarked before he could send her back to the mainland, much to his annoyance.

Coming across her file on his grandfather's desk had sparked Ryan's curiosity. Finding two photos had sent shock waves through him. Safiya-Ameerah Farid. According to Jarred, she was supposed to be on her parents' yacht cruising to New Zealand. What the hell was she doing working for Zoe?

He hadn't slept well last night. Then, this morning, the treasure hunters hadn't departed until after eleven. It hadn't helped matters that he'd needed to debrief with Garcia, which meant he'd arrived at Sanctuary Cove after the ferry had departed again.

The runaway princess was in for a surprise when she realized it was him standing on the sand waiting for her. She surfaced, lifted her goggles, and flailed about in the shallow water as she made several attempts to pull off her flippers. He found himself chuckling until she finally stood, all five foot-eight of tantalizing curves, knocking the breath out of him. Safiya-Ameerah in a leopard print bikini did not bode well for his ongoing health or sanity.

"Shit."

It was bad enough he had treasure hunters on the island, who might or might not be responsible for the break-ins and assault. The last thing he needed was this provocative woman drawing their attention and sidetracking him. It was bad enough she had a starring role in his dreams, just out of reach, tormenting him with her alluring body and sensual lips. Their dance at Nick's wedding had been a major miscalculation. Along with his moment of madness at the Gala Fund Raiser. If tabloids got wind of Safiya alone on Curra, the paparazzi would arrive *en masse*.

"Double shit." No woman had ever disconcerted him like this.

Safiya hesitated, raising a hand to shade her eyes. "Ryan?"

He should never have told her about his childhood home. It made a perfect hideaway for a spoilt heiress, notorious for running away when things got tough.

"Wait, I'm coming." She began wading toward him.

A groan escaped. Her words had his cock twitching. He was trying to keep a low profile. Her arrival would put an end to that unless he could get rid of her quickly.

"What are you doing here, Safiya?"

"Hello, Ryan. Isn't it a fabulous day? I adore your island."

"Answer my question."

She gave a light shrug, causing her plump breasts to rise and fall. He fought to keep his gaze above her chest, only to snag on her slender neck. She stopped in front of him, her lips curving into a radiant smile, revealing perfectly aligned snow-white teeth. "I'm assisting your sister to remove Crown of Thorns starfish. They're destroying the coral."

He blinked, her words slowly registering, bringing his gaze to her incredibly sensual eyes. "I know what they do, Safiya. What I don't understand is … Never mind. My sister has a photo of us together at Nick's wedding. Does she know who you are?"

"What photo?"

"It was taken as we came back into the marquee, after our chat by the harbor. I assumed you sent it to her. There is one of you with Madeline as well."

The color drained from her face. "I didn't send any photos."

"Then it must have been Nick. This is a complication I don't need." Zoe would become a matchmaking pain in the ass now that she'd seen that photo. If she detected his attraction to Safiya there would be no stopping her. Even his sister's various businesses wouldn't keep her from interfering in his love life.

"I applied to rent one of Zoe's cabins almost a month ago. We got talking and switched to face time. She offered me a job and I took it. Don't worry, Zoe hasn't said anything, so she couldn't have recognized me."

He silently cursed. "I find that hard to believe." He could just imagine Zoe, lonely and starved of female company, recognizing Safiya then latching onto her, hoping it would bring him home. He'd bet his Harley, Zoe planned to bring Safiya to Magnetic Island in two weeks.

Damn. He should be in Sydney at Simon's birthday bash.

"You're so lucky." Safiya pouted, drawing his gaze to her full lower lip. "You and Zoe ran wild all over this island. I've never had that freedom."

He raised an eyebrow. "Safiya, your father *owns* an island off Fiji."

"He didn't own it when I was a child, and I've never been allowed to roam on my own, a freedom you took for granted. Even your American friend is jealous."

"You've met Adam Garcia?"

"Yes. Zoe introduced us when I arrived. He's a little scary and extraordinarily quiet, but I doubt he misses much. Zoe thinks he needs some tenderness after what he's been through."

"God help him." Their remote island thrived in its anonymity. Bringing the ex-Navy Seal here to recuperate and watch over Zoe had seemed a good idea. Garcia, a six-foot-four bear of a man, much like Talos, would be almost invincible when fully recovered. The fact he'd worked for the NSA bothered Ryan, but the American insisted his job had been more intelligence gathering than anything. *Yeah, right.*

Ryan grunted. He'd hadn't foreseen Zoe taking Garcia under her wing, making it her personal mission to cheer him up. The thought of Safiya spending time with the American grated even more. An annoyance Ryan could well do without.

"Safiya, your father and brother will have my head if I don't send you back to Sydney. You're taking advantage of my sister's generosity."

"Zoe offered me work and a cabin. I accepted. My father agreed if I check in with him every week. He promised no bodyguards." Her eyes narrowed. "Did he send you?"

"If your father knew we were both on this island, he'd send his personal bodyguards to retrieve you and beat the shit out of me."

"He wouldn't dare." She frowned. "Zoe said your fishing trip isn't for two weeks and you always stay on Magnetic Island. Why?"

"My reasons are personal." Ryan crossed his arms, planting his feet wide. He'd have to rethink things. Having Safiya on the island would create nothing but trouble. Hell, anyone who read the tabloids would recognize her.

"Safiya, I'm quietly investigating two break-ins and an assault as a favor to my great-uncle. I'm also concerned about a group of treasure hunters who are out of control and dangerous. I would really appreciate you joining your parents."

"Sorry, no can do. Adam told me about the break-ins and Zoe warned me about the treasure hunters. I suppose the rest of your Steele Ops friends are here too?"

She sounded so vexed he laughed. "The boys are in Sydney. It's just me and Garcia."

"I see." She tilted her head considering him. "Adam told me to snorkel here this afternoon and to stay away from Palm Beach, but he wouldn't say why."

"I went spear-fishing there yesterday and a bunch of drunks attempted to plough me down with their yacht."

Safiya paled. "Obviously, they didn't see you."

"They saw me, warned me off, and made several attempts to run over me, before stealing my runabout."

She touched his arm, causing muscles to twitch. "Why would they do such a thing?"

"Treasure hunters chasing shipwrecks." Ryan shrugged. "Probably thought I was a rival treasure hunter called Miguel. At the very least, they wanted to frighten me off."

"Did you report them to the police?"

"I did."

She tilted her head like a curious puppy. "Aren't shipwrecks protected?"

"Yes, but it doesn't stop treasure hunters seeking fame or fortune. Every few years, old rumors surface, which are followed by a new batch of fortune hunters."

"I can see how a 15th or 16th century Galleon might come to grief on the treacherous reefs. Zoe told me there could be as many as eight hundred wrecks around the Great Barrier Reef. Maybe there is a treasure." Her voice rose with excitement.

Ryan groaned. "My sister is a damn chatterbox."

Safiya beamed, her dark eyes lighting with anticipation. "Sunken treasure. I've only been here five hours, yet Currawong Island is fast becoming an adventure. No bodyguards, no rules, and the freedom to be like any other twenty-three-year-old. Tonight, I'm having dinner with Zoe and Adam at the pub. Want to come?"

"I'm undercover."

"Right. Well after dinner we're going to walk along Turtle Beach. Zoe said there might be a batch of baby turtles scrambling into the ocean. Are you sure you don't want to come with us tonight?"

"Safiya, you can't stay."

The hurt in her eyes almost flayed him, but Ryan had re-read the background check Simon had done on Safiya-Ameerah Farid Gibbs. Since the age of fifteen, she'd been outwitting minders and bodyguards. Absconded from several topnotch boarding school, earning her the moniker of Runaway Princess. She'd dropped out of two universities.

She moved closer, the plea in her eyes compelling. "You can't deny me a chance to live a little and do some good in the world. The moment people discover my identity, they change." Her fingers left a trail of sparks as she ran them along his arm. "I crave being as carefree as Zoe. I may be wrong, but I don't think she has an envious or devious bone in her body. Everything she needs is right here on Currawong Island. Please let me stay. You won't regret it."

"Hah! Famous last words."

Safiya sashayed away, drawing his gaze to the triangular scrap of material covering her curvy butt. "If you change your mind, the menu tonight is tapas, and there will be Spanish music."

Hell, manipulation should be her middle name. The pub would be a magnet to the treasure hunters. Safiya's smile and mouthwatering curves would cause a stampede of testosterone.

"Safiya … wait." In all honesty, he couldn't leave Garcia to protect Zoe *and* Safiya against a bunch of idiots, deranged enough to mow him down. So much for covert surveillance.

Ryan wondered if it was too much to expect none of the locals to recognize him. It had been twelve years. He'd wear a cap and sunglasses. Sit at a table on the deck.

He jogged up to her. "I could do with a night out."

Her eyes lit. "Great. I'm sure Adam would enjoy your company. How's six o'clock?"

"Fine." Was she happy he'd agreed to go, or that Garcia might like it? An unwanted prickle struck. "Don't say anything to Zoe yet, just tell her Barnacle Bill wants her to drop by the boatshed. You can pick me up there."

"Zoe will be so surprised. Wait! I was told except for emergency vehicles, a minibus and one taxicab, there are no cars on the island. How can we pick you up?"

"Don't tell me Zoe made you walk from the ferry?"

"No, she sent a hilarious lady named Shirl who owns a beat-up taxicab. Zoe and Adam were tied up at the Surf Shack. We did pass some golf carts though."

"That's how most people get about or do their shopping. The transport ferry only brings delivery vans, the odd tradesman, and building materials."

"Which is why it's so quiet." She glanced toward the almost impenetrable foliage curving around the edge of the sand. "I love it." She beamed at him, her open smile radiating happiness.

"So do I." He cleared his throat, dragging his gaze from her face to the clusters of palms nestled among the eucalyptus grove, secluding Dutch land and their private beach from Coral Cove Road. It had grown thicker in twelve years.

It surprised him Garcia hadn't mentioned Safiya. He might be recovering from a range of injuries, but his eyes and mouth still worked. He knew how to use a phone. Ryan had stewed over many things early this morning, as he lay concealed on Rocky Point, his binoculars glued to the larger group of treasure hunters, before they motored off to the outer reefs.

Maybe Garcia wasn't into women. One thing for sure, the man had an astounding tolerance for pain. A week ago, he'd been ambushed and beaten badly before his attackers tossed him off a cliff. Hanging on to a tree root with broken ribs and a dislocated shoulder took some serious mind control.

Safiya touched Ryan's arm, jogging him out of his thoughts. "When I arrived, I saw shops and the pub, but where are all the houses?"

"The majority of people live at Paradise Beach and Oyster Bay. There are smaller settlements at Whale Point, Blue Haven, and Sunset Beach. If you'd gone in the other direction, when you got off the ferry, you would have seen a lot more houses."

"I noticed Coral Sea Road is sealed. Does it go all the way around the island?

"Pretty much." Ryan met her amazing eyes. "It's the main road, which starts at Sanctuary Cove and circles the island. There are walking trails going inland."

Safiya dropped her snorkel and flippers into a large beach bag then picked up her towel. "Adam put a drone up to show me the island. It resembles a star fish with ten stumpy legs." She rubbed her body dry then wrapped the towel around her torso. "I can see how Shark Bite Bay got its name. There were five sharks cruising about, and that cliff face rises out of the ocean like a giant wave about to break. I'd love to climb that mountain."

Ryan stiffened. "Stay away from Morcago Lookout. It's off limits."

"In that case I'll climb to Kingfisher and Heron Lookout. Adam said there is a koala sanctuary, if I want to get up close and personal with them."

"Did he?" What else had Garcia offered to show her? His job was to keep Zoe safe, not get sidetracked by Safiya. Fuck, jealousy was a bitch. "I could take you hiking to Kingfisher Lookout early tomorrow morning once the treasure hunters leave. On the way up, we'll cut through the koala sanctuary then stop for a swim at Cascada Falls. It's one of my favorite places on the island. We'll be back in plenty of time if you'd like to do Zoe's whale shark adventure swim." If she got to swim with the giant mammals, and explore the island, it might be enough to get her to leave on Monday's ferry.

"Really?"

"Sure." He was a fool, asking for trouble.

"So, you're not casting me off the island?" Her mischievous glance settled on his crossed arms.

It went against his better judgement, but he couldn't burst her bubble. "You can stay for now. However, I want you to promise you'll keep away from the treasure hunters."

"I promise. Are you staying at your parents' house?"

"No. Barnacle Bill's Boatshed."

"Why? It's not as if you need to hide from Zoe anymore." A smile curved her plump lips. "We could all sit on the porch in the evenings and watch the sun set over the ocean."

The thought almost choked him. No way was he going to watch romantic sunsets with her, the woman he should avoid at all costs. They were just too different. "Other than Bill and Zoe, I haven't had anything to do with my family in years."

"Whyever not?"

"Long story, but the bottom line is my best friend fell to his death while abseiling. I was held responsible, and my family didn't stand up for me. My father decided it would be better for me to finish my education on the mainland and never return to Curra. An inquest cleared me, but the damage was done. I left the island and refused to come back."

"Oh, my God, Ryan." She winced, reaching out with her hand to touch his chest. "They banished you from your home?"

"This is the first time I've been back since I was sixteen. I don't expect anyone to welcome me with open arms, which is why I'd prefer to keep a low profile."

"That explains why Zoe sometimes looks so sad when she speaks of you. I'm sorry you lost your friend, and that you were blamed. I don't understand why your family didn't stand by you. Surely, they knew you wouldn't intentionally hurt your friend. If you want to talk anytime, I'm here."

Ryan kicked at a piece of sun-bleached driftwood. "Do you know, besides Nick, you're the only other person to say that. Thanks, Saf."

Bewilderment touched her features for a moment before she smiled. "Seriously, I meant it. We all need someone we can trust to talk things through with, otherwise we bottle them up and stew on them. It isn't healthy." She glanced up toward Kingfisher Lookout. "I should unpack and get ready for our date."

"It's not a date, Safiya."

"It's a date with friends."

She slipped on a pair of flat sandals then tramped along the beach, leaving him to follow, which soon became a torturous pleasure. The Sheikh and Gibbs would have Ryan's head if he dared lay a finger on Safiya. A hike alone up a mountain wasn't his brightest idea, yet anticipation grew by the second. He'd have a 360-degree view of the surrounding reefs. The perfect place to scope out what the treasure hunters were up to.

They climbed the steps from Dutchies Beach to Dutchies Bluff. It might be the smallest headland on the island, but all five acres had belonged to the Dutch family since William Dutch claimed it in 1870. The house had been built to blend in with the natural habitat and overlooked two private beaches, sheltered from the east by Kingfisher Mountain, the south by Whale Point Headland, and the north by Sanctuary Cove.

He trailed Safiya onto the front porch then waited as she opened the screen door and strolled in. Not locked. That would have to change. He glanced either side of the wide hall, noting new bedspreads on Zoe's and his parents' beds. His father's study hadn't changed, nor had the hall runner. The back of his neck tingled, as if the ghost of a childhood friend haunted the house, looking for him to go on their next adventure.

Entering his grandparents' house yesterday had made him just as uncomfortable, as if he'd been a thief. At least finding Safiya's photo had vanquished his guilt, and the historic files were now secure in Sergeant Hawthorne's safe.

Safiya pushed open Ryan's childhood bedroom door and entered. His breath caught as he gazed around the room. New paint and a flowery bedspread on a double bed gave the room a completely different look. His posters, single bed and old desk were gone. As were his dart board, trophies and comics. Lucky he'd taken the gold sovereigns Bill gave him on his twelfth birthday, and the one he'd found in the cave, or they would have disappeared too. That first sovereign and reading his great-great-grandfather's diary had been the start of Ryan and Zane's infatuation with finding a hidden treasure. Had his parents thrown his prized possessions away or stuffed them in a box somewhere? Bill might know.

"It's as if I never existed."

Safiya spun around. "This was your room?"

"Yes."

She grimaced. "Zoe said it's more for show than anything. Nobody stays."

"I'm not surprised. My aunt rarely visited but always stayed at the pub when she did." He turned on his heel and strode down the hall to the kitchen. It had been updated and new tiles laid. He poked his head into the dining room, oddly pleased to see the large family table and familiar cabinet full of fine china and glassware.

"When you speak of Currawong Island, it's clear you love the place." Safiya squeezed past to stand in front of him. "Have you really never come home?"

"No. In between deployments, my mates and I hung out together. Sometimes we'd come up this way, but we'd fish off Magnetic Island, which is closer to Townsville."

Ryan had been blown away by how fast he'd bonded with the boys. They'd lost one member of the team to a suicide bomber, and another left due to PTSD, but Jack Callaghan had recovered and would be joining them on a fishing trip later in the year. Something they were all looking forward to, especially after Jack's run in with mercenaries in South America. Apparently, a beautiful redhead had a lot to do with his survival in the Amazon Jungle and positive mental outlook.

"Did you ever meet up with Zoe?"

"Yes, and Barnacle Bill more recently. We'd catch up in Townsville or on Magnetic Island. No one knew."

Safiya glanced out the huge kitchen window. "Except for birds, it's so peaceful. How many people live on the island?"

"I believe there are now close to four hundred permanent residents. In the school holidays the camping ground at Rocky Point can hold about eighty tents and we get the odd yacht or two most weeks."

"The ferry took two and a half hours. I wouldn't like to cross in rough seas."

"It doesn't run in rough seas or bad weather. It's not uncommon to be cut off for weeks at a time. As a teenager, I dreamed of having my own sea plane to fly tourists from the mainland. My mate and I wanted a catamaran to do day trips on the reefs and we planned to build an eco-friendly resort and make a fortune." Ryan closed his eyes as memories surged, threatening to overwhelm him.

Safiya touched his arm. "I saw a small school. Does it cater for all children?"

"It's an early learning center and primary school. The older kids either do School of the Air, travel back and forth each week or board in Townsville for the term and come home for holidays. Townsville is brilliant for kids into sport."

"What did you and Zoe do?"

"We boarded with our aunt who now lives on the Gold Coast. When things went belly up, my great-uncle took me to Perth where I lived with a retired army pilot."

"Aha! Which is why you became a Blackhawk pilot."

He chuckled. "No. When I was eighteen, six Sikorsky Blackhawk helicopters arrived from New South Wales for a month-long counter-terrorism training exercise. I became hooked, so joined the army and got into the Blackhawk program."

"That's where you met Jarred Steele and the others?"

"No, only Nick. We did our training together then flew a few tours in the Middle East. After one tour, we returned to find Jarred Steele waiting for us. He requested we join an elite unit he was putting together. That's where we met the rest of the boys, and I did my paramedic training."

"So, you left the army a year ago and now use your paramedic and pilot skills for Steele Security?"

Hell yes, more than he'd expected, but he couldn't admit it. "We provide security for visiting VIPs and dignitaries, high-end fund-raising events like Tuesday night, and some government gatherings."

"Like that Secret Cyber Summit in the Lau Archipelago, where Adam was attacked?"

Ryan clenched his fists. If Garcia had leaked sensitive information, he wouldn't get a job with Steele Security. "I can't comment on any of our jobs."

"I was on my father's island, remember. I listened at the door when you and Nick were talking to Madeline about the cyber conference. You formatted a plan to drop in covertly to join the rest of your team. Adam mentioned he'd recently been in Fiji. It doesn't take a genius to add two and two together."

Safiya traced a finger aimlessly over the granite benchtop. "It appears the men who tried to run you down want the fabled treasure, no matter who they hurt to get it. You need to stay vigilant."

Hell, Safiya was too astute for her own good. He should alert Jarred to her presence, which meant he'd be obliged to inform Gibbs and the Sheikh about the treasure hunters. At best she probably only had two or three days free of bodyguards.

"I'm out of here. Lock the door after me." Ryan ran a hand through his hair. He wasn't looking forward to Gibb's or the Sheikh's wrath. Safiya would see it as a betrayal. He would make it up to her with an impersonal tour of the island's best kept secrets.

Fuck, who the hell am I trying to fool? Spending time alone with Safiya excited him. Her empathy came across as genuine. Madeline's cutting dressing-down and dare had made him want to look deeper. This damn attraction between them demanded it. What could it hurt to spend a few hours with her?

CHAPTER SEVEN

"Did Barnacle Bill say why he wants me to stop by the boatshed," asked Zoe.

"No." Safiya rummaged through her makeup purse, keeping her head down.

"That's really odd." Zoe brushed Safiya's mascara over her fair eyelashes. "I swear my great-uncle is acting really weird lately." She handed the mascara to Safiya then twirled in front of her floor length mirror. "Thank you for braiding my hair and lending me this gorgeous dress. I love it."

"You're welcome. I still think it's a crime to tame all those wild curls." Safiya sent a critical eye over the powder-blue sundress smothered in white daisies. With a shirred bodice, it molded to Zoe's breasts perfectly, while the flared skirt flattered her slim build. "If you love it, keep it. I'll make another one."

"You made this?"

"Yes, my ... a lady taught me to sew during the long winter months in Switzerland. The shirring takes forever by hand. Thankfully, a sewing machine can do it much faster. If you have one, I can teach you?"

"Yes, please. My grandmother has one. I can't believe how well we get on. It's like you were meant to come here." Zoe beamed. "You're the sister I've always wanted."

"Really?" Safiya swallowed the lump in her throat, blinking furiously to ward off tears. "That's the loveliest thing anyone has ever said to me. I'd love a sister."

"Done." Zoe wrapped her in a bear hug. "You're my dream come true, Fia."

"Don't make me cry."

A sharp knock interrupted their special moment.

"Time to go," Adam called in his deep, gruff voice.

"Coming." Zoe squeezed Safiya's hand. "You could be a much-needed rainbow for Currawong Island."

"At least that's better than being called a storm, and there's a pot of gold at the end of a rainbow."

"Rainbows appear after storms. Maybe you're the treasure." Zoe giggled, dragging Safiya to the door. "Let's make this a night we'll never forget." She opened the door and almost ran into the big American. "Adam! Don't you look handsome?" She stretched up and kissed his cheek. "Seriously, all my Christmases have come at once."

Adam's stunned expression drew a laugh from Safiya. "Just go with it. We're deliriously happy tonight."

"Hmm." He stood back as they preceded him out of the house.

Once he'd locked the front door, they piled into a golf cart. Safiya took the rear seat while Zoe drove with Adam beside her. She fiddled with the flared skirt of her navy and white polka-dot dress. The sweetheart neckline and fitted waist flattered her curves. A present from her maternal grandmother, who Safiya had loved. Wearing it tonight had been an impulse she couldn't resist. Nanna would have been so happy Safiya had found a place and people she liked enough to build a future.

Happiness had only ever been short-lived for Safiya, yet she could barely contain her excitement. There'd been magic in the air since she'd seen the island for the first time. She stilled, lost in a whirlwind of precious moments. When her gaze had first locked with Ryan's on her father's Island last February ... Dancing barefoot with him at

Nick's wedding in April … Enthralled as he'd described Currawong Island's beauty and uniqueness … Ryan standing up for her against Jamal … Ryan rescuing her from the kidnappers … The anguish and uncertainty in his eyes when she'd said goodbye and wished him well.

No, she wouldn't think of *that* moment. Instead, she'd focus on the heat in his gaze earlier. His offer to take her hiking. The dimple in his cheek when he grinned. His vulnerability when speaking of the past. Her newfound freedom. She would create a special niche for herself on the island and build on her friendship with Zoe.

"You okay, Fia?" Zoe smiled over her shoulder. "You look miles away."

"I was thinking this is a fairytale. I feel like Cinderella, only instead of finding my glass slipper and a prince, I've found a sister and mystic island. Does that sound crazy?"

"Crazy but true. Given time we both might find our princes." She giggled and nudged Adam. "You're already a knight in shining armor. Is there a prince hiding in there too?"

"No." He shifted about, as if uncomfortable with Zoe's compliment.

"Too bad. If you see any, point them in our direction. We're here, Fia."

"Oh." Safiya studied the bright blue boatshed.

A sign with *Barnacle Bill's Boatshed and Fishing Charters* printed on it hung from rusty chains. Two huge wooden doors had been pushed to either side, giving a wide vista of the sea beyond. Stepping inside, she took in the expansive size. A small glassed-in office took up one corner, the desk cluttered with paperwork. Fishing nets and rods hung from hooks along one wall. Wooden stairs hugged the other, leading up to a closed-in mezzanine level. Barrels and large coolers were shoved haphazardly under the stairs. Two small tenders lay upside down in the middle of the concrete floor. A pair of slip rails disappeared into the ocean, where a big boat shifted gently with the rise and fall of the tide. Behind her Zoe and Adam were still at the golf cart, arguing the merits of fairytales.

Footsteps descending the wooden stairs drew Safiya's attention.

Her heart skipped a beat. Ryan wore caramel loafers, a soft-green shirt, tucked into cream pants and a white straw Panama hat. With his tanned physique, blue eyes, and sandy hair, he looked like he belonged on a yacht in the French Riviera.

For a moment they stared at each other. The heat in Ryan's gaze sent thrills through her. Her breath hitched.

A high-pitched squeal erupted behind her. "Ryan!" Zoe clattered across the concrete in her white sandals, leaving Adam at the door. "What are you doing here? I can't believe it." She threw herself into his arms. "It really is Christmas."

He hugged her tightly. "I'm here on the quiet, Zo, and only for a few days."

"Why?"

"To check on you and look into the break-ins and assault, as a favor to Bill."

"This is why Uncle Bill wanted me to stop by. You're my surprise?"

"Yes, but also because I need to keep a low profile. I'm coming to the pub with you, Adam and Safiya, but I've asked Gar... Adam to book a quiet table out of the way."

Zoe giggled. "You mean Fia?"

"Yes, that's what I said."

"No, you said Sa-fee-ya." She raised an eyebrow at Safiya. "Didn't he?"

"Yes." Safiya licked her lips. "We are acquainted, Zoe. I'm sorry I didn't tell you, but I honestly didn't expect Ryan to be here. I wanted us to get to know each other before ... before you heard things about me. I wanted you to form your own opinions."

Zoe blushed. "I asked Nick to send me photos of his wedding, so I recognized you, which is why I was so excited you wanted to work here. We've hardly had a chance to dig deeper. What sort of things would I hear?"

"I'm—"

"She's my ... girlfriend." Ryan's announcement rendered Safiya speechless.

"Girlfriend?" Zoe squealed. "Fia, you really could be my sister."

"Wait!" Safiya sent a silent plea to Ryan. She valued Zoe's friendship and trust too much to risk losing it through a lie. "We hardly know each other. I met your brother in February on my father's Fijian island."

"Your father has his own— "

"That's irrelevant, Zo." Ryan interrupted, strolling over to draw Safiya against his side, his hand gripping her hip firmly. "I know enough to want us to be exclusive."

Safiya frowned at Ryan. "I want Zoe to know everything, even if … she ends up despising me." She forced a smile for Zoe. "I'm hoping you will at least give me a chance."

Ryan's fingers tightened. "Safiya, let's do this my way."

"No." She swallowed. "Zoe, I've never had the freedom you take for granted. My father is a sheikh, and my mother was his interpreter. They married in secret so they could continue to work together. I've spent most of my life being raised by an au pair, and tutored at home, before being sent off to boarding schools." If she weren't so serious, she would have laughed at Zoe's stunned expression.

"If I told other students who my parents were, they called me a liar. It's hard to argue against an internet search engine. Everyone I've ever trusted, has left me, or betrayed me. I came here to get away because my father believes I need protecting from fortune hunters."

"That's horrible." Zoe shook her head slowly. "Ryan's not a fortune hunter."

He snorted. "The Sheikh decided to buy me off anyway."

"What?" Safiya pushed his hand away and whirled on him. "You're lying."

"He offered me fifty thousand to walk away. I told him you have the right to choose who you form relationships with, so he raised it to five hundred thousand."

"When?"

"An hour ago. Your brother gave him my number."

Heat suffused her face. "I can't believe it." Except she could. Her father's lawyer had bought off two men to save her reputation. This however was underhanded and inexcusable. Like everyone else, her parents assumed her an airhead. That her father would make such a deal, proved his low opinion of her character. Her judgement. Her intelligence.

"Oh, Fia. I'm so sorry." Zoe hugged her. "You can pick your friends, but you can't pick your relatives."

"No." Safiya tried to laugh. It came out as a choked sob. She mustered her courage and lifted her chin. "Did you accept his deal, Ryan?"

"No. I told him as politely as I could to fuck off."

"You should have taken the money. It would serve my father right."

"I can't blame him for testing me, Safiya, but I've fought hard for my honor. Anyway, it's a bit hard for me to walk away from you when we're on an isolated island."

This time she did laugh. "At least it will give my father some sleepless nights."

"Excuse us a moment, Zoe." Ryan took Safiya's hand and drew her across the boatshed. "While we're on the island, I think it best we let everyone believe we're dating. It will deter the treasure hunters and give you breathing room, while you decide what to do." He grinned. "If Zoe thinks we're together, she won't drive us crazy playing matchmaker."

"I don't want to lie to your sister."

"Give me and the boys a week to sort things out then I'll tell Zoe the truth."

"All right, one week. Wait, you and which boys?"

"I spoke to Jarred before you picked me up at the boatshed. He's bringing our fishing trip forward. The boys will be staying in Zoe's cabins." He lifted her chin, his gaze intense. His breath brushed her ear, tickling the sensitive shell. "If we're to convince people we're involved, I should kiss you."

She breathed in his spicy cologne, the scent as mesmerizing as the invitation in his eyes. Her heart raced; her breath caught. "That is … probably a good idea."

He touched his lips to hers … once … twice … three times. Feathered caresses that drew her into him. His hand skimmed her back, hot through the material of her dress, sending warm tingles cascading through her. He nipped at her lower lip, soothed over it with the tip of his tongue. With a smothered moan, she opened her mouth, inviting him in to deepen the kiss.

A world of difference separated her limited experience of groping hands and rushed kisses to this enthralling engagement. Long denied cravings rose from deep within, bringing forth a boldness she'd only encountered with him. She sank into him, reluctant to break this magic spell. Her breasts pressed against hard muscle, making her want to slip her hand under his shirt and touch his warm skin. He held back, even though his desire was evident, as if her pleasure mattered more than anything else.

"I know the lass is stunning, lad, but I didn't expect you to fall, hook, line and sinker the minute you cast your rod."

Barnacle Bill's voice made Safiya freeze. Shocked and embarrassed by her brazen behavior, she couldn't look at Ryan. Her hands shook as she withdrew them from his biceps to clasp them behind her back. Completely at sea, she watched Barnacle Bill plod down the wooden stairs, careful not to spill whatever he had in a white mug with a yellow sunflower on it.

He shook his head slowly. "In my day, only a betrothed man kissed his intended so thoroughly, or perhaps a scoundrel with no concern for a lady's reputation."

Ryan raised Safiya's chin, his touch gentle. She had no choice but to meet his amused gaze. "Then it's time you met my girlfriend, Bill."

"Your ... I'll be damned." Barnacle Bill stomped over. "Why didn't you say so yesterday?"

"I wanted to keep it low-key a while longer. We haven't been dating long."

"That's the best news I've had in years." Bill held his arms wide. "Welcome to the family, lass."

"Thank you, Bill." Safiya accepted the bear hug, embarrassed by the spiraling lie. Ryan wasn't the only person who strived for an honorable reputation. She clung to hers by her fingertips, yet nothing she'd achieved sold magazines like: *SHEIKH'S SECRET DAUGHTER SEEN*

SHOPPING IN PARIS. SHEIKH'S SECRET DAUGHTER ALMOST ABDUCTED FROM SYDNEY GALA EVENT. She could imagine the latest headline if news they were dating got out. *SHEIKH'S SECRET DAUGHTER DATING SECURITY GUARD.* Her photo would be plastered over every newspaper. Ryan would be labelled a gold digger.

"We should go," called Adam. "The table's booked for six-fifteen."

"You're welcome to join us, Bill." Ryan caught Safiya's hand. "It's only a short walk."

"Reckon I will." Barnacle Bill winked at Safiya. "Ryan's return has been long overdue. I wouldn't miss this for the world." He put down the pretty cup and stomped off after Zoe and Adam.

Ryan's fingers tensed round Safiya's hand before he released her. It wasn't her fault he was here, yet her presence had compromised his mission and would expose him to people he didn't want to see. Guilt ate at Safiya as Ryan closed and locked the shed doors.

"Did Bill have your trophies and comics?"

"Yes, and my dart board." He didn't retake her hand as they strolled side-by-side through a small park, although she could sense his gaze on her as she looked about. Was he regretting their kiss? Or reliving it like her?

Zoe's happy laughter burst through Safiya's chaotic thoughts. She glanced at Ryan to see him smiling indulgently at his sister. *This isn't about me. Ryan would risk all to keep Zoe happy and safe.* Safiya could only imagine what it would be like if he felt that way about her.

RYAN SLID on his sunglasses as they crossed Coral Sea Road. A colorful array of two and four-seater golf carts crammed the parking area. He wasn't particularly concerned about being recognized, as Bill's Panama and the sunglasses would conceal his identity while the sun held out. Hopefully, they'd leave before darkness fell. If he didn't go inside all should be well.

Several family groups were already gathered at tables along the wide veranda. He didn't look for familiar faces. Inside, two acoustic guitarists strummed out a soft Spanish melody. As barely any chatter could be heard, he guessed the audience inside were enthralled by the guitarists' talent.

Zoe, Bill, and Adam were already seated on the far side of the furthest table as Ryan trailed Safiya along the veranda. He silently cursed as all conversation ended and every person on the veranda focused on Safiya. He couldn't blame them, her beauty and aristocratic bearing demanded attention.

The guitarists broke into a Spanish Rumba, breaking the momentary hiatus. At least no one paid Ryan the slightest attention.

Once they were seated a young waiter handed out the tapas menu, took their drinks order and hurried off.

Bill rubbed his hands together and grinned at Ryan. "I feel as happy as a pig in mud."

"I can tell." Ryan fought an impulse to look over his shoulder. He couldn't shake the sense of being stared at.

Bill leaned across the table. "We've got a sailing regatta planned for late October."

"Really?"

"Zoe approached the council with the idea and then she got some big sponsors on board. We've got five months to get ready." He leaned closer. "Which is why we can't afford negative attention focused on Curra."

"Fia." A child screeched behind Ryan then a small body clambered onto Safiya's lap. He beamed up at Safiya. "It's still my birfday."

"Happy birthday, Robbie." Safiya gave the little boy a hug. "Don't tell me you've run off from your mommy again?"

"Nah. She's there." He pointed over her shoulder. "Did you buy me a present?"

"Robert John Curran. Don't be so rude."

Ryan glanced behind as the woman who'd reprimanded the boy extracted herself from between two other young boys at the next table.

Camilla. Still pretty, although plumper and looking a bit worn out.

His gut flipped as she handed a young baby to the solid guy across the table.

Tommy. Ryan turned away. Those children could have been his if Camilla had stuck by him. If she and Tommy hadn't betrayed him. If Zane hadn't died.

"Hello, Bill, Zoe. How are you settling in, Fia?" Camilla stood at the end of the table. Her curious gaze flicked to Adam, who gave her his marble impersonation. She shivered and quickly transferred her attention to Ryan, where it lingered, yet she showed no sign of recognition, only feminine interest.

"I'm settling in well, Camilla. I've had a lovely afternoon, snorkeling, and enjoying this beautiful weather." Safiya cast Ryan a quick glance. "I can't wait to go exploring."

Camilla gave a careless shrug. "There's not that much to see." She looked from Ryan to Zoe. "We heard another man arrived by seaplane yesterday. Aren't you going to introduce me to your visitors?"

"Of course. This is Adam; he's recuperating after an accident." Zoe sent Ryan a look. *What should I do?*

He removed his sunglasses and hat. It would cause hostility if he didn't at least acknowledge the woman. "Hello, Cammy. It's been a long time."

She blinked several times before her face paled. "Ryan?"

"I flew in on the sea plane yesterday."

"It's been twelve years since you left." Her animosity came at him in waves. "We didn't think you were ever coming back. Why now?"

"The island council invited me." They could explain the rest if they wished to. No way would he give anyone the satisfaction of knowing how much he'd longed to come home.

He'd had twelve years to mourn the death of his best friend. To relive the following week and the accusations hurled at him. To remember the humiliation and despair as he sat through the inquest, alone and lost. He'd admitted to being obsessed with finding treasure. He never once tried to conceal his involvement. If it hadn't been for Bill and the lawyer, Ryan might have been charged with manslaughter. There were still several accusations to be address and repudiated if he could be bothered.

"Is that you, Ryan?" Tommy sidled up to Camilla. "You're back?" At least he sounded friendly. Surprisingly, he hadn't grown taller than he'd been at sixteen, which had to be three inches shorter than Ryan's five-foot-eleven.

"Tommy, this is… Fia. Fia, this is Tommy."

"Hi." Safiya's open smile had Tommy gaping like a floundering fish, until Camilla nudged him. He adjusted the baby in his arms and looked to Ryan. "Where are you staying?"

"With Bill. I plan to do some fishing while Zoe and my girlfriend get acquainted."

"Your girlfriend?" Camilla's attention shot to Safiya.

"I didn't want to say anything until Ryan arrived." Safiya placed her hand on Ryan's tense thigh. "What better way for me to get to know Zoe and the island than to work here for a while."

The interest in Tommy's eyes irritated Ryan. Safiya's beauty and curvy build were certainly eye-catching, but surely Tommy could be less obvious.

Camilla scowled at Tommy as she took the little boy's hand. "Come on, Robbie, your ice-cream will be here in a minute."

"Yay." Robbie clambered off Safiya's knee and scampered after his mother.

Tommy hesitated, pulling his shoulders back. "I'd love to catch up. We could go fishing any day after I finish work."

"Maybe next time. I've got friends arriving Monday."

"I was once your friend, Ryan." Color rose in Tommy's cheeks.

"Yeah, until you betrayed me."

All color bleached from Tommy's tanned face. "You knew?" His shoulders drooped. "It all happened so fast, and you were gone before I could muster the courage to tell you. Then there didn't seem much point. I didn't know how to contact you." His eyes implored Ryan for understanding. "I'm sorry." He strode past his own table and into the pub, where the guitarists were now playing an intricate version of the *Flamenco*.

"What was that about?" Bill scratched his head, sending his mop of white hair into disarray.

"Ancient history." Ryan looked away. *Tommy hooking up with Cammy behind my back. Abandoning me when I needed my friends most.*

Their drinks arrived as a man and woman somewhere in their early forties stopped at the end of the table, their curiosity evident by the way they kept glancing between Garcia, Fia and Ryan.

"Hi, Joanne. Hi, Paul." Zoe smiled openly at them. "You taking the night off?"

Joanne nodded. "We're not open tonight. Figured all the action would be here. Hiya, Bill." Ryan picked a Scottish burr to her accent. She looked around the table. "Who are your visitors, Zoe?"

"Oh, this is Adam, he was a seal in the US Navy, and is recuperating after an injury. This is my brother Ryan and his girlfriend, Fia. She will be working with me for a while."

"Your brother?" asked Joanne, unable to hide her surprise.

"Hi." Ryan raised a hand.

"Everyone, this is Joanne and Paul Kilgour. They own the Angler's Point Café. Great place for breakfast or pizza and pasta."

They still looked confused. Probably because they hadn't even known he existed. The rumor mill would soon clarify things for them. They launched into small talk, asking Zoe how her businesses were faring, leaving Ryan to his beer.

Safiya slid closer. "I may be wrong, but is it possible Tommy's carrying a load of guilt over what happened to your friend?" She kept her voice low.

"Tommy wasn't there." The guilt that came with the memories gnawed at his gut. Under the table, his leg bounced. A nervous twitch he thought he'd grown out of.

"What happened, Ryan?" She dropped her hand to his thigh, the gentle rub of her palm soothing. "Believe it or not, I'm good at listening and thinking things through logically."

With a sigh, he dragged his hand through his hair. Safiya was stubborn enough not to let the subject drop. "My friend's name was Zane. He fell to his death while abseiling off Morcago Ledge. He ignored two crucial rules. Never abseil without a harness, and never abseil alone."

"If you weren't with … Zane, why were you blamed and banished from the island?"

"No one believed me. An old man swore he saw two boys on the cliff face in some sort of struggle. One fell, and the other climbed back up and disappeared."

She scrunched up her nose. "So, Zane wasn't alone. The question is, who beside you, could have been with him?"

"No one. At the inquest, the old man admitted to drinking heavily the night before and sleeping off a hangover at South Point, which is a far distance across the bay. His evidence was ruled inadmissible. To identify anyone from that distance was impossible. Our abseiling trainer vouched for my integrity and skill. He agreed I thrived on adrenalin, but insisted I always put safety first. He said Zane was the impulsive one. The judge ruled it death by misadventure. Zane got impatient and did the climb on his own."

"You don't agree?"

It felt cathartic to talk about Zane's death with someone who didn't judge, who could see things from an outsider's angle. "Zane wouldn't have used just a rope to descent. He would have used his harness and carabiners, which would have saved him from falling."

"You're sure?"

"I …" Ryan wasn't sure of anything, except for his father's sickening accusation.

Don't lie, boy. I found your harness and helmet. You left your best friend's broken body on the rocks and ran away like a coward. I will not have you sully the Dutch name. It would be best if you finished your schooling on the mainland and stayed there.

Ryan rubbed his chin. "I plan to discover the truth and clear my name, Safiya."

"Good." Her fingers tightened on his thigh. "But there's nothing you can do tonight. You should make the most of the time you have with your sister and Bill. Enjoy the music and have a little fun. It will do you good."

CHAPTER EIGHT

Safiya tapped her sandal to the lively music. She'd eaten her fill of a variety of tapas dishes, consumed two glasses of sangria and laughed at Bill's outrageous stories. Even Adam had cracked an occasional smile. Safiya had never had so much fun. She'd never been this carefree, and she liked how Ryan interacted so easily with his sister and uncle.

All evening people had been calling out greetings to Zoe and Bill, most eyeing Safiya, Ryan and Adam with open interest. Somewhat subdued, Ryan had kept his back to the other tables, although curiosity ran rife in the pub tonight.

"Want to dance, Fia?" Zoe scrambled from between Bill and Adam. "I love this song and don't want to dance on my own."

"Sure." Safiya followed Zoe.

Darkness had descended long ago, and most families with children had left. A woman, Safiya assumed to be Camilla's sister left with the three boys and baby, so Tommy and Camilla could stay. They'd gone inside to sit at the bar.

Ryan had joined in the conversation, although it was obvious to Safiya he would rather be anywhere else. He probably wasn't even aware of his jiggling knee knocking against her leg, or that he'd completely shredded a drink coaster.

Memories had to be hitting him hard. He hadn't elaborated on his friend's death, yet Safiya's concern went much deeper than idle curiosity. She wanted to be there for him. To understand him and help if she could. Maybe later, away from flapping ears, they could talk about it further.

Inside, every chair and table were occupied, the audiences fixed on the two male guitarists. Twins by the look of them, and handsome. Loud laughter drew Safiya's attention to a far table, where six men played a drinking game. Judging by the glares from the crowd, their behavior had become annoying.

Fishing nets, anchors, life-saving buoys, and an ancient ship's helm decorated the walls. She eyed the empty dance floor with trepidation. "Why isn't anyone else dancing?"

"Too scared to make the first move," Zoe called, rolling her shoulders and hips, as she sashayed onto the dance floor. "Come on, Fia. Let's get this party started."

A burst of laughter escaped Safiya at Zoe's uncoordinated and out of beat movements.

Zoe shrugged and laughed back. "I know, but who cares."

That did it for Safiya. If Zoe could live in the moment, she would to. She loved Zoe's bouncy spontaneity. When they'd first chatted over the net, Safiya took Zoe to be an eighteen-year-old, blonde surfer girl. Her springy, long curls so out of control, she'd never get a comb through it without conditioner. She'd been stunned to discover Zoe was twenty-two and running several businesses on her own. She didn't answer to anyone and if people didn't like the causes she supported, or how she danced, that was their problem, not hers. They were worlds apart yet, from the first moment they'd met, a friendship had bloomed.

Catching the beat, Safiya spun around Zoe, moving in, back-tracking, shimmying, and twisting, giving every part of her body a workout. It had taken dancing barefoot with Ryan to remind her how much she loved dancing.

Zoe began mimicking Safiya, resulting in much laughter. Some from their audience. Others began clapping, and Camilla joined them on the dance floor. Not the least flustered by their amused audience, Zoe threw herself about entirely at odds to the beat.

They were having so much fun, it wasn't long before they were all breathing heavily, and still they danced on. The guitarists upping the tempo until Safiya thought she'd collapse from spinning. It was exhilarating and freeing.

A group of teenagers joined them, everyone intent on mimicking Zoe's crazy antics. Safiya's hair collapsed from its twisted top knot and tumbled down her back, the clip falling at her feet. Before she could retrieve it, Ryan appeared before her, picked it up and slipped into his shirt pocket. She couldn't help but admire his muscled thighs. She'd tried not to dally on the green shirt clinging to his solid chest and broad shoulders. He shared his sister's lively blue eyes and sandy hair. He had to be close to six feet, a perfect height for her five-feet-eight inches.

His serious gaze locked on her. "I believe I owe you a dance." He took her hand and drew her close to sway in time to a much slower tempo.

She raised an eyebrow. "Aren't you worried you'll be recognized?"

"Too late. News spreads like wildfire on Curra. As your boyfriend, people would think it odd if I didn't dance with you. Aside from that we're saving you from being approached by some unsavory drunks."

Confused, she glanced over her right shoulder. The teenagers had quit the floor. Adam danced slowly with Zoe, maneuvering her about easily tucked inside one massive arm. She looked like a deliriously happy, dainty fairy. Camilla and Tommy were dancing together, although they didn't look at all relaxed. Tommy looked drunk, which might be why.

Raucous comments drew Safiya's attention to the group of six men, who now stood by the dance floor, making no attempt to lower their voices or disguise the offensiveness of their comments. All of which were sexist and unwelcome. A frisson of disquiet skittered down her spine.

"Ignore them." Ryan's warm breath tickled her ear, sending a thrilling tremor straight to the center of her womanhood. She wanted to kiss him, climb him, claim him.

The drunken louts' comments got louder and sleazier. Then everything happened at once. One shoved Tommy into a table, sending drinks scattering then he grabbed Camilla's arm, attempting to dance with her. Another two went for Zoe. Safiya had never seen a man move as fast as Adam. He twisted in front of Zoe, sent his good elbow ploughing into one man's face, knocking him to the ground. The other, he grabbed by the throat, lifted then hurled him across the floor. Two more men came at Ryan.

"Go sit with Bill, Safiya." Ryan took two strides before doing some sort of roundhouse kick thing, striking one man in the solar plexus, which sent him tumbling to join the two stunned men on the floor. Ryan ducked to avoid an incoming punch. The guy hit a wooden post instead and howled. Ryan grabbed the man's other arm and twisted it behind his back. The man screamed.

Adam went after a man who'd staggered to his feet. He punched him so hard he flew backward, hitting the floor hard. People were shouting and screaming so loudly Safiya couldn't understand a word.

One of the guitarists leaped in front of Safiya. "Sebastian, guard that blonde girl. I'll guard this one."

"No, I'm okay." Safiya pointed at Camilla, who was struggling to get away from the man gripping her arm. "Can you please help her."

Ryan beat him to it. Striding across the floor, he reached for Camilla's free arm, pulled her aside then smashed his fist into the man's nose so hard, it was a wonder his head didn't decapitate. He dropped, boneless to the floor, a pool of blood spurting from his nose. Another man came at Ryan.

"Behind you," screamed Safiya.

He twisted, blocked a punch with his forearm then drove his fist into the man's stomach, doubling him over, before the man dropped to his knees. Ryan gripped the last man standing by his shirt then drove him back against a brick pillar. "Get your friends and get out of this pub." He shoved him hard again. "By the way, it's illegal to captain a boat under the influence of alcohol or drugs. I'm the man you and your friends attempted to kill yesterday."

"I don't know what you're talking about." The man tried to shove Ryan away.

Ryan didn't budge. "This is a friendly warning. Don't fuck with me or anyone else on this island." He slammed the man against the bricks again.

"Okay, okay."

Silence reigned as Adam strode over, his focus locked on the man Ryan had pinned against the pillar. "As friendly warnings go, you got off lightly tonight. This guy—" he nodded at Ryan, "is capable of much worse."

The guitarist beside Safiya held up his clenched fist. "*Bravo.* Those idiots got exactly what they deserve." He spoke in Spanish, a language Safiya knew well.

"They did, didn't they." She smiled. "You play beautifully by the way. We were really enjoying ourselves." She watched Ryan and Adam escort the treasure hunters out of the pub.

"You are Spanish?" The excitement in the guitarist's voice made her smile. His brother launched into a vibrant rendition of a tango, and she had to raise her voice a little. "No, I'm officially Swiss, but I speak several languages. Spanish is one of my favorites. Do you live on the island?"

"No, my brother and I are recreational divers, on holiday. We have a yacht in the Marina. It's called *Capricorn*." His eyes sparked with interest. "I am Alejandro Oliveira. My brother is Sebastian. We are from Valencia."

She smiled. "It's nice to meet you, Alejandro. I'm Fia. I've been to Valencia. It's a beautiful city."

"*Gracias.* Your boyfriend is skilled in hand-to-hand combat. What does he do for a living?"

Boyfriend. If only that were true. "Ryan used to be in the army. Now he works for a security firm in Sydney. He spent his childhood on this island. Are you diving for fun or searching for shipwrecks and treasure?"

His lips twitched. "Shipwrecks. My brother and I believe the Spanish discovered Australia before the English Captain James Cook. We have ancient maps of a coastline that we believe is the east coast of Australia. It would be tremendous to prove such a thing." He had an engaging smile and friendly demeanor. She couldn't help but like him.

The patrons clapping for Sebastian made it increasingly hard to hear Alejandro. "What's in it for you?" She yelled, just as the clapping finished, drawing many eyes.

"Recognition."

Aware of a presence beside her, Safiya looked to find Ryan. "*Hola*. I mean Hi."

"I didn't know you spoke Spanish?"

"There are a lot of things you don't know about me, Ryan. This is Alejandro Oliveira. Alejandro, this is Ryan Dutch."

"Dutch? Your family were among the first settlers on this island. I have met Bill."

"Then you've heard all the old rumors." Ryan shook Alejandro's hand. "You play well."

"*Gracias*. I must return to my brother. If we do not play, we do not get paid." He met Ryan's gaze. "Be careful. We have come across those other men in the Caribbean. They are trouble." With a smile for Safiya, he paced away.

"What were you talking about before I came over," asked Ryan.

She gave Ryan a rundown of her conversation with Alejandro. "He's a nice guy."

"Hmm." Ryan caught her hand. "You wanted to see the baby turtles?"

"Yes, I do." They'd almost made it to the door when Frankie Ellis blocked their way.

"Hello again, Fia. I apologize for those drunken louts. That sort of behavior is not tolerated on Curra."

"Frankie, you have nothing to apologize for. I assume you know Ryan."

"Hello, Aunty Frankie." Ryan's fingers tightened around Safiya's. "How are you?"

The elderly lady gave a light shrug. "As well as can be expected for a woman my age. Thank you for coming to Camilla's assistance. Along with the rest of the council, I appreciate how you must feel."

"Do you, Aunty Frankie?" His fiery gaze skimmed the pub's patrons. "I wasn't given a chance to defend myself. I was accused of something I didn't do and betrayed by all the people I thought cared about me."

Safiya gasped. "Ryan!"

Ignoring her, his gaze shifted to Camilla and Tommy now sitting at a table. "I lost everyone and everything important to me that day. I wouldn't be here now if I wasn't worried about Zoe."

Even though the music prevented the crowd from hearing their conversation, Camilla didn't seem to know where to look. Had there been something between Ryan and her?

Ryan's attention returned to Frankie. "I don't believe any of you appreciate how I feel. If it weren't for Bill —." He rolled his shoulders. "I haven't returned because the council requested my help. I'm here because Bill asked, and I plan to clear my name. Goodnight, Aunty Frankie."

"Ryan." Bill followed them onto the wide porch. "There was another witness that day, who chose not to come forward."

"What witness?" demanded Safiya. She would gamble her life on Ryan's honesty. There had to be more to this awful incident than met the eye.

"Who?" The disbelief in Ryan's eyes almost made her cry. Hadn't he been through enough?

Bill shuffled closer, his face laden in gloom. "I was fishing off the rocks on South Point that morning. I saw one person in a red helmet on top of Morcago Ledge. I assumed it was you and grabbed my binoculars from the golf cart. As I watched, you fell several meters, ending upside down and tangled. I radioed for help, but then Zane appeared at the top of the ledge. He immediately threw a rope down to come to your rescue, without a helmet or harness."

Bill swallowed. "It looked like you panicked and latched onto

Zane. There was a scuffle and he fell." Bill shook his head. "No way could he survive a fall from that height. You managed to right yourself and climb up. I assumed you'd gone for help."

Tears ran down the old man's face. "I'm sorry, lad. You were only a boy, and you would have been in a state of shock. I've never forgiven your parents and grandfather for the way they treated you. I did what I could, but it broke my heart. I've replayed that day over and over because, you were a skilled climber. You always stepped forward when guilty of some childhood prank. I never knew you to lie and you certainly weren't a coward. I stayed quiet because my evidence would have destroyed your life."

Safiya struggled to draw a breath. She glanced at Ryan to find him staring at Bill in bewilderment. If he were guilty, she'd expect remorse, guilt, or shame.

"I wasn't there, Bill. I'd been grounded for getting bat shit on my shoes. It wasn't me." The confusion in his expression and desperation in his voice tugged at her heart.

"Ryan." She squeezed his hand. "If it wasn't you climbing with Zane that morning, who else would attempt such a thing?"

"Nobody. Zane would never allow a novice near Morcago Ledge."

"Yet someone attempted to climb down. Who would Bill mistake for you?"

All color drained from Ryan's face. "I can only think of one person, but …."

"Lad, I'm sorry." Bill punched his thigh. "I should have spoken up sooner."

"Yeah, you should have. All these years I thought you believed me. The truth is a kick in the guts. I'll find out who is behind the break-ins then I'm out of here."

Adam clamped a hand on Ryan's shoulder. "Go back to the boat-shed, mate. Sleep on it."

Safiya followed Zoe and the two men down the front steps then turned to give Bill an encouraging smile. After all, he'd done his best by Ryan.

The elderly man stood with his shoulders bowed, tears in his eyes as he watched Ryan walk away. She hoped his confession wouldn't destroy his relationship with Ryan. Perhaps honesty wasn't always the best policy.

CHAPTER NINE

The golden sand of Turtle Beach took on a gray tinge under the cloudy moonlight. Without any public lighting, most of the beach lay shrouded in a blanket of black, much like Ryan's mood. The gentle, rippling waves breaking on wet sand the only indication there was an ocean out there. Not the best night for fledgling turtles to make their way into the sea.

Hanging back from Zoe, Safiya and Garcia as they ambled down to the shoreline, Ryan kicked off his loafers, threw them onto the pile of other shoes and dug his toes into the cooling sand. His resentment had affected their small hunting party, but for the life of him, he couldn't put aside tonight's revelations. He'd been preoccupied wallowing in his misery.

For so long he'd believed Bill and Zoe to be his only allies on the island, when in fact Bill had believed him guilty, just like everyone else. They'd never spoken of that day, which now seemed inconceivable. He'd been pretty messed up. If he'd known how to prove his innocence, he would have. What hurt most, had to be that Bill had believed him a liar and coward. All this time he'd thought Ryan responsible for Zane's death, while the real culprit had gotten off scot-free. It was a fucking kick in the guts.

His churning stomach and roller-coaster emotions made him want to throw up. If Bill had come forward, the charge of involuntary manslaughter would have stuck, unless a guilty conscience forced the true culprit to come forward. It seemed unlikely.

With everything he'd faced in the last twelve years, he'd never experienced a fury like this, which meant he had to get it under control. He calmed his breathing and thought of his team. Jarred would tell him to stay focused. Sam would insist he make no assumptions. Talos would counsel Ryan to get his anger firmly under control. Simon would say, "dig deeper." Of all the boys, Nick would understand best and say, "Fuck that, let's get the guilty bastard."

He glanced at two silhouettes now walking toward the sand hills. They weren't his enemies. Zoe had never stopped loving him. Garcia was doing an excellent job of looking after Zoe, and he'd given Ryan a nod of support.

Rolling his shoulders, Ryan forced his murderous thoughts to the furthest part of his mind, to be examined later, along with a plan of attack. The clouds parted to allow the moon's light through. He didn't want to search for baby turtles. He wanted to drown his anger in a bottle of Scotch.

"Are you okay, Ryan?" Safiya stood several feet away. "Is there something I can do to make you feel better?"

He almost laughed. "That's not a question you should be asking me tonight, Safiya-Ameerah. My emotions are running high." He strolled forward, purposely crowding her. "Give me an inch and I might take an aggressive mile."

"Fiddlesticks. You're not a bully." She set her fingers on his arm and caressed his skin. "I know what it's like to be surrounded by people, yet alone in the world. To have accusations leveled at me that aren't true." She stroked his wrist then linked her fingers through his.

Her empathy sure felt real. "Zoe is worried about you. The three of us should sit down and talk things through." Tears glistened in her eyes.

"Why is that, Safiya-Ameerah?"

"Because we believe in your honesty and integrity. You can trust us to standby you."

Sincerity rang in her voice. Her slim fingers held on tightly, conveying genuine comfort. Standing this close to her wasn't a good idea, yet it gave him a pleasant sense of calm warmth, which he clung to. Hell, he wanted to grab her with both hands and never let her go.

"Hey, Ryan," called Zoe. "Me and Adam are going to call it a night. Why don't you walk Safiya back via the beach? I'll be at home if you want to talk over a hot chocolate." Her voice sounded oddly vulnerable.

"You okay, Zo?"

"I … I don't want you to leave because of what happened tonight. I've missed you."

He strode over and gave her a hug. "I've missed you too, Zo. Bill should have told me the truth. I should have come home and sorted things out years ago. It's long overdue."

"So, you'll stay?"

"For now. I want to clear my name and figure out who is behind the break-ins."

"I'm glad." She glanced past his shoulder. "Do me a favor and see if you can find some hatchlings for Safiya." Her hold tightened and she lowered her voice. "She's one of those people who make everything better and brighter, Ryan. Don't let the past screw this up. You both deserve to be happy."

Guilt hovered over Ryan as he watched his sister's and Garcia's silhouettes disappear into the darkness. The last twelve years had to have been tough for Zoe, yet she'd never complained or sulked. She was another of those people who made everything better and brighter.

He strolled back to Safiya and gripped her small, soft hand, determined to indulge her curiosity, and end the evening on a happier note. "If we find hatchlings, don't use your cell phone's torch. It confuses them."

"Why does light confuse them?" whispered Safiya.

He grinned when she shoved her phone into the clutch hanging from her shoulder. "They use the moonlight to guide them into the ocean. It's why this beach has no houses or lighting nearby. There are so many coastlines around the world crammed with bright lights and skyscrapers, the hatchlings get confused. Instead of scrambling into the ocean they go toward the lights. With traffic, domestic animals and birds, hatchlings don't stand a chance."

"That's terrible." Safiya stepped carefully across the sand. "I'm scared I'll stand on one."

"Don't panic, the females bury their eggs deep and now that the clouds have cleared, you'll see the turtles clearly if they decide tonight's the night." He noticed a mound that looked promising. "Let's sit here for a little while."

"Okay." She sat beside him; her gaze locked on the black ocean. "Can I ask you a question?"

"Sure."

"Why do you think Zane climbed down the cliff without his harness and safety gear?"

Her question was the next best thing to throwing a bucket of ice cubes at him. He held his head in his hands. "I don't know. After all our training, it's something neither of us would do."

She wriggled closer and rubbed his back. "What if Zane came along, saw a person he thought was you, hanging upside down, and panicked?"

"Zane knew I could right myself. We practiced things like that all the time. It had to be someone who'd tried to descend on his own, and Zane arrived too late, then for whatever reason, didn't have time to get into his harness. We hid them close by the day before."

"It was Tommy, wasn't it?"

Ryan scratched his head. "Tommy is terrified of heights. He refused to take abseiling lessons. Refused to come as an observer on any of our weekend climbs. Wouldn't even watch our videos. I never believed another person had been on the cliff face with Zane, but I couldn't figure out why my harness was found above the ledge. I never once considered Tommy. I'd heard he'd been caught in Camilla's bed the night before and they'd been grounded, like me that Sunday."

"Why were you grounded?" Safiya traced a pattern on his back, which soothed as much as distracted him.

"I came home Saturday with bat shit all over my clothes. My parents were furious when I admitted we'd found a cave inside Morcago cliff face. That Sunday morning, they left me to mow the lawns and went off to a council function, until all hell broke loose."

"Didn't anyone see you mowing the lawn?"

Ryan shook his head in disgust. "You can see how private the place is. It was hot and I was mad with my parents for confiscating my phone and grounding me. I found a shady tree and went to sleep. If I'd mowed the bloody lawns, they might have believed me and not some drunk who woke up on South Point from an all-night bender."

"Did you try to clear your name?"

"Of course. I demanded to know who the witness was. I told them he was lying. I was furious at my parents for grounding me. If I'd been with Zane, he wouldn't be dead. I couldn't believe they were accusing me of causing my best friend's death. Of leaving his smashed body on the rocks. My father brought my harness and helmet home. I will never forget the disgust in his eyes, or what he said to me. Discovering my girlfriend was cheating on me with Tommy was another kick in the guts I didn't need."

Safiya flinched beside him. "Camilla?"

"Yes."

"What about the police?"

"The old sergeant questioned me for hours before Bill took me to the mainland. As Zane's legal guardian, and an elder, Aunty Frankie could have expelled me from the island, but she didn't. I'll never forget the desolation in her eyes though. But unlike my parents, she at least came to the inquest."

"Thank goodness you had Bill." Safiya squeezed his arm.

"Yeah. He'd been a sniper in the army, before buying his fishing boats. He wasn't a big talker and to be honest he scared the shit out of me back then. It was Zoe who saved me."

"How?"

"She dragged up the courage to ask Bill to set up email accounts for us and then she'd sneak messages to me. After I joined the army, I'd fly across from Perth every so often and we'd met up in Townsville." Ryan shook his head. "I had no idea Bill saw someone on the cliff with Zane. His testimony would have seen me charged. Why didn't he ever say something?"

"Probably because you'd been through enough and he wasn't convinced it was you."

Movement in the sand distracted Ryan. It was a relief to change the subject. "There!" Ryan pointed to a small crater where the sand appeared to be moving of its own accord. He leaned back on his hands and stretched his legs. "It could take a while, so you might as well get comfortable."

She drew up her knees and hunched forward, her gaze locked on the crater. "It's like quicksand, isn't it? Tumbling in on itself."

"Believe me, quicksand doesn't look like that. It can be under an innocent mud puddle or patch of wet sand."

"You've seen quicksand?"

"I've been stuck in it. Luckily, the boys were within yelling distance, and I'd only sunk a few feet. It locks you in solid and the pressure on your legs is horrendous. If you sink chest-deep without help, you're a goner."

"So, how would a person get out by themselves, if they hadn't sunk too far?"

"By wriggling to the edge in small movements, and if possible, holding onto something firm to drag against it. Doesn't always work though. The deeper you sink, the harder it is to get out. The boys had to throw a patchwork of branches and small saplings down just to get close to me. They almost ripped my arms off before poking saplings around my legs to create air pockets. Not an experience I ever wish to repeat."

"Thank goodness they were with you."

"Yeah." Movement caught his eye as the first hatchling broke through the sand. "Look."

Safiya squealed and clutched his thigh. "It's so tiny. I've seen them on documentaries, but I never realized." She flashed him a wondrous smile. "It's so cute. Thank you for taking the time to show me, Ryan."

"You are very welcome, Safiya-Ameerah."

Her fingers tightened, sending a surge of lust straight to his already half-erect cock. He shifted, thankful her attention swung back to the hatchling, giving him the chance to drag his shirt out.

Another two hatchlings broke through and Safiya cooed in delight. He could easily imagine the sounds she'd make in the throes of sex, and it wasn't helping.

"They're so tiny and awkward. It must be exhausting fighting to get to the surface and then down the beach."

Ryan watched six more hatchlings tumble over the edge of the crater, all scrambling in the right direction. There would be at least another hundred hatchlings making the same trek tonight. Further over, a misguided sibling began scrambling up the beach.

"Oh, no, that one's going the wrong way." Safiya scrambled over the sand on her hands and knees, drawing Ryan's attention to her nice ass. "I'll just point him in the right direction."

He flung himself after her, catching her ankle. "Don't touch it."

She flipped over then lay staring up at him. "Will my skin burn it?"

"No, but you'll affect its survival. Baby sea turtles imprint on the sand where they hatch. The oil in your skin can interfere with their imprinting process."

"I didn't know."

"Most people don't. It's why this beach is protected. During summer, when most turtles hatch, this beach is patrolled night and day."

"So, the females only lay their eggs on this beach?"

"Usually. It's not common to see hatchlings this late in the year though. The females leave a trail in the sand when they arrive and leave, so it's easy for Zoe to flag the nests." He hovered over her, fighting his own body not to close the gap and press her into the sand. To lose himself in her soft curves.

Safiya raised her hand, hesitated then stroked his cheek. "Ryan?"

"Yes."

She licked her lower lip then bit it. "There's something I'd like to do, if you're agreeable?"

He held in a groan of surrender. Whatever she wanted, he'd give her. He prayed it would be more than a kiss. He needed to hold her in his arms tonight. Fuck regrets, he could only hope she felt the same. "I'm easy. What is it?"

CHAPTER TEN

Safiya rolled him onto his back, jumped to her feet and held out a hand. "Come on. Let's leave these little darlings to do what nature intended. I'd like to stroll home along the beach and hear about your childhood adventures."

Disappointment weighed heavily as he accepted her hand then kept it as they strolled to the water's edge. She wasn't conforming to the spoilt, self-centered heiress he'd expected. It seemed with her, he couldn't make assumptions, even based on Simon's intel. "We'll walk around the headland, it's the long way home, but well worth it."

"We won't meet anyone, will we?"

"Probably not, but it's possible." Ryan glanced at Safiya. "Has anyone taught you how to defend yourself?"

"What? Why?" She looked about frantically. "Do I need to?"

He laughed. "No, I'm asking if you can you defend yourself."

"Oh, of course. I've done a defense course."

"Right, so if I were to do this—" He lifted her against his chest, trapping her arms. "...You could easily escape?"

She giggled. "I could but you're not doing anything I find threatening."

"My mistake." He ran to soft sand, where he fell to his back, before rolling, so he lay on top of her, pinning her hands either side of her head. "You're vulnerable. Alone. Mine to do what I want." He released her hands. "Show me how you'd escape."

"Why on earth would I want to escape?" She cupped his face with both hands, her gaze locking with his for a moment before she drew his head down and kissed him.

He lost himself in her eager touches, exploring her mouth, savoring the sweet taste, relieved to be able to drown in her kisses without an audience. She was a dream to kiss. He had no idea if they'd ever have a meaningful relationship, but their chemistry was off the planet, and it scared the fuck out of him.

He traced the silky shape of her calf, grazed the back of her knee with his fingers, slid his palm over her thigh, the skin smooth under his touch. Her murmur of encouragement had him curling his fingers into the hem of her dress, inching it up over silky underwear. Her breasts pressed against his chest, nipples hard and inviting. He'd prefer her naked on a soft mattress, where he could lose himself in her curves and make love with her until they were breathless and sated. The sand wasn't the place. "Safiya, do you want this?"

"Yes." She squirmed, pressing herself into him, her movements urgent, her hands making a mess of his hair. "The house is too far away, and Zoe will be there."

"True!" He grinned down at her. "I've got a better idea." Jumping up, he swung her into his arms and ran, anchoring her safe against his chest, laughing at her girlish giggles.

Reaching the small park above the sand, Ryan lowered Safiya's feet to the soft grass, holding her close. She ran her hands up his chest, over his shoulders and into her hair, drawing him back into another intoxicating kiss. As he savored her mouth, he slipped a knee between her thighs, rubbing against her heat. She moved against him, moaning his name. He found the globes of her bottom and lifted, bringing her against his erection. She wrapped her legs around his hips, igniting his blood.

Their kisses turned frenzied. He sank to his knees, laying her on the grass. He wanted his hands and mouth on her breasts, needed to bury his fingers and tongue in her wet heat. Pushing up on his hands, his gaze fixed on her silky, white panties. "I know this is madness, but I've wanted you since we met on your father's island in February. I've never had this strong an attraction to any woman, and I can't fight it tonight."

"Wait!" She scrambled from under his widespread knees, drew her legs in close to her chest then fumbled with her dress, pulling it down until even her toes were hidden. "You think it's madness?"

He raised his eyes, surprised to find her looking at him with a wounded vulnerability. "What's wrong?"

She swallowed. "Why would you call this madness and fight our attraction? Are you saying this is a one-time thing? That you're still not interested in a real relationship with me?"

He sighed. "Safiya. You don't stick to anything. You've been pampered all your life and haven't had to work for anything. I would bore you in no time."

"So, I'm okay for a roll in the grass, but nothing more?" She shoved him hard, knocking him off balance. "You're right. We wouldn't suit. I'm not into arrogant, selfish jerks."

"Safiya!" Ryan sat up and crawled to her side. "I'm sorry, I thought we were on the same page." He reared back to avoid her fist, not that she'd do much damage. He was more concerned she'd hurt her fingers. "Stop!" Having no choice but to capture her flying fists, he held them firmly against his chest. "What are you so upset about?"

"I don't sleep around." She pulled away and jumped to her feet. "I had one short relationship in my first year at Uni. That cheating creep turned out to be a bodyguard, paid to keep an eye on me. My second relationship was at a London university and even shorter. I thought I could trust him, but he suddenly saw me as a cash machine. When I dumped him, he spread rumors I was an easy lay and had the hots for my roomy's boyfriend."

"Shit, I'm sorry." Ryan stood. "That's why you dropped out of Uni?"

"Well done, Einstein." A sob caught in her throat. "I'm going back to the house."

"Safiya, I really am sorry. Let's start over."

"No, we are done." She stalked across the grass toward the road.

"Wait. Safiya." He'd taken two strides when an explosion detonated somewhere behind him. He dived for Safiya, taking her down hard. "What the fuck?" He rolled to see a fireball shoot into the sky to the north. Whatever had blown up, it was big.

"What was that?" Safiya pushed against his chest, scrambling away when he released her.

"I don't know, but I'm going to find out." He sprinted over to where they'd left their shoes, grabbed them, and met Safiya at the edge of the road, just as Garcia and Zoe came hurtling round the bend in the golf cart. They skidded to a stop.

"Get in," yelled Garcia. "That explosion came from the Dugong Marina."

"Do you have a fire engine on the island?" Safiya called as she jumped in and slid to the far side.

"Yes," Zoe called over her shoulder. "The fire station is beside our police and emergency services' building, on the other side of Dugong Marina." She hit the accelerator. "Maybe it was one of the marina's diesel pumps."

Ryan placed Safiya's sandals on the floor between them and leaned closer. "We need to talk."

"It's no big deal. Forget it."

It was a big deal, and he wouldn't forget it, but right now, they needed to find out what exploded, and if anyone had been injured.

It took five minutes to reach the town center, only to find their way blocked by golf carts parked haphazardly. A crowd had gathered at the entrance to Dugong Marina, watching in horror and fascination as flames shot into the air behind the clubhouse.

"Fuck, it's Bill's boatshed." Ryan leaped out of the golf cart and sprinted across the park. The fire truck, an ambulance and police wagon blocked his way. Two firefighters held the fire hose, directing the powerful water jet over what used to be the boatshed.

Sergeant Hawthorne jogged over. "Am I glad to see you. After what happened at the pub, I thought for sure you'd be in that inferno."

"Why?"

"Frankie Ellis said you left the pub after subduing six drunk treasure hunters. She heard Adam Garcia tell you to go back to Bill's boatshed and get some sleep."

"I went to Turtle Beach with Zoe, Garcia and ... my girlfriend. Where's Bill?"

"Isn't he with you?" The sergeant looked beyond Ryan.

"No, we left him at the pub."

"I didn't see him. I will need you and Adam Garcia to drop by the station first thing in the morning, to give statements regarding what happened tonight." Sergeant Hawthorne turned back to the inferno. "Christ, I hope Bill wasn't in there."

Ryan's gut clenched. That didn't bear thinking about. "What the hell did he have in the boatshed to cause such a big explosion? It sounded like a bomb going off."

"Nothing that would make an explosion like that," called a firefighter. "I fish with Bill regularly and, other than a bit of diesel and paint, there wasn't anything dangerous in there.

Sergeant Hawthorne eyed Ryan. "You were in special forces. Any idea what would make an explosion like that?"

"My first thought is Bill had an old land mine from his days in the army, or dynamite, but that's impossible." Ryan didn't like the way Sergeant Hawthorne's steady gaze scrutinized him. He stepped away for some privacy so he could give Jarred a call and update him. Before he answered any more questions, he needed advice from a man he trusted. Looking back at the inferno, he prayed Bill had gone off to visit one of his mates.

SEVEN HOURS AFTER THE EXPLOSION, with the first rays of sun breaking across the water, Ryan leaned against a tree trunk, exhausted. His heart plummeted as he stared at the burnt-out remains. He'd answered Sergeant Hawthorn's questions, expecting Bill to turn up any minute. He'd spent hours, calling at the houses of Bill's mates. He'd searched Bill's charter boat and would have searched the trawler, only it was padlocked from the outside. He'd combed the Dutch estate and its private beaches. It was better than standing here twiddling his thumbs with Sergeant Hawthorne and the firefighters watching his every move.

He'd returned two hours ago to find the firefighters had found a body, leaving Ryan battling with shock and disbelief as he struggled to keep it together.

"Jesus!" Ryan wanted to throw up. He ran his hands down his clammy face. He couldn't believe Bill was dead, but who else could it be? He'd walked away from Bill last night in a foul mood when Bill had been the only adult to stand by him. To think he'd never see him again or hear his embellished stories or go fishing together. It tore Ryan's heart out. Nausea rose in his throat. He needed to focus. Figure out what the hell blew up.

Over the years, he'd seen the damage dynamite or even a small bomb could cause. It was obvious from the huge crater in front of him that the origin of the blast came from under Bill's mezzanine living quarters, which made no sense. Sergeant Hawthorne had been just as bewildered but kept harping back to Ryan's knowledge of explosives. Finally, the cop had gone off to take photos and tag pieces of metal and debris strewn around the park.

Ryan's attention shifted to where two ambulance officers were loading a covered stretcher into the back of the ambulance. The charred body had been found under a pile of metal sheeting, too hot to touch until ten minutes ago. Ryan clenched his fists. Thanks to his time in Special Forces, he'd seen entire villages burned to the ground by terrorists. Few had escaped incineration, but it had never hit him like this. He couldn't stop shaking.

"Go home and get some sleep," called Sergeant Hawthorne. "I'll be in touch."

Ryan gave the cop a nod but didn't move. Instead, he watched wearily as Tommy and the other firefighters climbed aboard the truck, one eyeing him with narrowed eyes. They reversed through the park. With all the water, their tires left deep grooves in the saturated grass.

Sergeant Hawthorne clamped his hand on Ryan's shoulder. "I'll need you, Fia Gibbs and Adam Garcia to stay put until things are sorted. Detectives and police from the Bomb Squad and Arson Investigation unit are on their way. They will need to speak to you."

"You know where to find us, Sergeant."

"I'm leaving my constable to keep an eye on things here. Don't touch anything." He strode over to his wagon, got in, and drove out of the park. That's when Ryan noticed Frankie Ellis off to his right, her arms stiff by her sides, staring at the blackened mess. He had no idea what to say to her, or if she'd speak to him. She'd known Bill all her life.

She looked his way. "That wasn't Bill." She touched a hand to her chest. "It's not his time yet."

Ryan's focus returned to the ambulance. Frankie's predictions were legendary. To his knowledge, she'd never been wrong. He thought back to the day before Zane died. Camilla had sworn Frankie predicted Ryan would be the one to leave the island. Against all odds, she'd been right. As the ambulance drove away, Ryan turned back to Frankie, but she'd vanished. For the first time in hours, hope bloomed in his chest.

The body would be kept at the clinic until it could be flown to Brisbane for DNA testing and identification. All he could do was pray and keep searching day and night until those tests came back.

Ryan rolled his shoulders and massaged his neck. Garcia had taken the girls home hours ago, thankfully before the firefighters found the charred body. Something Ryan hadn't been prepared for. The last two hours had passed in a foggy haze of desolation and disbelief. If it were Bill in there, he didn't know how he would break the news to Zoe.

The heavy wop-wop-wop of a Sikorsky Blackhawk drew Ryan's tired eyes to the western sky. Instantly a massive load of tension shifted as he watched the chopper fly in a wide arc then lower to the helipad behind the emergency services building.

Relief hit him like a tidal wave. Jarred, Sam and Nick had arrived. He wouldn't have to face this alone.

Two gentle arms wrapped around his waist as the familiar, delicate fragrance of Safiya filled his nostrils, followed by the aroma of coffee and freshly baked pastry.

"Was that ... Bill?"

Lifting his face, he met her distressed gaze.

"We won't know until the DNA tests come back."

She sniffed then hugged him, rubbing his stiff back in long, soothing strokes. He sank into her comforting embrace, too exhausted to play the hardened soldier. Absorbing her kindness as the weight of his exhaustion almost overwhelmed him. The purity of her white singlet under his filthy hands brought him out of his funk. He tried to ease away.

She tightened her hold. "I'm here for you, Ryan."

A bleak numbness had devoured him since the firefighters found the body. Slowly, Safiya's warmth permeated the chill inside his heart. He wrapped his arms around her, holding her against his chest for several minutes, breathing in her soft, flowery fragrance.

"Hey." She leaned back, bringing both hands to his cheeks. "You need to eat and get some sleep. I've got coffee and croissants."

"I'm not hungry."

"You need sustenance, Ryan. It's going to be a long day." She turned away, taking her heat with her. "Here." She placed a croissant in one hand and a warm mug of coffee in the other. "I don't want to have to use my angry voice. Now eat and drink."

He cracked a weak smile. Her white top, arms and one cheek were caked in ash. "Yes, ma'am." He scoffed down the ham and cheese croissants and coffee, grateful for her thoughtfulness, especially after what he'd said last night. He owed her an apology.

"I'm sorry about last night. I'm an idiot. Will you please forgive me?"

"Of course." She worried her bottom lip. "I've decided to stay and help Zoe, while I decide my future. We had a long talk last night. She knows everything."

"Safiya—"

The pounding of boots on the ground broke his deliberation. He looked toward the marina, surprised to recognize Talos, Simon, Sam and his ex-military German Shepherd, Ajax. The three men slowed to a walk, their gazes taking in the destruction.

"Your team must have been on that big helicopter." Safiya squeezed his hand. "I'm glad your friends are here for you."

"The Blackhawk is a surprise."

Safiya released his hand. "I don't see Jarred Steele."

"Probably grilling Sergeant Hawthorne while Nick shuts down the chopper." Ryan stood as an emergency vehicle stopped at the edge of the park. A tiny, blonde dynamo jumped out then stepped carefully around rutted clumps and puddles, her ponytail swinging wildly when she almost lost her balance.

"Who's that?" Safiya clambered to her feet and stepped back.

"Our robotics engineer." Ryan stood. "She's one in a million and has an arsenal of robotics and drones."

He smiled when Madeline exited the front of the vehicle. If ever he needed an investigative journalist, it was now. He frowned as another woman and man in navy coveralls exited the emergency service's vehicle. They went to the rear of the vehicle and began hauling large cases onto the ground.

Ryan's attention shifted to his friends as they crossed the grass. "Am I glad to see you boys." Swallowing the lump in his throat, Ryan held it together as his friends surrounded him. Ajax gave a woof and licked his hand.

"Thanks for the heads up, mate." Sam clapped him on the shoulder then nodded toward the man and woman pulling safety helmets and black cases from the rear of the vehicle. "She's from the bomb squad and he's from Arson Investigation. After your phone call last night, Jarred called Gibbs. We picked up those two and another detective in Brisbane."

"How you doin', mate?" Talos gave Ryan a fist bump. "Gibbs is concerned about his sister, so he asked for our help. Apparently sending our best man to protect his sister isn't enough anymore."

"What the fuck?" Ryan tensed. "Are you saying Gibbs hired us to spy on Safiya?"

"Not exactly. You were coming here to check on Zoe anyway and Jarred knew you wouldn't let anything happen to Safiya."

Simon clapped Ryan on the shoulder. "Hey, mate. If it makes you feel better, Gibbs is aware Jarred sent *you*."

"Fuck."

Sam frowned at the charred rubble. "You're right. It looks like a bomb or dynamite exploded. Has Bill turned up?"

Ryan drew in a deep breath. "They found a body. It will take a few days to get the DNA results back."

"Shit." Sam ran a hand over his head. "Geez. I'm sorry, mate."

"Until I have solid proof, I'm not ready to accept it's Bill." Ryan rubbed the bristles on his jaw. "The police are going to suspect I blew up the boatshed. Bill is worth a fortune and I'm his heir. That could be seen as motive, especially as I left the pub last night in a bad mood, after speaking to Bill."

"Shit." Talos stared at the wreckage. "Any chance Bill kept dynamite in the boatshed?"

"Nope. It might have something to do with the recent break-ins. Rumors of hidden treasure have been around since the early 1900's, which means we get treasure hunters. No way could this be the result of exploding oxygen tanks."

Ryan cursed. Twelve years ago, he'd sworn he'd never set foot on Curra again. Never search for its fabled treasure. He'd broken one vow. It looked like he might have to break the other before anyone else got hurt.

He glanced around his friends faces. "If it was Bill in that shed, I'm concerned he may have been murdered or kidnapped because of a rumored treasure. If so, Zoe may be in danger too. I'm going to need help protecting her."

"You've got it." Darius' gaze dropped to his filthy coveralls. "I've brought my drones."

Madeline pushed between Sam and Talos to hug Ryan. She leaned back, grimacing when she realized her blue blouse was now covered in ash. "Did you find our great-uncle?"

"We found a body." He clenched his teeth. He couldn't handle sympathy right now.

"Oh no." She hugged him again. "Where's Safiya?"

"Safiya?" He shouldn't be surprised Madeline knew about Safiya. They were friends. He glanced around, surprised to find Safiya missing. "Damn. If she heard I'm here to spy on her, she's probably gone to find something to kill me with."

CHAPTER ELEVEN

A tear ran down Safiya's cheek. She'd barely known Bill, but he'd welcomed her and made her laugh with his stories. If it were him in that fire, he would have died a horrible death.

What would have caused such a huge explosion? Poor Ryan, he'd come back to the island knowing he'd face hostility, but he'd done it for Bill and Zoe.

She kicked at a bunch of sticks in frustration. She didn't know what she could do to help Ryan and Zoe. Last night Zoe had turned to Adam, as well she should. It didn't take a genius to see they were besotted with each other. Adam had held Zoe on his lap for hours, cradling her against his chest, holding her gently as she slept. As for Ryan, he had his friends now.

Safiya's dream of a romantic relationship with Ryan seemed as likely as finding pirate treasure. Ryan may have apologized, but he'd never see her as anything other than a spoilt heiress who didn't fit into his world. He thought more of the robotics engineer than he ever would of her. Except, he would have made love to her last night, if she hadn't baulked at his thoughtless words. She wished she could rant and rave or scream out her frustration, but that wasn't her way.

She jumped off the wooden boardwalk, landing in soft sand. For several minutes she stood on Sunset Beach and stared at the burnt-out wreckage of Barnacle Bill's boatshed. Bits of twisted metal and burnt beams were scattered over the sand and through the shallow water. Most had tags on them or two-sided evidence markers beside them.

Her misery hardly compared. How could she be so selfish? Ryan might need an alibi, which she could provide. Maybe there was something else she could do for him before she left the island. Ask Tommy if he'd moved Ryan's harness the morning Zane died. Help Ryan win back the respect of his family and the people on Currawong Island.

As she wandered along the water's edge, avoiding the incoming tide, she considered various ways of achieving such a task. Would Ryan thank her? Realize she was much more than he thought? Want a real relationship? Who was she fooling? When he'd seen that petite little blonde, he'd forgotten Safiya existed.

She stubbed her toe on something wedged in the sand. Bending down, she realized it was one half of a mug with a coral-red lipstick on the edge. It had a yellow sunflower like the mug Bill had carried down his stairs last night. Had it come from the boatshed? She looked around for something to stick in the sand so the police found it. Her gaze fell on a small flag attached to a canoe wedged in the sand further down the beach. "Perfect." She ran over and reached for the flag when her brain registered the canoe's contents. A roll of thickly twisted string, duct tape, assorted small pliers, a packet of matches and what looked like giant firecrackers wrapped together. "Dynamite."

"Oh my God!" Dropping to her knees, Safiya tried to comprehend what she was seeing.

"Whatcha got there, young lady?" The female voice came from behind. Rearing back, Safiya looked up at a woman in blue coveralls, a cap, and sunglasses. She had a police badge on her sleeve.

"I think I just found dynamite or really big firecrackers."

"Step away." The woman wore a pair of sterilized gloves. "What did you touch."

"Nothing. I … didn't touch anything." Safiya's voice shook as she scrambled to her feet. "There's part of a cup over there with lipstick on it that I think came from the boatshed. I was looking for something to flag it."

The policewoman didn't answer, instead she pulled out a phone. "Roger, get down to the beach. There's a canoe here with dynamite in it. Yeah. Bye." She glanced at Safiya. "What's your name?"

"Safiya Gibbs. I work for Zoe Dutch. Do you think someone purposely blew up the boatshed?"

"I can't comment on that. Where can we find you if we have questions?"

Safiya pointed up to Dutchies Point. "I'm staying up there."

"Okay, thanks. You can go now."

Safiya backed away, unsure whether she should go back to Ryan or ring her brother.

If this turned into a murder investigation Ryan could be in serious trouble. Her brother would know what to do. She turned away, trying not to run. Her knees and joggers were caked in wet sand, but she couldn't be bothered washing it off, her only aim was to get help for Ryan as fast as possible.

Reaching the locked gate, Safiya punched in the code Zoe had given her and followed the path through the dense foliage that circled high above Dutchies Beach. She couldn't get her mind off the dynamite. Things had just gone from dire to drastic. Who would want to blow up the boatshed, or worse, kill Bill?

Adam stood on the porch with both hands on his hips. He had to be as tall, if not taller than Ryan's friend Talos. Adam looked beyond her, as if searching for someone. "What's happening down there?"

"They found a body, but ..." She swallowed. This was the hard bit. "Ryan said, it ... wasn't recognizable. He won't accept it's Bill."

Adam slammed his fist into his thigh. "Zoe's going to be devastated if it is Bill."

"I know." She mounted the front steps, her feet as heavy as bricks. "Ryan's team flew in on the big helicopter."

"I figured as much. They will come in handy keeping all the nosey parkers out. I'm over all the damn do-gooders dropping in and upsetting Zoe."

"Madeline Shaw is with them and a robotics engineer. Dainty, blonde, very pretty."

Adam didn't appease her curiosity, just acknowledged her comment with the lift of his chin. "Zoe rang her parents. She wanted them to know about the fire before they heard from someone else. Thanks for staying with her last night." He glanced over his shoulder at the open front door. "Should I break the news to her or wait for Ryan?"

"I don't know. He could be a while."

"I've locked the gates and Zoe's gone to her room, so I'll see what happens. Have you eaten anything this morning?"

"No." Safiya fiddled with her bracelet. "I'll grab a croissant now. I imagine Zoe's parents and grandparents will take the first flight home, so we can probably expect them tomorrow or Wednesday. I'll shift my things into one of the studio cabins."

"Might be best. Once they arrive, I'll move to the large cabin, closest to this house."

"Okay." As it had two bedrooms, she figured he'd share with Ryan's friends. That left a one-bedroom cabin and a studio for Madeline and Darius.

"You look exhausted, Fia. Why don't you try to catch some sleep?"

"I am exhausted. I'll see you later, Adam."

"Yeah, later." He paced over to a wicker chair and sat, his gaze sweeping the landscape. There wasn't anything relaxed about his posture. Alert and on guard.

A slither of envy hit Safiya. Adam cared for Zoe. It was obvious in the way his eyes followed her everywhere. How he leaned down and gave her his full attention. He wouldn't leave his post until he heard movement in the house. Zoe was a lucky girl.

After one croissant and two cups of tea, Safiya stripped her bed and remade it with fresh sheets. She shoved the items she'd unpacked into her suitcase then gave the room a quick dust. It had been a pipe dream to think she'd find her niche on this island. With one final look around the flowery bedroom, she rolled her suitcase out the side door to one of the golfcarts and loaded it. She returned to the house to throw her used sheets and towel in the washing machine and leave a note for Zoe.

Adam hadn't moved from the porch, so with a heavy heart, Safiya drove down the main drive. Zoe had given her a tour of all four cabins yesterday, letting Safiya choose which ever one she wanted once the thieves were caught. She'd picked a studio cabin overlooking Dutchies Beach.

Safiya took the first left-hand trail then veered left again at a fork. This trail took her to the cute, white cabin she'd adored at first sight. It's small porch only had room for a potted golden palm and a cane egg chair which hung from the pergola. Its vibrant blue cushions beckoned Safiya, but she resisted, instead unlocking the French doors, and opening them wide. Looking across Dutchies Beach, she spied Adam standing on the porch. Too far away to make out any features other than his height. He gave a wave then returned to his vigil. She appreciated his concern for her safety.

Surrounded by ferns, palm trees, breaking waves, and bird chatter, Safiya breathed in the ocean air. She could detect the faint stink of burned timber and ash, yet it wasn't anywhere near the putrid, nauseating smell of last night.

She took a moment to let the peacefulness wash over her then walked around the side of the cabin to look out over the amazing aquamarine blues of the sea. A solitary yacht lay anchored off Sunset Beach. The glint of sun on glass caught Safiya's curiosity. A woman in a white dress and broad brimmed hat stood at the bow; her binoculars trained on the two police officers trawling Sunset Beach. The beautiful black and tan German Shepherd ran along the water edge, his nose to the ground.

Turning back to the woman on the yacht, Safiya was surprised to see the binoculars pointed at her. Whoever the woman was, she didn't seem fazed at being caught snooping. Instead, she returned her attention to the beach briefly then entered the cabin. A minute later the yacht motored toward Dugong Marina. Safiya focused on the italic scrawl along the side of the hull.

Sea Sprite. She'd check the marina later. She thought of the broken cup with the lipstick smudge. Had it come from Bill's boatshed? Why was the woman so interested in the beach? Could it have something to do with the dynamite? Safiya's spine tingled. She had plenty of questions. Now she needed answers.

AN HOUR LATER, after unpacking enough clothes for two weeks on a tropical island, and visiting the grocery store, Safiya strolled along the marina's boardwalk. Sunset Beach and the small park behind the clubhouse were taped off with blue and white incident tape, blocking access to the boatshed. With so few yachts in Dugong Marina, the *Sea Sprite* stood out like a neon sign. On the wharf beside it, a young guy hunched over a broom, sweeping the boards.

"Hello," she called out.

He lifted his head, revealing red-rimmed eyes. "Hi."

It took a second for her to realize he'd been the deckhand on the ferry. She remembered belatedly he worked for Barnacle Bill. News must have spread. "Are you okay?"

"Yeah. Got me chores to do. I get paid to keep the wharf clean."

"You do a good job. I'm Fia."

"Josh. My parents own Butler's Grocery Store."

"Hi, Josh. Do you happen to know who owns *Sea Sprite*?"

He glanced across at the yacht. "It's a rental out of King's real-estate office."

"Do you know the lady who just brought it in?"

"Sorry, only just got here. Didn't see anyone."

"No worries. Take it easy."

"You too." He bent to his task again.

Not knowing what else to say, Safiya retraced her steps along Dugong Marina's boardwalk then walked across the road. She strolled past the pub, where it sounded like quite a crowd had gathered inside. The next block contained Jody's Beauty Hair and Nails, Michelle's Ladies Wear, and a bakery. She crossed the grocery store's carpark then quickened her pace past the police station to Golf Cart Rentals. Recrossing the road, she walked back along a pretty, beachside pathway, passing the Medical Center, a lane that ended at a helipad and the huge Blackhawk. Next, she passed the Ambulance Station and Emergency Services' building, and the Tourism Office. Finally, she came to King's Reality. To her surprise, she found Camilla sitting on a desk, talking to an older lady holding a baby. Both women dabbed at their eyes.

Too late to keep walking, they'd seen her, so she pushed the glass door open. "Hi, Camilla. How are you?"

"Okay, you?"

"Fine. I'm sorry I didn't tell you I'm Ryan's … girlfriend on the ferry."

"It's okay. I'm glad Ryan and his friend were there last night. How is he?"

"Upset. In shock. It's hard to comprehend."

"Yeah, tell me about it. Barnacle Bill is … was an iconic figure around here. My grandmother refuses to accept he's gone."

"Is that Frankie?"

"Yes. She and Bill have known each other since they were kids. She has a photo of them as teenagers. I think they may have been sweethearts, but then he left to join the army and Frankie married my grandfather, who died fifteen years ago. Frankie has an uncanny ability to predict the future but … who else could it be? No one else is missing."

"I don't know, Camilla, but Ryan feels the same."

The woman holding the baby sniffed. "Zoe must be devastated. She was closer to Bill than the rest of her family. I'm Dawn King. Camilla's mother and Frankie's daughter."

"Hello, Dawn. I'm Fia."

"Sorry, I should have introduced you." Camilla turned to her mother. "Fia is the one I was telling you about. She's working for Zoe."

Dawn King wiped another tear away. "We heard an explosion

started the fire. My son and son-in-law are volunteer firefighters. They said they are at a loss to explain it."

"Until the arson investigation report comes through, we won't know anything for sure."

Dawn King waved her hand towards the window. "We'll know soon enough. Pete Hawthorne called a meeting at the pub to see if anyone knows anything. Is there something we can do for you before we head over there?"

"Oh, yes. I believe you hire out a yacht called *Sea Sprite*."

"We do, but there's a problem with the radio. Until it's fixed, she's not for hire."

"I saw it off Sunset Beach earlier. There was a woman on board."

"Couldn't be the *Sea Sprite*. We haven't hired it out for weeks. Might be those two brothers who played guitars at the pub last night. They've got a similar looking yacht."

As neither Camilla or Dawn were wearing a white dress, Safiya scrambled for another tact. "Who normally hires it?"

"Tourists, locals who want to take visitors out for the day, or who want to go diving. Over summer, it's in high demand. My family take it out whenever we get the chance."

"Did either of you happen to notice a lady in a white dress in town this morning?"

"No, why?" asked Camilla.

"She looked familiar. I thought I might know her. Well, I should get back to Zoe. See if there's anything I can do. Bye."

"Bye," called both women.

Out on the footpath again, Safiya wandered past the Ferry Terminal Office then crossed the ferry access road, her mind racing. Who would have the gall to take out a yacht without hiring it, especially as it wasn't for hire? Someone who knew they'd get away with it. She would keep her eyes open for a woman in a white dress.

Returning to the golf cart, Safiya made her way back to the Dutch House. She'd left a message for Zoe to call her if she needed anything. Poor Zoe, she'd been a mess last night and this morning. She'd confessed her wish was for Ryan to move back home, but now their parents would hate him more than ever. Safiya consoled her friend as best she could, finally leaving her sobbing in Adam's arms.

She parked the golf cart under the carport then grabbed her two grocery bags and walked to her studio. She'd left the French doors and windows open, figuring it would air her cabin. Other than the ensuite and walk-in robe at the rear of the cabin, she had everything she needed in one space. A couch and coffee table, queen bed with side tables, kitchen, a dining table for two and large windows to let in light and fresh air. She'd gain a friend, privacy, a beautiful view, and a job, if she stayed.

Yes, she had everything she needed. Was it too much to ask for a special man to share her life? To love and cherish her? To put her above all else?

If she could only have one wish, it would be for Ryan to be that man.

CHAPTER TWELVE

Fury and frustration built in Ryan's chest as he paced his parents' back porch. The phone inside the house trilled, which only added irritation to his mounting emotions. It hadn't stopped ringing since he and his team arrived home. Zoe didn't need a constant stream of do-gooders wanting to drop by with their condolences or questions. She needed peace and quiet. The ringing cut off. He heard Zoe's shaky voice.

"Hello, this is Zoe. Thank you, Mrs. Kilgour. Ryan and I appreciate your offer, but we have everything we need. Yes, some close friends arrived this morning. No, we haven't heard anything since you last called. I will. Thank you."

Ryan swung around and glared at Sergeant Hawthorne. "The coroner's office must have given you some idea when we'll know if it's Bill's body. They took a sample of my blood. Surely, that will speed things up?"

"We won't know anything until the autopsy is completed. There's a legal process to follow. Same as determining the cause of the explosion."

"I know there's a bloody process, but we need to move quickly. Bill did not store dynamite in the boatshed. Somebody wanted him out of the way. Why?"

"As I said, there is a process to follow."

"This is bullshit." Ryan slammed his fist into a hanging pot, sending it smashing across the concrete pavers. Dirt, shards of plastic and flowery plant matter spewed everywhere.

"Shit." He kicked the largest clump of entwined roots and clumped dirt. "I'm not sitting on my ass, while rumors run riot. I will not be accused of something I didn't do."

Jarred pointed to an empty chair at the outdoor table. "Sit down, Major. No one is accusing you of anything. You have witnesses confirming your whereabouts last night. People ready to swear you had a good relationship with Bill."

He appreciated Jarred's and his friends' support, but what he needed were answers. "That might not be enough, Colonel. I was accused of something I didn't do twelve years ago. The case against me was dismissed, but it meant nothing. Mud sticks." He threw himself into the chair. "I want the motherfucker who did this." The phone trilled again. "That does it! I'm going to stop these busy bodies once and for all." He pushed back the chair and stormed inside. "Don't answer that, Zoe."

She snatched her hand back to her chest. Her puffy eyes widening as she backed up to the breakfast bar. "Ryan?"

He pulled out the power plug, picked up the base-set and stuffed it under his arm. "You don't need this, Zo." His gaze switched to Garcia, who'd been sitting at the table drinking coffee. He stood, his hands fisted, as if he might lash out at Ryan any second.

"No more calls. Take Zoe down to the private beach. Sitting on the sand where nobody can disturb her is what she needs right now."

The tension went out of Garcia. "Yeah, she does. I'll take care of her."

"Thanks." Ryan turned on his heel and strode back outside, dumping the phone set on top of the barbeque. Sergeant Hawthorne stood well out on the grass, his phone to his ear. Ryan's

mates hadn't moved from the table. Each watching him with concern.

"Sorry about that." He threw himself into his chair and picked up a beer. "I appreciate your support, and Madeline's offer to play tourist to dig around a little, but we need to work out a plan of attack.

"I've got my Identiscan program with me," stated Simon. "I can photograph the treasure hunters and anyone else of interest to see if they have criminal records or ties with organized crime. Darius is planting hidden cameras about the place and is keen to get her drones up in the air."

"Great. Does she have a small drone with a strong light?"

"Yes, she does. I'll get it for you."

"Thanks." Ryan looked to Jarred. "I've spoken to Garcia. He won't leave Zoe's side. As an extra precaution, I've locked the front gates. So many people have been coming and going this morning, it was driving me insane."

"Understandable. I've spoken to Inspector Gibbs. He promised to tell us what he can, which might not be much. The boys can mingle with locals, keeping their ears alert for anything of significance. I will liaise with Sergeant Hawthorne and Gibbs."

It's a start." Ryan took several deep swigs of his beer, relishing the cool liquid in his throat. "It's possible this has nothing to do with the treasure hunters. Someone might have it in for me. They might be getting at the people I care about as payback for my friend's death." He glanced at Sam. "Could you patrol the estate with Ajax?"

"No problem. I think you and Zoe should keep a low profile for now. Stay out of sight."

"I agree." Jarred rolled his shoulders. "You need sleep. You're a walking zombie on a short fuse."

"I can't sleep. There's something I need to check on. I'll take Safiya with me. It will kill two birds with one stone."

"What is it and where will you be," asked Talos.

"I want to check if anyone has been on Morcago Ledge recently. There is a cave system inside the mountain. It's where Zane and I thought the treasure might be, which is why I need the drone. There are hiking trails across the center of the island, so it's unlikely we'll meet anyone."

Jarred taped his fingers on the table. "Just a heads-up. Sheikh Farid knows about the explosion and could decide to drop anchor off the island. Having a super yacht show up is going to draw a lot of attention."

"It's going to piss Safiya off too." Ryan rubbed his forehead. A tension headache had been nagging him for hours. He wanted Safiya safe, but if she left now, they'd never get to know each other. "Ask Gibbs to delay his father."

"Consider it done."

Ryan closed his aching eyes. Having his team here lifted the load he'd been carrying since the explosion. A long hike would help take the tension out of his body and spending time with Safiya lifted his shattered spirit. He pushed thoughts of Bill away. He refused to mourn his uncle until he had proof the body was his. Until then he'd hold onto hope. If he let down his shields now it wouldn't be pretty.

"Right." Ryan skulled the rest of his beer. "I'm going to grab a few things and head over to Safiya's cabin." He met Simon's intent gaze. "I'll need that drone."

"Yep, no worries. If you find any treasure, don't forget your mates."

"I've lost one mate over it. I'm not losing any more."

AFTER PUTTING the groceries away in the neat little kitchen, Safiya made a mug of tea. It was a relief to sink into the cane egg chair and contemplate her next line of enquiry. She'd almost fallen asleep when Ryan came striding up the path, his face and hair clean. He still wore the clothes from last night with a pair of work boots. He carried a bulging backpack over his shoulder.

"Hello, Safiya-Ameerah. Why'd you take off this morning?"

"I thought you'd appreciate time with your friends. Are they staying in the other cabins?"

"Yes." He dumped the pack on her porch. A bundle of T-shirts fell out. "I lost my stuff in the fire, so the boys loaned me some essentials. Darius bought me a few necessities."

She chewed her bottom lip, debating whether she had the courage to ask about the blonde.

He crossed his arms. "I can see you have a question. Ask away."

Curiosity won out. "Your robotics engineer is very pretty."

"She is."

"I suppose she'll stay in one of the smaller cabins."

"Zoe put her in the one-bedroom cabin, closest to the gate."

"Will you be staying there too?"

He raised an eyebrow. "As she's engaged to Simon, and they'll be sharing the only bed, I don't think they'd appreciate my presence, even on the couch."

"She's engaged to Simon?"

"Yep. We met Darius on our last mission. She's a woman of many talents."

"I could tell you hold her in high esteem."

"I do. She may be tiny, but she's got a backbone of steel and will do whatever it takes to protect those she loves. Simon's a lucky guy. She's become special to all of us."

Safiya squirmed. How she'd love to be valued like that. Forever the optimist, she'd never give up hope. One day she'd find a man to love her. To appreciate her. To cherish her. Her gaze returned to the backpack. She could see what looked like rope. "Where are you going to stay?"

"I'm moving in with you."

"What?" If he thought—

"I'll sleep on the couch. As we're supposed to be together, it will look strange if I bunk down with the boys."

"I don't see why, they're your friends and it's a two-bedroom cabin. You could sleep on their couch."

"The whole team is here, Safiya. Sam, Talos, Nick and Garcia are taking the biggest cabin. Simon and Darius are in the smaller one. Madeline claimed the other studio, so Jarred will sleep on her couch."

"Is Madeline okay with that?"

"She has no choice. Until we get the people targeting her, she's under his protection."

"Can't you stay at the main house?"

"I need to make sure you're safe. Someone could be trying to hurt the people closest to me, plus my parents and grandparents will be arriving in the next few days. They wouldn't want me in the house."

"Then what makes you think they'll allow you to stay in one of their cabins?"

"The cabins belong to Zoe. Bill loaned her the funds to build them on his land."

"His land?"

"My great-grandfather split the property in half. Being the eldest, my grandfather had first choice. He chose the other side with the house. Barnacle Bill got this side and the private beach below. When he— If it is Bill who died in that fire, I inherit all his assets. Zoe will inherit the other side when our parents pass on."

Safiya's gaze shot across the cove to the Dutch House. "Ryan, what if people think you blew up the boatshed after finding out Bill hadn't told you the truth? Anyone could have heard your conversation at the pub." She held a hand to her chest. "We need to prove your innocence."

"We don't yet know what caused the explosion."

"I found a bundle of dynamite sticks in a canoe on Sunset Beach. I didn't touch it, but a police officer caught me looking at it."

"Dynamite?"

"Yes."

"Jesus. It makes sense, but who the hell would blow up the boatshed?"

"There was a woman on a yacht watching the beach with binoculars. She might be involved."

"Probably a curious tourist."

"I don't think so. I clearly saw *Sea Sprite* on the side of the yacht. Josh Butler told me it's for hire, but when I asked Dawn King about it, she said the yacht hasn't been rented for weeks because the radio doesn't work. She thinks I confused it with another yacht. I didn't."

"Who is Josh Butler?"

"A teenage deckhand I met on the ferry. He also works on Bill's fishing boat, and he told me his parents own the grocery store."

"I remember Josh. The last time I saw him, he would have been about five or six. Would you recognize the woman again?"

"No, she wore a wide brimmed hat and sunglasses. She was watching me too."

He picked up the backpack, pulled out the clothes and hoisted it onto his shoulders. "You got hiking boots with you?"

"Yes. Why?"

"Get them. Bring bottled water and snacks if you have any. I promised you a hike today, and it's time I checked something out."

Safiya stared at him for several heartbeats. "It's the treasure, isn't it?"

"Let's call it a remembrance hike. Garcia is keeping an eye on Zoe. And I've asked Sam to patrol the estate with Ajax. We had to lock the gates to keep well-meaning busybodies out. I thought you might enjoy a hike and the view from our highest point."

She almost fell out of the egg chair. "Give me five minutes to change and make some sandwiches." She ran inside, grabbed her bikini, a pair of socks, T-shirt and tights then shut herself in the bathroom to change. He wanted her help. The thought made her pathetic heart swell with happiness. A couple of hours with Ryan beat a lifetime without him. She could only pray he'd let down his guard enough to see the real her.

She couldn't rein in her optimism. She had two weeks to show Ryan he had her all wrong. Two weeks to help him prove his innocence. Amazingly, her parents were honoring their promise to give her space and privacy. She hadn't spied any of her father's security guards.

She thought of Barnacle Bill's tortured eyes last night and drew a deep breath. They had two weeks to discover if he'd died from a terrible accident, or his boatshed had been blown up on purpose. The thought sent a shudder through her. What if there was a killer on the island? Why target Bill? She gasped. Maybe Zoe and Ryan were in danger?

CHAPTER THIRTEEN

Suggesting they hike to Morcago Ledge hadn't been Ryan's best idea. Neither would be allowing Safiya to lead the way through the koala sanctuary. He couldn't keep his eyes off her curvy hips and butt. At least she kept her gaze straight ahead or up in the trees, oohing and aahing when she spotted koalas, or the echidna she'd insisted on videoing as it went about foraging in the dead leaves and sticks.

Ryan had taken the longest route he knew, desperate to get away from well-meaning busybodies, who'd he likely snap at.

"Ryan, look!" Safiya stopped so suddenly, he ran into her.

"Sorry." He steadied her with his hands on her waist, then couldn't seem to let go. "What did you see?

"There ... beside the tree."

He couldn't help smiling. They were surrounded by trees. Movement caught his eye as a rock wallaby bounded away. "Argh."

"I've never seen so much wildlife in one place. What are those pretty birds?" The wonder in her voice had him glancing up.

"Rainbow lorikeets and that's a blue-tipped kookaburra."

"Where?"

He pulled her closer then pointed out the bird watching them.

"It's beautiful." She took a swig of water. "What sort of trees are these?"

"The ones with koalas were eucalyptus, these hairy ones are stringy barks, and the gray ones are iron barks. We are going to walk through a gully soon that's mostly rainforest."

"How do you stop cats and dogs from killing the native wildlife?" She stepped away, much to Ryan's disappointment.

"There are no cats on the island, and dogs have to be contained in a fenced yard or kept on a leash if out walking."

"What about the German shepherd that arrived with your friends?"

"Ajax is ex-military. He doesn't attack anything unless it's on command, or one of us is threatened. He won't touch wildlife. If the council want our help with the treasure hunters, they'll have to suck it up."

"Ajax. Great name." She lifted her cap to wipe her forehead. "How far to the waterfalls?"

"The most impressive one is about ten minutes away. Just up ahead there's a huge boulder, if we squeeze between it and the rainforest monstera, there's a trail that will take us to Cascada Waterfall."

She giggled. "*Cascada* is Spanish for waterfall. Maybe it was named by Spanish sailors." She turned away to continue along the worn trail.

Ryan followed, enjoying their easy banter. "Where did you learn to speak Spanish?"

"I had a linguistics tutor when I lived in Switzerland. She was supposed to teach me English and German, but I have an ear for languages, so she also taught me Spanish, Italian, and French. I continued my studies as a teenager and then chose to do a linguistics degree at university, which didn't work out, so I did my degree through Open University."

"You speak five languages?"

She laughed. "Actually, I speak eight. I'm also fluent in Arabic, Portuguese, and Greek."

"How did Simon not know that?"

"It's not something I broadcast. My family don't even know." She laughed again. "Comes in handy when I want to eavesdrop on people."

"Geez Louise, I don't know anyone who speaks eight languages. As part of our training, the boys and I had to learn passable Arabic. Jarred and Sam also speak Persian, and Talos speaks Greek."

"I'm not surprised, seeing as you were Special Ops soldiers." Safiya sat on a fallen tree and removed her cap to fan her flushed face.

Ryan joined her on the dead tree. He found their interaction brighter than losing himself in morbid thoughts of Bill's death. "Madeline said you spent time together earlier in the year."

"Yes." Safiya stretched out her legs, drawing his attention to her shapely calves and golden skin. "We found we have a lot in common. I'm looking forward to catching up with her later." She pinned him with a mischievous look. "Okay, you've learned something about me that isn't common knowledge. Tell me something about you?"

Ryan stretched out his own legs. "I ride a Harley."

"Come on, something intriguing, that few people would know?"

He laughed. "I own a two-bedroom apartment overlooking Sydney Harbour."

"Not good enough. Adam told us he'd been staying there with you."

"Right." Ryan scratched the stubble on his chin, trying to come up with something intriguing. "I have a tattoo on my chest."

"Show me."

"Can't we wait until we get to the waterfall?"

"No, show me now." She reached for his shirt.

"Okay." He pulled it over his head, enjoying Safiya's stunned silence. He worked hard to stay in shape, but the appreciation in her eyes boosted his ego.

She swallowed then reached out to trace the dolphin and seal frolicking in waves tattooed on his chest. "You're him."

"Who?"

"The boy who saved Pong after Ping towed her into shore. You swam with them regularly until you left the island."

"How do you know?"

"Josh Butler told me it was one of Barnacle Bill's stories. He said the boy named the seal Pong because her farts stank."

"That's true." Ryan grinned, enjoying the touch of her fingers gliding over his chest. He raised his hand and traced his thumb over her full lower lip. "Safiya."

Her breath hitched. "Yes."

Her questioning gaze brought him back to earth with a thud. He'd been about to kiss her. He stood and shoved his shirt into the backpack. "You're going to love the waterfall. There's a deep pool we can cool off in."

She blinked a couple of times. "Sounds like a plan. Lead on."

He had no trouble finding the huge boulder, although it didn't look quite as large as it had twelve years ago. "Stay close and watch the rock doesn't graze your skin. It's a pretty tight squeeze." He pushed the monstera away as he forced his way past the enormous plant. They came out the other side where the old trail had grown over. He'd assumed local kids would have discovered the hidden trail to Cascada Waterfall. Obviously not.

"Do you think there's any truth to Alejandro's claim?"

"The Spanish guitarist?"

"Yes. He wants to prove his Spanish ancestor discovered Australia before James Cook."

"It's possible. Captain Cook sailed down the east coast in 1770, but there's always been rumors of pre-Cook shipwrecks off the northern coast of Queensland." Ryan held a palm frond aside for Safiya. "As a kid I read of rumored Portuguese and Spanish Galleons. There was even a Japanese pirate, supposedly carrying gold and silver coins. There are many who believe James Cook used Portuguese or Spanish maps to aid his navigation of Australia's east coast."

"So, it is possible?" She trudged along behind him for several minutes in silence. "Zoe told me there are as many as eight thousand wrecks off the coasts of Australia, and only two thousand have been found."

"I'm not surprised." Ryan grimaced. "Imagine navigating the world in a leaky wooden ship with no engine. Bill had a diary full of interesting facts his great-grandfather discovered. Someone broke into his boatshed last week and stole it, along with a very old saber."

"It has to be that group of treasure hunters … or Alejandro and his brother?"

He frowned at the disappointment in her voice. "Maybe. Best to stay away from them." He took another few strides then stopped and looked over his shoulder. "Listen."

She cocked her head. "The waterfall."

"Yep, it's not far. Come on."

Five minutes of tramping through sub-tropical rainforest brought them to the top of Cascada Waterfall, where the foaming water mass plummeted to the depths below. The power of nature never ceased to amaze Ryan. He held his face up to the fine spray of cooling mist then glanced at Safiya. Her eyes were alight, her smile wide.

"It's majestic, isn't it?"

"Yes, and magical. Let's make a wish each." She grabbed his hand. "Humor me, Ryan. What can it hurt? It's so magical we should make two wishes."

"Okay." He breathed deeply, reaching out with all his senses. *I wish for Bill to be alive.* The falling water thundered down to the pool below, yet he could hear bird chatter and leaves rustling. There were so many other things he could wish for. Clear his name. Discover who was responsible for the explosion in Bill's boatshed. Find Bill's diary and saber. Have the respect and admiration of everyone on Curra. Yet, right at this second, one wish overshadowed all else. He wanted to prolong this easy camaraderie with Safiya. Get to know her.

She squeezed his fingers. "Now you have to believe they will come true." Not waiting for an answer, she stepped closer to the rock edge. "How do we get down?"

"Carefully." He led the way, fitting his boots to sturdy rocks and gripping tree roots. "It's a deep pool, so if you feel yourself falling, push out as far as you can."

"Let me guess … You jumped from the top when you were a teenager?"

"Yeah, but we borrowed dive gear and checked for submerged rocks first."

"Borrowed?"

He chuckled. "Bill assumed we wanted to dive off the beach."

"I bet he did." She sighed. "You and your friends must have had a wonderful childhood."

"We did." Which made Ryan's loss so much worse. He'd soldiered on. While serving his country, he'd kept himself busy training and learning incredible skills. He'd filled his life with new friends, and leisure activities that left little room for morbid memories.

Reaching the rock ledge around the pool, he held out a hand and helped Safiya down the mossy bank.

"Stick your feet in and cool off, I'm going for a swim." He dropped the pack, unlaced his boots then dragged them off along with his pants and dived in. The icy water took his breath for a second then he surfaced and swam to the other side. Safiya had it right. This place held magic. In less than a minute he felt completely refreshed, lighter.

A loud splash had him twisting round, worried Safiya had slipped on the mossy rocks. "Shit, where is she?" He kicked out, taking two strokes before she popped up in front of him, grinning and wearing her skimpy, leopard print bikini.

"This water is freezing." She laughed then dived again, giving him an eyeful of her leopard print covered butt. The cold water lost the ability to cool his desire.

"Hell." His wish had come back to bite him, and he couldn't do a thing about it.

She popped up in front of the frothy curtain of water. "What are you waiting for?"

"Damned if I know," he muttered. She had him by the balls. There had never been another woman he wanted so desperately. Maybe if he gave in, made love to her, and got whatever this was out of his system, he could move on. "No." What the hell had gotten into him? He wasn't the kind of guy who took advantage of a woman to ease a bout of lust. He had hands for that.

"Ryan? Is something wrong?"

Oh, yeah, but he couldn't admit it. "Just admiring the view." *Shit, I'm an ass.* "Don't go any closer, there's a lot of clout in that falling water."

"Where's it coming from?" She kept her head above water, propelling her arms and kicking, her gaze on the cascading water as she swam toward him.

He swallowed and moved until his feet found the pebbled bottom. "Up higher on the mountain is a larger pool and Kingfisher Falls. There's a natural spring, but because we get such a heavy rainfall between November and April, the waterfalls never run dry."

"It doesn't look like anyone comes here." She'd almost reached him.

"Cascada Waterfall isn't on any tourist brochures. Only locals know about it. Or they used to." He glanced around the edges of the pond then up the banks, unable to locate any evidence of human tracks, other than theirs. "Me, Zane, and Tommy found it as kids. We didn't tell a soul." This had been their secret place.

Safiya rolled over then breast-stroked the last few feet to him. "I love this place. Thank you for bringing me here." She meant to kiss him. He knew it with every fiber of his being. She reached for his biceps, hanging on as she maneuvered to press her lips to his check.

He wasn't interested in a sisterly kiss. Ryan caught her hips and lifted her against his chest, sabotaging her lips with all the desire that had been mounting since they'd first met. She molded to his body as if made for him, wrapping her legs around his waist, her arms around his shoulders. He lost all common sense. He deserved a little magic, after all he'd lost. He'd take a little pleasure and worry about the fine print later.

"Ryan." She moaned, grinding against him, giving him the permission he desperately required. He had her clasp undone and bikini top off in less time than it took to draw a frantic gasp of air before diving back into the sensual haven of her mouth. Her naked breasts against his chest fueled his lust.

He pushed a hand between them, spreading his fingers wide to cup her left breast. She more than filled his hand and he hummed with pleasure. Safiya had breasts a man could feast on for days.

"Geez, woman, have you any idea what you do to me?"

"If it's what you do to me, yes." She kissed the corner of his mouth, cheek, eyelids, leaving her neck free for the taking. He couldn't resist laving, kissing, nipping, lapping up her soft cries of ecstasy.

The inferno within his body raged. "Saf, I want my mouth on your breasts."

"I want that too."

He staggered to the edge of the pool then lowered her to a relatively smooth rock. She instantly leaned back on her hands, proudly displaying her assets, like a mermaid calling besotted sailors to their deaths. He kneed her legs apart, sinking into the cradle they provided then lowered his head to her right breast, flicking his tongue over the erect nipple.

"Yes." She arched further, pushing her nipple into his mouth.

He grinned and closed his lips, sucking hard. It wasn't enough. He leaned on one elbow for balance, so he could caress her other breast, while feasting on this one.

"Yes. Yes. Yes."

Her breathy little gasps delighted him. He couldn't wait to watch her orgasm. Raising his head, he stared into her sexy eyes. "You have been driving me crazy for months. I want to explore every inch of your body then have my way with you, but not here. Not yet." He grinned. "I didn't bring a condom."

"Okay," she panted. "I want that too."

"Thank fuck." The scent of her arousal almost tipped him over the edge. He licked his lips, struggling with this strange new beast inside him. "I won't do anything you don't want."

"I trust you, Ryan. I've been imagining this for months."

Geez, she'd kill him. He'd been softly caressing her breast, now he squeezed.

"Your scent is intoxicating. I can't get enough of it, the way your hips sway when you walk, your laugh, your vibrant come-get-me eyes, these beauties." He lowered his mouth, worshipping first one breast then the other.

She squirmed. "I've wanted this since the day we met."

He raised his head again. "On your father's island?"

"Yes. I liked the way you smiled at me and flirted before you knew my identity. Before my brother warned you off."

He nodded, remembering Gibbs' warning and the coolness directed at Safiya. At the time, Ryan figured she'd been part of the additional staff brought in to cater for his mates' double weddings. Until Simon told him she was Gibbs' flighty sister. The daughter of a sheikh.

"Enough reminiscing." She arched. "Kiss me."

"Yes, ma'am." He layered kisses across her collar bone then over her fullness of her breast to her nipple, rolling it with his tongue then closing his teeth and gently tugging.

She quivered, cried out and squirmed.

He watched his hand as he traced over her ribs to her hip then down her smooth thigh and back up. His erection pulsed against his belly. Only a callous jerk would take her here on the rocks. When they made love for the first time, he wanted it to be in a bed. He wouldn't do anything to harm this new fragile bond developing between them. For now, he needed to touch and taste her. Pushing up on one arm, he lifted over her leg, rolled to his side then pulled the black cord holding her bikini together. She immediately pulled the other side undone.

He brushed his fingers over her tight, dark curls then through her soaked folds to her clit.

She jerked, crying out. "Yes, touch me there."

"You're so wet, Saf. I can smell your arousal. It's intoxicating."

She gyrated against his fingers. "Harder."

He pushed a finger inside her hot, tight haven, mimicking what he'd do with his cock. Her sheath coated his finger in juices that he couldn't help but remove for a taste. "Delicious."

"Don't stop." She grabbed his hand, forcing it back between her thighs. "Make me come."

"Oh, I will, honey. I promise." He pushed two fingers inside, curling them as he rubbed back and forth.

"Yes, like that." She lifted her hips, meeting his thrusts, her pupils dilating with desire.

"You're soaked." He spread her juices, circling the hard little nub then pushing inside her again.

She trembled, her sheath squeezing his fingers. "Ryan, I'm coming."

"Yeah, come for me, Saf." He rubbed her clit faster, while capturing a nipple and sucking hard.

She bucked, crying out his name, shuddering then stiffening under his fingers and lips. He flicked her engorged nub, prolonging her orgasm.

"Please, no more," she grabbed his hand, digging in her nails as she tried to hold his hand still. "No more."

He pressed his whole hand against her soaking folds. "You're amazing."

"Wow." She held on tight, her eyes wide with wonder. She licked her lips. "I've never come from a guy touching me." She blushed. "Not that I've been with a woman."

"You're welcome." He liked being the first man to give her an orgasm. "Saf, I need to taste you properly."

"Taste me. Oh, God, I don't think I could handle that right now. I don't even know if I want you to do that. It's…"

He raised an eyebrow. "Another first?"

The color in her cheeks brightened. "I told you, I've been with two guys, and we weren't together long enough to get around to that."

"You'll like it, I promise. Let me give you this, Safiya?"

"What about your pleasure?"

"Soon." He eased back, sinking into the water, allowing it to cool his ardor, then he pushed her knees wide, looking his fill. She was a smorgasbord of erotic delight. Her folds glistening with her juices, her plump breasts lifting with every ragged breath, her dark eyes hazy with passion. "Wriggle down closer then lie back."

"What if someone sees us?"

"We'll hear anyone way before they get here. Move down, babe."

She sucked in her lower lip, clamping down on it with her teeth then did as he'd requested. "This better be good, because I've never been so vulnerable in my life."

He chuckled. "Trust me, Safiya."

She eased back on her elbows then waved a hand regally. "Okay, continue."

He barked out a laugh. "You're adorable, Saf."

"Hmmp." She hesitated then slowly spread her legs. He'd swear she didn't mean to be provocative, but his hard-on got harder.

Crawling between her legs, he lowered his head and inhaled her arousal then spread her thighs wider with his shoulders, his attention focused on her patch of curls and glistening folds. Easing his hands under her thighs, he gripped her butt, lifting her to within inches of his mouth and blew.

"Oh," she gasped, her legs locking round his shoulders.

"Easy, darlin'" She was so sensitive this wouldn't take long. His erection throbbed against his stomach. This thing between them was unlike anything he'd experienced. It was as if his body demanded its true mate, leaving his brain floundering to catch up. Each time he learned something new about her, it hammered home just how wrongly he'd judged her. One look into Safiya's sensual eyes and his brain lost its battle. He wanted her more than he'd ever wanted anything in his life.

CHAPTER FOURTEEN

Safiya gloried in her newfound confidence. Ryan had the power to hurt her more than anyone ever had, but she would risk it for the chance of true happiness. It was like he'd infected her with a non-returnable, highly contagious love potion, drawing her to him without anything to grasp on to. After their very first conversation, he'd hooked her better than any fish.

She jolted at the first touch of his tongue sweeping through her slick folds. She couldn't help but cry out when he circled her clit, sucked then thrust his tongue deep inside her.

"So good." She moaned. "Don't stop."

He drew her sensitive flesh into his mouth then speared her with his tongue, thrusting deep until she was quivering and gasping. She could smell her own arousal and relished it. He gripped her butt so hard she'd probably have fingerprints. That thought died a quick death when he ruthlessly devoured her, his stubble raking against her sensitive skin, arousing her beyond endurance. She screamed, bucking against his mouth, shuddering, her sheath clenching around his tongue as she rode out another overwhelming orgasm.

When she could finally reengage with the world around her, she was cocooned in his arms, sitting across his thighs with his erection pressed against her hip. "Wow."

His arms tightened. "Yeah."

Looking up she found him smiling wolfishly, his lips and chin wet with her juices. He dipped a hand in the water then splashed his face, wiping away all traces. "You orgasm spectacularly, Safiya."

"Err, thanks." She squirmed, embarrassed by her brazen behavior. "I'm really hot. Time to cool off?"

"My thoughts exactly." He scooped her up then strode through the shallow water and dropped her into the freezing water. She came up spluttering. "Ryan?"

His lips twitched. "You are one extremely hot lady. I'm just cooling you down a little so we can move on." He gave her a cheeky smile, which she returned.

"The waiting will make it so much more exhilarating." She giggled. "Win, win."

"You're one in a million, Safiya-Ameerah." He closed the distance then pulled her into a bear hug. "I will need something to tide me over though." He lowered his head and kissed her, so deeply and thoroughly her knees threatened to give out.

As if waking from a deep sleep, his words sluggishly registered. He'd said the robotics engineer was one in a million. Her heart swelled. Ryan couldn't have given her a higher compliment. It was heady stuff. She wanted to jump for joy, dance and laugh. Instead, she pulled him and fell backwards, taking them both underwater. When she came up for air, she had a choking fit from laughing underwater.

"You are a wicked woman, Safiya."

"You needed cooling off too. Shall we continue to Kingfisher Lookout?"

"Race you to the other side." He gave a boyish laugh and dived.

She couldn't hold in her own laughter. His despondent mood from this morning had been replaced by a cheeky guy intent on giving her pleasure of one kind or another. He'd have to face the reality of Bill's death soon enough. If she could give him a few hours of light-heartedness and companionship, she would.

An hour later she stood on top of the world with three-sixty-degree views of the island and surrounding ocean. Currawong Island was pure magic. The emerald hinterland and the shimmering azure blue of the surrounding ocean were more than a picture postcard of the ideal island getaway. It promised adventure, freedom, relaxation.

She sucked in a lungful of the crisp, salty air, her gaze sweeping over Rocky Point and Palm Beach before dipping to the treacherous reefs to the south-east of the island. A chill feathered her spine as she studied the sheer cliff across the bay and the boulders lying at the base of the treacherous drop. Majestic, yet terrifying.

She shook her head in wonder. "It must have devastated you to leave all this."

"Yeah." Ryan stood beside her, his hands on a round metal rail. "For the first month, I struggled through each day. I imagined it over and over. After another month, my father called, but I refused to speak to him. To anyone except Zoe or Bill. It was my decision never to return."

"You must have been lonely."

"I hit rock bottom." He sighed. "Not long after I arrived in Perth, I caught a bus to the beach. I swam until exhaustion made it impossible to take another stroke. A lifeguard on a jet ski picked me up. Said if I wanted to prove my stamina, I should join the beach club."

"Oh, Ryan …" She ducked under his arm and hugged him. "Did you?"

"Yeah. Being near the ocean helped, and the mate of Bill's who I lived with kept me busy teaching me his style of martial arts. He encouraged me to join the army after I became obsessed with Blackhawks."

She gazed over the cove below. From the dark blue of the water, she knew it would be deep. Instead of sand, rugged boulders ringed the edges. On the far left, beyond a wide river inlet, the sheer cliff rose out of the sea. "Is it just me, or is there something eerie about this cove?"

He stiffened. "It's not just you. This is Shark Bite Bay. It's deep enough to attract big sharks, and …" He pointed to where she'd been looking. "… See how that inlet looks like the open mouth of a great white?"

"Yes. From up here it looks exactly like the head of shark." She turned fully, leaning back against his chest. "That's a scary-looking cliff." When he didn't answer, she glanced up. "Oh … is that …?"

"Morcago Ledge."

She shivered. It was a long way to fall. "Are there bats on Curra-wong Island?"

"Why?" Ryan's hard voice caught her by surprise.

"Just that Morcago is close to *murciélago*, which is Spanish for bat."

He spun her around. "Are you sure?"

"Yes, why?"

"There are bats inside that mountain." Ryan looked past her shoulder toward the cliff. "Zane and I found writing on the wall of a cave. *Cueva de los murciélagos.* I'd forgotten that."

"The English translation is bat cave."

"That is where I got bat shit all over my clothes and why my parents grounded me." He shook his head. "Zane wouldn't descend without me, or his harness. He would have had the shits with me for not turning up, but he would have come to find me. I know he would."

Safiya sucked in her lower lip and thought for a minute. "I think we can confidently say, someone he knew tried to descend that cliff and got into trouble. What if Zane found them hanging upside down and didn't think he had time to get into his harness. The person he tried to rescue could have been in a panic. I'm guessing they panicked and Zane lost his grip and fell."

Ryan's fingers dug into her waist. "Tommy would have been petri-fied, so it makes sense, but why didn't he come forward? Why leave me to take the blame?"

"We will have to ask him. Would Zane have told anyone else about the cave?"

"No, but Tommy couldn't keep a secret if his life depended on it. He's got a heap of cousins. That could be why he feels guilty."

Safiya ducked as something swooped low over their heads. "Wow, what was that?"

They looked up at a large bird gliding in circles above them, it's wingspan enormous.

Ryan chuckled. "It's Darius' sea eagle drone."

"That's a drone?" She couldn't believe the beautiful bird of prey wasn't real.

"I told you she was clever."

Safiya watched the bird glide out over the ocean until it disappeared. "Isn't she afraid it will go out of range and crash into the ocean?"

"No, it's got plenty of range. I'd say she's sending it out to spy on those treasure hunters. She now knows where we are too. I'd like to hike around the cove to Morcago Ledge?"

"You intend going over there?"

"Yes. We can eat our snacks there, then I want to check something out."

The thought of Ryan returning to the scene of his friend's death worried Safiya. He'd been through enough turmoil today, but if it were something he needed to do, she'd keep her thoughts to herself and try to lighten the mood. "We will certainly have a fabulous view to enjoy over lunch."

Eating sandwiches up close and personal to Morcago Ledge was far scarier than she'd anticipated. Much to her horror, after they'd eaten, Ryan pulled out a harness and helmet. "What are you doing?"

"I want to put a small drone into the cave Zane and I found." He anchored a thick rope to a tree using silver lock bolt things. "I'm perfectly safe, Saf. I do this for a living."

"Maybe so, but it's a long way to the bottom." Her stomach turned at the thought of him going over the treacherous ledge.

He winked at her. "Relax, I'll be back up in ten minutes." He buckled the harness at his waist then pulled on his helmet. "Move right back and do not come near the edge."

"I have no intention of coming near it. Please be careful."

"Always." He leaned down and kissed her lightly before backing to the lip of the cliff. "Nothing's going to get in the way of making love to you, Saf." He leaned way back and stepped over the edge.

She froze, her heart in her mouth. Terrified didn't come close to what she was experiencing. It was a struggle to breath, her hands shook. Her stomach flipped and perspiration trickled down between her breasts. Who in their right mind would step off a cliff?

She didn't know how much time passed, but it felt like hours before Ryan crawled over the cliff top. He was drenched in sweat and solemn. "Are you okay?"

"Yeah. We need to get back to the Dutch House."

"Did you find something?" She stood, wincing as blood returned to her feet. *Note to self. Don't sit on feet so long without moving.*

"I found a passage that descends into a large cave, but I crashed Darius' drone into a pool of water." He unbuckled his harness and took off the helmet. "I'd kill for a drink."

She ran to the backpack and pulled out a fresh bottle of water. "Here."

"Thanks, Saf. You're the best."

"Flattery isn't going to cut it, Mister. I'm not happy with you jumping off this ... this big rock. I'm sure to have nightmares tonight."

"Not if I'm with you, honey."

THEY ARRIVED at the Dutch House gates to find Adam and Talos leaning against the sandstone pillars. Both said hello to Safiya then gave Ryan a nod. Men and their mannerisms.

"You head over to your cabin. I'll catch up with you later." Ryan squeezed her arm. "Thanks for the company, Saf." He strode over to Talos.

Adam opened a gate for Safiya then fell in beside her. "Sergeant Hawthorne requested we all stay out of town this afternoon. He suggested we go look for whales. I think a change of scenery would be good for Ryan and Zoe."

"I agree. Our hike did Ryan a lot of good."

"I thought it might. Zoe's got the charter boat ready to go."

Forty minutes later, Safiya sat on a cushioned bench with Madeline, Zoe, and Darius at the stern of the *Francine*. Darius looked as dainty as a ballerina. She was cheerful, friendly, and couldn't keep her eyes from drifting to Simon, who returned her gazes with heated promises and little touches whenever they were close. It was clear they adored each other.

Inside the cabin, Ryan steered the boat while talking quietly with his friends as they watched live footage from a drone high above the yacht belonging to the large group of treasure hunters. Ajax stood with his head through the safety railing, every now and then barking at ping and pong who'd followed them from Dutchies Beach. Talos and Adam had stayed behind to keep visitors out.

Safiya drew a deep breath. It was a magnificent afternoon. Not a cloud in the pretty blue sky, the ocean as calm as a lake, and a faint breeze to cool her skin. It would have been idyllic, except Bill's death hung over them like a wet blanket. All the way out they'd kept Zoe busy asking her about her encounters with whales, dolphins, and giant manta rays.

Nick took over the wheel and Ryan came to sit beside Safiya. "We've been watching the treasure hunters. The larger group are two kilometers north of us on a yacht named *Winner takes all*. The Spanish brothers are working on their yacht, *Capricorn,* in Dugong Marina. We sighted a couple of whale sharks if you'd like a closer look?"

"Yes, please."

Zoe jumped up. "I've got stinger suits and gear if anyone wants to swim with them."

"Not me," called Nick. "I'm not interested in playing with sharks."

"Whale sharks," corrected Zoe. "They eat plankton. Don't be a scaredy cat, Nick." Her smirk lifted Safiya's spirits. Zoe had been in a deep depression since the fire at the boatshed. No one wanted to believe that Bill was dead, but facts were facts. Who else could it be?

"I'm not a scaredy cat, Zoe," complained Nick. "But once you've been surrounded by great whites, it's something you never want to experience again."

"Surrounded?" Safiya stared at him. "What happened?"

"My chopper was shot down. Long story, but some quick thinking by my mates and Ava saved my life."

"What?" Zoe glared at Ryan. "You never told me that story."

"I'm not surprised," volunteered Sam. "Seeing those sharks closing in on Nick scared the hell out of me too."

Zoe paced over to a large plastic tub and began handing out stinger suits, gloves, snorkels, goggles, and flippers. Once fully equipped, Safiya looked out over the calm ocean. She hoped swimming with the whales would give Zoe and Ryan a little relief from their heartache.

"What's that?" yelled Darius. "Over there." She pointed to a massive shape just beneath the surface to their right. Suddenly an enormous gray whale with a white underbelly breached the surface, rising out of the water then bellyflopping down again. Everyone rushed to the port side of the yacht, gasping in awe.

"It's so close," Safiya pressed against the rail beside Ryan, staring at the water, eager to see the whale again.

"There's another one," called Madeline, pointing behind the yacht. "This is amazing. I've never been so close to whales."

"Me either." Safiya clapped her hands as another whale breached the water. "They're magnificent." A whale lifted its tail high then forcibly slapped it down, then did it repeatedly. "I think it's waving to us." She glanced at Ryan. "What kind of whales are they?"

"Humpbacks." Ryan stood beside her, resting his hand on her lower back. "Each year, between April and November, Australia's eastern and western coastlines becomes a playground to these acrobatic displays."

"They're amazing." Madeline leaned out as a whale slapped the water with its tail, rocking the boat and tipping her off balance.

"Careful." Jarred clasped his arm around her waist. "I don't want you falling in."

"Thanks, Chief." She rested against him. "I can always trust you to keep me safe."

"Never doubt it."

When Jarred didn't move away from Madeline, Safiya's interest spiked. There was something about the way they interacted that intrigued her. She'd never noticed an intimacy between them, but now she thought about it, Jarred's gaze rarely left Madeline.

Safiya's gaze shifted over the men. They wore black stinger suits, which showed off their broad shoulders, sculptured peaks, and tight butts. Yet, it was Ryan who captured most of her attention. She caught him checking her out too.

"Okay, gather round," called Zoe. "Sam has spotted a couple of whale sharks really close to us from the drone. Ajax needs to stay on the boat with a spotter in case of an emergency, but we can take it in turns to swap out." She held up a finger. "Don't forget to keep a four-meter distance from them, especially their tails. You do not want to get swiped by their tail flukes. Any questions?"

"What about real sharks?" asked Safiya. "Will we be safe."

Zoe held her hands wide. "I can't promise we won't see a shark, but in the two years I've been bringing people out here, I've never had a problem. There is a huge misconception that sharks automatically attack humans. They can be curious, but more often are afraid of us. If you see a shark, don't panic."

Nick grunted. "Right. Don't panic. With us fellas in the water, they'll leave you alone, Safiya. More meat on us." He winked at her then turned back to the screen he'd been watching.

Swallowing her nerves, Safiya put on her mask and gloves then picked up her flippers. Her heart raced madly as she shuffled after Madeline and Zoe to the side of the boat, where Ryan held a panel open.

"Holy hell." Jarred gripped the rail as he stared into the water. "They're massive."

Safiya gasped as two huge whale sharks glided past. Even though she knew they only ate plankton, their sheer size overwhelmed her. They were as long and wide as a bus. "I don't know if I can do this."

"I'll be with you, Saf." Ryan cupped her cheek. "Remember, they don't eat meat."

"Right."

Zoe slipped into the water, closely followed by Sam, Jarred, Madeline and Darius. Safiya gave herself a mental shake. *I can do this.* She pulled on her flippers then sat on the edge of the boat, waiting until Ryan dropped in. Taking a deep breath, she slid into the water and with Ryan beside her, caught up to the others, then snorkeled above the two pre-historic giants.

Within minutes, she'd forgotten her fears and transcended into a fantastical new world, swimming alongside, under and above the two whale sharks as they meandered through the water, not the least concerned by the tiny humans interloping. They moved so leisurely, it seemed they were suspended in the water by invisible strings.

Witnessing Zoe kicking like a dolphin as she swam alongside was an experience on its own, one Safiya tried to imitate. The slightly bigger whale shark had a reddish-brown skin with white spots, the other bluey-gray with white dots.

Realizing Zoe was pointing behind Safiya, she turned as a massive, flattened, black shape appeared from the depths, then another and another. *Shit. Shit. Shit. Shit.*

Ryan caught her hand and squeezed. He held up his other hand, his thumb and first finger forming a circle, while his other three fingers stayed straight. *It's okay.* Then he pointed up.

She nodded, gasping when she surfaced. "What are they?"

He grinned. "Manta Rays. They'll come close but won't hurt you." He dived again.

Not wanting to lose him, she followed, kicking hard to catch up then almost freaking out when one of the giant rays swam straight at them, its massive wings flapping like a bird. At the last minute it did a barrel roll, exposing its white underside. Ryan reached out, his fingers brushing against its body. Another appeared and did the same thing.

Coming up for air, Safiya quickly dived again, to see five enormous rays circling their group. With her heart in her mouth, she copied Ryan and held out her hands as a giant ray came at her. It rolled, close enough for Safiya to run her gloved fingers down its underside.

I love this place. She wished she didn't have to keep going up for air. Diving again, she almost landed on the reddish-brown whale shark as it came up under her. It was so close, Safiya reached out and slid her hand along its body as it glided below. She barely recovered from that wonderful experience when the bluish gray one swam alongside her. Again, she reached out and ran her fingers along its body, then quickly kicked away as its tail loomed close.

Surfacing, she looked toward the boat. Zoe and Madeline were waving for her to come back to the boat.

Ryan surfaced in front of Safiya, a look of wonder in his eyes. "That was out of this world."

"I know. For the rest of my life, I will remember these magic minutes with wonder and awe." She snorkeled alongside Ryan to the boat, surprised to find everyone on board, waiting for them. She pulled off her flippers. "Are we heading back?"

"Yes." Jarred took her flippers, allowing her to use both hands on the ladder then waited for Ryan to climb up. "Talos rang. Someone broke into your father's study. I'd suggest they watched us leave then took the opportunity to break in."

Ryan tore off his mask. ""The gates are locked." How'd they get past Talos and Garcia?"

"Talos said there are drag marks in the sand, most likely from a kayak, and one set of footprints leading up Dutchies Beach then another set going back into the water."

Ryan frowned. "Could be one of the Spanish brothers? Their yacht is in Dugong Marina."

"What about the other group?" asked Safiya. "Do we know if they're all on their yacht?" She hated to think Alejandro or Sebastian were behind the break in.

"Too hard to tell," called Nick. "We haven't seen more than five onboard, so one could have stayed on the island. I'll keep an eye on them." Safiya noticed Nick wasn't wet. The great whites had obviously well and truly scared him out of the ocean.

"I've had enough of this bullshit." Ryan strode over to Zoe. "How ya doin', Zo?"

"Why would someone break into Dad's study?"

"They could be after the file on the history of Currawong. Hopefully, the police will get fingerprints. I promise you I will find them." Ryan's gaze found Safiya as he hugged his sister, his eyes fueled with anger and determination.

Rage welled in Safiya, so much so, she turned away to face the ocean. That large group of treasure hunters did try to run over Ryan, but were they behind the explosion and break ins? Was the explosion retaliation for Ryan whipping their asses at the pub. Had Bill's death been accidental? Maybe they weren't involved. Maybe it was the woman in the white dress or the Spanish brothers. Whoever it was, she wanted them caught and punished. They deserved the karma coming their way, and so did the person who let Ryan take the blame for Zane's death.

She could kiss her evening of debauchery away. There was important sleuthing to do.

CHAPTER FIFTEEN

"Hell." Ryan stood in the middle of his father's study. It was a shambles. Broken glass covered the rug from where the thief had gained entry through the window. Drawers, books, and papers were strewn across the room. Nothing had been left on the bookshelves. A fist had been punched through the dry wall, leaving a gaping hole. The forensic guy had left dark smudges and dust over every wooden surface. It would take a while to bring the study back to its usual pristine order. He'd already boarded the broken window in case it rained.

First thing first. Ryan squatted and brushed the glass into the dustpan. Irritation was the least of his mindsets. Sergeant Hawthorne and the detective had left, unable to do much without a clear fingerprint or an eyewitness.

The euphoria of lavishing pleasure on Safiya at the waterfall, then swimming alongside her with the whale sharks and manta ray had long passed. He couldn't remember a day of such highs and lows. He'd fought all day to block the image of the charred body. He refused to accept he'd lost Bill, but who else could it be? For the old guy to die so horrifically after cheating death so many times during his years as a soldier on the front line was damned unbelievable. It threatened to send Ryan over the edge. He needed distraction. He needed to be doing something to find the person behind the explosion. Bill did not keep dynamite in the boatshed, and he certainly wouldn't blow himself up. Someone had to have seen something.

Emptying the glass into a bin, he picked up the chair and rolled it in under the desk. He grabbed the bucket of soapy water and a cloth to clean off the fingerprint dust. Staying busy helped calm his mind. Safiya had driven off with Zoe and Garcia to pick up supplies for dinner, which made Ryan uneasy. If someone was targeting his family, he didn't want Zoe or Safiya leaving the estate, but as they needed food, Sergeant Hawthorne had given his approval, and his escort. It was a small consolation. Garcia wouldn't let anything happen to Zoe and Safiya, yet Ryan couldn't shake the uneasiness growing within him.

Darkness had fallen. The boys had set up a command center in the largest cabin. They would be monitoring cameras set up around the Dutch estate twenty-four-seven.

Once he'd dried the shelves and desk, he returned everything to its place, as best as he could remember. He stacked the files in a neat pile on the desk for his father to sort. His stomach was a ball of twisted knots at the thought of informing his father the study had been trashed, but he couldn't put it off any longer. Nonsensical compared to the deadly missions he'd survived.

Taking a deep breath, he keyed in the number Zoe had given him and held his breath as it connected and rang three times.

"John Dutch speaking."

The sound of his father's voice, so clipped yet familiar caught Ryan by surprise. It took him a moment to regain his wits.

"Who is this?"

"It's Ryan. Hello, Dad."

There was a long pause then. "Has something happened to Zoe?"

No how are you? It's been a long time. We've missed you. We're sorry for how we turned our backs on you. Ryan drew in a deep breath. "Zoe's fine. I have her well protected. I'm calling to let you know someone broke into your study. I think they were searching for grandfather's historical file on Currawong."

"Good grief. Did they get it?"

"No. I gave it to Sergeant Hawthorne for safe keeping."

"I see. Is there any news on the explosion or … the body they found?"

"Not yet."

"I hear you got into a fight with this latest batch of treasure hunters. Did you provoke them? Is this payback for something you've done?"

His father's words cut deep but came as no surprise. For some reason he'd always expected the worst of Ryan. "I've done nothing to provoke them. The break ins began before the council asked for my help. I'll find out who is responsible… and while I'm here I'm going to figure out who was with Zane on Morcago Ledge twelve years ago?"

"So, you *still* insist it wasn't you? I found your harness and helmet."

Ryan cleared his throat. "This was just a curtesy call to let you know about the break in. Goodbye, Dad." He ended the call and stared out over the ocean. Aside from his grandmother, he'd never managed to please his parents or grandfather. He'd never fitted the mold they expected. He'd been too carefree. Too adventurous. Too independent.

He was about to leave the study when his phone began vibrating. He checked the ID then swiped to answer. "Colonel?"

"You or Nick had anything to drink?"

"No. Why?"

"I need you to fly the detectives and the body to Townsville Army base."

"Now?"

"Yeah. The quicker we get things happening, the sooner we'll have answers. They've got everything they need and will be communicating through Gibbs. Meet me at the Blackhawk."

"Garcia hasn't brought Zoe and Safiya back yet?"

"They are with me and Madeline. We didn't get anywhere at the police station, so we've been speaking to older residents about your friend's death. Safiya and Madeline work in tandem like well-oiled, fucking pistons, barely taking a breath as they hammer people with questions. We've been told the previous sergeant left a lot to be desired. He didn't check the top of Morcago Ledge until after it had been trampled by dozens of feet. Any evidence would have been compromised or destroyed."

"Yeah, I know." Ryan appreciated Safiya's desire to prove his innocence, but she wasn't a local. He needed to talk to Tommy and the elder he'd once been close to. Frankie Ellis knew everything that happened on Curra. Whether she would talk to him was another thing. Zane had been her grandson and she'd raised him from a toddler.

"I'll grab Nick and be there in twenty." Ending the call, Ryan headed to the largest cabin to update the others and collect Nick.

THE FLIGHT to Townsville had been mostly silent. As Nick shut down the Blackhawk, Ryan watched the police leave with the body. He still couldn't accept it was Bill. His whole being fought the idea as his emotions threatened to overwhelm him. He climbed out of the cockpit and slammed the door. His feet felt like lead weights as he followed Jarred and Nick to a waiting Jeep. They were driven to the officers' mess where the base commander had organized a late dinner for them. Ryan hadn't eaten since lunch with Safiya on Morcago Ledge, but he couldn't stomach the thought of food. Transporting the body to the mainland had killed his appetite.

Jarred clamped his hand on Ryan's shoulder. "I've been invited to dine with the base commander. Make sure you eat something."

"Will do." Ryan sat opposite Nick while they were served a roast dinner. He tried a mouthful, but struggled to swallow it. All day he'd prayed Bill would show up with some outrageous excuse for missing in action. Now he couldn't block the memory of Bill's choked apology at the pub. Ryan laid down his knife and fork. Losing the only adult who'd given a fuck twelve years ago ripped his soul apart. Bill had stood by him when his own parents couldn't stand the sight of him. He'd mentored Ryan for years. He'd been more a father than great uncle. For once it seemed Frankie Ellis was wrong. With a choked sob, Ryan pushed back his chair and dropped his head into his hands, his upper body shaking as grief consumed him.

A hand clamped his shoulder and held firm. "Let it all out, mate. There's nobody here but us." Nick's words gave him small comfort. "You need to grieve, or you'll explode. I don't know how you've held it together so long."

Ryan grabbed a serviette and wiped his nose. "Who the fuck blew up Bill's boatshed? Did they know he was inside?"

"I don't know, mate, but we'll find them. None of us will rest until we find Bill's killer."

"Thanks." Ryan cleared his throat and sat up straighter. "If the explosion is tied up with a rumored treasure, then it's time I settled a few scores."

IT WAS after zero two hundred when Ryan kicked off his heavy boots on Safiya's tiny porch. He hadn't felt this dog-tired in a long time. The breeze coming up off the water was enough to shrivel his balls. On impulse, he checked the French door, expecting it to be locked. It opened, annoying the crap out of him.

Damn it, woman. There are dangerous people about. Locking it behind him, Ryan peered through the darkness. He could see Safiya curled up under the bedcovers and hear soft, steady breathing. Anyone could have snuck up on her. Shaking his head, he placed his wallet and watch beside the bed then peeled off his flying suit and paced to the bathroom. He needed to wash off the strain of the last seven hours, shave and clean his teeth.

His stomach growled, reminding him he'd barely eaten since lunch.

Finished in the bathroom, Ryan checked on Safiya. In the shaft of light coming through the open bathroom door, he could see she'd kicked off the covers. She wore a tank top and sleep shorts, her hair a loose mess around her shoulders. He frowned at her agitated movements and breathing. She looked to be in the middle of a nightmare.

He'd intended to sleep on the couch and see where they stood in the morning. Instead, he switched off the bathroom light then crawled onto the bed, surprised when she whispered.

"We need to stop the bat-shit, crazy motherfuckers before they kill anyone else."

Ryan almost choked, holding in his laughter. *Bat-shit, crazy mother-fucker.* He'd never heard Safiya say anything so coarse. She must have picked up that particular phrase from Jarred. It was one of his favorites. "We will, Saf."

Lying on his side, Ryan drew her against his chest, spooning around her butt then spread his hand over her belly. She instantly relaxed.

Ryan sighed with contentment. This is what had been missing in his life. She wasn't the woman he'd been searching for, but she seemed to be the woman he needed. Time would tell.

She wriggled closer, pressing against his cock. "Ryan?" she mumbled drowsily.

"Hi," he returned with a grin. "You okay?"

"Uh-huh." She snuggled closer, placing her hands over his. "Are you?"

"Yeah. Go back to sleep."

"This is nice." She exhaled then relaxed again.

He waited until her breathing settled into soft, steady breaths then nuzzled her neck, drawing in her flowery scent. "Sleep well, Safiya-Ameerah."

Safiya registered the heat surrounding her while still half asleep. It took another moment to recall her whereabouts and realize who lay wrapped around her. Bliss consumed her. It felt amazing to be held so protectively. So intimately.

She'd stayed up late with Madeline, catching up as they waited for the Blackhawk to return. Madeline's relationship with her husband never cease to amaze Safiya. It was obvious they cared about each other, yet they didn't call each other every day, or week for that matter. *Very odd.*

Since meeting Ryan and his team, Safiya had made a point of studying the men, especially when interacting with the women they obviously loved.

The thing that stood out with each couple was their intimate connections. The way they'd send affectionate glances to each other, or how they touched each other. In the men's case, a soft kiss to her forehead, his hand lightly resting against her lower back, or a caress on her cheek with the back of his hand.

Safiya smiled. Her favorite interaction was when the men stared intently into their women's eyes then almost always, tucked a whisp of hair or curl behind her ear.

In the case of the women, they'd reached up and place a feather light kiss on his cheek, or brush fingers as they passed, or place a hand on his chest.

Safiya sent up another wish that she'd find that with Ryan. Her thoughts jumped to Madeline's interactions with Jarred, which were just as confusing. She often caught them watching each other warily. What was that about? Safiya frowned harder.

"You done thinking, Saf." Ryan's drawl against her neck sent delicious shivers skimming over her skin. "From the expressions crossing your face, you've come up with every scenario possible for my being in your bed, and what you should do about it."

Shout hallelujah. "I didn't realize you were awake, and I was thinking about your friends' relationships." She rolled so they were face to face. "How could you see my expressions?"

"Mirror on the wardrobe door. You were frowning, smiling, chewing your lip, and smiling again. Must have been an interesting thought process?"

"It was. What time did you get here?"

"Two-ish. I'm not happy you left the door unlocked, Saf. Anyone could have sneaked in."

"I knew Sam and Ajax were patrolling, and you *did* say you'd be staying here."

"Thanks." He palmed the back of her head, bringing her close enough to kiss, and he did, at his leisure, long lazy, tender kisses.

He ran his thumb over her bottom lip, never taking his eyes off hers. Sensation exploded under his sensual touch. She wanted nothing more than to throw herself in his arms, give him anything he asked for. Feeling bolder, she scooted closer. She reached up and ran her fingers down his cheek and across his smooth chin. "You shaved."

"Hmm, didn't want to graze your delicate skin."

She licked her lips, anticipating which delicate skin he referred to. Nothing existed except the two of them. They could've been lying in the eye of a tornado for all she cared.

His gaze dropped to her tank top. "This should go."

Her nipples immediately puckered. She grabbed the edge and hauled it off. "Better?"

"Much." His wicked grin elicited more moisture between her legs. She pressed her hand to his rock-hard chest, her pulse erratic as she traced his defined muscles and tattoo. It was so sexy. She could understand why the other women loved touching their men's chests.

His warm breath on her neck sent delightful shivers shooting in every direction. He shoved his fingers in her hair, tilting her head until she had no choice but to meet his eyes again.

"You sure you want this," he asked, staring at her so hard she shivered. Here was the special forces soldier, who did what needed doing, no quarter given. Yet, he still had enough chivalry in him to do right by her.

She swallowed, her heart hammering. "I want you more than my next breath, Ryan."

She'd barely got his name out when he moved. He ravished her mouth without restraint, devouring her like she belonged to him and no one else. She could feel his heart thudding against her chest, his erection hard against her belly. It was no simple kiss. He was a conqueror, claiming his woman. Excitement raced through her, making her even wetter and bolder.

Sliding her hand down his chest, she circled his flat stomach, before sliding over his hip and squeezing his butt. He was hard everywhere. Their tongues danced and dueled as if recognizing their one true lover. Giving in to instinct, she slid her hand between them, closing her fingers around the thick, hard length, which jerked.

He groaned then rolled onto his back, taking her with him. "Let's get rid of your shorts. I need you naked and straddling me, now."

She almost swooned with his dirty talk. This was a side of Ryan she'd never seen. Quickly she did as he'd asked, kicking off her sleep shorts and straddling him, standing up on her knees, unconcerned with her own nudity as she took in his magnificent body. He was a work of art. "You're beautiful."

He scoffed. "I'll accept good-looking and fit, but you're the beauty, Saf." He reached up with both hands and palmed her breasts. "Every glorious inch of you."

She pressed into his hands. Neither of the two men she'd been intimate with touched her with such reverence. Neither had paid her such sexy compliments. Neither had given her pleasure like Ryan.

"Shuffle closer. Sit on my stomach."

Her eyes flew open. "Your stomach?"

"Yeah." He gripped her hips, moving her forward to exactly where he wanted her, almost on his ribs. "Sit."

She did and gasped as her sensitive folds touched his hot skin. She squirmed, unable to help pressing against him harder.

He groaned. "You're so wet, Saf. I can feel your arousal soaking my skin." He pushed his fingers between them, rubbing against her swollen skin. "So wet, for me."

Words were beyond her. She could only pant, gasp, groan and gyrate against his questing fingers.

"Beautiful." Ryan reached for her breasts, his fingers spread so he could torment both nipples at once, while his other hand worked magic between her legs. He pushed two fingers inside her, thrusting against her clitoris.

"Harder." She begged, thrusting against his fingers. "Do it harder. I'm so close."

"Come for me, Safiya. Come with my fingers inside you."

"I …." Her legs shook hard. She threw her head back as orgasmic bliss slammed through her body, until Ryan's touch became almost painful. She grabbed his wrist, pushing it away. "No more." As weak as a newborn kitten, she collapsed on his chest, burying her face against his neck. "I'll never be the same again."

He chuckled, stroking her back in lazy circles. "I love the way you come with such uninhibited abandon, Saf. It's the sexiest thing I've ever seen."

"Really?"

"Yep." He rolled, spreading her legs wide with his knees. "Still okay?"

"Yes." She ran her hand over his shoulder. "I want it all, Ryan."

"Words to make me hard. Give me a sec." He reached across to the bedside table then sat back on his heels and rolled on a condom. "Where were we?"

"You were about to make love to me." Safiya reached out to touch him, but Ryan caught her hand. "Later."

He balanced on one hand beside her hip then fitted the head of his erection against her wet center with the other. "Tell me what you like, Saf?"

"I like everything you do to me."

He chuckled. "What's your favorite position?"

"Oh. I've only done it this way, but I'm open to suggestions."

He nudged in a little. "I take it your past lovers were fools, or in too much of a hurry. They obviously didn't take time to give *you* pleasure." He nudged in further then palmed her breast, taking her breath away.

"As I only did it once with each jerk, they didn't get the chance."

"Once?" He frowned. "We're going to talk about that, after I've had my way with you."

She lifted her hips, pushing against him, sighing as he sank in further. "I'm only interested in talking about making love with you."

He pushed in all the way and sighed. "Wrap your legs around me and hold on."

She did, clutching his shoulders so he couldn't get away. She whimpered when he pulled almost all the way out. Her whimper died a quick death when he plunged back in, then did it again. She was so wet they made a slapping noise every time his balls hit her butt. Sometimes he slowed, rolling his hips, and grinding against her, then he'd speed up, thrusting hard and fast. His hand left her hip, sweeping up her body to palm her breast.

She could feel her body tightening. "I'm going to come again."

"I want to you watch you come around my cock."

"Oh, yes." Her climax hit hard, wrenching a scream from her throat.

"That's it. Yes, Saf. Squeeze me tight. I'm gonna explode." He ground into her. Groaned, then collapsed on top of her, nuzzling her neck. "Beautiful." He rolled onto his side, wrapping his arms around her, holding her against his chest as he caressed her bottom.

Unable to gather enough energy to move, and happy to stay exactly as they were, Safiya murmured, "Can we stay like this forever?"

"I'd like to sweetheart, but I have a feeling the others will come knocking soon."

"Damn."

He chuckled. "What was with the bat-shit, crazy motherfucker lingo?"

"What?"

"You were talking in your sleep."

She groaned. "I heard Jarred say it to Adam. It's very fitting."

"Thank you, Safiya. That means a lot to me."

"You're welcome."

He put a finger under her chin and raised it until she met his eyes. "Why did you only have sex once with those guys?"

Her face warmed and she squirmed. "Do we have to do this?"

"Yeah, we do. I can't understand any guy thinking once was enough with you."

"Oh!" She licked her lips and took a deep breath. "I met Ian Hudson in my first year at Sydney Uni. He seemed to be everywhere I went. Sometimes he'd smile at me. Other times he'd stop for a chat. After five or six months we started meeting for coffee at my favorite café, or he'd come to parties with me. It was nice. I felt safe. After a few months, he started kissing me. Not as passionately as you, but it was nice. I trusted him."

She swallowed. "One night, he got a little more amorous, touching my breasts and saying he wanted me. I thought why not? It wasn't a great experience. I wasn't... ready. He left straight after."

"Bastard." Ryan kissed her forehead. "Don't tell me he was a fucking scalp collector?"

"Not exactly. He always wanted to know my movements. That night was no different. He asked what I was doing the next morning. I told him I had to stay in and study for an exam, but I changed my mind and decided to study in my favorite café. I was in a back booth when he came in with a blonde girl. They were all over each other.

"The waitress had seen me there with Ian enough to realize I might make a scene. That was the last thing on my mind. I wanted to shrivel up and die. When I pushed, she told me he was getting it on with heaps of Uni students. That he'd boasted to her about being a rich girl's bodyguard and earning a small fortune to make sure she didn't come to harm. That's when the penny dropped.

"I rang my father and asked if Ian Hudson was being paid to keep an eye on me. My father said yes, it was for my safety. I was so angry; I asked my father if Ian's salary included taking my virginity, then I hung up and marched over to Ian's table. He almost choked on a doughnut. I told him if he was wise, he'd get out of town fast. Not that my father would kill him, but I was as mad as..." She smiled. "A bat-shit, crazy motherfucker."

"Good girl." Ryan kissed her forehead again. "Go on."

"I wouldn't take my parents' calls for weeks, and that blonde girl told everyone I broke up her relationship with Ian. I couldn't go to my favorite café or parties without hearing degrading comments. I enrolled in a university in London, where I'd been accepted to continue my linguistics degree. I'd told my parents I was doing an arts degree because I'd wanted to surprise them. I never got round to telling them the truth."

"Struth, Safiya. I'm so sorry." Ryan held her tighter.

"Yes, well. My second disastrous romance was toward the end of the following year. I'd recently made friends with a girl called Stacy, and we decided to share an apartment on campus. She had a serious boyfriend, so wasn't there much, but we got on. I'd learned not to tell people who my parents were. Jason Clarke was my roomy's boyfriend's brother. We started hanging out as friends whenever he came to London. He was always short of money, so I'd pay my way and sometimes lend him money to get home. He found a picture of my parents I'd hidden in my bookcase. My father was wearing a *thawb*, it's what Arabic men traditionally wear."

"I know what it is. Go on." Ryan rubbed her back soothingly.

"I decided to take a chance and told Jason they were my parents, but he couldn't tell anyone as their marriage had to stay a secret. He asked a lot of questions then googled my father. Of course, his search revealed my father wasn't married. I showed Jason a photo of me with my parents.

"The following weekend he showed up with flowers and took me out to dinner. We came home and did the deed. It wasn't what I'd hoped it would be. He said he'd see me the following weekend and left. He rang the next night asking for a lot of money. I refused and he got nasty, threatened to tell my parents we'd had sex. When that didn't work, he threatened to tell my roomy I'd been trying to get it on with her boyfriend."

"Jesus." Ryan's other hand clamped on her hip. "I'd like ten minutes with the slug."

She shrugged. "I stood my ground. Jason went through with his threat and Stacy turned on me. Our friends did too. Jason said if I gave him the money, he'd come clean, otherwise he was going to the tabloids. I rang my father, who said he'd pay Jason off, which in turn made me so furious I quit Uni. I hate liars. I hate people betraying my trust. I hate that no one's ever taken the time to get to know me. My parents and brother figured where's there's smoke, there's fire, and that I'm promiscuous. I didn't speak to them for over a year."

"I don't blame you." Ryan stroked her face. "I'm amazed you trust anyone. How did you finish your degree and survive, financially?"

"My maternal grandparents died and left me their house. I sold it and enrolled in Open University, worked part time jobs, and kept to myself. I always sensed or caught the private detectives or bodyguards my father sent to spy on me, so I got really good at evading them, which meant moving, changing jobs, disappearing until another one tracked me down. We patched things up about a year ago."

"Fuck." Ryan shook his head. "I'm so sorry for everything you've been through, and for what I've said to you."

"It's okay. We're starting over, remember." She kissed his chin. "I trust you, Ryan."

"Thank you." He frowned. "There is something I need to tell you, and it's really bad timing, but it's only fair you know."

No, no, no, no, no. She pushed back. "Please don't say you're seeing someone else?"

"I'm not, I swear. I just want you to know—"

Safiya jumped as someone hammered on the French doors. "Yo, Ryan, you awake?"

"Hell, that's Nick. I need to see what's up. We'll continue this conversation later." He jumped off the bed. "Yeah, mate, give me sec."

"Yikes." Safiya leaped off the bed, ran to the chest of drawers and grabbed a bikini, shorts, and top. She didn't want to miss out on any news, but the only man she wanted to see her naked was Ryan. "Give me five minutes."

CHAPTER SIXTEEN

Once the bathroom door closed behind Safiya, Ryan grimaced. He needed to explain he wasn't being paid to spy on her. That he hadn't known her father had hired Steele Security to keep her safe. "Shit." She'd been let down by so many people in her life. This could push her over the edge. He had no doubt she could disappear. People did it all the time. He couldn't let that happen. Now that he'd found the woman of his dreams, he'd never let her go.

Pulling on a T-shirt and a pair of boardshorts Nick had lent him, Ryan slipped his wallet into his back pocket, strapped on his watch then donned a straw hat. If he wanted to blend in, he needed to look like he was on holiday. After hearing Safiya's wrenching story, he'd love to beat those jerks to a pulp, which would only bring him trouble. He'd get Simon to track them down. Jarred would make sure Ian Hudson never worked in personal protection or security again. As for the Jason Clarke, blackmail was a serious offence, which he would soon regret.

He unlocked the door, opening it to find Nick observing the ocean. "Morning."

Nick looked over his shoulder. "How you doin', mate?"

"Better. Thanks for being there for me last night."

"No worries. You've done it for me often enough." Nick gave a nod toward the expanse of grass before he stepped off the porch, taking several strides before stopping to wait for Ryan.

"What's up," asked Ryan.

"Jarred wants a round table, now." Nick's troubled eyes flicked back to the cabin. "You're not getting in over your head are you, mate? Safiya is gonna hurt you."

"I'm going to have to disagree there. There are things I need to tell you and the other boys about Safiya's life. It's fucking heartbreaking. I intend to make a personal call to her parents. It's time they knew the truth about their amazing daughter."

Nick's lips thinned. "You've fallen for her, haven't you, mate?"

"Yeah, I guess I have. Give me sec." He paced back inside then tapped on the bathroom door. "Safiya, I've got to go meet with the team. I'll be back as soon as I can."

"Okay. I'll catch you later."

"Later." He stared at the door for ten seconds then bit the bullet. "Thanks for trusting me, sweetheart. I won't let you down, and... I just wanted to say, you're beautiful, inside, and out."

The door swung open and Safiya hugged him tight, before leaning back to stare him in the eyes. "I think I love you." She didn't give him the chance to reply, before kissing him. Not that he could think of anything to say.

"Yo! Ryan. Quit kissing the lady and let's go. Jarred's not a happy boy this morning."

"Yeah, yeah." Ryan stole another kiss then stepped back. Safiya's hair hung in a braid over one shoulder. She wore cute green shorts and a red bikini bra, which showcased her plump breasts and couldn't disguise her stiff nipples. He groaned. "Later, beautiful."

"Later, handsome." She sashayed back into the bathroom and shut the door.

He stared at the door, wondering how he'd gotten so lucky.

"Mate?" called Nick. "Get your head in gear." He rolled his eyes. "Your other head."

Ryan looked down at his bulging shorts. "Smart ass." He pulled on his loafers then left the cabin, closing the door. He'd need to get another key from Zoe.

They ran the short distance to the largest cabin, where the French doors stood wide open. Simon and Darius sat on one side of the dining table concentrating on two laptop screens. Jarred sat at one end, talking on his phone.

Madeline had a fully cooked breakfast laid out on the kitchen bench. She clapped her hands. "It's ready, everyone. Help yourselves."

"Thanks Madeline." Ryan rubbed his stomach. "I didn't eat much yesterday."

"I heard." She patted his shoulder. "Your sister is taking me and Safiya out for breakfast. Sergeant Hawthorne said it would be fine."

"Breakfast?" Jarred cocked one eyebrow. "Who are you snooping on?"

"No one in particular, Chief Steel Feather." Madeline grinned at Ryan. "If we happen to come across something of interest, all the better." She blew Ryan a kiss then strolled out of the cabin.

Jarred glared at Ryan. "What the fuck was that?"

"Don't ask me, Colonel." Ryan raised his hands in surrender. "She scares me sometimes."

Jarred grunted. "Bloody woman scares me all the time. Plate up your breakfast then grab a seat. We've got a lot to discuss."

"Smells great," called Talos coming out of the bathroom.

"I'm starved." Sam yawned as he and Ajax entered through the back door. "Garcia is manning the front gates. He's not happy about Zoe going off with Madeline and Safiya." Sam grinned at Ryan. "I think our American friend has the hots for your sister."

"I think the feeling is mutual," muttered Ryan, still not sure how he felt about a romance between Zoe and the ex-Seal. He quickly filled his plate then took a seat, listening intently as Jarred shared his offer of assistance to the unreceptive detectives yesterday.

"I've spoken to Gibbs this morning. He will keep us informed of developments and findings. One point worth mentioning. After we discovered the break-in yesterday, Garcia headed over to Zoe's Beach Shack. A canoe and kayak were missing. The canoe turned out to be the one Safiya found on the beach yesterday. Darius' drone spotted the kayak this morning. It's tied up in Dugong Marina."

Jarred briefly covered last night's flight then they got down to planning surveillance of the treasure hunters, and the best way to get head shots for Simon's Identiscan program.

They were on their second coffee when Jarred checked his watch. "What time does the ferry arrive tomorrow?"

"Eleven hundred hours." Ryan glanced at each of his friends. "I'm not sure how my father will react to us staying in the cabins. I'm apologizing early in case things get ugly."

"You've got nothing to be ashamed of, Major." Jarred's gray eyes had gone cold and hard. "We are your family, not the people who donated to your gene pool."

A grin spread over Ryan's face. "Colonel, that's the nicest thing you've ever said to me."

"Make the most of it, I'm not given to sentiment very often."

"Yes, Colonel." Ryan met Jarred's gaze. "If we're done discussing the treasure hunters, there's something else I'd like to make you all aware off."

"Oh." Jarred's eyes narrowed. "I assume it's about Gibbs' sister?"

"Yeah." Ryan laid down everything Safiya had told him and his own observations, without mentioning anything intimate. By the time he finished there was a stunned silence.

"Poor Safiya." Darius wiped a tear away. "What can I do to help?"

Ryan smiled at Simon's fiancée. "Be Safiya's friend. Help me track down the two guys who betrayed and hurt her. It's time they got a truck load of karma."

Jarred opened his mouth then closed it and nodded. "See to it, Simon." He stood. "Anything else?"

Everyone shook their heads.

"Good, let's get those mother —" Jarred's gaze shot to Darius. "The people responsible for blowing up Bill's boatshed, and whoever is behind the robberies and assault. I'll be with Sergeant Hawthorne if anything comes up. What's your plans, Ryan?"

"There's someone I need to speak to, if she'll allow it, then I'll come back and help."

"Call if you need backup," warned Sam. "You don't need to do this alone."

"Thanks. I will." Ryan gave them a salute then left the cabin. He retraced his earlier path along the narrow, gravel road to the back gate. Zoe had given him the keypad combination, so he didn't have to go the long way or jump the fence. The trail down to the beach wasn't as steep as he remembered, although much more overgrown.

Reaching the beach, he took a moment to enjoy the morning sun on his face, the solitude, breaking waves, and bird calls before moving on. Several seagulls ran away from a fish carcass, squawking at the interruption. At the other end of Sunset Beach, he caught the lingering odor of burnt timber, his heart aching at what remained of Bill's treasured boatshed. When the legalities were settled, he'd have the wreckage cleared and maybe build a new boatshed for Zoe.

He looked through the park to Dugong Marina, and out to Angler's Point, where a café now stood. Bill's large block made an ideal site for Ryan's long-ago dream. *The Flying Dutchman. Charter Boat, Seaplane and Helicopter Tours.* Bill would have loved that.

BREAKFAST WITH ZOE and Madeline had been wonderful. To have what felt like real friends chatting about everyday things made Safiya deliriously happy. Zoe insisted on paying the bill, shooing Safiya and Madeline away. As she stepped out of the Angler's Point Café, Safiya read the sign on the building next to the Marina's clubhouse.

"National Parks and Wildlife Service." She sneaked a peak in the window. Tommy Curran stood at the front counter, which surprised her as it was Sunday. "Do I dare?"

"Dare what?" asked Madeline.

Safiya frowned. "Has anyone told you why Ryan left this island?"

"Not officially, although I heard Jarred and Sergeant Hawthorne discussing it. Sergeant Hawthorne said Ryan was cleared, but it was a messy investigation. Any evidence the old sergeant might have found was lost due to laziness."

Safiya shot a quick glance at Zoe, who was still chatting to Joanne, the Scottish lady who owned the café. "Do *you* think Ryan lied?"

"Of course not. I've known him almost five months. Not long in the scheme of things, but I've observed him during some intense missions. Ryan is conscientious, dependable, and brave. His team-mates trust him with their lives. If he said he wasn't on that cliff face with his friend, then he wasn't."

"That's how I feel too, especially after meeting Tommy Curran at the pub Friday night. He was Ryan's other friend back then. He's feeling guilty about something. That's Tommy sitting at the desk." She jabbed her thumb at the window behind her.

"Right." Madeline glanced at the café. "I'll keep Zoe busy while you talk to him."

"I will. Thanks, Madeline."

"If you need me, scratch your head, and here, take this." Madeline reached into her own hair and withdrew a long, wooden hairpin that looked like a chopstick. "I never leave home without a weapon. Stick that in your hair. Stab him in the throat if you have to."

"Oh...kay, thanks. I won't be long." Safiya plastered a smile on her face then pushed the door open. "Hello, Tommy. Just the man I need to speak to."

He stood up. "Hello...?"

"Fia. Ryan's girlfriend."

"Yes, I know who you are. What can I do for you, Fia?"

"I would like to ask you, if you know or suspect who was on Morcago cliff face with Zane the day he died?"

"What?" Tommy's face paled.

Safiya gave a light shrug. "It wasn't Ryan?"

"I ... I don't like what you're insinuating."

"I'm not insinuating anything, Tommy. If you know anything that could help Ryan clear his name, I would appreciate you telling me." She smiled. "Ryan would appreciate it."

He rubbed his forehead. "It was a long time ago. We were

teenagers. Everyone knew Ryan and Zane were obsessed with finding treasure. It could have been anyone."

"Besides you and Camilla, who else knew about the cave? Tell me about that day? What was going on between you and Camilla?"

"Christ." He leaned on his elbow, gripped his chin in his hand and sighed. "I never meant to hurt Ryan, but he took Camilla's infatuation for granted. Zane and Ryan were always off on another adventure or quest, the more hair-raising the better. I was terrified of heights, sharks, caves, getting caught in off-limit areas. Neither of them feared anything."

"Did they ever put themselves, or you in danger?"

"No, but because of my fears, they'd often disappeared on their own then they'd tell me about their latest discovery when they got back. I hated being left behind but hanging out with Camilla made up for it. I had a crush on her before Ryan registered her hero worship and asked her to go steady."

Safiya wanted to hurry him along but feared he might clam up. "I can understand your hurt and disappointment. What changed things?"

"While Ryan and Zane searched for treasure, me and Camilla hung out more and more. She was frustrated with what she called their bromance. The week before Zane's death, we'd taken our flirting further. Zane caught us kissing and threatened to tell Ryan. Camilla begged him not to, because she didn't want to destroy our friendship." Tommy shook his head. "I was a lovesick fool and would have done anything for her. If she wanted to flirt with me to make Ryan jealous, I wasn't going to stop her, because I hoped she might fall for me, and she did, eventually."

"I can see you genuinely care for her." His devotion to Camilla was obvious in the way his face softened as he spoke.

He nodded. "I do."

"What happened the day you went to Morcago Ledge?"

"Ryan upset Camilla by saying he had no intention of getting married straight out of school and he'd never leave the island. He and Zane planned to use the treasure to set up a tourism business.

Camilla wanted to get married, live on the Gold Coast. Run her own café. Ryan and Zane descended the cliff face, found a hidden cave then climbed up again. I knew they'd found something important by their excitement. Ryan joked that they'd found bats. Camilla had the shits with Ryan, so I walked her home then we..." Tommy blushed.

"You made love?"

"Yeah. I promised I'd take care of her. Later, I went to see Zane and asked what else they'd found. He said they'd found some cave drawings. I told him if there was treasure, I wanted a share, because me and Cammy might have to get married. Zane lost it and we got into a punch up. He lived with his grandmother, Frankie Ellis. I didn't realize she had family gathered in the back yard. Zane and Camilla are cousins, so most of their relatives were there."

"Go on, what happened?"

"We were throwing punches and yelling at each other. Lots of stuff came out. Camilla's mother and Frankie broke up the fight."

"That's how people knew you and Camilla had been intimate?"

"Yeah. I wanted to tell Ryan myself. Explain how I'd always loved Cammy, but my parents read me the riot act then grounded me for eternity. The next morning, I was consoling Cammy over the phone when my father told me about Zane. I tried to talk to Ryan, but his father wouldn't allow me through the gate. A few days later, Barnacle Bill took Ryan to Townsville while the police did an investigation. Cammy and I were interviewed and our statements presented at the inquest, but I never got to speak to Ryan."

"You didn't try to get in contact with him?"

"I asked his grandmother if I could ring him. She said she didn't have a number or know where to reach him. She said he didn't want anything to do with any of us. Zoe said she didn't know anything either, but I guess she did."

Safiya chewed her lower lip. "You didn't ask Barnacle Bill?"

"Hell no, he scared the shit out of us all back then."

"So, you're saying, it wasn't you on the cliff with Zane?"

"It wasn't me, but if I hadn't confessed to sleeping with Cammy,

Zane wouldn't have lost it. No one would have known about the cave or the drawings or any damn treasure."

"Who do you think was on that cliff face? Who did Zane try to save before falling to his own death?"

A deep flush crept up his face. "After the accusations hurled at Ryan, I'd never hazard a guess, but I have noticed a renewed interest in the treasure. Those Spanish brothers have been asking questions about the treasure and hanging out at the Angler's Point Café. The other group of treasure hunters are reckless idiots. Tell Ryan to watch his back."

"I will. Any other newcomers?"

"Paul and Joanne Kilgour arrived about three years ago. They keep to themselves most of the time." He shrugged. "You're not local unless you're born on Curra or lived here twenty years."

"Thanks for speaking to me, Tommy." She walked out of his office, lost in thought.

"How'd you go?" asked Madeline.

Safiya grimaced. "Tommy feels guilty about his relationship with Ryan's girlfriend back then, which got him into a fight with Zane. He claims things were said about a cave, drawings, and the rumored treasure. There were many people around who could have heard." Safiya looked round. "Where's Zoe?"

"She wanted to talk to that young guy on the wharf." Madeline pointed. "He worked for Barnacle Bill and Zoe wanted to check he's okay."

"That's Josh Butler. Let's join them." Safiya tried not to show her eagerness as they approached but Josh might well be a fountain of information. "Hi, Josh. Sorry to interrupt, but were you near Sunset Beach yesterday?"

"No, I was making deliveries for my dad. Why?"

"There was a break-in at the Dutch House. Someone used a kayak to sneak in via Duchies Beach. They left the same way. I was hoping you might have seen them."

"They used one of my kayaks." Zoe hissed. "At least they left it tied up in the Marina."

Josh's eyes widened. "Hey, I did see a guy in a kayak. I'd just delivered cartons of chips to the ferry. He paddled between the *Sea Sprite* and Barnacle Bill's trawler, then ran along the wharf and up the steps toward the Marina's Clubhouse. I raced over and tied up the kayak so it wouldn't float away."

Safiya stepped closer. "Did you recognize the man?"

"I didn't see his face. He was wearing a cap and sunglasses, but there was something familiar about him."

"Young, old, tanned skin, pale, clothing?" pressed Safiya. "Anything you remember might help us identify him."

"Not young, not old. He wore dark pants and a long-sleeved, checkered shirt. I think it's the shirt I recognized, but I can't remember who I've seen wearing it."

Safiya patted his shoulder. "You've been a great help, Josh. If you remember, or see him, will you please call me straight away?"

"Sure."

Safiya dug around in her purse for a piece of paper and came up with an old receipt. "Anyone got a pen?"

"Here." Madeline passed Safiya one of her business cards and a pen. "Write your number on the back." She looked at Josh. "Hi, I'm Madeline. Don't approach the man. He could be dangerous."

"Okay. If I see him, I'll get in touch." He nodded at Zoe. "Thanks for offering me a job. I didn't want to have to move to the mainland."

"Come and see me at the Surf Shack next week and we'll fill out the paperwork."

"Sure, Zoe." He gave an awkward wave then headed off along the boardwalk.

Safiya rubbed her hands together. "Ready to do a little snooping, ladies?"

"Sure." Zoe glanced round. "Who are we snooping on?"

"Yes, but we're going to need a distraction."

Tell us more," murmured Madeline. "What do you have in mind?"

"I want to look inside the *Sea Sprite*. Maybe the lady in the white dress left something on board. I'd also like to check the yacht beside it. *Capricorn* belongs to two Spanish brothers. They would love to prove the Spanish discovered Australia first. For that reason, they may be responsible for the break ins."

"Let's get the paddle boards," suggested Zoe. "I can pretend to teach you the basics here in Dugong Marina. The ferry doesn't operate on weekends, so we won't get in its way."

Madeline narrowed her eyes. "I'm sure we can distract the Spanish brothers, especially as it might lead us to the person or people behind the explosion and break ins."

"Why is the ferry here?" asked Safiya.

"It's kept here over the weekend. In case we need an emergency evacuation, due to a bushfire or cyclone warning. It leaves early Monday mornings to take workers and students to the mainland. Comes back at eleven then leaves again at one. Fridays it arrives at eleven, heads back at one then comes back with the students and workers at six-thirty and stays."

Safiya looked around. "So, we basically have the marina to ourselves."

"Not quite." Zoe pointed down into the water, where a dolphin and a seal were bobbing up and down, as if listening.

"Hello, Ping. Hello, Pong," called Safiya. "Would you like to join us paddle boarding?"

As if understanding her perfectly, the seal barked and the dolphin propelled itself back in the water, making a clicking noise.

Safiya considered the seal and dolphin. "If only they could tell us who used the kayak, or who the woman in the white dress is."

CHAPTER SEVENTEEN

Wishful thinking wouldn't get Ryan anywhere. He had no idea how long he'd stared at the boatshed debris, lost in nostalgia as he recalled so many conversations with Bill. They'd been good for each other. Bill had no children, had never married, but he'd taken on the responsibility of supporting Ryan, and along the way, they'd grown close. He'd changed Ryan's life for the better. To think they'd never go fishing together again gutted Ryan.

With a final nod, Ryan strode on to Dugong Marina, taking his time to examine the Spanish brothers' yacht. They hadn't gone out today.

Crossing back through the park, Ryan stopped to watch the island's only bus pass by. A much older version of Steve Thomas raised a hand, then returned his attention to the road. Striding along the grassed footpath away from town, Ryan took in the changes on the opposite side of the road. Curra now had a two basketball courts, more tennis courts, a new football stand for spectators and a swimming pool.

He stopped at the green cottage he'd visited many times as a kid. This had been Zane's home, where he'd lived with his grandmother, an elder of the Bindal People. Ryan had taken it as a personal privilege when she'd allowed him to call her Aunty Frankie.

The woman he sought sat on her front verandah, knitting. "Hello, Aunty Frankie. Can I speak to you?"

Frankie Ellis dropped her knitting in a basket beside her then slowly stood. He thought she intended to snub him and go inside the house, but she stepped forward, reaching out to hold onto a rail. "Hello, Ryan. It's about time you came to see me."

Moisture blurred Ryan's vision. He cleared his throat and walk up the short, brick path. "I wasn't sure you'd want to talk to me."

She nodded. Close up, he could see her face and neck carried more wrinkles than the last time he'd seen her. Her hands shook. She'd been a close friend of Bill's. Closer than most people probably knew.

"Dear boy, I've been waiting a long time for you to return. Come, give me a hug."

Ryan did, wrapping is arms around the elderly lady and holding her gently.

She sniffed. "I remember holding you like this as a youngster. You've grown."

He laughed. "Yeah, I guess I have."

"Into a fine man." She eased back and waved toward the gate. "You can take me for coffee. It's been a long time since I had a handsome young man to take me about. You can tell me about that lovely girlfriend of yours." She led the way to the gate.

"You want to lock up first, Aunty Frankie?"

"Nothing worth stealing." She linked her arm around his then tapped her forehead. "Everything of value is up here. Memories to treasure."

They crossed the road, then as they walked along Dugong Marina, Aunty Frankie, pointed out changes Ryan hadn't noticed. "The club house has been extended and modernized. That's a new Parks and Wildlife office alongside it."

Ryan frowned at her upbeat attitude. Maybe she was in denial. "Aunty Frankie, I know you were close to Bill—"

"Still am, dear boy. The body they found is not Bill. If it were, I would feel it here." She touched her chest. "No, something has happened to him, but he's not dead."

"You really believe that?"

"I do."

Frankie had always been gifted. Everything she'd ever predicted came true, even his own departure from the island. "I pray you're right, Aunty Frankie, but who else could it be?"

"Someone up to no good."

Ryan looked through the Parks and Wildlife window and noticed Tommy behind the tall counter. Giving him a nod, Ryan and Frankie continued to the Angler's Point Café in silence.

Every table out the front and inside the café had been taken, the Sunday morning patrons eating, drinking, and chatting. He recognized four of the treasure hunters from the pub at a table out front, their faces sporting bruises of varying colors and severity. One had a tape over his nose. Two had swollen black eyes. They gave Ryan death stares.

All conversation died as Frankie proudly led the way through the café to the open back deck and a table overlooking the ocean. There were no other patrons on the back deck. Ryan sent off a text to Jarred, letting him know four of the treasure hunters were in the café. Simon and Darius most likely already knew, but just in case.

"It's much nicer out here, Ryan. I didn't want anyone listening in to our conversation."

He glanced back inside, recognizing three faces. He received a couple of hard stares and one friendly nod. "Aren't you concerned you might cop flack associating with me, Aunty Frankie?"

"No one would dare. You probably remember this place being Tommy's father's bait shop. A Scottish couple moved here about three years ago. Paul and Joanne Kilgour. They bought Doug Curran out then gutted the place. They do pizza and pasta Monday to Friday nights. Food tastes good, but there is something about those two that bothers me. They ask too many questions and throw a lot of money round. Bill doesn't trust them either."

"Is that so?" He'd get Simon to check them out.

Joanne Kilgour came out to take their order. "Good morning, Mrs. Ellis." She barely spared Frankie a glance, before locking her gaze on Ryan. "Sorry to hear about Bill's boatshed. Any idea what happened?"

"Not yet. There will be a full investigation."

"We saw the big helicopter fly in and then out again last night and we heard it fly back in early this morning. What's that all about?"

"It brought in police specialists yesterday and took them back to the mainland last night. That's all I can tell you."

"Any news on the body?"

"No." He looked across the table. "What would you like to drink, Aunty Frankie."

"Good morning, Joanne." Frankie squinted at the menu. "I'll have a cappuccino and cinnamon toast. What would you like, my boy?"

"I'll have a flat white, thanks, Joanne."

She hesitated a moment then took the menus and hurried off. If he had to guess, it was to impart this latest bit of gossip to any customers interested.

Ryan tapped his fingers lightly on the table. "I'm sorry I didn't get to talk to you before Bill took me away, Aunty Frankie."

"Probably for the best. Losing my grandson nearly killed me. I didn't talk to anyone for weeks. I needed time to come to terms with it."

"Aunty Frankie, how come you didn't predict Zane's death?"

She sighed. "I did occasionally feel a great loss when I looked at him, but figured it was to do with his parents car crash." She rubbed Ryan's hand. "Bill spoke to me before he left the pub Friday night, before that explosion. Had something he wanted to get off his chest."

Ryan leaned forward. "What did he say?"

"That you weren't with Zane that day. He'd suspected as much but couldn't prove it, which is why he never told the police. He said he'd had an idea who the real culprit is and planned to speak to them. To make things right. Heartbroken, he was. What do you think was used to blow up the boatshed?"

"Dynamite."

"That makes sense. It was a powerful explosion. Bill intended to set things right Saturday morning and apologize to you. Those young men you warned off at the pub have been causing problems. Hanging around the boatshed, annoying Bill with questions about the treasure. I suspect the body found will be one of them. Bill's not dead, but someone wants us to think he is. He told me you'd inherit everything, made sure he'd legally tied things up so no one can contest his will. I don't know who else knows, but you get everything when he does eventually die."

"Not everything." Ryan smiled at her. "Bill sent me a copy of his will. You get a nice stipend."

"Silly old fool." She wiped her eyes. "What are you doing about finding him? He's got to be on the island somewhere."

The strength of her conviction lifted his spirits. "My boss and colleagues arrived on that helicopter. They are here to help me. If Bill is …. We will find Bill and those responsible for Steve Thomas' assault, the robberies, and the explosion. Bill wants his great-grandfather's diary back, and the saber they stole. I plan to clear my name too."

"And?"

He smiled. "One of my friends has a program that will identify anyone with a license, passport, or criminal record. I will get him to check out all those treasure hunters."

"Good." She squeezed his fingers. "As for clearing your name, I know the truth is important to you, but when it comes out, there are people who will be traumatized. Many won't be able to forgive themselves for doubting you. Treating you so badly. Abandoning you."

"I don't care. I want the truth acknowledged. I deserve to be exonerated."

"Yes, you do."

Ryan narrowed his eyes. "Did you believe I caused Zane to fall? That I ran off and left him?"

"When they told me Zane was dead, I collapsed. Your father sedated me, which turned me into a zombie. Even though I was wallowing in misery, I watched the ferry depart. You stood at the rail, bow-shouldered and sobbing. It's one of the saddest things I ever saw."

She huffed. "It took me weeks to join the land of the living again. When I did, the whole incident just didn't add up. You and Zane were always off adventuring, but neither of you were reckless. I questioned the man who said he'd seen you. He'd been drinking but swore he saw two people on the cliff. It wasn't good enough for the prosecutor, especially after he spoke to us elders. We believed you were where you said you were, and that Zane had been on the cliff alone. I didn't know Bill had seen two people as well. If the elders had known, we would have questioned the young people and figured out the truth twelve years ago. After the court case, the elders went to your parents. We demanded your return, but were told, you didn't wish to return."

"It's the truth."

"Your parents and grandfather shut themselves off after that. I asked your grandmother where you were. She didn't know. It was so frustrating."

"You can say that again." Tommy stood in the doorway holding a takeaway coffee. "I asked your father if I could ring you. He said he had no contact details as you'd wiped everyone from Curra out of your life. He thought you were in Western Australia but couldn't be sure. He said you'd given Bill instructions you never wanted to see or speak to any of us ever again."

"I was hurting for a long time, Tommy."

"So were we." Tommy walked inside the café.

A balding guy with a short, brown beard stepped past Tommy. He wore a black apron with Angler's Point Café printed on the front. Ryan recognized him from the pub.

"One cappuccino and one flat white." Paul Kilgour placed the drinks on the table.

A teenage waitress placed Frankie's cinnamon toast on the table, smiling shyly at Ryan before scurrying back inside.

Paul Kilgour hovered.

"Oh my." Aunty Frankie licked the froth off her top lip. "Their prices are a little high, but they make an excellent cappuccino." She took another sip, eyeing Paul Kilgour until he returned inside the café. "Is there anything else you'd like to know before I go home for a morning nap?"

Ryan smirked. "Actually ... there is. When did you and Bill become so friendly? I remember him being a loner when he retired from the army. Hell, he rarely spoke to anyone. Us kids were terrified of him back then."

She chuckled. "We knew each other as children. We were seriously dating before he joined the army. He asked me to go with him, but I wouldn't leave Curra."

"He named his charter boat the *Francine* after *you*?"

"Yes." She exhaled. "Bill came back to the island a different man, kept to himself, didn't mix much. Had no time for your father and mother." She looked off into the distance. "Two months after you were taken away, I went to see him. I've never been so nervous. I dragged up my courage to confront him because I was worried about you *and* Zoe. You were so close. I insisted on knowing where you'd been sent. If you were safe. Who was looking after you? When were you coming home?"

Frankie stared off into the distance. "Bill looked at me so long and hard, I expected him to slam the door in my face. Instead, he gruffly told me I'd best come upstairs, which I did, fearing something terrible had happened to you. He made a pot of tea and told me you were living with his mate in Perth. You were devastated by Zane's death but going to school. You were struggling to come to grips with Tommy and Camilla's betrayal and your parent's distrust. I insisted he keep me informed and promised it would go no further. He told me Zoe had come to see him, begging to know how she could contact you. From that day we slowly became close again."

Frankie sniffed again. "As the years passed, he'd share your news and achievements. There wasn't a prouder man alive. He loved you like ... a son."

Ryan looked out to sea, blinking hard. "I loved him too. I'm going to find him, Aunty Frankie."

"I expect no less. Well, look at that?" She pointed to the café's roof, where a beautiful eagle loitered, as if magically suspended in the air.

"It's a drone, Aunty Frankie. Try not to draw attention to it."

"Oh, how exciting." She beamed. "My lips are sealed, but it won't do you much good when the storm hits."

Ryan looked up into the clear blue sky. "What storm."

"Late tonight. I can feel it in the air."

"Really?"

She chuckled. "I heard the weather forecast this morning. I doubt the ferry will be going to the mainland tomorrow morning."

"Mind if I join you?" Tommy held a chair in one hand, several feet away. "I didn't want to interrupt anything earlier."

"Of course, you're welcome to join us." Frankie waved him over. "I'm sure you two have a lot to catch up on, and I might learn something in the process."

Tommy looked embarrassed. "You know everything there is to know about me, Aunty Frankie." He placed the chair between them, sat and looked at Ryan. "I'd love to know what you've been up to all these years if you can tell me. I've heard plenty of rumors all weekend."

"I bet you have." Ryan's lips quirked. "What do you want to know, Tommy?"

"Everything. Where'd you go. When did you join the army? Is it true you flew helicopters in Special Forces?"

"I finished school in Perth then joined the army so I could fly Blackhawks. After a few years I transferred to the Special Air Service Regiment. We did more tours overseas then last year, instead of signing on for another four years, I opted out, to work for Steele Security."

Tommy frowned. "But aren't Special Force soldiers' hard core and trained in all types of fighting and weapons? You were a chopper pilot."

Ryan chuckled. "We had to train just as hard as the other guys and learn anti/counter surveillance, reconnaissance, close quarter fighting. The physical training is murder, but we worked so well as a team, they kept us together. I'm also a paramedic."

"That's awesome. Do you ever regret leaving? I mean if you'd stayed, you probably would be running that tourism business you and Zane were always on about."

"If I could turn back time, Tommy, I would. I regret not being there to save Zane. Thankfully, the army was the making of me. I had no choice but to change my life. Now I have five brothers who will always have my back."

"And you've got a determined girlfriend," muttered Tommy.

When Ryan frowned, Tommy's face heated. "Fia called by my office earlier. She told me you plan to clear your name and go after the person you believe was with Zane that day?"

"Did she?"

Tommy fidgeted with his empty takeaway cup. "What good will dragging up the past do?"

"I want the people I once respected and loved to know the truth. I was judged unfairly because my harness and helmet were found on top of Morcago Ledge. I was too young and distraught to defend myself or prove my innocence. I lost the trust and respect of so many. I lost my friends and my home."

"You're right." Tommy exhaled. "It's time the truth came out."

"Good heavens." Frankie leaned sideways, looking beyond Ryan. "What in the world?"

Twisting, Ryan glanced across Dugong Marina to where women in bikinis were struggling to stand on paddle boards. One had sandy-colored, frizzy curls, hanging round her shoulders and a slim build. The other could only be described as a blonde bombshell. He blinked hard. *Zoe and Madeline.*

Their high-pitched squeals drew Joanne, the treasure hunters and most of the café's other customers to the stone wall. Ryan's mouth dropped. Zoe was lurching back and forth along her board, arms cartwheeling for balance. He'd never seen such a pantomime. His sister had been paddle-boarding for years. The two Spanish brothers were leaning over the bow's handrail, laughing, and yelling encouragement.

His gaze switched to Madeline, swaying and staggering. The reason she didn't fall in was her excellent balance. What were they doing and where was Safiya? Up to her ears in mischief if he had to guess. He just hoped she realized a large audience were up here behind the wall, privy to the unfolding antics in the Marina. Or was that the point?

The patrons weren't the only ones watching. Jarred stood at the top of the ferry ramp, his arms crossed as he took in the scene playing out on the water. Ryan was too far away to see his expression, but he could imagine a severe scowl.

Frankie chuckled. "This should be interesting. While those two young Spanish men are fascinated by the girl's theatrics, your girlfriend is on their yacht below deck."

"Bloody hell, Safiya." Ryan went to stand, but Frankie tapped his arm.

"You'll draw more attention by racing down there. She asked to go aboard. I'm guessing to use their amenities. Sit back and enjoy the show. You're close enough if… *Safiya* needs you. She's much more a Safiya than Fia."

Damn, he'd misspoken. He could only hope no one else had been close enough to hear or recognize the unique name. The last thing they needed was paparazzi invading the island, or one of the brothers cornering Safiya below deck.

CHAPTER EIGHTEEN

Once inside the *Capricorn*, which had been surprisingly easy to achieve, Safiya glanced around the untidy mess in the cockpit, galley and eating area. Alejandro or Sebastian had stuff everywhere. Clothes, wetsuits, shoes, used food containers, dirty dishes in the sink, and pots on the stove. There were ocean maps covering two side windows and scattered over one end of the dining table. Even the curved, cushioned bench seat was crammed with books, note pads, and life jackets, leaving only enough room for one person to sit either end. On the wall above the kitchen bench a cork board covered in notes and photos masked another window. One photo of the brothers with a large group of divers caught Safiya's attention. An ancient canon and what looked like bricks of gold lay at their feet. They were all smiling broadly.

She rifled through everything, looking for anything resembling a diary. It saddened her to think Alejandro and Sebastian might be behind the robberies and explosion, but she wouldn't stop searching until she knew one way or the other. Not for one minute did she believe Bill blew himself up. That lovely old gentleman loved Ryan and Zoe. He'd face things head on, not end his life because of an unfortunate mistake.

Creeping down a narrow set of four, deep steps, she found what should be a sleeping berth on the left. Instead, the beds had been removed for storage. Safiya stepped through the disorder carefully. Eight scuba tanks and several spear guns lay on one side. On the other were what she assumed were two motorized underwater machines. They had an enclosed fan at one end and handlebars over a torpedo shaped cylinder with a large headlight at the front end. At the back of the berth were cardboard boxes of tinned food, packets of toilet rolls, two gas cylinders and stacks of wrinkled clothes. No diary.

The bathroom on the other side of the hull was tiny and needed a good clean. She flushed the toilet for good measure then washed her hands. The master berth at the bow had two single beds forming a V of open space between them. Both beds were unmade and the tiny shelves above were crammed with bits and pieces. There were long, horizontal windows high on the side walls, curtained which meant the only light came from a window in the ceiling. A cupboard door hung open, so she snooped inside and found two pairs of black leather shoes, ironed dress shirts, and pants. Every drawer contained items of clothing strewn through them, but no diary. She pulled a drawer from under one bed and found blankets and winter clothing. Opening the drawer under the other bed, she gasped. There were two rifles and lots of boxes of bullets. Her breathing became ragged as her heart raced. She quickly went through the bookshelves built into the bow above the beds. Some were in English, some in Spanish. No diary.

She could hear Madeline and Zoe shrieking and the two brothers laughing and offering to go to their aid. In a hurry to get off the yacht, Safiya rushed up the steps to the saloon area and checked in and around the cockpit's console and under the captain's chair. In the middle of the wooden walkway, she noticed a brass ring so knelt and pulled a hatch open, revealing the engine and very little room to move about. It looked oily and other than a spray can, there was clearly nothing of interest down there.

After shutting the hatch, she lifted the cushioned seats to peak underneath. She found an inflatable life raft and more life jackets. She searched the kitchen drawers and cupboards, stopping every now and then to check what the brothers where doing, but they stayed hanging over the bow, calling out instructions, or offering to swim out and help the girls. Madeline and Zoe kept up their banter, almost falling in before recovering their balance.

Madeline yelled out that she couldn't swim, to which Alejandro and Sebastian promised to rescue them if necessary. The brothers' laughter sounded genuine, like they were nice guys. After one more look around, Safiya strolled out the back of the cabin then with a quick glance left and right, jumped onto the wharf and ran to the back of the *Sea Sprite*.

She was surprised to find the back sliding door unlocked. Thanking her lucky stars, she slipped through then shut the door and examined the interior. This yacht had a different layout to the *Capricorn* and was immaculate. Not a thing out of place. She quickly went through drawers, cupboards, lifted cushions, then went down three steps to check out the bathroom, side berth and main berth. All beds were made and neat as a pin. Nothing to indicate who used it last.

Coming back up to the main area, she stood for a moment, allowing her gaze to rove, stopping when she noticed a scrap of paper caught near the rear door. Snatching it up, she exhaled in disappointment. It was a grocery docket from Butlers Independent Grocer.

"Wait." It had a date and time stamp. What if it belonged to the lady in the white dress? Was there a way to check who had been in Butlers' store on that day at that time? She could ask Simon. He seemed to be able to find anyone or anything.

An outboard engine caught her attention. Running to the cockpit, Safiya stared in horror as a rubber dinghy shot into the harbor, its churning backwash slamming into the girls' boards. Zoe managed to stay upright, but Madeline went flying. She surfaced, flapping about in the water, gasping, and choking. One of the brothers dived into the water and began swimming toward Madeline. Another man reached her first, flipping her on her back. He hooked both his elbows under her shoulders then began kicking toward the wharf. Madeline kept hitting his arms. Had she panicked, or was she trying to make the man let go?

Slipping out through the rear sliding door, Safiya closed it then tucked the docket into her bra cup, before climbing over the back of the yacht, onto the wharf. A cough had her looking up the Marina's rock wall. Her eyes widening at the amount of people standing behind the wall, most watching the action in the water. Ryan, Aunty Frankie and both the Kilgours were focused on Safiya.

"Uh-oh." Caught red-handed. There wasn't much she could do or say, so she may as well go with it. She waved then blew Ryan a kiss. She could always say she heard the yacht was for hire and wanted to check it out.

"Did you not like our toilet, *Fia*."

She whirled around to find Alejandro standing at the stern of his yacht. An amused grin on his face. She forced a laugh. "I was curious to see the inside. Mrs. King told me the *Sea Sprite* is for hire. I thought it might be fun to go out scuba diving one day."

"You are welcome to come with me and Sebastian any time."

"Thanks. I might take you up on that one day, when I'm not working. See you round."

"I hope so, Fia." He gave a wave then made for the bow of his yacht again.

Espionage wasn't really her thing. With her heart pounding madly, Safiya glanced along the wharf to see the man who had rescued Madeline standing with his arms crossed. Jarred's soaked clothing clung to his broad back and muscular frame. He said nothing as Madeline waved her arms about, pointing at the water and then his chest. Safiya couldn't catch her words, although it looked like Madeline was working herself into a mini tantrum.

Jarred stepped forward, picked Madeline up and threw her back into the Harbor.

Madeline surfaced and screeched, "Chief Steele Feather, you're going to pay for that."

Safiya giggled then climbed down a ladder to her board and paddle. She'd almost reached Zoe when she heard an engine roar to life. Looking along the Marina, she saw the same dinghy, with four men aboard. It came straight at her, blasting a horn before turning away, sending a wave of backwash crashing into her board. She lost her balance and fell into the water, surfacing seconds later without her paddle. She kicked madly, pushing the board ahead as she formulated the dressing-down she'd give those morons.

Something slammed into the board, shearing off a piece of fiberglass.

"What?" Another object hit then another and another, the last sending a bit of board into her shoulder. "Ouch." She glanced at her shoulder, shocked to see a shard of fiberglass embedded in her shoulder and a thin trickle of blood running down her chest.

"Oh no." She began thrashing about in the water and lost her grip on the board. Her shoulder burned. She had to get to the wharf before sharks caught the scent of her blood. "Help!"

"Safiya, don't panic. I'm coming," yelled Ryan.

She looked up as he dived off the wharf.

Thank God.

He surfaced and swam toward her. She tried treading water with both arms yet moving her injured shoulder made her woozy and nauseous. "Help me."

Ryan's strong arms caught her against his solid body. "I've got you, Saf. I've got you."

"Something hit my board and a bit of fiberglass flew into my shoulder."

"Someone tried to fucking shoot you." He flipped her on her back.

"What?" She was shaking so badly her voice wobbled. "Why?"

"I don't know." He hooked his arms under her shoulders and suddenly they were moving backward fast. The pain in her shoulder made her cry out. "Ryan?"

"I've got you, sweetheart."

"I hope so, because if I black out, I don't want to sink to the bottom of the harbor and get eaten by sharks. Don't let go of me, Ryan."

"I won't. We're almost at the wharf. I'm going to pass you up to Jarred, okay?"

"Okay." She cried out as he bumped her shoulder, then she was being lifted above the water. She opened her eyes to see Jarred reaching for her.

She almost passed out as he hauled her into his arms then against his chest. "Let's get her to the Medical Center. Get in the golf cart, Madeline. I'm not leaving you here."

"What about Zoe?"

"Garcia's looking after Zoe. You're coming with us."

Safiya looked up the rock wall where dozens of people were watching them. Had one of them tried to shoot her? Jarred passed her to Ryan in the back of a golf cart. She moaned as agony shot through her shoulder.

Ryan kissed her forehead. "I'm sorry."

"You didn't do anything."

He met her pained eyes. "What did you hide in your bikini?"

"A grocery docket. I'm hoping the woman in the white dress dropped it on the *Sea Sprite* and we can access the cameras at Butler's Grocery store."

"Clever girl. Unfortunately, that docket could be the reason someone just tried to kill you. Have you still got it?"

She poked her fingers inside her bikini bra and felt around, eventually finding a soppy bit of mush. "Waterlogged. Doesn't matter. It was dated Saturday morning at nine-sixteen."

"Great work. Simon should be able to access the store's cameras and zoom in on the check outs at that exact time."

"Who would want to kill me?"

"I don't know, but Frankie Ellis may have seen something, or one of the café's customers. Hang in there, we've arrived at the Medical Center."

She hissed as Ryan lifted her in his arms then again when he stepped out of the golf cart. He held her as if she weighed nothing. She was aware of Jarred and Madeline keeping pace on either side, but it meant little. She could only focus on Ryan's soft blue eyes, watching her anxiously. A door opened, breaking their connection.

Safiya glanced at her shoulder and cringed. The sliver of fiberglass stuck out like a giant splinter and there was blood over her arm and chest. The sight made her gag. "I hope it doesn't get infected. I don't want to die, Ryan. I just found you."

"I won't let you die, sweetheart." He strode forward, his shoes squelching on the floor.

"I'm so glad you were at the Marina." She frowned. "Why were you there?"

"I was having coffee with Frankie Ellis at the Angler's Point Café." He lay her on a bed and leaned over her. "I will figure out who did this, Safiya. You have my word, but I can't concentrate unless I know you're safe." He gently brushed her cheek with the back of his fingers then leaned closer and kissed her forehead. "Will you promise me, you won't go off on any more evidence-finding quests?"

She'd promise him anything if he kept touching and kissing her with such … She blinked several times. He was touching and kissing her like his teammates touched the women they loved and respected? She closed her eyes, fearful to open them again and discover this was all a dream.

"Safiya, sweetheart, talk to me."

Not a dream. She opened her eyes to find him leaning over her, watching her with concern. "I promise not to—"

"Right, let's see what we've got here." A man with graying hair and a nurse appeared on the other side of the bed. "Hello, young lady. I'm Dr. Michaels and this is Nurse Natalie. I'm the locum while Dr. Dutch is away. I hear someone shot at you?"

"I heard that too. Will I have a scar?"

He chuckled. "Maybe a tiny one. We'll have you back on your feet in no time."

"Good." She turned her head away. "I don't want to watch, but can Ryan stay?"

"I don't have a problem with that." He must have indicated for Ryan to move further down the bed, because Ryan shifted beside Safiya's legs, and the nurse took his place.

Over the next twenty minutes Natalie sterilized Safiya's shoulder, gave her four jabs of anesthetic, which stung worse than wasp bites. Dr. Michaels then removed the shard of fiberglass, cleaned out her wound, and put two stitches in her shoulder. Natalie finished off the procedure by applying a dressing and then placing Safiya's right arm in a sling.

Ryan didn't leave Safiya's side and kept them all entertained with his childhood adventures on the island. She'd never been so aware of a man. Ryan's gaze rarely left her face, gave Safiya a comfort she'd never experienced. Her heart swelled, knowing he would do anything in his power to keep her safe. He genuinely cared for her. This wasn't an act. He wasn't being paid to spy on her. This was real. When a tear ran down her face, he gently wiped it away and set about distracting her with more stories.

Finally, Dr. Michaels gave the okay to leave and wished them well. Safiya had barely put her feet on the ground, when Ryan swept her up in his arms and carried her out into a waiting room, where Madeline and Jarred jumped up from their chairs. Jarred wore a white singlet and Madeline wore his blue shirt.

Jarred gave a nod. "All good?"

"Yep." Ryan winked at Safiya. "As good as new." He carried her out to Shirley Thomas' taxicab then placed her gently on the back seat beside Madeline and buckled the seatbelt.

"I want you to go back to the cabin and take it easy for the rest of the day. Madeline will stay with you, until I get there."

A seaplane flew low overhead, cutting off her reply. She caught his hand and held on until the plane's engine quietened. "Where are you going? Don't do anything dangerous."

He smiled then leaned in and kissed her forehead. "Jarred and I are going to scout round the Angler's Point Café and Dugong Marina then have a chat to Sergeant Hawthorne."

"Oh." She pulled him closer and whispered, "Be careful."

"I will." He stood back and looked over the roof of the taxicab. "Thanks, Shirl."

"No worries, Ryan. Good to have you back." Shirley swung into the taxicab and grinned. "Never had a shooting on the island before. It's got everyone's knickers in a knot."

"News travels fast." Safiya smiled. "Luckily, I wasn't hit by a bullet,

Shirl, but a bullet hit my paddle board and sent a splinter into my shoulder."

"Same thing, luv. Alrighty, let's get you home." Shirley buckled her seat belt, cranked up the music, then after one or two kangaroo hops and the exhaust backfiring, they were off. Whether they would make it home in one piece was anyone's guess. Safiya grabbed the seat in front at the same time Madeline grabbed the handhold above her door. Their eyes met and Safiya had to bite her lip to hold in her laugh.

Madeline leaned close and muttered. "It would really suck to survive a sniper only to run off the road in this beat up old taxicab, wouldn't it?"

They both giggled and the last remnants of tension left Safiya. She had friends who cared about her. Coming to Currawong Island was the best decision she'd ever made. Now she just had to survive a sniper and get her happy ever after.

She looked at Madeline to find her deep in thought. "What were you and Jarred arguing about on the wharf?"

"He couldn't believe an intelligent woman like me, could be so scatterbrain as to paddle-board in a deep harbor when I can't swim."

"What, you really can't swim? I thought it was an act to keep Alejandro and Sebastian's attention off me."

"Of course it was an act, but Chief Steel Feather didn't give me a chance to explain that. He was too busy scolding me for my foolishness."

"Why do you call him Chief Steel Feather?"

Madeline's lips spread in a wide grin. "Because Jarred loves to order me around. He frustrated me so much once, I told him he could stick his steel feather up his ass. I won't tell you what he said in reply. Now I use the moniker to tease him."

"Hmm." Safiya studied Madeline's pensive expression then smiled. "I think Jarred Steele has a soft spot where you're concerned, Madeline."

"I have a soft spot for him too … and the rest of his team."

Safiya's heart ached for the sadness in Madeline's voice. "If you're not happy with your life, Madeline, it's up to you to change it. Go after what you want. Who you want."

"You're such a romantic optimist." Madeline inhaled deeply then reached for Safiya's hand. "Other than Elliot, I never really had close friends, until I stumbled across the Steele Ops guys and Jane in Vietnam."

"How did that happen?"

"Elliot asked me to drop off important documents to a Mr. Steele on my way to a job interview."

Her lips twitched. "Short version of a complicated story. One minute I was cooing over Jane's beautiful baby and the next I'd been crash tackled into the pool by Jarred. Then a sniper targeted us and suddenly I'm locked down under Jarred's protection. It's an entertaining saga for another day, but that's how I became friends with Jane and Kallie. I'd met Ava in London about a year ago, but we really gelled during a Steele Ops mission back in February. I only met Darius recently, yet we're destined to be good friends. You ladies are five of the most incredible women I've ever met. I trust you all."

Safiya swallowed the lump in her throat. "I'm delighted to be counted as a close friend. I never had that either. What of your husband?"

Madeline squeezed Safiya's fingers. "Elliott and I will always be friends, but ... we pretty much lead separate lives these days."

"Why?" Safiya couldn't understand such logic. "Don't you want to be together?"

"It's complicated. Elliott has a lot of responsibilities. I'd like to have a family, but it must be with a man who would put us above all else."

"I agree." Safiya mulled that over for a moment. "My father and mother are still very much in love." Safiya exhaled. "I just wish they hadn't kept their marriage and children secret. It's been too high a price to pay."

Madeline clasped Safiya's hand between hers. "I've researched your father's family and the empire he controlled before stepping aside. His position as head of the family demanded his complete attention. The fact he resisted a traditional Middle Eastern marriage and remained faithful to your mother speaks for itself. If they'd admitted the truth, your mother would have been forced to give up her career and remain within the family compound, rarely seeing her husband. She would have been treated like an outsider, a foreigner. Your brother would have been treated like a prince and given everything he desired. You would have been raised traditionally by your grandmother, possibly kept from your mother, and then married off to achieve a prosperous alliance. I know you believe you were abandoned by your parents, but they did what they thought best for *you*."

Safiya's heart thudded frantically at Madeline's account. Her parents hadn't been lying. "How did you know this, Madeline?"

She grinned. "I'm a very good investigative journalist with contacts all over the world."

Safiya glanced out the window, surprised they hadn't reached the Dutch House. Nothing looked familiar. "Where are we?" She had to yell for Shirl to hear her over the music.

"I'm giving you a tour of the island. That man with Ryan gave me a fifty to take the long way home." She took a bend a bit too sharply and swerved, zig-zagging a couple of times before she got the car back on the right side of the road. "Sorry about that. This is the scenic route."

"Great." Safiya glanced at Madeline to see her doubled over, shaking with silent laughter.

Shirl hit the accelerator, sending dirt and dust shooting up behind them. "Hold on to your hats, it's not far. I'll get you home without anyone shooting you, or my name's not Shirl Thomas."

CHAPTER NINETEEN

Frustration ate at Ryan. He couldn't believe someone had shot at Safiya. At least she'd be safe in the cabin with Madeline. Talos and Ajax wouldn't let anyone on the estate.

Ryan ran a hand through his hair then strode after Jarred, Sam and Nick. They combed the pathway above the Marina, being the most likely place for the sniper's position. Further along from the café, Nick found an unused bullet. The ground between a palm tree and the rock wall had been trampled. The tree would have concealed the sniper from the café's customers and onlookers, all of whom would have been preoccupied with the action below. No easy task hiding a rifle. He glanced at the Angler's Café. "The Kilgours need looking into."

Jarred gave a nod, his attention also focused on the café. "I'll send Simon a text."

After dropping the bullet off at the Police Station, they hiked back to the Dutch compound. Ryan wanted to check on Safiya then he'd help Darius and Simon examine footage from the drones. Hopefully, they'd find something.

As Ryan closed the gate, his cell phone chimed. "Aunty Frankie … What's up?"

"I've been told your parents arrived on that seaplane. You might want to check on your guests. I've got room here if you and your friends need somewhere else to stay."

"Err, thanks, Aunty Frankie. That's really good of you."

"Take care." She ended the call, leaving Ryan staring into space. He hadn't expected his parents and grandparents to fly in, and he certainly hadn't wanted Zoe to face them alone.

At least Garcia would be there, hopefully preventing any unpleasantness. If there was one thing Ryan knew for certain, it was John Dutch Snr and John Dutch Jnr shunned public confrontations. As did Ryan's mother. Under no circumstances was dirty washing ever aired in public. What happened in the home, stayed in the home. Thank fuck he was no longer a boy.

They strode up the main drive to find Madeline, Safiya, Darius, Simon and Garcia sitting outside the large cabin, surrounded by suitcases, duffle bags and the metal cases Simon and Darius carted their valuable computer equipment and drones around in.

"What the hell is this?" muttered Jarred.

Ryan sighed. "I'd say they've been thrown out of the cabins."

"You're fucking kidding me?" Jarred strode over to Simon and Darius. Sam and Nick followed. Ryan headed for Safiya who still looked pale. She went to stand, but Madeline put out a hand, indicating she stay sitting.

That said enough for Ryan. He went down on his haunches beside Safiya then placed his hand on her back. "You okay?"

She nodded. "I'm fine."

"What happened?" He addressed his question to Madeline.

"Your father called by the cabin and asked us to leave. We are waiting for Shirl and her taxi. Zoe tried to intervene, insisting they were her cabins on Barnacle Bill's land, and she'd hired them out to us, but your father threatened to call the police."

"Shit." Ryan glanced at Garcia. "Where's Zoe?"

"Trying to reason with your father and mother. How the hell did those two narrow-minded bullies produce a sweetheart like your sister?"

Ryan's lips twitched. "What? You don't think I'm a sweetheart too?"

"Fuck off. Your sister is a breath of fresh air. I only left her because she insisted on it. She knows I'm not leaving the estate without her."

"Where will we stay," asked Darius. "I was under the impression there isn't any available accommodation on the island."

"We're staying with Francine Ellis," offered Ryan. "She's got two spare bedrooms and a sunroom out the back us fellas can bunk down in. Let me give her a call." He strode a few paces away then brought up his contact list, thanking his lucky stars Aunty Frankie had offered her home.

"Ryan, my boy. I've been waiting for your call."

He couldn't help chuckling. "I need to take you up on your offer, Aunty Frankie. We've been tossed off the estate."

"I half expected it. Come on over and bring your friends. I'll need some help making up beds and you'll have to get in groceries before the storm hits. It'll be nice to have some company."

"Thanks. I'll send the others over now and follow soon with Zoe."

"That is wise. There's something you both need to hear, before it's rubbed in your faces by those who think they're better than the rest of us."

He frowned at her words, unable to guess what she could be referring to, but he'd deal with one thing at a time. "Okay, Aunty Frankie, we'll see you soon." He hung up and turned to his friends. "We'll stay with Francine Ellis. Her house is within walking distance and backs onto Sunset Beach. It's thirty-nine Coral Sea Road." He nodded toward town. "Fourth house on the left, beside the park. Load the luggage in Shirl's taxi and she can take the ladies."

Jarred strode over. "I'm coming with you."

"So am I," insisted Safiya, awkwardly getting to her feet. "Your parents won't want to cause a scene in front of strangers, especially your girlfriend."

He smiled at her. "They don't know about you, Safiya."

"Yeah, they do." Simon handed him today's paper, folded open on page five. "Your father flung this at me when he came calling."

Ryan's mouth dropped at the color picture of him dancing with Safiya at the Gala and the headline above it.

SHEIKH'S SECRET DAUGHTER DATING SECURITY GUARD

"Fuck." He began reading the first paragraph aloud. "Sheikh Tariq Zakour Farid's only daughter has surprised many, including her own family by running off with a security guard. It is unknown where the couple met or how long they've been dating. There is speculation however, that the couple are on an island off Queensland. Sheikh Farid and his Australian born wife have only recently divulged they've been married for thirty-three years and have a son and daughter. A close friend of the family revealed the Sheikh is most concerned for his daughter, as she is a prime target for gold diggers. We were unable to reach Sheikh Farid for comment."

"Damnation." Ryan went to crumple the paper.

"No." Safiya used her good hand to snatch it. "It's a nice picture of us."

He sighed. "This will be all over the island by tonight. Tomorrow's ferry will be full of reporters. We won't get a moment's privacy."

"Then we have one day to figure things out and clear your name." Safiya raised both eyebrows. "It should be a piece of cake for an investigative journalist and six Special Forces soldiers."

Talos barked out a laugh. "I like this woman, Ryan."

"Yeah, me too." He turned to the main house. "First thing first. I need to check on Zoe."

"Wait for me," called Safiya. "I'm coming for moral support."

Ryan caught Safiya's free hand, thankful to have her and Jarred by his side. He'd take all the moral support he could get.

As they approached the house, raised voices caught Ryan's attention. "Let's go round the back. Sounds like they're on the terrace."

Seeing Zoe facing off against the three people who should be in her corner had Ryan seeing red. He'd recognize his parents anywhere. They'd aged, as had his grandfather. John Dutch Snr had bowed shoulders and a paunch. Ryan's grandmother, Pam, stood apart, holding on to a walking stick. Ryan's mother, Carol, looked as stylish as she always had, so out of place on an island like Curra. Her short hair and glasses were different. John Jnr stood as stiff as his father. Neither were warm, easygoing men.

Ryan couldn't remember ever seeing any displays of affection, even toward their wives or each other. His grandmother had been the one to cuddle Ryan when he was a child. Zoe had told Ryan their grandmother spent a lot of time with their Aunt Marilyn, on the Gold Coast.

No one heard Ryan, Safiya and Jarred approaching, due to John Snr's booming voice. Ryan stopped behind them, curious to hear what he had to say.

"Why didn't you do as we demanded and keep your distance from that no-hoper."

Zoe shook her head. "Grandpa, Ryan is my brother and I love him. He's not a no-hoper, and he wasn't responsible for Zane's death."

"Poppycock. The boy was a daredevil, always on some dangerous lark with those friends of his. He could have been a doctor if he'd buckled down, but he'd rather look for treasure than study. It was only a matter of time before one of them was seriously hurt."

His mother waved a finger at Zoe. "We forbid you to have anything to do with your brother. How can you speak of him with such devotion? He hasn't wanted anything to do with you in twelve years."

"You're wrong about that, Mother. I've been in contact with Ryan since he left the island. We regularly text, email and have been physically catching up whenever he has leave. I've met his friends and even holidayed with them. Ryan is a hero. He's been in the army's Special Forces for years. He's served our country, completing dangerous missions all over the world. Zane did not die because of Ryan. He died trying to save someone else who tried to abseil down Morcago Ledge."

She drew a deep breath. "You were so quick to blame Ryan. You never took the time to hear him out. You never cared enough to support your own son, which you should have done, whether you thought him innocent of guilty. You are atrocious parents. This was Ryan's home. He'd just lost his best friend. Shame on you."

She hauled in another deep breath. "I will never forgive any of you for what you did to my brother. Ryan is here with his Special Forces team at the request of the Island's council."

She had hardly taken a breath, talking over his parents and grandfather each time they attempted to butt in. It was so unlike his quiet little sister. Ryan wanted to crow with pride, yet he couldn't let her stand against them alone.

Leaving Jarred and Safiya, he stalked forward, around his parents and grandfather to put his arm around Zoe's shoulders. "I love you, Zo, and I appreciate your support."

He stared at their parents and grandfather, amused to see their mouths gaping open. He hadn't really thought about their reactions, but of course they would notice the physical changes. He'd grown much taller and bulked up in the last twelve years. They'd also be able to see the determination and hardness in his eyes. Realize he'd done well without them. Nothing they said had the power to hurt him anymore. He was proud of the man he'd become. He had nothing to be ashamed of. Crossing his arms, he stared them down.

"I'm here to do a job for the council and to clear my name." With that he caught Zoe's hand and towed her around them to join Safiya and Jarred.

"You're just like your parents," called his mother. "It's all about the next adrenaline rush or adventure. You'll never settle down."

He swung around. "What the hell are you talking about?"

"Carol." Ryan's father tried to cover her mouth.

She shook him off. "We are not your parents. We agreed to adopt you, after your mother died in childbirth. Bill was your father and it's time you knew the truth."

"Bill?" An icy dread threatened to freeze the blood in Ryan's veins, followed by a steel band tightening around his chest. Somehow it made sense, yet he struggled to get his head around the fact Bill and an unknown woman were his biological parents, not these indifferent, hard to please, cold people. Bill was his father.

Ryan felt sick in his gut. He should have been told. "Is Zoe your natural child?"

His mother lifted her chin. "She's an IVF baby. My sister donated the eggs."

Blown away, Ryan couldn't get his mind around all this information. It was like he'd walked into an alternative reality. Carol's confession echoed around his brain leaving him reeling.

Zoe fingers tightened in Ryan's hand. She stood there with tears welling in her eyes before they spilled down her cheeks. She turned into Ryan's chest and sobbed. "I didn't know."

"Of course you didn't." Safiya stalked forward, stepping around the elder Dutch members, ignoring the gasps her presence caused. She wrapped her good arm around Zoe. "Nothing's changed, Zoe. Your still Ryan's sister and my friend."

Zoe sniffed. "Thanks, Fia." She looked up at Ryan, her lips curving slightly. "Actually, I think you're my uncle."

He tightened his hold. "Technically, but if you dare call me Uncle Ryan, I'll toss you in the ocean."

"Okay." She sniffed again. "I love that you're my brother."

"I love that you're my sister, Zo." He focused on his father and mother. "I couldn't figure out why you seemed to resent me, but now it makes sense. You wanted a child you could mold to your way of thinking. Not an independent kid with a mind of his own and a free spirit. You used to swear I lacked the intelligence and fortitude to be a doctor. That I wouldn't go anywhere in life. You were wrong. I joined the army and became a Blackhawk pilot. I've flown hundreds of retrieval and rescue missions. I'm a qualified paramedic and have my seaplane license. I own my own apartment." He ignored his parents shocked expressions and put his arms around both girls' shoulders, steering them toward the house so Zoe could pack what she needed. He glanced at his grandmother, sitting on a chair by the terrace table. She had tears in her eyes and was smiling at him then she winked, surprising the hell out of him.

They'd reached the back porch when Ryan realized Jarred wasn't with them. "Safiya, will you help Zoe pack what she needs?"

Safiya shot a quick glance behind them then nodded. "Of course. We'll meet you out the front of the house."

"Thanks." Ryan waited, curious to see what Jarred had planned.

The Colonel hadn't moved, but now stood facing Ryan's parents. "I am Colonel Jarred Steele. Major Ryan Dutch is one of the finest soldiers, paramedics, and Blackhawk pilots I've ever had the privilege to serve with. He is a decorated soldier and now works as part of a special ops team under my command. On occasion we still assist the Australian Government in sensitive operations. You should be extremely proud of Ryan. I am."

Blown away for the second time today, Ryan waited for Jarred to join him. After a nod of gratitude, they strode around the house to wait for Zoe and Safiya. He'd thought of Sam, Talos, Nick and Simon as brothers for years. He'd respected Jarred, looked up to him, even though there were only five or six years between them. From today, he'd think of Jarred as another brother.

Ten minutes later, Zoe and Safiya came onto the front porch with a backpack and carryall. Ryan took them both. "Let's go."

The journey by foot to Frankie's was completed mostly in silence. Each of them deep in their own thoughts. Yet the minute they knocked at the front door; they were swamped by their friends. Madeline hustled Zoe and Safiya into a bedroom they'd be sharing. Nick gave Ryan and Jarred a chin lift then led the way through the house to the back patio, where Aunty Frankie sat as proud as a queen at the head of her outdoor table. He soon found out Simon and Darius had claimed the other spare bedroom and the rest of them would be sleeping in the sunroom, as he'd predicted. Several minutes later Talos and Sam joined them, loaded with cartons of beer, wine, and enough groceries to feed everyone for a week.

The lump in Ryan's throat took a while to clear. He met Safiya's shining eyes, reading her empathy, and understanding as she placed a beer in front of him. Aunty Frankie had outdone herself. The table was loaded with cooked sausages, fresh rolls, and salad. His stomach growled, reminding him he hadn't eaten for hours. When Safiya slid onto the wooden bench, he joined her, placing his hand on her thigh. "Thank you, Safiya-Ameerah."

As if she understood all he was thanking her for, she smiled. "You're welcome." She squeezed his fingers. "I had a conversation with Tommy earlier. He told me he got into a fight with Zane the night before his death."

"What about?" This was certainly a day of revelations.

CHAPTER TWENTY

Still reeling from Safiya's conversation with Tommy, Ryan barely registered his friends thanking Aunty Frankie for her hospitality. He'd gone through a range of emotions from confusion and disappointment to intense grief, anger, and hostility. His head ached with a piecing throbbing behind his right eye. His gut churned so badly, he feared one bite of food would come straight back up. The others were about to tuck into lunch when the doorbell peeled.

"You expecting visitors, Aunty Frankie?" asked Zoe.

"No, luv, but there's bound to be a mountain of curiosity after the shooting."

"I'm nearest, I'll get the door," offered Darius. She ran off and a minute later came back with Tommy. "This guy says he's a friend of yours, Ryan."

Ryan came to his feet. He'd been expecting Tommy, but it still tore his heart apart to see his old friend standing there, cap in his hand, flushed and obviously uncomfortable.

"Hi. Ryan, can I speak to you in private?"

"Hey, Tommy. These are my friends. Jarred, Talos, Sam, Nick, Simon, Madeline, and Darius. You've met Safiya and of course know

Aunty Frankie and Zoe. Whatever you have to say can be said in front of everyone."

"I'd prefer to speak to you on our own."

"Nonsense, Tommy," called Aunty Frankie. "I thought you might call. Say what you have to and get it off your chest, then you can join us for lunch."

He looked like he wanted to turn tail and run. Instead, he took a deep breath. "I swear it wasn't me on the cliff with Zane, but it could have been one of his cousins. I got into a fight with Zane the night before and stuff came out about the cave and … me and Cammy."

Aunty Frankie put a hand to her chest and gasped as if she'd just figured something out, but she didn't say a word.

Safiya clambered off the bench and padded barefoot over to Tommy. "Tell Ryan what happened that night."

He swallowed. "After being with Cammy, I decided if there was a treasure, I needed to help find it, so I could set Cammy up in her own café. I planned to tell you about me and Cammy the next day and hoped you'd understand. I knew I'd never be able to give Cammy what she craved, so I went to see Zane. He told me you were meeting at Morcago Ledge at ten the next morning. Because I'd been caught with Cammy, it was only a matter of time before he heard, so I tried to reason with him, but he lost it. He said I wasn't part of the group anymore and we got into a fight. I went home but decided to go early and climb down to the cave myself."

"On your own?" Ryan narrowed his eyes. "You were terrified of heights."

"I know. I got there and dug out your harness and helmet, but I couldn't do it. I couldn't even get close to the edge. I went home, hoping you'd forgive me and Cammy and share the treasure, if you found it."

"Why didn't you say something?" asked Ryan.

"I tried to see you, to explain about me and Cammy, but your parents wouldn't let me through the gate. We heard you'd left the island. You didn't come to Zane's funeral. Cammy was sent to relatives in Mackay, and I was shipped off to Brisbane to finish school.

When I came back, I went to see your grandmother, but she didn't know where you were."

Ryan exhaled. He'd hoped it hadn't been Tommy and could see how Zane's death had affected Tommy.

Safiya touched Tommy's arm. "Barnacle Bill said the person he saw on the cliff was tangled in the ropes. It had to be someone without climbing experience. They must have panicked."

"That's what I figured."

The back screen door slammed against the house, and they all turned to see Cammy glaring daggers at her husband. "Tommy Curran. What are you doing?"

"Cammy, I'm making things right."

"No, you're not. I should never have told you I was coming to see Ryan. You are not taking the blame."

"What? No, I wasn't."

"Ah." Aunty Frankie smiled. "This is more like it."

Tommy strode over to Camilla. "This is my fault. If I hadn't got into a fight with Zane, he'd still be alive and none of your cousins would have known about the cave. I didn't want you talking to Ryan. I love you and the boys."

"What are you talking about?"

"You have enough guilt eating you, Cammy. Your mother told me you were plagued by nightmares in that year following Zane's death. I know you love Ryan, but he'll never love you like I do."

"You know squat, Tommy. For a start, Ryan has a girlfriend. Safiya-Ameerah Farid. She's an heiress, almost an Arabian princess. I barely made it through school, and I've had four kids with the man I love. I'm not interested in Ryan, but Zane is dead because of me."

She turned to Ryan. "Tommy told me about his fight with Zane, so I sneaked out the next morning and went to Morcago Ledge. I planned to find the treasure, so me and Tommy could run away together. Go live on the Gold Coast and open a cafe."

Ryan crossed his arms, mainly to hide his clenched fingers. How he wished they'd never found that cave. "So, you went to Morcago Ledge. What happened?"

"I found your harness and helmet by a tree. It didn't look that hard and I wasn't scared of heights, but my foot got caught and next thing I'm upside down and I couldn't get untangled. I screamed for help. Zane yelled to stay still and climbed down with a rope."

She sobbed. "He'd just got me untangled when a piece of rock fell from above and hit him. Zane fell, without making a single sound. It's tormented me ever since. I managed to get back up and couldn't stop shaking and crying. I ran home for help, but Zane had already been found, and he was dead. I went berserk. Your father had to sedate me. When I could function again, you'd left Curra. I tried to speak to your parents, but they wanted nothing to do with me or Tommy."

"Why didn't you speak to me or one of the elders, Cammy?" asked Aunty Frankie.

"My mother rushed me off to Mackay, where I stayed until I finished school. When I came back, I confessed to the old sergeant, but he said it wouldn't bring Zane back or do any good. I decided to wait until Ryan came home, but you never did."

Ryan blew out a long breath. "Wow." He rubbed his skull, trying to sooth the pulsing pain ricocheting around his brain. Even his heart hurt. Nothing was as black and white as he'd assumed it would be. The devastation on Tommy and Camilla's faces spoke volumes. He didn't have it in him to lay into them for his suffering.

"Thanks for clearing things up, Camilla. I'm relieved Zane wasn't conscious when he fell. He wouldn't want us blaming each other either."

Ryan turned to Aunty Frankie. "If you can let the other elders know, I'd appreciate it, but I don't want a fuss made. We've all paid enough."

"I will."

He turned back to Tommy and Cammy. "There is something you can both do for me."

"What," asked Tommy.

"There's plenty of food. Stay and join us for lunch?"

Tommy and Camilla stared at him in shock then each other then back at him. Camilla's eyes filled with tears. "You want us to join you, after what we did?"

"The past can't be changed, Camilla, but it did redirect my life for the better, and you two seem to be happy. Come on, sit down. I'd like you to join us."

Talos shifted sideways so Camilla and Tommy could squeeze onto the opposite bench. They looked stunned, but as Ryan organized a thorough search of the island, they visibly relaxed and offered suggestions as to where Bill might have gone. Ryan didn't miss the sympathy on everyone's faces. With Bill still missing, and no clue as to where he might be, it made sense that the body found in the burned-out shed might be Bill. Ryan could only pray Aunty Frankie was right, and the results of the autopsy report would come through soon and provide some answers.

He noticed Aunty Frankie slip away and figured she meant to phone the other elders. Within an hour, all the elders would know the truth. He hoped Camilla wouldn't be snubbed or judged. God, how he wished Bill would walk through the door, so they could talk things through. Ryan wanted to hug the old guy and tell him how much he loved him.

The others were tucking into Aunty Frankie's caramel tart when the doorbell rang again. Ryan was even more surprised when she showed his grandmother onto the back patio. Pam Dutch suddenly looked much older than her seventy-five years. For a moment she seemed overwhelmed by all the people sitting around the table, then she lifted her chin, and using the walking stick, hobbled to Ryan's side.

"I'm sorry to disturb your lunch, but it's important I talk to you." She glanced quickly at Zoe, sitting beside Garcia, still looking pale and terribly sad. "It has to be now, as I'm leaving on the ferry tomorrow. I'm going to live with Marilyn permanently."

Ryan stood and offered her his arm. "We can talk inside, if you'd like privacy?"

"No, I know everyone here is close to you." She carefully lowered herself onto the bench beside Safiya then shuffled along, before tapping the wooden seat. "Please sit."

He glanced around the table, noting everyone was just as interested as him to hear what she had to say.

"May I have a glass of wine?" she asked. "I need something to fortify me."

Safiya grabbed a wine glass then poured his grandmother a Chardonnay.

"Thank you, dear." Pam smiled at Safiya. "You're very pretty. I'm glad you see the good in Ryan. He might have been after treasure as a child, but he's no gold digger." She looked around the table. "I would appreciate no interruptions, otherwise I'm likely to lose concentration and forget something."

She took a sip then carefully placed the glass in front of her. "Let me start by saying, Bill was a good man, and I'll miss him. The times he stepped in when his brother, my husband was berating me, is too many to count. They were nothing alike. Bill was the black sheep of the family, but the better man. As a child he roamed all over the island and refused to go away to boarding school. He was wild at heart but yearned for adventure. He only ever truly loved one woman, but she didn't want to leave Currawong." She pointedly looked at Aunty Frankie then took another sip of wine.

"My son is like his father, a loner and impatient. John happily went away to boarding school, then university to study medicine, following in his father's footsteps. When he qualified, he came back and joined his father's practice."

She took a much bigger sip of wine. "Marilyn, my daughter, is fourteen years younger than John and completely different. They don't get on. Marilyn wanted to spread her wings, travel, be a hairdresser. Maybe she got that from me." She smiled.

"When Ryan refused to go to boarding school, I asked Marilyn if she'd let him board with her in Townsville, which she did and then she took in Zoe too. She loved having the kids."

"What happened to Aunt Marilyn," asked Ryan.

"When Zoe finished school, Marilyn sold up everything and opened a new salon on the Gold Coast. She now has a lovely home and a very nice husband. They never had children." Pam finished her wine then looked at Ryan. "Bill told me your mother was an adrenalin junkie. Her career in the army was the most important thing to her. She was one of the army's few female pilots back then. He said she was forty when they met."

Ryan raised his eyebrows. "Really?"

"Yes. He was surprised when she decided to go ahead with an unplanned pregnancy and keep the baby. They were living together when Bill was deployed overseas for six months. He got back a week after she'd gone into labor, and sadly died of complications. She had no family that Bill knew of, so he found himself with a tiny baby and didn't know what to do. He brought you to me."

Pam pushed her wine glass closer to Safiya, who immediately topped it up. After a sip Pam continued. "John and Carol had been married three years by then, so I suggested they adopt you. Bill agreed, as he had no idea what to do with a baby on his own. It seemed to work out well. Then when you were six, Zoe came along, thanks to Marilyn donating eggs."

She smiled at Ryan. "You loved your little sister. Sadly, you didn't conform with my son's and daughter-law's view of the perfect son. Your grades were poor. You hated school on the mainland. You loved to run wild and refused to go to boarding school. When Zane died, your parents and grandfather shunned you. They insisted you'd brought shame on the Dutch name. They wouldn't listen to reason. You were inconsolable and disgusted with us all."

"That's why Bill agreed when I asked him to take me away." Ryan huffed in disgust.

"After the hearing, I begged Bill to take you to Marilyn, but he refused. When he came back without you, I asked where you were. He said you were better off and safe. I never forgave my husband, or son and daughter-in-law for what they did to you. After years of being meek, I grew a spine."

A tear ran down Pam's face. "I'm happy you've found a nice girl and you have your friends. If you can forgive me for not standing up for you, I'd like to be a part of your life."

Ryan took a deep breath. His brain was struggling to take it all in. Nothing was as he'd believed. Other than Aunty Frankie, his grandmother was the only soft influence he'd had in his life. As a child, he'd spent more time in her kitchen than his own house. More time pottering in the garden with her than talking to his parents. He looked up as Zoe scooted round the table and hugged their grandmother. Zoe was such a softy. As Garcia said, a sweetheart.

He hugged the frail woman. "Thank you, Grandma. It means a lot to me to know you were in my corner."

"Thank you, dear."

Ryan kissed her forehead. He'd always think of her as his grandmother. "I'd like to stay in touch. How about you stay a while, and have a slice of this caramel tart?"

Another tear ran down her wrinkled cheek. "I would love some caramel tart and another glass of chardonnay." She held up her empty glass.

They all laughed.

The doorbell rang again, and Ryan put his head in his hands. "I don't think I can take any more revelations today." What he wanted to do was take a long, solitary walk to deal with his churning emotions, to process everything, and to figure out where Bill could be.

"Alrighty, looks like this is the place to be." Shirley Thomas marched out of the house smiling broadly at everyone around the table. Her fizzy red hair stuck out from a colorful scarf wrapped around her head. She plonked a crockery dish crammed with all manner of sliced and chopped fruit in the middle of the table. "Frankie told me she had house guests, so I thought you might like a fruit salad. Phil's coming with the whipped cream." She looked over her shoulder and yelled. "Phil, stop yakking and bring that cream out here."

Phil immediately scurried out the back door, ahead of Darius. "Hold ya horses, woman, I was just talking to this lovely young lady." He'd removed his cap, revealing a row of stitches across his forehead.

The island's bus driver handed his wife the bowl of cream then gave Ryan a nod. "Good to have ya back, mate. I thought that might be you I passed this morning. About time you came home and cleared things up. Ya haven't got a spare beer, have you?"

"Sure." Ryan slid off the bench and strode over to an open cooler. "4X okay?"

"My oath it is. Thanks, mate." Phil unscrewed the lid and took a long swig then exhaled. "It's a dreadful business about Bill. He was good man. One of the few who honestly cared about Curra and our people. I can't understand why anyone would blow up the boatshed. It's gotta be those bloody treasure hunters."

"We'll know soon enough." Ryan held out his right hand and shook Phil's. "It's good to see you, Phil. Do you remember anything about your assault? Anything you might have remembered since speaking to Sergeant Hawthorne?"

"Nah. I was walking the dog past the museum and thought I heard a noise inside. I figured it couldn't hurt to look. I unlocked the door, turned the lights on and everything looked fine in the main room. I left Daisy there and went to check the office. I remember hearing the door creak behind me, then whack ... something hit me in the head, knocked me off my feet. I came to with Daisy yapping in my ear and blood everywhere."

"Hi, I'm ... Safiya." Safiya smiled at Phil. "Would Daisy recognize your attacker?"

Phil beamed. "You're Ryan's girlfriend. I recognize you from the today's paper. I get it online. I think Daisy would know the culprit, but it wouldn't stand up in court." He winked. "You've got a good man in Ryan."

"How would you know, Phil? I've been gone twelve years."

"I fished with Bill. When he'd had a few drinks, he liked to boast about you and that team of yours. Was as proud as punch, he was. Once told me he loved you like a son."

"I am his son, Phil." Ryan looked down the garden, fighting to keep control over his rolling emotions. He couldn't care less about gossip.

He wanted everyone to know he was Bill's son. He wanted to shout it out from Heron Lookout.

A small, soft hand slid into his. "What do you say, we get out of here?" Safiya's expressive, dark eyes looked up at him in compassion. "I think you need some space to think."

He chuckled. "What I need is a kayak so I can check out the island's coastline."

"Okay, but I'm coming with you. We work better together."

CHAPTER TWENTY-ONE

Accepting Ryan needed to mull things over, Safiya sat quietly in the front bucket-seat of the tandem kayak, watching the passing scenery for any sign of Bill. She held little hope, yet Frankie was convinced he was alive, somewhere. During lunch, Camilla and Tommy backed Ryan's statement, that Frankie's sixth sense and predictions were never wrong.

Ryan paddled with steady strokes, occasionally modifying their direction. Garcia had dropped them at Paradise Beach, where they'd selected one of Zoe's two-seater kayaks and two life jackets. Frankie had lent them two wide-brimmed hats to hide their identities and protect them from the sun. There'd been no one on the beach, so they made it into the water without having to speak to anyone.

Safiya noticed a church up on the narrow headland they were approaching. It looked rather solitary and unkept.

Ryan must have noticed her preoccupation with it, as he stopped paddling and leaned forward. "Pelican Point. When I was a kid, that was the Anglican Church. Zoe told me it's been locked up for years, but she'd love to buy it and turn it into her home. It could be somewhere Bill might go if he wanted to drown his sorrows. I'll make sure it's on the search list."

"Is he the type to go somewhere to drown his sorrows?"

"I wouldn't have thought so, but he was distraught at the pub."

Ryan paddled around Pelican Point. "Oyster Bay is where most locals picnic and gather. Up ahead is Rocky Point and Curra's only camping ground."

She could see two dome tents. "Is that where the treasure hunters are staying?"

"Yes. I installed a motion camera on the side of the amenities block so that we can monitor them when they're about. What we need is good headshots to run through a program Simon invented. He can slip in and out of secure data bases without leaving a footprint. We can identify anyone, if they've had their photo taken for a government agency or judicial system almost anywhere in the world."

Safiya glanced over her shoulder. "Surely that's illegal?"

"No comment." He chuckled.

They rounded the headland and Safiya sighed at the picturesque beach set against a backdrop of hundreds of swaying palm trees, and a steep mountain of forest rising behind. "It's stunning."

"Welcome to Palm Beach. There's a sandbar, which makes it a safe beach to swim. This is where the treasure hunters have been mooring their yacht. As they won't be in for a few hours yet, we should walk along the beach and check out the park."

"Good idea." Safiya pulled out her camera. "It's like paddling into Paradise."

"During the holidays it's packed with tourists, so the council employ lifeguards to patrol. Zoe has a thriving business."

Ryan propelled them through water so clear, Safiya could see stingrays half buried in the sand, and colorful fish darting every which way. A loud yap right beside her, almost propelled Safiya over the side of the kayak. She whipped around to see a black head, huge black eyes, and whiskers. "Is it Pong?"

"Yes." Ryan tapped the side of the kayak. "Here comes Ping. Watch out."

"For what?" Safiya whipped back around as a silvery dolphin leaped out of the water then slam dunked, sending a wave of water over Safiya, and drenching her. "Oh, oh." She spluttered. "I knew I should have stayed in my bikini. Will they bite?"

"No. Hold these." Ryan passed her his paddle and life jacket then tore off his shirt and slid over the side of the kayak. His two old friends immediately popped up in front of him, barking and clicking. Safiya watched in amazement as the dolphin and seal allowed Ryan to stroke their faces and rub their bellies, then Ryan tried to swim toward the beach, towing the kayak, except his two friends kept cutting him off. It was as if they didn't want him to reach the sand, or maybe they wanted him to stay and play. It was the funniest thing to watch.

Eventually Ryan swam back to the kayak and managed to climb on board without it capsizing. "Looks like we're not walking on Palm Beach today."

"Why?"

"These two have something they want to show us."

"Really?" Safiya sent him a skeptical frown. "They told you that?"

"It might be nothing, but they used to love to show me interesting things. It started with Ping bringing me Pong, who was caught up in a fishing net."

"So where are they taking us?" Safiya handed Ryan his life jacket then the paddle. She kept his T-shirt on her lap.

"Let's find out." Ryan drove his paddle into the water, and they surged forward, out to sea again. "It might be something that's fallen off a yacht. They once took me to Turtle Beach because they'd found a cooler floating in the water. It had a six-pack of beer inside. Me, Zane, and Tommy drank the lot then fell asleep on the beach. We woke up with headaches and sunburn. I was grounded for the next two weekends."

They rounded the headland of Shark Bite Bay and Safiya shivered. She looked up at Morcago Ledge and gasped, her eyes almost popped out of her head.

"Shit." Ryan stopped paddling. "That's the treasure hunters' yacht. What are they doing in the middle of Shark Bite Bay?

"Climbing up Morcago Ledge." Safiya pointed at the cliff face, where two men in helmets were tentatively working their way up the rockface. She could see a trailing rope that had been anchored to the cliff below them. Another three men were scrambling over the rocks below. "I think they're looking for your bat cave."

"It won't do them any good," muttered Ryan. "Only a skinny kid can squeeze through the narrow gap. My coming back and Bill's death must have stirred up talk of Zane's death. Those idiots have probably heard about our obsession with finding treasure. It makes sense someone mentioned Morcago Ledge. They probably heard about it in the café this morning."

He shook his head. "I'm more concerned with why Ping and Pong want me here. He began paddling again, following the dolphin and seal.

Safiya kept watch on the men. "We should search their yacht; in case they have Bill or his diary."

"I can see a dinghy perched on the rocks. Maybe the other guy is further around the rocks. I'll paddle to the far side of the yacht. Let me know if they spot us."

"Okay. Look." She pointed up at a large eagle circling. "Is that one of Darius' drones."

"Yep, which means she will send help if we need it."

Safiya's nerves were jumping about like fleas on steroids. "At least our kayak, hats and life jackets are blue, so we don't stand out."

Her phone chimed, so she leaned forward to unzip the waterproof bag and retrieve it before the chimes got louder. "It's my brother." Frowning, she raised her phone to her ear. "Hello, Zac."

"Hi, Saffy. Are you okay?"

Wow, her brother hadn't called her *Saffy* since they were kids. "I'm fine."

"Can I speak to Ryan?"

"Ryan?"

"Yes, Safiya. I know he's with you."

"You do?"

"Before you go off the deep end, I'm investigating the death of William Dutch, Ryan's great-uncle, as a favor to Jarred Steele. I just spoke to him. He told me about your injury and that you were kayaking with Ryan, so please put him on."

She handed her phone to Ryan. "He wants to speak to you."

Ryan raised an eyebrow then rested the paddle across his thighs and lifted her phone to his ear. "What's up, Senior Inspector?"

Safiya couldn't hear her brother's words, but Ryan's eyes flared then narrowed as he stared toward the horizon. "Are you sure?" He listened again, swallowing then rubbed his forehead. "If that's true, where the hell is he?"

Safiya kept her gaze glued on Ryan's face. It was obvious something had happened. His eyes darted to the cliff then to the treasure hunter's yacht and back. His hands were shaking.

"I'm in Shark Bite Bay. There's a drone above us, so Jarred probably knows, but I may need back up. Five of the treasure hunters are at Morcago Ledge. Not sure where the sixth guy is, but after your bombshell, I have my suspicions. I'll board their yacht and see if I can discover anything useful."

"What's happened?" Safiya waved a hand in front of Ryan. "Is it about Bill?"

"Yes." He held up his free hand, silently asking her to wait. "I know you want Safiya kept safe. I will protect her. Can you ask Sergeant Hawthorne to authorize a door-to-door search and request he allow us to assist?"

Safiya held out her hand. "I want to speak to Zac."

Ryan nodded. "I'm handing you back to Safiya. Keep me informed." He passed her the phone than began paddling for the yacht.

"Me again, Zac. Don't think I'm leaving the island any time soon. I intend to help Ryan find out what happened to his great-uncle."

Her brother sighed. "I figured as much and I'm trusting Ryan to keep you safe for now, but Safiya, you're on an island where a string of violent incidents have taken place. I've requested Jarred Steele escort you to the ferry tomorrow. You will only get in the way and distract everyone if you stay on the island."

"No." Too livid to say another word, Safiya ended the call. Jarred might be scary and intimidating, but he couldn't make her leave. She really hoped her family hadn't broken their word and hired Jarred to spy on her. At least Ryan wasn't in on it. She twisted and met Ryan's intense gaze. "What's happened?"

"Jarred rang the coroner's office. Preliminary tests show the body in the boatshed is a young man, and with the lack of smoke in his lungs, the forensic physician believes he was dead before the fire started."

"It's not Bill?" Safiya's eyes welled. "Do they know how the man died?"

"There's damage to his skull, although that could be from falling debris or the explosion."

She worried her lower lip "We have to find Bill."

"I know." Ryan paddled strongly toward the yacht. "First we'll check he's not on board this yacht then I'll tear the island apart until I find him."

Safiya gulped. She really didn't want to get on that yacht. These treasure hunters could be behind this morning's shooting. Her heart pounded as they neared the yacht. She kept darting glances back at the cliff to see if anyone had noticed them. The two men climbing the cliff had made little progress but were nearing the halfway mark. The men beneath were heaving small boulders aside, as if searching for a hidden cave entrance. It seemed like wasted energy to Safiya. If there had been a cave entrance, it was hidden under tons of heavy rock, which must have sheared off the cliff and crashed into the sea a century or more ago.

Ryan paddled to the stern of the yacht, out of sight of the men. He stood, placed the paddle on the yacht's deck then hiked himself up. Watching him tie off the kayak, Safiya could only pray they weren't discovered.

He held out a hand. "Hold on to me then stand. I'll lift you up."

"Why?"

"I need you up here as my lookout." He opened the side railing.

Her legs shook as she took Ryan's hand then stood. She'd barely got her balance when he lifted her easily on to the back deck of the yacht. They both crouched, then Ryan signaled her to stay low and peep through the window facing the cliff. He ran through the saloon then disappeared down some steps.

Safiya did as he asked, rarely taking her gaze off the men. Ping and Pong were also keeping a low profile, popping up every now and then before diving deep. She was smiling at Pong's underwater antics when she saw two shapes below him. Two divers behind propeller machines. They had odd round objects attached to their backs. She jumped back, sealing herself to a panel of wall. Why were two divers underneath the yacht?

She risked a glance back at the cliff and frowned at the five men. Who was under the yacht? Alejandro and Sebastian had propeller machines, but what were they doing here?

She slid along the wall then ducked and crept inside. Staying low, she hurried down the steps to the sleeping quarters. The first berth had bunks, sleeping four. The one opposite had two single bunks. She found Ryan in the berth under the bow, rummaging through papers. It was crammed full of stuff, much like *Capricorn*, the brothers' yacht.

Ryan looked up. "Everything okay?"

"There are two divers under the yacht," she whispered. "I think it might be Alejandro and Sebastian, because they're using propeller machine things."

"Diving sea scooters. Did they see you?"

"I don't think so. They had strange round things on their backs. What would they be doing under this yacht?"

"Nothing good. Maybe trying to disable the propellors, or ... Shit, we need to get off this yacht, right now." He grabbed her good hand and almost dragged her up the steps.

"Why? What do you think they're doing?"

"After what happened to Bill's boatshed, I'm worried they're attaching limpet mines to the hull. If that's the case, we need to get the hell out of here."

He held the kayak steady then helped her carefully step in and sink into the front seat. Ryan passed her the paddle, then untied the rope, stepped into the kayak, and shut the gate rail. Once seated, Safiya handed him the paddle and they were off. Ryan cut through the water like an Olympian athlete going for gold.

"Why aren't you heading for the shore?"

"It's all rocks. Nowhere to land. We're heading for South Point. I could be wrong, but just in case, we need to get out of here. I don't want to get blown up or blamed for something I haven't done." He knocked his paddle against the side of the kayak in a rhythmic tattoo, before paddling hard again.

Within seconds Ping and Pong zoomed past.

She laughed. "You called them."

"Yes. It's an old game we used to play when I took my kayak out. I don't want these two anywhere near that yacht if she blows up."

"Did you find anything useful?"

"Not really. They've a huge map of the island and outer reefs. They could be holding Bill in one of their tents. Text Jarred to check them out now." He gave her Jarred's number, which she texted straight away.

"If the yacht's going to blow, we should warn Darius to get her drone away."

"Good idea. If those divers did plant Limpet mines, they'll allow time to get clear."

Safiya sent off another text then looked around. "Where's the divers' boat?"

"Probably entered the water round the headland then used the sea scooters to get here."

"They mustn't know about the sharks in this bay."

"They would have been told. There was a savage attack sixty years ago. Great whites attacked an injured whale and her calf. My great-grandfather wrote about it in his diary. There were so many sharks it was a feeding frenzy. No one has been allowed dive or swim here since."

"Great Whites." She swallowed, searching the water frantically.

"Relax, Saf. It would be one in a million chance for a great white to bother us. I know they sometimes attack surfers, but that's because the underside of surfboards reminds them of sea lions. If you stay out of the sea at dawn and dusk and steer clear of schools of fish, you should be fine. Those divers could have been wearing shark shield wrist bands. They omit an electrical current that confuses sharks, or so I've heard."

"Ping and Pong shouldn't be here." Safiya did another frantic search for Ryan's friends.

"They've gone. I told them to race me home."

"Thank goodness."

They'd just rounded the headland when an almighty boom blasted behind them. Safiya screamed then gasped as flames shot into the sky. "We never would have survived that."

"No. Text Darius again. See if she can fly the drone around and find those divers."

"Okay. I'm on it."

A minute later Safiya's phone pinged. She read the message aloud. *"Didn't get your message in time. My eagle must have been hit by debris. We are on our way."* Safiya sank back into her seat, relieved on one front, worried sick on another. "I hope Bill's okay."

"Wherever it is, he must be there against his will. Maybe he saw or heard something?"

Safiya's heart ached for Ryan. He sounded downcast. To discover Bill was his real father and his mother had died in childbirth, had to be tearing him apart. She didn't know what she could do to help him. Looking north, she blanched. Dark clouds were building in the distance. She'd heard Northern Queensland often got hit with fierce storms and cyclones. She really hoped this wasn't one of those times. Zoe had said big storms were part of life in the tropics, and it wasn't unusual to get a ten-minute downpour then the sun would come back out. Maybe that's all it would be.

They rounded the headland, and she noticed a tiny little cove. "How pretty."

"That's Coral Cove." Ryan tapped the side of the kayak again. They waited a minute or two then he tapped it again. "Come on guys, where are you?"

Safiya searched the water. "I hope they didn't go back to the yacht."

"I saw them heading this way. Their hearing is incredible. I'm just wondering if they're trying to convince someone to help us."

"Would they do that?"

"I think so. There's never been a need before, but they're incredibly intelligent creatures." He'd hardly finished speaking when a silver dolphin zoomed past then shot out of the water and dived again. Behind her, Safiya heard Ryan deeply exhale. "They're okay"

"Where's Pong?"

"Beside us, on your left."

Safiya glanced down and laughed. Pong's head bobbed about as if laughing at her. She reached out and patted him. "Hello, Pong. I'm so glad you're safe."

He barked then flipped over, splashing her again.

"Here comes the cavalry," called Ryan.

Looking ahead, Safiya felt her whole body relax. The *Francine* churned through the water toward them. It still had a way to go, but she could see several people out on the bow. Now that they were safe, she took the time to study the small cove. A golf cart with a green canopy had been parked above the beach. "Could that golf cart belong to the divers?"

"It's possible. I'll ask Sergeant Hawthorne if he knows who owns it."

Five minutes later the yacht's engines slowed, and it came alongside the kayak. Talos leaned out from the open gate in the rail and plucked Safiya out of the kayak as if she were as light as a cat. She winced as her stitches pulled a little, but was grateful to be out of the water, away from any roaming sharks.

"Thank you, Talos."

"My pleasure." He set her down on the deck then caught the rope Ryan threw across. Once Ryan and the kayak were on board, Zoe pushed the throttle and the yacht surged forward. When they didn't turn for home, Safiya walked over to Zoe to find out why.

Darius preempted her. "Jarred wants us to check for any floating debris that might show those guys are up to no good, and I want to find my drone. Did your brother reach you?"

"Yes. He told Ryan the body found was a young man. Bill wasn't on that yacht, but they could be keeping him somewhere else. Did you see anything from the drone?"

"Yes, the two divers leaving the yacht, but without my drone I don't know where they went. Simon hacked into the camera at Butlers Grocery store. He's got three possible suspects if you want to go below and check out the video."

"Definitely." Safiya hurried down the steps and found Simon and Madeline sitting side-by-side on a single bunk. "Can I see?"

"Sure." Simon patted the bed. "There are three cash registers. I've checked twenty minutes before your time zone to cover when our four suspects entered the shop. It only shows the backs of them, so I've cut straight to the time we're interested in. I can only identify two people."

"Okay." She leaned in closer and watched the screen as Simon brought up the video recording. She immediately recognized Sebastian and Alejandro Oliveira at one register. The person at the next register she recognized too. "That's Paul Kilgour." The third guy along wore a cap and kept his face down or turned away from the camera. Sebastian and Alejandro left the store. Paul Kilgour picked up a pack of sparkling water and followed. The other guy paid cash for several large packets of chips and two bottles of soft drink then left the store, keeping his face down.

"Play it again, slower." Safiya concentrated on the unknown man. She could make out fair hair reaching his collar, and a bandage on his right hand. "He could be the treasure hunter who punched a pole when Ryan ducked. Play it again." She spied a flash of white near the door. "Play it again, and this time watch the door. I caught a flash of someone standing there."

"No worries." He hit replay and they watched a slow rerun, which caught the bottom half of a woman in a white dress.

"Who is it?" asked Madeline.

"I don't know, but someone in town yesterday morning must have seen her. Simon, are there any cameras on the outside of the store?"

"No, but there's one out front of the ferry terminal." Simon's fingers raced over his keyboard, and he brought up another video stream. "I haven't had a chance to examine it yet."

They leaned close again as the audio played on a fast mode. Simon paused and slowed it every time a person or golf cart passed. "There," called Madeline. "It's her and a man walking across the road from the grocery store. Can you zoom in?"

"They're too far away. The pixels will be too distorted."

"I'll ask around," volunteered Madeline. "See if anyone remembers her."

The engines slowed.

"Let's go up top." Simon closed his laptop. "The more hands we have the better chance we might find something before it sinks."

CHAPTER TWENTY-TWO

It wasn't Bill. It wasn't Bill. The chant wouldn't leave Ryan's head. He'd prayed Frankie was right, but deep in his soul he'd been terrified that for once she had it wrong. Bill had to be somewhere on the island. It was a toss-up whether to punch the air in exhilaration or throw up as his gut churned with anxiety.

Had the firemen missed Bill under the rubble? He didn't think so, but once he'd seen the charred remains, Ryan had descended into a fog of bleak emptiness. If Bill's body had been there, the detectives would have discovered it. They'd bagged anything they thought important. They wouldn't miss a body.

He leaned over the yacht's rail, racking his brain for where Bill could be. His gut instinct told him, wherever it was, Bill had to be there against his will, if he wasn't dead. He needed to get to the camping ground and tear the place to pieces. If necessary, they'd continue with the house-to-house search. Checking abandoned or closed buildings as a priority.

The yacht rounded South Point headland. Ryan's gaze shot to Morcago Ledge. He spotted the five men in their dinghy, speeding toward the floating debris. He didn't want to waste precious time, but these idiots might know something. *Wherever you are Bill, I'll find you.* He sent up a prayer his father was alive.

From his position on the port side of the yacht, Ryan could see into the saloon-cockpit. His pulse quickened when Safiya emerged from below deck. She glanced around, her gaze searching until she found him. Her faltering smile cracked his heart. He'd misjudged her so badly. She was kind, thoughtful and sexy as hell. He needed to tell her Steele Security had been hired by her father to keep her safe, before she found out herself and jumped to the wrong conclusion. It would have to be later, when they were alone, after they found Bill. This wasn't the place or time, yet it had to be a priority. He didn't want to lose her.

"Hi, handsome." She smiled and sidled against him, protecting the arm across her chest. "You okay?"

"I'm hanging in there." He wrapped an arm around her waist, drawing in her light, flowery scent. "Tonight, we need to have a serious talk."

"Oh?" She tortured her lower lip. "You're not planning to dump me, are you?"

"No, but we can't talk now. I need to concentrate on finding Bill. Hopefully, later today we can find somewhere private and have a heart-to-heart chat."

"I'd like that."

"Good. We're coming up on the wreckage. Stay on board. There'll be dead fish from the explosion, which might draw sharks."

Safiya shivered. "I don't want you in the water."

He smiled. "I'll use the kayak. We may have to take those guys on board, so keep your distance. I don't trust them."

"Neither do I."

The yacht's motor cut off and with the aid of a boat hook, Talos pulled in anything floating, he could reach. Ryan took the kayak and paddled out further, picking up everything he could. The treasure hunters dinghy puttered to a stop near Ryan, the men looking stunned. None of them seemed to know what to do or say.

Talos waved them over to the back of the yacht. "Know anyone who would want to blow up your yacht?"

"Only this stupid idiot." A dark-haired guy with a bruised face pointed to his ginger-haired friend. "Andy must have left the fucking gas on."

"He turned the gas off, Kyle," yelled the guy with the bandaged hand. It was the fricken oil all over the engine. I told you we needed to get it serviced. Now we don't have a boat and all our stuff is gone."

"Shut your gob, Mitch. The engine wouldn't blow up without something igniting it."

"Enough," roared Talos. "It wasn't the gas or the engine. There were two divers under your boat. We saw them from a drone we were flying."

"Two divers?" The guy called Kyle glanced at his friends. "What the fuck?"

"Who are you lot?" asked the guy called Mitch, looking from Garcia to Simon to Talos.

"That's irrelevant," answered Talos. "You boys are in a shit load of trouble."

Ryan appreciated Talos not dobbing him and Safiya in. He paddled closer and addressed Kyle, as he seemed to be their leader. "You boys got any enemies?"

"Plenty, but not in these waters. Maybe the Oliveira brothers wanted us out of the way so they could have all the glory."

Ryan zeroed in on the guy with the bandaged hand. "Did you get that from punching the pole or breaking into Barnacle Bill's boatshed?"

"Hey, we had nothing to do with that," yelled Kyle.

"Why were you climbing Morcago Ledge?" called Safiya, hanging over the yacht's rail with Darius, Zoe, and Madeline.

The five men visibly straightened, their interest in the four attractive women obvious.

"We were talking to a young guy called Josh at the pub Friday night," volunteered the ginger-haired guy. "He told us about a cave some kids found in Shark Bite Bay years ago. Joey decided to hang around and ask Barnacle Bill. The rest of us went back to our camp site. Now Joey's missing. We can't find him anywhere."

Ryan's gaze shot to Safiya then back to the group of men. "I was one of those kids. The only thing inside that cave are bats. There is no treasure. Morcago Ledge and this bay are considered dangerous and off limits. I'm the guy you attempted to run down with your yacht, while drunk. That's attempted murder. You smashed a glass in the pub and could have hurt someone badly. That's assault with intent. You admit Joey hung around to talk to Bill before the boatshed blew up. Sergeant Hawthorne will want to talk to you. You'll be lucky if you're not charged."

"Hey, we didn't know about this bay being prohibited," called a fair-haired guy. "I'm Brad Yates, and I'm happy to leave. I just want to find my brother, Joey."

"Fair enough," called Ryan. He didn't want to cheese these guys off, or he might never find Bill. "The body found in the Boatshed isn't Barnacle Bill. If you know where he is, now would be a good time to come clean, before a task force of police descends on the island."

"We never touched the old man," called Kyle.

"Wait? Do the police think it's Joey?" asked Brad, his face ashen.

"They haven't identified the body. I suggest you talk to Sergeant Hawthorne as soon as we get back to Dugong Marina and file a missing person report."

Ryan looked at the bits and pieces floating among dead fish. "Pretty much all your things have been blown to smithereens."

"Our passports and clothes are back at the camp site," said Andy. "Not much use staying here without a yacht and our diving gear. I'm outta here on the next ferry."

"What the fuck," yelled Brad. "What about Joey?"

"He's your brother. You figure it out," shot back Kyle.

They'd drifted to the back of the yacht. Talos reached out and pulled them alongside. "Climb aboard. You won't be going anywhere until that body is identified and Bill is found. Did any of you break into the museum and assault the man who came to investigate?"

"No, we're not interested in museums," replied Kyle as he jumped onto the deck. The others followed then Talos tied off the dinghy.

"What about breaking into the big house on Dutchies Bluff," asked Garcia.

"It wasn't us," said Brad. "We haven't broken into anything. Can we get going. I need to know if Joey's…" He choked then looked down at the deck.

"We'll know what happened soon enough," called Darius. She held up a battered and torn sea eagle. The Island's council gave us permission to fly the drones, and I've been filming for days."

Ryan's lips twitched at her lie, but hey, if it got a confession, he was all for it.

The five men looked uncomfortable then Kyle shrugged. "Look we hung around the boatshed Friday night to talk to Barnacle Bill but got sick of waiting. Joey volunteered to stay, so we went back to the camping ground. That's the truth. We don't know where the old man is."

"Take a seat," called Talos. "We're heading back to Dugong Marina."

Ryan checked on his sister, relieved to see her smile at Garcia. The big man had been hovering near Zoe from the minute the five treasure hunters boarded the yacht. He stood beside the wheelhouse, arms crossed, staring coldly at them.

Ryan chuckled. "Where's your sling, Garcia?"

"Don't need it." Garcia's lips twitched. "Seals are a lot tougher than you SAS guys."

"In your dreams, mate." Talos gave Garcia a two-finger salute before leaning back against a side wall, never taking his gaze off the men either. They had to be feeling intimidated with two six-foot-five, irritated giants standing over them. The five men sat along the stern's bench seat, their heads bent, avoiding their silent guards. They were as quiet and solemn as the headstones in a graveyard, perhaps realizing the full impact of their situation. They'd be lucky to get off the island with only a warning never to come back. Sergeant Hawthorne could easily have them charged with reckless behavior, attempted murder, assault, and trespassing.

Ryan looked up at the darkening sky in the far north. They were in line for a big storm late tonight or tomorrow.

The trip back to the Marina didn't take long and Ryan wasn't surprised to see a crowd gathered as they motored in. Sergeant Hawthorne, Jarred and Sam were on the wharf waiting.

Pete Hawthorne took charge immediately, waving the five treasure hunters off the boat, then he and Garcia left, escorting the men to the police station for interviewing.

Jarred stood back, waiting until Ryan and Safiya joined him. "You two will need to give statements later. Don't leave anything out. Thanks to the drone we have you and those divers on video before the explosion, so *you* won't be implicated. On another front, Sam and I searched the tents and amenities. No sign of Bill."

Ryan moved closer. "One of the treasure hunter's is missing. Joey Yates. My gut tells me it's his body the firemen found, but where the hell is Bill?"

"Sergeant Hawthorne has been given approval for a door-to-door search, and Gibbs got permission for us to assist. We'll split up into pairs. A number of locals have offered to help and Darius is sending up another drone to watch for runners. She and Simon will be working out of the police station, coordinating everything. The army is sending out foot-soldiers by chopper to help with the search, but they can only spare two Blackhawks, so we need to work fast. A severe storm is predicted to hit late tonight, so the soldiers need to be back in Townsville before it arrives."

"Fair enough. Safiya and Madeline will want to help too."

"I'd prefer they stay with Frankie."

"They won't." Ryan strode beside Jarred toward their teammates and a large group of people.

Nick stepped forward. "You want to search anywhere in particular, Ryan?"

"An abandoned building and the cliff top. I know Darius can send up a drone, but the tree canopy is fairly thick. We need to get moving. It'll be dark in a couple of hours."

Safiya turned to him. "Go. Me and Madeline are heading over to Frankie's house."

Ryan met Jarred's raised eyebrow. If only everything were that easy. "Okay, keep your phone handy, Saf, and ring me if Bill turns up."

"Of course. Stay safe." She stretched up and kissed his cheek. "Don't take any risks. I don't want to lose you."

"That goes both ways, Safiya-Ameerah."

Her beautiful smile touched his heart. He could only hope the day ended well, and they could celebrate Bill's safe return around Aunty Frankie's table, then he'd take Safiya to the *Francine.* Tell her how he felt and with luck, spend an hour worshipping her body. They could sleep there the night. The incoming storm would allow them complete privacy. It would be a perfect ending to a horrendous day of revelations. He watched Safiya walk over to Madeline then they left the Marina. He sent up a silent prayer to any deity who might be listening. *Please help me find Bill alive. Please give Safiya and I the chance to find happiness.*

RYAN WIPED HIS FOREHEAD. He stank. Sweat soaked his T-shirt. He crawled out from under Phil and Shirl Thomas' house and brushed the spider webs off his cloths. He headed to the small garden shed and ducked his head inside. It was crammed with rusty garden tools, paint tins and several old lawn mowers. Nowhere to hide a fully grown man. Nick was in the roof cavity. They weren't leaving any space unchecked. With the help of locals and twenty-four army personnel, they'd searched every house, business, garden shed, back yard toilet, garage, abandoned building and church.

The screen door opened and Nick strode out and down the back steps. "Where to next?"

"It's a long shot, but I want to climb to Heron Point and scour the trail to Morcago Ledge then hotfoot it across to Kingfisher Lookout."

"Bill's an old guy, Ryan. I can't see him climbing to the lookouts."

"He might be in his early seventies, but he's fit. Come on. Do you know where the rest of the boys are?"

"Yeah. Sam sent a text a while ago. They've been over every beach and are now combing the golf course. The soldiers are checking the koala sanctuary before they return to Townsville.

"What about the marina?"

"Yeah, it was done earlier."

They jogged most of the way up the trail to Heron Point then, in a lather of sweat, set off for Morcago Ledge. By the long grass on top, no one had been there for years. Ryan's gut churned. They were running out of places to check. No boats were missing, so Bill hadn't been taken off the island or left of his own accord.

"Let's go. There's still Kingfisher lookout." He led the way, searching for any disturbances along the trail. His heart sank when they reached the lookout to find no trace of Bill there either.

Darkness had fallen when Ryan and Nick reached town again. They were bone tired and filthy. He didn't know what else he could do. There wasn't one building, boat or yard that hadn't been searched.

Safiya had been sending him texts throughout the afternoon. She and Madeline had joined forces with Frankie and several other women to feed the volunteers. They'd cooked biscuits and cakes in the pub's kitchen then served them with tea, coffee, or bottled water to the searchers. It was wonderful to see the whole community come together. Safiya had also texted that his parents and grandparents had got involved. Maybe the confrontation had done some good. During the search, quite a few older people apologized to Ryan for misjudging him and told him how proud they were of his achievements. It went a long way to healing his soul, yet he longed for good news about Bill. He'd now been missing for forty-eight hours. He could be lying in bushland, hurt, and dehydrated, maybe gagged, and tied up, unable to call for help. He was an elderly man and if they didn't find him soon, it might be too late.

"Come on, Bill. Where are you?"

CHAPTER TWENTY-THREE

Anxious and at a loss to know what to do, Safiya sat on Frankie's front porch. She'd spent several hours watching the purple storm clouds gather and now a heavy stillness hung in the air. The heavy tread of two people alerted her to their approach. The moment she noticed Ryan and Nick trudging toward the gate, she ran to meet them. Other than the streetlamp, it was pitch dark. They looked exhausted.

"Any news?"

Ryan shook his head. "The soldiers have returned to Townsville and a missing person alert has been issued on the mainland."

"At least that's something."

"I need to ring Ava, otherwise she'll worry." Nick clapped Ryan's shoulder twice then strode up the path and into the house.

Ryan gave Safiya a tired smile. "Thanks for all you did this afternoon. I appreciate you ladies helping to keep the searchers fed."

"It was no trouble. I'll run you a bath with Epsom Salts. It will ease your tired muscles."

"I just want a shower then I'll go back out. There must be somewhere we've overlooked."

"No, you won't." She grabbed his hand and towed him into the house. "I've saved you some cottage pie. Once you've eaten you are having a healing bath. Frankie says the storm will hit soon, so there's nothing else you can do tonight." She hassled him into the kitchen then retrieved his dinner from the warm oven. "Eat."

He sat at the small table and played with the pie, barely eating enough to feed a sparrow.

"You need to eat, Ryan."

"Tell Frankie I'm sorry, but my appetite's shot."

"I know this will come as a shock to you, Ryan, but I cooked the pie and I'll be very disappointed if you don't finish it."

"You're full of surprises, Saf." His lips thinned. "Makes me ashamed of that comment I made at the Gala."

"What comment?" She knew yet keeping his mind off Bill might get food in his stomach.

"When I asked if you knew how to cook."

"Oh, that comment." She pushed his plate closer, and sat beside him, pleased when he tucked in, knowing it was only to please her. "To make you feel even worse, I've completed on-line classes in cake decorating, seafood, Asian, Italian, French and Spanish cuisine. I love experimenting with different styles of cooking."

"Hell, what can't you do?"

Be free to live my life the way I want. Gain the admiration of my parents and brother. Find true love. She shook away the negative thoughts. Things were changing for the better. "I can't fly a Blackhawk helicopter."

He'd been watching her closely, probably picking up on her melancholy. When he reached out and cupped her cheek she sank against his side. "Neither can most people, Safiya, and very few speak eight languages. You're a remarkable woman."

"Thank you." She hugged him, then eased away as a door opened.

"You're back," called Jarred. "When you've got a minute, we're in the sunroom."

"No worries, boss." Ryan winked at her. "Thanks for the pie."

"Stay right where you are." She stood and placed her hands on her hips to glare at Jarred. "Ryan's hungry and exhausted. He needs to finish this pie then have a long, hot, soak in the bath. You have ten minutes."

"Good God, another interfering woman. That's all we need." Jarred's lips twitched, taking the sting out of his words. "Bring your pie to the sunroom, Major. It appears we're on the clock."

"Yes, Colonel." Ryan lifted his plate in one hand and stood, leaning over to kiss her lightly, before following his boss, his expression sobering.

Safiya pranced to the bathroom. She'd stood up to Jarred Steele and he'd indulged her. It was a sign of respect she hadn't expected. She knew he'd been a Special Forces Colonel, in charge of a squad of elite soldiers, and according to her brother, didn't take flake from anyone and always put his men first. He cared about Ryan.

She had the bath three-quarters full when the door opened and Ryan stepped inside, looking wearier. "Strip and get in this bathtub."

"Yes, ma'am." He gave her a lopsided grin then dragged his T-shirt over his head. He bent to untie his boots, but she beat him to it, using her right hand. Her left shoulder still ached and if she tried to lift it too high, the stitches pulled.

"Sit on the edge of the bath and let me help." She disposed of his boots and sweaty socks quickly. "Up."

He stood and she went for his pants button then zip. He turned away and shoved everything down, giving her a nice view of his butt as he stepped out of his clothes and into the bath. He sighed as he sank under the warm water. "Fuck, this feels good."

"Lean forward." Using the hand pump, she squirted liquid soap onto a washer then scrubbed his back and shoulders. "Lay back." She almost chuckled when he did exactly as she ordered, resting his neck on the towel she'd rolled up earlier. He closed his eyes and exhaled. She scrubbed both his arms and chest, then gently wiped his face.

"Keep your eyes shut. "She squeezed her own rose-scented shampoo onto his head and massaged it in deeply, taking extra time to really push her fingers into his scalp. "Tilt your head forward." She poured fresh warm water from Frankie's water jug over Ryan's head, until all traces of shampoo were gone. Using only one arm had its limitations, yet somehow, she got the job done.

"Lean right back." She scrubbed each of his legs, trying and failing to ignore his erection peeping through the bubbles. Obviously, even when exhausted, men could get excited by a woman's touch. She grabbed the nail brush and worked on his fingernails, hard to do one handed, but they needed scrubbing. When she sat back on her heels and glanced as this face, she was surprised to find him watching her, his eyes blazing with lust. Her own arousal soared to life, making her antsy. She had to remind herself he was exhausted.

"All done. I've got fresh clothes for you; in case you need to talk to your friends before bed."

"You missed a spot." He raised one eyebrow, daring her to take up his challenge. Well, she was game, even if it would leave her hot and horny. Soaping the washer again she bathed his testicles then paid special attention to his erection.

He groaned. "Is the *Francine* still in Dugong Marina?"

"Yes, why?"

"We're sleeping onboard tonight. I want to fall asleep with you in my arms. Go grab whatever you need while I shave... and make one quick phone call. I should be no more than ten minutes."

She couldn't help grinning. "Yes, sir." She ran to the kitchen, grabbed a zip-top shopping bag, and threw in some fruit. Having spent a few hours on the *Francine*, she knew the galley was stocked with tea, coffee, long-life milk, biscuits, and bottled water.

By the rumble of male voices in the sunroom, Ryan's team weren't done talking. Darius, Madeline, and Frankie had gone to bed ages ago. She tiptoed to the bedroom she was sharing with Madeline and Zoe then eased the door open. Madeline lay on the bed reading. Zoe was sound asleep on a camp bed under the window.

"I thought you'd be asleep," Safiya whispered so as not to wake Zoe.

"No." Madeline watched as Safiya threw underwear, shorts, a tank top, her hairbrush, and toiletries in the bag. She closed her book. "Looks like someone is in hurry to go somewhere."

"Ryan and I are sleeping on the *Francine* tonight. We'll be back in the morning."

"Really?" Madeline chuckled. "Half your luck. Enjoy."

"I will." Safiya slipped on her runners and a light jacket then tiptoed back to the kitchen. She didn't want Frankie waking and asking awkward questions. She was reaching for the sunroom door when it opened, and Ryan came through. "Ready?"

"Yes." He took the bag from her to add his own clothes and a toiletry bag, before zipping it closed. "Let's go. The boys know where to find us if there's news."

"Great." She wasn't going to think negative thoughts. Bill was alive, and they would find him tomorrow.

As they stepped off the porch a couple of raindrops hit Safiya's face. "It's started."

"Come on." Ryan hitched the bag on his shoulder, then grabbed her good hand. "It's only a couple of minutes to the Marina."

Jogging hurt Safiya's shoulder, so they had to power walk, which meant they weren't even halfway to the Marina when the heavens opened, saturating them in seconds. At least it gave them something to laugh about, and the insulated grocery bag kept their other clothes dry.

It was almost impossible to see through the sheeting rain as they climbed aboard the *Francine*. Thunder rumbled above and the occasional streak of lightening lit the deserted marina. It was a relief to get the hatch unlocked and retreat out of the drenching rain. Once below in the galley, she stood shivering like a wet dog, dripping all over the floor. "That was exciting. I'm guessing there isn't a clothes dryer on board?"

Ryan laughed. "No, but we don't need clothes tonight." He unzipped the shopping bag and grabbed his toiletry case. "And we have dry clothes for tomorrow."

She giggled. "Lucky. I don't think the locals are ready to see me naked."

"Your optimism is one of the things I love about you." He stilled, probably realizing he'd used the L word. When she continued to smile, he lifted her chin then captured her lips. Who was she to object?

Lost in sensation, she was barely aware of his tongue tracing the seam of her lips or moving her backward. She opened, allowing him to deepen their kiss. She loved the way he explored her mouth, tasting and nipping her lips, as his hands gently stroked her body. She loved how he took the time to tenderly caress her, before drawing her against his erection, driving her deeper and deeper under his seductive spell. Every place his fingers brushed, massaged, or caressed, came alive. She couldn't help but moan when he eased away.

"I'm not going far." He dropped to his knees and tugged her runners off, then unbuttoned her shorts, sliding them down her legs, along with her panties. Her whole body heated as his gaze lingered on her thatch of dark curls. When he raised a hand and traced his fingers through her soaking folds, she jerked, cried out then widened her stance, inviting him to explore further.

"You like that, Safiya-Ameerah?"

"God, yes. You know I do."

He stood and undid her sling. "Can you move your arm without your shoulder hurting?"

"Yes. It only hurts if I lift something or put pressure on it."

"Good." He pulled her thin straps off her shoulders then slid her tank top down her arms and body, until she could step out of it.

Her face warmed again at being completely naked in front of him.

"Hey, stop torturing that lip." He ran his thumb over her lower lip, easing it away from her teeth. "There is nothing to be anxious about."

"It's okay for you. You're more experienced than me. I feel awkward and exposed. It would help if you were naked too."

For a moment he stared into her eyes then he cupped her cheek. "This... thing between us is bigger than anything I've experienced, Safiya. With you, I'm constantly floundering. I've wanted you physically from the moment we met. When I discovered who you were, I fought my desire, especially after hearing all the crap Simon dug up. I apologize for how fast things have happened between us, but I don't regret a second of it. I want you more than I've ever wanted any woman." He kissed her lips then her nose and forehead. "Getting to know the real you, made me realize what a jerk I've been. If you want to slow things down, I'm okay with that. I want you in my life. I don't care who your parents are, or what your brother thinks of me. I'm not rich, but I do okay. I'm not interested in your father's money. He can cut you off without a dime for all I care. I want you for so many other reasons."

He chuckled. "Sorry about the verbal diarrhea, but honestly, I'm happy to hold you in my arms tonight, if that's all you want. We can slow things down until you're comfortable with deepening our sexual relationship. No pressure, I'm ready and willing whenever you are, Saf."

"Thank you." She stretched up and kissed him. "We have moved fast, however, it felt right. You feel right. I trust you, Ryan. I love that you were attracted to me when you thought me a waitress. I love that you couldn't resist me. I feel the same. Since meeting you in January, I've fried my brain trying to figure out how to accidentally run into you."

She pressed closer. "I've driven my brother and Madeline mad with questions about Steele Security, hoping to get snippets of infor- mation about you. I've watched you interact with your mates and the women in their lives, which impressed me. I've never been obsessed or curious about any man, until I met you. I don't need my father's money to be happy. I need you. I want you. I desire you."

She drew in a deep breath, terrified her next words might scare him away, but unable to stay quiet any longer. "Ryan, if you want to hold me and sleep, I'm perfectly fine with that. If you want to make love, I'm not going to argue, because … I love you." There, she'd said it.

His eyes flared, yet all she could detect was flagrant desire. "Come here."

She only had time for a quick breath before he devoured her mouth. The bed butted the back of her knees, forcing her to sit before she fell. He kicked off his runners then stripped off his T-shirt and shorts. She barely had time to squirm up the mattress before he parted her thighs and fell on her, lapping up her aroused juices with his tongue. It wasn't a gentle seduction, he meant to bring her to completion fast.

He hummed low in his throat. "You taste divine. I can't get enough of you." He teased her nub, suckling and circling then thrust two fingers inside her, until she was squirming and bucking against him. It was too much and not enough. He touched the center of her desire, relieving one pulsing need, while tormenting another. Pleasure pooled low in her stomach. Her breasts felt full and heavy. Sensation screamed through her body. Her legs shook then she cried out, stiffening as euphoria rushed blindly through her, causing her to clench the muscles around his fingers.

"You're so responsive, Saf." Ryan wiped his mouth on the back of his hand then grinned. "Can you balance on one hand, if I help support you? I want to take you from behind."

God, another first. She couldn't wait. "I think so." Twisting around, she rested her left hand, loosely on the bed, then pushed up to her knees with the right hand. She glanced over her shoulder to see Ryan rolling a condom on. He met her eyes and grinned. "Ready?"

"You bet."

He clamped a hand around her hip then rubbed the hard length of his erection along her wet folds. It was so sensual, raw desire engulfed her again. She pushed back against him.

"Easy, darlin'." He nudged into her an inch and held still. "You feel fantastic. So wet and tight." He pushed deeper and groaned. "I can't go slow, Saf. I want to take you hard and fast."

"I want that too."

He gripped both her hips firmly then surged inside her, retreated then thrust home hard, rocking into her faster and faster, his testicles slapping against her butt. Another climax began building deep inside. Ignoring the slight twinge in her shoulder, she fingered her clit, rubbing hard and fast as she pushed back, meeting his every thrust.

"That is so fucking erotic, Saf." He pushed her fingers aside and took over.

"Ryan." She arched and cried out, "I'm coming."

He thrust deep and came with a guttural roar. "Oh, yeah."

A moment passed as they both gasped for air before Ryan pulled out. He dragged back the covers and gently lowered her to the bed. "I'll be back in a sec."

She lay in a state of sensual bliss, too replete to move an inch as the storm raged outside, isolating them from the rest of the world.

The mattress sank, then Ryan lifted her in his arms, laying her down again so her head sank onto a pillow. He covered them then spooned in behind her, placing a featherlight kiss on her sore shoulder. "Thank you, Safiya-Ameerah. For everything you've done today and for taking care of me tonight. I desperately needed some tender loving care."

"Any time." She smiled, drifting off content and blissfully happy. She'd found what she'd been searching for. Love, trust, desire, friendship, and respect. The storm could rage away all night long, she was safe and exactly where she wanted to be.

It seemed she'd only closed her eyes when her phone pinged twice. Cracking one eye open, it surprised her to see daylight streaking between the curtains above. It took a moment to realize where she was and that the rain had stopped, and who was softly snoring behind her. Smiling, she eased out of bed, picked up her runners then tiptoed to the galley, intending to nip up to the Angler's Point Café for coffee and croissants. She used the bathroom then quickly dressed before reading the first text.

I found the guy. He's on BB trawler. I will keep eye on him til you get here. Josh.

"Wow." The trawler was further along the Marina. Why would anyone be on Bill's trawler? She needed to wake Ryan, but first she'd better check the other text.

My darling, Safiya, your father and I need to apologize for so much. Ryan Dutch phoned us last night. He thought it time we appreciate how special you are and stressed all the ways we've let you down over the years. I had no idea you speak eight languages. It took a stranger to make us aware of things we should have known. Please forgive us. You probably now know your brother hired Steele Security to keep you safe. What you might not know is your father offered Ryan Dutch a substantial amount of money to walk away. He refused the offer, darling.

Ryan had told her about being offered money. She read the crucial bit again. *You probably now know your brother hired Steele Security to keep you safe.*

Betrayed again.

Jarred Steele had sent Ryan to keep an eye on her. Could she believe anything he'd said? Safiya pushed her fist into her mouth and bit down hard to hold back her heartbreak and tears. She'd opened old wounds by telling Ryan her worst experiences. There had been plenty of opportunities for him to tell her the truth. Why hadn't he?

When she had herself under control, she looked back into the cabin to study his handsome face, relaxed in sleep. He'd been so loving last night. His caresses and kisses so exhilarating. His words heartfelt. He'd taken time to give her pleasure before taking his own.

It couldn't be an act. She loathed confrontations but walking away from Ryan without knowing the truth would eat at her for the rest of her life. The last thing she wanted was to hurl accusations and wrongly accuse him of betrayal. She mentally shook herself. Bill's life could be in danger. For once, she would not run away. She would stand tall and confront Ryan after they found Bill.

She slipped on her runners then shook Ryan's shoulder. "Wake up. We need to check Barnacle Bill's trawler."

Ryan rolled over and smiled. "Good morning, Safiya-Ameerah."

"Hurry. Josh sent a text. He said the man who stole Zoe's kayak is on Bill's fishing trawler. He might lead us to Bill. I'm going to follow him."

Ryan leaped out of bed. "Not without me. Text Jarred while I get dressed."

"I don't have his number. I'll text Madeline." While Ryan ducked into the bathroom, she quickly sent off a text, hoping the whole team didn't descend and scare off a potential lead. She couldn't risk the guy getting away, so she dashed up the steps and opened the rear door. Nothing stirred on the wharf. *Where's Josh?*

Ryan caught her hand. "Stay on the wharf and if things go south, run like hell."

"Okay." She had to jog to keep up with Ryan's long strides. She noticed an empty birth where the *Capricorn* was usually moored. She was positive it had been there last night. The trawler was at the very end mooring. There was no one on deck or in the wheelhouse.

Ryan stopped at the stern of the trawler. "Hello, anyone onboard?" When no answer came, he dropped her hand and climbed aboard, slowly edging along the port side to the wheelhouse. He disappeared inside.

Safiya screwed up her nose at the disgusting, fishy smell. No way could she work on a trawler. Shopping at the fish markets was bad enough. She walked back and forth, looking, and listening for any signs of trouble. What was taking Ryan so long? Had he found Bill?

A muffled clunk made her jump. Had Ryan fallen or been attacked? She sent another text off to Madeline. If things had gone south, someone needed to know where they were. She hoped whoever Josh had seen had left the trawler, but had Josh followed?

She sidled along the port side and stepped into the wheelhouse. A set of steps descended into a dark galley. "Ryan?"

A pained croak had her heart racing. She held on to the rail and descended slowly. The galley, dining area was rough and cluttered. Peeping around one side of the steps, she noticed two sets of bunks. She gasped. Bill lay very still on the bottom one. "Oh, my goodness!" She ran forward, stumbling to a stop when she noticed Josh huddled on the floor against the back wall.

"Josh?"

He made a muffled noise, shaking his head from side to side.

"What's wrong? Where's Ryan?" She swished the grubby curtain aside to let in light then gulped. Josh had been gagged and his hands tied behind his back. His nose looked broken, and one eye almost swollen shut.

"Uh-oh." She'd made a tactical mistake following Ryan.

A creak had her whirling, barely catching a glimpse of checkered shirt before excruciating pain exploded in her head as something hard slammed into her skull.

CHAPTER TWENTY-FOUR

The sudden whirring and clanking of the trawler's diesel engine sent a jolt of alarm through Ryan, but he had bigger things to worry about. He was locked in the trawler's dark hull. He'd found Bill, unconscious in the bunk. Josh had been beaten, and God only knew whether Safiya had gone for help or followed him on board. No matter what he'd hoped, he hadn't been expecting to find Bill on the trawler. Not after it had been searched yesterday.

"Fuck."

He should have guessed the man holding Bill would make sure the searchers didn't board the trawler. Paul Kilgour's word wouldn't be questioned. *The bastard would have slit Josh's throat if I hadn't handed over my phone and climbed down here.*

Safiya would get help, or the boys would figure something was wrong, but how long would it take? By the cold calculation in Joanne Kilgour's eyes, she'd be more than happy to put a bullet in each of their captives then feed them to the sharks. Not happening. The bitch had to be the woman in the white dress.

Ryan felt his way around the hull and engine, looking for something to use as a weapon. The highs and lows of the last few days raced through his mind. He had too much to live for to have a pair of treasure hunters destroy his and Safiya's chance of happiness.

The Epsom salt bath and Safiya's body scrub had taken care of his sore muscles and lifted his spirits last night. She was so much more than anyone realized. He could only thank his lucky stars he'd been given the chance to comprehend that for himself.

Stalling her, so he could call her father before they left Aunty Frankie's last night had been a gamble, which could have backfired. Thankfully, after the Sheikh's initial cool reception, he'd agreed to hear Ryan out. If they now saw Safiya in a positive light, he'd achieved what he'd set out to do. His only regret was he hadn't got to tell her he hadn't been aware Steele Security had been hired to keep an eye on her. He cringed, knowing it would devastate Safiya, especially after those callous jerks at Uni betrayed her. He had to get out of here and make her understand.

With the engine clanging and grinding so loudly, it was impossible to hear what was happening above. Where were they headed? Where was Safiya? A sickening dread seeped through his veins. His sixth sense kicked in, which he never ignored. Safiya was on board, he felt it in his bones. Breaking into a sweat, he climbed back up the ladder, stretching his hand out, feeling for an auxiliary light switch. He didn't have time to waste.

The boys would notice Bill's trawler missing from Dugong Marina and follow their instincts. They'd send up a drone and have a bird's eye view of the trawler. The Kilgours had to be after the treasure, but were they working alone? His fingers collided with a plastic box and a protruding switch.

"Yes." Light lit up the engine room. The toolbox he'd been looking for sat on a shelf under the ladder. His relief knew no end. He slid a metal file alongside his foot inside his runner then grabbed a couple of clamps to sabotage the diesel fuel line. He had to disable the trawler before they got too far from the island. As the engine coughed and spluttered, he used a chisel and hammer to dislodge one of the rusty hinges of the trap door. He had to trust his team would work out what had happened to get a rescue plan happening.

Ryan hesitated. The Kilgours might be willing to negotiate the release of their other hostages if he led them to the treasure. He'd do anything to save Bill and the Safiya, the woman he wanted to spend the rest of his life with. The thought should have shocked him, yet nothing had ever felt so right. But first he needed to get Bill and Josh medical attention.

A heavy dread descended, yet he'd been in worse situations, surrounded by unfriendly, radical militants, stranded in hostile territories, desperate for backup or retrieval. He'd lost one team-mate to a suicide bomber in Afghanistan and another to PTSD. Over the last six years there'd been many times where he feared for his life or the lives of his teammates, but this was different. If anything happened to Safiya, or Bill and Josh, he'd never forgive himself.

The engine died, leaving a heaviness in the air, partly from the heat it pushed out and partly from the rising humidity. He dropped the tools into the toolbox then flipped the light switch.

The bolt above Ryan shot back as he descended to the bottom of the ladder.

The hatch opened and a beam of light hit him. "Whatever you've done, you'd better fix it, or I'll throw the old man overboard." Kilgour bellowed.

"I'm willing to fix the engine if you hear me out. I have an offer that benefits us both."

"Oh yeah, and what's that?"

"Let the others go and I'll lead you to the treasure. I know exactly where it is."

"A likely bloody story. If you know where it is, why haven't you absconded with it?"

"I found it twelve years ago in Shark Bite Bay. The day before my friend fell to his death off Morcago Ledge. That's why I lost all interest in the treasure and left the island. There are … chests of gold and silver sovereigns, jewel encrusted sabers, challises, and … gemstones of every color, but we're going to need a stick or two of dynamite to get it out." Ryan's lies had grabbed Kilgour's attention. "The treasure is yours, if you agree to my terms."

Silence met his request then the hatch slammed shut. He could only pray the Kilgours were considering his deal. Several minutes passed then the hatch opened again.

"All right," called Kilgour. "Fix whatever you did to the engine then climb up here. Bill can stay onboard, but your girlfriend and the boy come with us. Don't try to be a hero. My wife will shoot to kill if provoked."

Shit, Safiya did followed me.

Ryan unclamped the hose then climbed the ladder. "You can start the engine again now."

Kilgour waved a handgun at him. "Turn around and put your hands behind your back."

Ryan complied, wincing as a zip-lock tie pinched his skin.

"Now, sit at the table and don't move," ordered Kilgour. He glanced at his wife, still blocking Ryan's view into the narrow berth. "Jo, send the boy up in ten minutes. I'll need him to watch for reefs and drop the anchor. Kilgour gave Ryan a pointed glare before leaving the galley

A bag of zip-lock ties lay on the table in front of Ryan. He waited until Kilgour climbed up to the wheelhouse then twisted so he could check out the bunk room.

Joanne Kilgour leaned against the door frame smirking. "One wrong move and your girlfriend dies. Remember that."

A WOMAN's voice woke Safiya. The throbbing in her head had to be the worst headache she'd ever experienced. She cracked her eyes, flinching as light from a porthole tried to pierce her brain. Soft sobbing caught her attention. She focused on Josh, huddled against a bottom bunk.

"Please let me go, Mrs. Kilgour. I promise I won't tell anyone."

"As if we'd believe that. You'd better hope Ryan Dutch holds up his end of the deal or a broken nose will be the least of your worries."

Safiya didn't dare move. So, the woman in the white dress must have been Joanne Kilgour, and the man in the checked shirt her husband, Paul.

One of them knocked me out.

Where was Ryan? What had Joanne meant by a deal? Unfortunately, the pounding in her head made it hard to concentrate. Bill and Josh needed medical attention. She needed to think logically. The floor under her vibrated with the pulsing of the engine. They were heading out into the ocean. That wasn't good. She hadn't caught a glimpse of the future she yearned for only to have it snatched away.

Thank God she'd sent Madeline those texts. Ryan's team did search and rescue missions all the time. Madeline would alert them straight away.

Over several glasses of wine Sunday night, Madeline had told Safiya about three missions she'd been privy to. Vietnam, Broome and on an island in the Lau Archipelago. It was mind boggling, scary stuff. This would be a piece of cake for a team of Special Force soldiers and a Navy Seal. It was only a matter of time before they arrived guns blazing. She prayed it happened before the Kilgours decided to throw their hostages overboard. Maybe Ryan had a plan that would save them.

She lay on a grimy floor in something sticky, surrounded by that disgusting fishy odor. She wanted to touch her head to feel if an egg had formed, but she didn't want to alert Joanne.

Glancing up, she flinched as the light coming in through a porthole drove sharp needles into her brain. Under the bunk in front of her, she could see life jackets, poles with steel hooks and a bunched-up fishing net. Maybe she could protect herself with one of those hooks. She gasped as a cramp spasmed in her foot. She rolled onto her back, groaning at the throbbing in her skull. She stretched out her foot. It eased the cramp.

"About time you joined the land of the living." Joanne Kilgour's Scottish accent gave Safiya a jolt. She'd hoped the woman had left the berth.

"What happened?" She needed to play the helpless victim and pray she got an opportunity to escape. Pushing herself to the back wall, she managed to at least squirm into a sitting position beside Josh. Something trickled down her face. Blood? That couldn't be good. Bill lay on the bottom bunk. She detected the tiniest rise and fall of his chest. He wasn't dead.

"What's going on?"

Joanne stood by the doorway, wearing a loose T-shirt, tights, and runners. She sneered at Safiya. "I think that's pretty obvious. Your nosiness has got you into trouble."

"Ryan?"

"I'm okay, Saf." His voice came from the galley. "The Kilgours have promised to let Bill and Josh go, if I lead them to the treasure."

"What about you and me?"

"*You* are coming along as collateral." Joanne's voice rose. She was almost salivating as she waved a handgun about.

Safiya hoped she'd achieved a look of surprise. "What treasure?"

"Your boyfriend didn't tell you?" The bitch cackled like a witch. "He found it years ago then left the island because his friend died. For three years we've been following leads, listening to rumors, searching the island and reefs."

"I don't know what you're talking about." Struggling to keep her balance as the trawler rocked from side to side, Safiya clasped Josh's arm. She'd always been a good sailor, but this rolling from side to side had her stomach churning. Wherever they were, it was choppy outside. "What's wrong with Bill?"

"The silly old fool tried to escape and ended up fighting Paul. We think he had a heart attack. Do anything stupid and Paul will toss him over the side."

"I'm not that brave," volunteered Safiya. "If you release Bill and Josh, I'm sure Ryan will do whatever you ask." She wouldn't give any such vow.

"I will," growled Ryan.

Joanne waved a tatty book at Safiya. "This is Barnacle Bill's great-grandfather's diary. It makes interesting reading. He mentions a history of wrecks in the reefs between this island and the coast of Australia. There is a passage about European men rumored to have been stranded here in the late 1600's, after a storm blew their galleon into to rocks on Currawong Island. Now we know it was in Shark Bite Bay." She hurled the diary onto the bunk with Bill.

Safiya grimaced. There'd be no reasoning with this horrible woman. She had no alternative but to encourage Joanne's greed and pray for a chance to escape. "I do remember Ryan telling me he found a cave system as a teenager with drawings on the walls."

"Hidden caves. No wonder the treasure wasn't discovered." Joanne gave a hollow laugh. "We may need to use a little dynamite to get it out. Make it look like a rock fall, which will encourage the council to keep people away from Shark Bite Bay."

"You blew up *Winner takes All*, didn't you?"

"I thought you saw us." Joanne shrugged. "After hearing those obnoxious idiots were concentrating on Shark Bite Bay, we decided it was time to do away with our competition."

"Were you responsible for the assault on Phil Thomas and the break-ins?"

"That was a complete waste of time. We've been biding our time for the last three years. Checking all the reefs, talking to old timers, earning their trust, blending into the community until it was nauseating. We'd heard about the diary but thought it would be in the museum. Took a while to track it down, along with a gold sovereign and a Spanish saber, which I have safe at home. We were still no closer to finding the treasure so decided to have a talk with Bill. We found him drunk and remorseful for ruining his relationship with his son."

Safiya cringed. This malicious woman wouldn't admit anything unless she intended killing them all. "You blew up the boatshed. A person died."

"One of those party boys, treasure hunters." Joanne shrugged. "He tried to stop us taking Bill out of the boatshed, so Paul hit him with a steel bar."

Ryan swore. "You left Joey Yates to die?"

"He was already dead. We set off the dynamite so people would think Bill blew himself up. Dramatic but effective, and it worked.

My God, this woman is pure evil. The fact she divulged her husband had kill Joey didn't bode well, but Safiya couldn't fall to pieces. If Ryan could stay calm when he must be consumed by rage, she would too. If this woman believed her a spoilt, naïve airhead, it might save their lives.

"You're welcome to any old relics. We won't say a word to anyone. Pinky promise."

Joanne blinked several times as if stunned then smirked. "If your boyfriend comes through, you'll eventually be found." She glanced at Bill, who hadn't moved. "It's not our fault he had a heart attack."

Narcissistic cow. Safiya had one last card to play. It was a long shot – an awfully long shot – but might be enough to scare these evil people into upholding their end of the bargain. "I'm glad we have a deal. If anything were to happen to me and Ryan, there are people who would hunt you down and it wouldn't be pretty."

"Really. Why don't you tell me what's so special about you two, Fia?"

"My real name is Safiya-Ameerah Farid. My father is Sheikh Tariq Farid. He's on his way to this island right now with his own security force. Then there's my brother. He's a senior inspector in the Australian Federal Police. Ryan belongs to a team of ex-Special Force Soldiers, who arrived on the island in that Blackhawk."

Joanne's hard eyes narrowed. "I don't believe you."

"It's the truth. Hurt us and I promise you will regret it."

Joanne kicked out so fast, Safiya didn't have a chance to avoid the impact. She screamed as agony exploded in her injured shoulder. Safiya curled in a ball, trying to breathe through the pain.

"Touch her again, and I swear I'll strangle you with my bare hands." Ryan's lethal words had Joanne whirling around. "Be careful, Mr. Dutch, or I'll lock Bill and Joshua down here and blow a hole large enough to sink this trawler. They'll drown and the sharks will gobble them up. No one will ever know."

So that was their plan. Black dots blotted Safiya's vision.

"Stand up, Joshua." Joanne waved her gun at the terrified teenager. "We're going up on deck. Behave or you'll end up in the fish hold.

Josh whimpered as he struggled to his feet then edged through the doorway, cowering, as if expecting a clout any second. As he climbed the steps to the wheelhouse, each thud of his feet echoed his despair. The resounding clunk of the hatch shutting and then a bolt sliding across, sent chills down Safiya's spine.

"I'm sorry, Ryan. I was hoping intimidation might work."

"Have a little faith, sweetheart." He stepped into the berth; his hands secured behind his back. I'll get us out of this. I'm counting on Bill to do more than lie there like a corpse though."

A gruff chuckle came from the bottom bunk. "Hoped you saw my finger twitching."

"Bill!" Safiya tried to stand, gasping as pain shot through her shoulder and more black dots clouded her vision. It was easier to stay where she was. A trickle of blood ran down her arm. Everything hurt. "You scared the life out of me. I thought you were unconscious. Joanne said you had a heart attack?"

"Not a heart attack. After the fatty, fried meal that woman served me, I had an Angina attack. Let me tell you, it damn well felt like a heart attack. I used to be a sergeant in the army. Been in some sticky situations over the years, but never expected to croak it that way. When I realized they thought I was on my way out, I played along."

He sat up, throwing his legs over the side of the bunk. "Hardest thing I've ever done, lying still while they bashed young Josh and you. But, after hearing their plans, I knew the only way to help was to stay quiet. My right wrist is broken, but I can walk and swim one armed if necessary." He picked up the discarded diary. It's good to have my diary back."

"We'll get your saber too, Bill." Ryan grinned. "I know you're my father. When I thought you'd died, my biggest regret was I hadn't told you how much I love you. I don't blame you for anything, Bill. Without you I would have gone off the rocks."

A tear ran down Bill's weathered cheek. "I've wanted to tell you for years but didn't have the nerve. Your mother was a hotshot pilot."

"You can tell me all about her later. I'll need you to fake your deathbed act a little longer and once we leave the trawler, call for help, if they leave the radio in working order."

"Paul smashed the wheelhouse radio the night he dragged me onboard." Bill winked at Safiya. "I've got an old backup radio stashed under this bunk and a life jacket. Where do you think Ryan got his intelligence? It wasn't just from his mother."

She grinned, her soul filling with gratitude and hope. "Don't take any risks. It's important you get off this trawler. I think they plan to sink it."

"Aye, they do. I wasn't looking forward to joining Davey Jones. Do you want me to cut you free, son?"

"Yes, but you need to put another one on, only make it looser. There's a bunch on the table." Ryan grimaced. "I have a file in my boot you can use."

Safiya gasped. "You can't climb that cliff, especially with your hands tied."

"Not with my hands tied. The other treasure hunters left their ropes and anchors. I'll use them. I'm going to need to blow a wider hole in the bat cave. With luck the explosion will alert the boys to our location, although, I'd be surprised if they aren't already monitoring the trawler."

The pounding in Safiya's shoulder made her nauseous and light-headed, but this was her chance to show Ryan her inner strength. He obviously had a plan, which she had to trust would work.

As Bill retrieved the file from Ryan's boot, she caught sight of the right side of his face and winced at his swollen right eye and cut lip. "They hurt you?"

"Paul got a few swings in, but let me tell you, so did I. I'm quite sure I cracked one of his ribs." He sliced through the plastic tie and slid the file back into Ryan's boot. How's your head?"

"Sore, but I'm more worried about my shoulder. There's some-thing wrong with it." She pressed against the wall so the sudden rocking motion of the trawler wouldn't send her toppling onto her damaged shoulder.

Ryan cursed. "It looks dislocated, and your head wound needs stitching."

"Terrific. My pain tolerance is at an all-time low." Her attempt at levity was ignored.

He dropped to his knees and kissed her forehead. "I'll do everything in my power to get us out of this, sweetheart."

"I know you will, Ryan. I wonder how they plan to sink the trawler?"

"Homemade bomb." Bill huffed. "They've stashed it in one of the fish holds and plan to set it off remotely."

"Fuck." Ryan blew out a breath. "They won't do it until I've led them to the treasure, which means you've got to get off the second we're out of sight. I'll fix Safiya's shoulder then you'll need to secure my hands again before that bitch comes back."

"Righto, son." Bill pulled out his leather wallet. "It won't be so bad if you bite down on this, luv, and try not to scream. I'm going to stick this diary in a couple of zip lock bags, so it doesn't get wet."

Inner strength. She nodded. "Do it, Ryan."

"Sorry, sweetheart, but this is going to hurt like hell. Sit up straight and lean against the wall. I'm going to pull your arm forward. With luck it will guide the ball of your arm bone back into the shoulder socket. Try not to fight me."

"Okay." She clenched her teeth around the wallet and thought about the beautiful babies she'd have with Ryan, if he hadn't betrayed her. She'd almost forgotten that soul destroying piece of news.

She moaned, biting hard as Ryan lifted her arm. *Too much pain.*

She regained consciousness to find a cold washer over her forehead and her shoulder on fire. "That's the most horrific pain I've ever experienced."

"You should have that arm in a sling, but if we strap it to your chest, you should be okay." Ryan moved about the galley quickly then came back with an emergency first aid kit. "They'll think you did this yourself, so we can't let it look too professional." He pulled out a narrow length of sponge. "The trick is to keep your arm and shoulder from moving."

"Okay, I'll try."

He tied one end around her wrist then pressed her hand to her chest and ran the length around her neck and back to her wrist, pinning it with a safety pin. "That will do for now."

"Thank you. What about Bill's wrist?"

"On it." Ryan made a similar sling then pushed it inside Bill's shirt. "Once we leave the trawler put that on and get out of here. Do you still have that inflatable dinghy in the equipment locker?"

"Yes, son. Don't fret, I'll get on the dinghy." He smiled at Safiya. "I have a confession to make, luv. Back in February, Ryan told me about an amazing girl he'd met on an island off Fiji. She had a beautiful smile and stunning dark eyes. Then in April, Nick Flanagan sent me photos from his wedding. Among them was one of you with Ryan. He'd written your name on the back. Ever since, I've been holding my tongue, hoping for Ryan's sake it all worked out."

Ryan smiled at Safiya. "She's one in a million, Bill."

Safiya heart rejoiced, and she returned his smile. "You have no idea how good that makes me feel."

He winked at her. "It's the truth. I only wish I'd discovered it months ago."

Safiya's spirits rose even higher. "Better late than never."

A loud clanging had Ryan dashing to a porthole. Safiya staggered to her feet, holding onto the bunk for balance then followed him into the galley. When she looked out a porthole, she yelped. "Ryan, look how close we are to those rocks."

"Yeah. They just dropped the anchor, but it won't hold once the tide is fully in."

She leaned into the grimy porthole and peered up at Morcago Ledge. It rose into the sky like an intimidating sentry. She could just make out a vertical crevice. No one could survive a fall from that high.

The ocean pounded against jagged, slippery looking rocks at its base. She jerked back as a small crane swung a metal tender out over the side. Josh sat on the middle bench, clinging to the side. Joanne sat behind him hanging on tightly. "They're launching a boat."

"Quick, Bill, tie my hands again then lie down exactly as you were before and don't move. Saf, slide onto the bench seat and shuffle along." Once Bill was lying on the bunk, Ryan slid in beside Safiya, just as the hatch above the steps opened.

Paul Kilgour stood at the top, holding a rifle to his chest. "Let's go."

Following Ryan up the steps and leaving Bill behind didn't sit well with Safiya, but it was the only way to save him. She prayed he'd be alright and get away safely. That the Kilgours wouldn't kill anyone else. She needed to tell her parents she loved them. Her dream of a happy ever after with Ryan was so close. If he genuinely loved her, she'd forgive him for not admitting he'd been sent to keep an eye on her.

As they passed through the wheelhouse, she caught sight of a tangled bunch of cut wiring. The Kilgours weren't taking any chances.

CHAPTER TWENTY-FIVE

Reaching the rocks and getting out safely would be a mission. Ryan could barely keep his balance. Feet spread, he relied on Safiya and Josh either side of him to stay upright. If they tipped over, he and Josh were done for and Safiya wouldn't have a hope against the rocks. He and Safiya wouldn't have made it onto the tender if Kilgour hadn't cut his zip tie. Unfortunately, he'd had another ready the minute they were on board.

He looked back at the Kilgours. "You need to release our hands. There's no way Josh or I can get out otherwise, and Safiya will need help."

"All right, but don't try anything stupid." Paul leaned forward and sliced through the tie, nicking Ryan's wrist.

Ryan immediately wrapped his arms around Safiya and lifted her across his lap. He slid sideways and put her between him and Josh then with one arm around her waist, gripped the side of the boat and yelled back at Kilgour. "You need to make for that narrow channel. It's going to be tight, and we'll hit rocks, but I'll jump out and try to keep the boat steady."

Kilgour nodded. He'd gone green around the gills.

Ryan coiled the bow line. "Josh, hold on to Safiya for me."

"Okay." The kid looked petrified.

The next minute had to be the longest of Ryan's life as they rose and fell with the waves. Kilgour fought to keep the tender aimed at the narrow opening. When they finally made it through the gap, the impact sent the others sprawling across the bottom of the boat. Ryan leaped out, found his footing then hauled on the rope. His arm muscles strained to keep the tender from being dragged back with the current. "Everyone out. Now!"

The Kilgours scrambled over Josh and Safiya, keen to save their own skins without a damn for anyone else. Josh helped steady Safiya, keeping hold of her hand as he jumped onto a ledge then pulled her across.

She landed awkwardly and stumbled.

Ryan released the rope to catch her. "Gotcha, darlin'."

"The boat!" Joanne Kilgour glared at Ryan. "You idiot."

"Safiya's safety is more important to me than your fucking tender."

"Forget the boat, Jo. It's not important." Paul Kilgour pinned Ryan with his cold eyes. "Where's the treasure?"

"Up there." Ryan pointed to the crevice, invisible from this angle. "It's a small cave and the only way in is to squeeze through a narrow gap. I slid through when I was sixteen. I won't fit now, but Joshua will. There are drawings on the cave walls showing a cave entrance right there." He pointed to the huge pile of boulders at the foot of the cliff.

"I can get Joshua up there and if he has a phone and flashlight, he can film the drawings, to prove I'm not lying to you. If he runs, he'll get lost in a maze of volcanic tunnels. I can lead you to the main cave, where the treasure is."

Kilgour scratched his chin. "I've got enough dynamite to blow the boulders clear."

"Not a good idea. The cliff face is covered in cracks. A big explosion at the base will collapse more of the cliff and block the tunnels and maybe the large cave. It would be heard all over the island. I'd like to place a small amount of dynamite in the crevice up there, just enough to open it up, so we can lower the treasure."

"Are the tunnels big enough to carry the treasure through?"

"They were, but I don't know if there's been any rock falls inside during the last twelve years. I'd have to have a look. If they're clear, we'll need strong bags to shift the treasure."

Kilgour's gaze flicked to the trawler then up to the cave and back to Ryan. "I agree to send Joshua into the cave to film the drawings, then I'll decide what we do. Don't get any ideas. Remember, I can blow Bill up with the press of a button."

"I'm not likely to forget." Ryan waved Josh over and checked his runners, relieved they were sturdy. "You ever abseiled before, Josh?"

"No, but I'm not scared of heights."

"Good to know." The poor kid had pissed his pants and would probably need therapy.

Ryan helped him into a harness left there by the other treasure hunters and tightened it. He attached carabiners and Belay plates and made a Prusik loop, attached that to the carabiner at the top of Josh's right thigh, which hopefully would save the kid from falling. Taking his time, he adjusted a harness for himself, passing a loop of rope through his own Belay plate then locked the loop through his central carabiner.

"I'll give you a quick lesson, Josh, then take you up. There's nothing to it, as long as you keep your head and don't panic."

"Okay." Josh stood still as Ryan showed him how to set his feet wide, lean back and place his feet carefully. "Don't let go of the Prusik unless it's to feed rope through the Belay plate." Ryan spent a little extra time showing Josh how to grip the Prusik to stop himself falling. Satisfied they could make it to the cave he turned to Paul, who had been silently watching. Unfortunately, he hadn't set the rifle down. Every now and then Ryan caught him texting and wondered who he was in contact with.

"Right, we're ready. We'll need a cell phone to film and a flashlight."

"Use the boy's phone," snapped Kilgour throwing it at Ryan. "I've taken the sim out, so you can't call anyone."

"Fair enough." Ryan scanned the treacherous rocks, searching for an easy way in and out of the water as he waited on Kilgour to scrummage through a duffle bag at his feet, keeping the rifle aimed at Ryan's stomach. He was too close to miss and a gut wound was the last thing Ryan needed.

Kilgour laid the phone and a flashlight on a flat rock then stepped back. "Pick them up, Joshua, and don't drop them."

The kid was scared witless and as white as a ghost as he picked up the items and returned to Ryan's side.

"Double cross us, Mr. Dutch, and we blow up the trawler and kill your girlfriend," promised Paul Kilgour.

Ryan stayed silent. He had to figure out a way to alert his mates, so they could get Bill to safety and rescue Safiya and Josh. He stared down Kilgour as fury surged through his veins. The minute he got the slightest opportunity, he'd beat the bastard to a pulp. "I'll fulfil my part of the deal as long as you don't hurt Safiya in any way." He turned to Josh. "Nice and easy, mate. I'll be right beside you. Let me carry those for you."

"Thanks." Josh handed over the phone and flashlight then did as Ryan had shown him and carefully climbed the cliff.

Halfway up, Ryan tapped Josh's arm. "The cave is full of bats, so once you're inside crouch down. Keep the flashlight's beam low until you get to the far wall then raise it slowly. Film the drawings then give me the phone. You're not descending with me. I want you to take the flashlight and go deeper into the cave system. Follow what looks like the biggest tunnel. It will take you to a huge cave where I want you to hide. If you hear us approaching, go dark. If anything happens to me, my friends will get you out. We're ex-Special Force soldiers, and they're close by with sniper rifles." At least he hoped they were. "You will be rescued, Josh."

"I'll never forget this, Ryan. Thank you."

"No thanks needed, mate."

Climbing the last few feet, Ryan clung to the edge of the bat cave's crevice and peered down on Shark Bite Bay. Bill's trawler rose and fell on the dark ocean swells, far too close to the rocks. The drop wasn't as terrifying as he remembered, but he'd only been sixteen. Since joining the army, he'd done tougher descents in much worse conditions.

Ryan eased to his right. "The opening is right here."

Josh climbed into the crevice. "Is there really a treasure?"

"I guess we'll find out." Ryan unclipped the carabiners then handed Josh the flashlight and cell phone. Be careful. I'll wait right here."

"The Kilgours are crazy, Ryan. How are you going to get away?"

"By using years of training and taking them by surprised." Ryan looked down at Kilgour far below. The snake had moved out from the cliff to stand by his wife. Safiya now had two guns trained on her.

I will rescue you, Safiya-Ameerah. I swear I will if it's the last thing I do.

Ryan leaned closer to the crevice and peered inside. He could see a beam of light at the back of the cave then it wavered and went out. A moment later Josh held out the cell. "Those drawings are cool, but that disgusting smell makes me gag."

"Yeah, I know. Okay, go hide somewhere safe and watch your step. I'm proud of you, mate. You're a brave guy. Working on the trawler gave you the strength to pull your body up here. You'd make a great soldier."

Josh nodded and backed away.

The squawk of a circling eagle drew Ryan's attention to the mechanical bird high above. Its presence eased his mind. With the live feed, his team could view everything as it happened. The recording would put the Kilgours away for a long time. He moved back from the crevice and began to descend.

Kilgour yelled something that was lost on the breeze and crashing waves. No doubt wanting to know why Josh wasn't coming down. He cringed when Kilgour raised his rifle, but no shot rang out. He couldn't risk killing his meal ticket. Phase one of the plan had worked. The rest would be tougher to achieve.

With a final jump to a level rock shelf, Ryan faced Kilgour. "The kid panicked and ran off into the caves with the flashlight. Not much we can do about it. Here check out the drawings."

"We'll find him later."

While the Kilgours watched the video in fascination, Ryan checked out the trawler. Bill gave a salute from the wheelhouse then ducked down.

Kilgour's eyes were almost dancing with delight. "What's your plan?" He stared up the cliff face.

"Give me another flashlight and half a stick of dynamite and I'll blow the crevice wider. We go in, get the treasure then get out. If anyone hears the rumble, they'll think it's a rock fall."

"Half a stick?" Kilgour looked dubious.

"Half a stick will blow a tree out of the ground. With the cracks up there, I'm certain it will be enough." Ryan intended to scare the bats down into the tunnels before he set the blast.

"I agree, but you double-cross me, and Joanne will blow up the trawler and Bill." Kilgour fished around in the backpack then pulled out a switchblade and stick of dynamite. He cut it in half then stuck a long fuse in and wound the excess around it, before handing it and a flashlight to Ryan.

"Do it quickly so we can get up there."

"That's my plan." It rattled Ryan to know Joanne had the detonator remote. He stuffed the dynamite down the back of his shorts then clipped the flashlight to one of his carabiners. It was a much faster climb without Josh. After yelling into the crevice several times and hearing no response, he shone the flashlight erratically over the cave walls. Instantly the rapid flutter of hundreds of wings reached him. Satisfied the bats had taken cover deep inside the cave system, he unraveled the fuse then wedged the dynamite in a tight gap, low in the crevice, hoping the blast wouldn't damage the drawings.

As Ryan reached the base of the cliff, he met Kilgour's excited eyes. "It's done. You can light the fuse. I'm going to pull this rope to the right, so the explosion doesn't destroy it."

"Yeah, yeah, get on with it." Kilgour lit the fuse then scrambled over boulders to his wife and Safiya at the rock ledge near the crashing waves. They were lucky the tide wasn't fully in, or they'd have been swept off the rocks. He'd like to see the Kilgours swept away.

Ryan shook his head in disgust and pulled the rope as far right as he could then held it down with a heavy rock and stepped out of falling rock range.

Twenty seconds later the boom shook the ground under Ryan's feet. He breathed a sigh of relief when the dust and smoke cleared enough to see a hole big enough to crawl inside the cave. Part two of the plan had succeeded.

Kilgour emptied out his duffle bag handing Ryan two compact little pillows. "They're backpacks. Fill them with the treasure then wear one on your chest and one on your back. I've got more we can carry in our hands."

"We've lost the tender," stated Safiya. "How do you plan to get back to the trawler?"

"We're not going back to town in the trawler. I've made alternative arrangements." Kilgour pointed his rifle at Ryan. "Get moving. We haven't got all day."

"Safiya can't climb as your wife dislocated her shoulder, and it'll take a while to reach the main cave. She's better off staying here."

"I don't care how you get her up there, but she's coming with us." Kilgour pulled out his cell and began texting, a sly smile plastered across his face.

Ryan glanced out at the empty ocean. Did Kilgour have a backup boat coming? Darius' eagle glided high above them on an updraft. Hoping he could get Safiya safely up to the cave and pull off the next part of his plan, Ryan removed his harness and fashioned another one from the ropes left by the cliff. Once he had the carabiners and Belay plates attached, he helped Safiya into the real harness, clipping her securely to his harness, her back to his chest. It would be slow going, but the anchor points would hold them. The Kilgours could just use ropes for all he cared.

The climb physically exhausted Ryan. By the time they reached the crevice every muscle in his body screamed for relief. It was as if a band of ninjas had used him for knife practice. Safiya had helped as much as she could by placing her feet, good hand, and fingers exactly where he told her, taking her own weight, and giving him a breather then clinging to the belay rope as he half carried, half hoisted her up the cliff face.

As they crawled inside the cave, the atrocious smell took him back to the day he and Zane discovered the drawings. He gagged, his nasal cavities burning from the pungent odor.

"Oh my God." Safiya gagged then pinched her nose, burying her face against his chest. "This can't be healthy to breathe into our lungs."

Kilgour crawled in behind them. "Both of you, back against the wall and stay there until Joanne gets up here." He undid his rope harness and dropped it to his wife.

"Aren't you afraid she'll fall," asked Safiya.

"No. We've been climbing for years." He slipped off his backpack and pulled out another flashlight then ran the beam over the drawings. "Amazing. Looks like a cave entrance was at the bottom of the cliff. It would have made a perfect place to hide treasure after a shipwreck."

Ryan didn't bother replying. He thanked his lucky stars he'd used one of Darius' small drones to explore the cave system or he would have been shitting himself.

Ten minutes later, Joanne Kilgour crawled into the cave and gagged. "Is something dead in here?"

"It's bat excrement." Ryan pointed to the back of the cave. "We go this way." He gripped Safiya's hand, keeping her close behind him as he shone the flashlight ahead and stepped into the tunnel he'd found twelve years ago.

Thirty minutes later, after taking several wrong turns that terminated in dead ends or crevices too small to crawl through, Ryan led the way into a large grotto with a pool of water in the center. It looked deep. He found the original entrance easily as it framed a mountain of boulders blocking any way in or out. Shining the flashlight's beam over the entire cave, the adventurer in him crowed. This grotto would have made an amazing secret base all those years ago. Zane and Tommy would have loved it. By the damp tidal marks on the walls, the water level rose significantly at high tide, which meant it had a way of getting in and out. There was no sign of Josh, but he could see fresh shoeprints in the dirt. The kid was hiding somewhere on the far side of the cave. He quickly scuffed over the prints.

The Kilgours shone their flashlights all over the cave, seeking the treasure. If it existed, he supposed it could have been dropped in the water or hidden under any of the overhanging ledges around its perimeter, or the hundreds of crevices he'd passed on the way down. It would take weeks to explore the cave system properly. At least low tide meant he could get a better look at the base of the cave.

An idea struck. He prayed he could pull it off. "The treasure was under one of these ledges. We were going to come back and drop it in this deep pool until we were old enough to claim it. My friend Zane might have done that before he fell to his death."

"Let's hope he didn't, or you'll be doing a lot of diving, Mr. Dutch," promised Joanne. "Start looking over that side." She spun away and bent to shine her flashlight in under rock ledges. Her husband made his way to the back of the cave, keeping his rifle trained on Ryan and Safiya.

Once they were on the far side of the pool, Safiya squeezed Ryan's hand and whispered. "Please tell me you have a plan?"

"I'm working it out as we go. Have faith, it's one of the things I do best."

"It's here! Jo, I've found it!" called Kilgour. "I can't believe it. There really are gold and silver sovereigns and jewels, Jo, come see."

"I am. I am." She ran over the rock floor as sure-footed as a mountain goat. "Glory be! We're rich. Even split four ways, we're rich."

Four ways? Ryan gripped Safiya's hand tighter and pulled her back into a dark recess, extinguishing his flashlight. "They have partners, Saf. That's why they weren't too worried about losing the tender. They have no need of us now, so we're going to hide. Stay close."

They'd only taken a couple of steps when another voice echoed in the cave.

"Nice work Mr. and Mrs. K. Need help carrying it out? We've got backpacks."

Safiya gasped. "That's Alejandro."

"Figures. Let's hope they can't be bothered to search for us."

"I don't think Alejandro would allow the Kilgours kill us."

"We're not important, Saf. Treasure fever does strange things to people."

As if to prove his point Alejandro spoke again. "Where are your hostages? We can't risk anyone reporting us to authorities."

"Shit." Joanne's curse echoed through the cave. "They must have run off into one of the tunnels. It could take hours to find them."

"It could take days," added Sebastian. "It's not worth our time. We need to get the treasure and leave these waters. We'll blow the tunnel up once we are clear of the cliff. Paul, do you have enough fuse if we leave a bundle of dynamite in this cave?"

"Yes."

"Good, we will entomb them and the boy."

Safiya shuddered against Ryan's chest.

"What if there's another way out," called Paul.

"Highly unlikely," answered Alejandro. "Now hurry, we can divide the treasure once we get back to the marina, then Sebastian and me are heading for Tahiti."

"What about us?" Joanne's shrill cry had Ryan cringing. "We should go with you."

"If you were to disappear straight away, it would draw too much attention. Leave it a month then sell up and go wherever you want."

"What should we do," whispered Safiya. "We need to find Josh and I don't want to be buried in here."

"Josh is right behind us. I followed his footprints in here and heard him shuffle back further. There is another way out, but it's going to be tricky, and we will have to move quickly."

Ryan held Safiya against his chest, stroking her spine as he listened to the Kilgours and Oliveira brothers gather up a treasure he'd lost interest in long ago.

Once the cave went quiet, Ryan crept to the tunnel's entrance. He switched off his flashlight and glanced around. A ball of daylight shone low on one side of the boulders.

"Yes." Flicking the beam on again, he picked up a rock as big as his hand. Satisfied it was heavy enough, he undid his Prusik loop and tied the cord around the rock then lowered it into the water, feeding out the rope as the rock sank. He ran out of rope before the rock hit bottom. Zane would have loved this. They'd have come back with scuba gear and flashlights to search. God only knew what was lying on the bottom.

Safiya and Josh were standing at the tunnel's entrance, holding hands as they watched him. He retrieved the rope then carefully made his way along the edge of the water toward the gap of light he'd seen. If he could make the gap wider, without any rocks falling, he could hopefully get Safiya and Josh out before Kilgour lit the fuse. He would have preferred to follow the group up through the tunnel system and pull the fuse out of the dynamite but it would be impossible without using his flashlight.

Seventeen minutes later, sweating like he'd run a marathon with a full pack, Ryan stood back and rolled his shoulders. Josh was breathing hard and just as sweaty.

The tide had started trickling in, but with luck they'd all get out without drowning. Ryan threw his rope harness aside. The last thing he needed was to get snagged, unable to free themselves. He looked to Safiya and Josh, pleased to see they'd discarded their harnesses too. Safiya had also taken off the sling but held her hand to her chest, verifying the pain he thought she had to be enduring. He could detect no sign of distress or panic. A gutsy woman, ready to do whatever it took to gain freedom. She'd fit right in with the other Steele Ops ladies. Josh stood beside her, as white as a sheet, chewing on his fingernails.

Ryan wrapped one end of the slim cord around Safiya's waist and tied a double bowline knot. "I'm going to keep you close so the cord doesn't get caught on rocks." He withdrew the file he'd hidden in his runner and cut through the cord then tied the end around his own waist. "I'll lead the way, give two tugs if you get stuck but until the tide comes in fully, we shouldn't have to put our heads under. Use the rocks to help pull yourself along. Josh, I want you to stay close behind Safiya and help her if she needs it."

"What if we can't get through?" Josh's voice shook as he stared at the gap they'd made.

"Don't worry, I noticed an eagle drone that belongs to my team's robotics engineer. If we have to come back into the cave, she knows where to start looking for us. My team will move heaven and earth to get us out. I'm fairly sure we can make it, but it may get tight. I'll assess things as we go."

"I trust you and I'll be right behind you." Safiya stretched up and kissed him quickly. "That's for good luck. I'll give you a proper kiss when you get us safely back to town."

He chuckled. "I'm counting on it." He helped her down into the pool then began the process of gripping moss-covered rocks as he worked his way along the narrow, enclosed channel of freezing water.

CHAPTER TWENTY-SIX

Tariq Farid ended the alarming call from his son and pushed his breakfast aside, his appetite destroyed. Fear gripped his soul as he looked across the table at his beloved wife, grimacing at the apprehension in her beautiful blue eyes. There'd be no sugar-coating Zakour's bombshell.

"Safiya and Ryan Dutch have been kidnapped and are being held on a fishing trawler anchored in an isolated bay of Currawong Island."

"Tariq." She clasped a shaking hand over her mouth. "Why?"

"Zakour said Jarred Steele thinks it's tied up with a treasure that likely doesn't exist." Tariq waved one of his new security guards over. "Stryker, please inform Captain Merrick we have a Code Blue. He needs to get us to Currawong Island as fast as possible. We may need to block or chase a fishing trawler. I'll also require Miss Blackett to ready the helicopter in case your team are needed to retrieve my daughter. You should be armed."

"Yes, sir."

Tariq's guilt threatened to engulf him. They were so close to making things right with Safiya. To lose her would destroy them. He reached over the table and took Dana's hand.

"Zakour assures me Jarred Steele and his men have the trawler under surveillance." He wasn't going to tell her about the couple holding Safiya. Treasure Hunters wanted by Interpol would be extremely dangerous if cornered. It would only add pressure to the suffocating guilt Dana felt for neglecting Safiya.

"We must trust Jarred Steele's people will rescue our precious daughter, and if they need back up, our crew are on hand to assist." The five ex-Navy Seals had come highly recommended after opting out of Special Forces to try a life at sea for a year or two. Miss Blackett had been a Night Stalker pilot. As luck would have it, they'd all been looking for a laid-back pace of life, just as he decided to take his wife and daughter on a cruise around the world.

Tariq hadn't blinked at the cost of hiring five Navy Seals and the Night Stalker for twelve months. He required trustworthy, trained personnel to join the crew of his super yacht and keep everyone onboard safe.

As the yacht surged to maximum speed, Tariq squeezed Dana's fingers. "Zakour insists Ryan Dutch is a man of strength and courage. He rejected my deal and stood up for Safiya. He is aware of the huge disparity in their backgrounds; however, I believe him an honest and proud man. He insists he loves Safiya and doesn't want a handout. If that is true, he will move heaven and earth to keep her safe."

"As you did with me, Tariq." She stood and came around the table, waiting for him to push his chair back so she could sit across his thighs. "You resisted me a long while."

"Ah, but while resisting you, I still spent most days with you by my side, darling. Right up to that ball in the Presidential Palace. It was impossible to ignore your sparkling eyes and the way you fit perfectly in my arms when we danced." He flicked her nose. "That you did not return my interest, annoyed me greatly, as did the many men vying to dance with you. Rescuing you from that lecherous ambassador was an honor. That he meant to kidnap you is something he'll never live down and has paid greatly for. I can only thank Allah I went searching for you and heard your scream. I still shudder at what could have transpired."

She frowned. "It took courage to accuse us of undervaluing Safiya's intelligence and neglecting her."

He sighed. "It shames me to realize our daughter is far more intelligent than we gave her credit for."

"Yes, which reminds me. I want to show you something." Dana scooted off his thighs and padded bare foot into the saloon. Several minutes later she returned and once comfortable, handed him a journal. "I found this hidden in Safiya's suite. It's a diary depicting the unpleasant events through her life, her achievements and most recently, the two happiest days of her life. Meeting Ryan in February and dancing with him at his friend's wedding in April."

Tariq flicked through the private journal. Stopping every so often to read one of the three languages he understood. His throat tightened. "Dana, I had no idea."

"Neither did I. It is extremely upsetting and yet she lives in hope of our approval." Dana wiped away her tears. "Safiya's grasp of languages is exceptional."

"I am ashamed, Dana. What else don't we know about our daughter?"

She dropped her head on his shoulder and hugged him. "I don't ever regret marrying you, Tariq. You are my heart, and we did our best to protect our children, but I should have stayed in Switzerland with Safiya. She isn't like Zakour."

"It would have drawn my family's and enemy's attention if I were continually flying to Switzerland to see you. We did what we thought best. The past can't be changed; however, with the help of Allah, we will have a second chance to make things right with Safiya."

Dana sat up then raised her hands to hold his face gently. "We must let her live her life as she wishes, and hope she allows us to be part of it."

"Yes, and if anyone can keep her safe, it's that young man."

Aware the six Americans had stepped onto the deck; Tariq kissed his wife's forehead then eased her off his thighs. "I need to speak to these men and Miss Blackett. With Allah's blessing, we will arrive at Currawong Island to find Safiya her normal feisty self."

"Please God." Dana clutched his hand then turned to the petite woman and five silent men. "Whatever you can do to assist in the safe rescue of our daughter would be appreciated."

Miss Blackett smiled, but not a flicker of emotion touched the men's faces as they waited for Dana to enter the saloon, before turning their gazes on Tariq.

He indicated they take seats on the outdoor lounge then followed. He'd read each of their files before hiring them, which were impressive. Meeting the men in person had left him reeling. He'd never been intimidated by any man, other than Jarred Steele, until that day. All were close to or over six-feet, broad shouldered and muscular. Each carried an air of menace and power. Yet over the last two weeks he'd found the men polite and obliging, especially to his precious wife and daughter. With these men and the highly skilled Miss Blackett ready to rescue Safiya, she had a better chance of survival then most kidnapped victims. He could only pray it was enough.

CHAPTER TWENTY-SEVEN

Safiya had never experienced claustrophobia until now, and it sucked. Struggling along against the incoming tide, surrounded by heavy boulders that could shift at any minute wasn't for the faint hearted. The second the dynamite exploded, the earth would tremble, rocks would fall, and they could easily be crushed, trapped, or drown. She also had to keep her mouth shut and breath through her nose, holding her breath as the incoming tide smacked into her face.

They only had five or six inches of air above their heads and if that got much lower, they'd have to dive under water and hope they could hold their breath long enough to reach the ocean. Smashing waves against deadly rocks awaited them. Their only other choice was to return to the cave and hope Ryan's team could arrange for them to be dug out. It could take days.

Her head and shoulder continued to pound, like someone was poking them with sharp sticks, making her nauseous, but Ryan had enough to worry about. At least the freezing water kept her from passing out.

She kept kicking her feet and dragging herself along the rocks, trying to take some of load off Ryan. Thankfully, they were moving through the narrow passage relatively fast. She prayed Bill had got off the trawler and made it out of the bay. She hadn't heard the inflatable's engine, but Ryan had assured her it had one and they wouldn't hear it inside the mountain.

Ryan's broad shoulders blocked the way ahead. He turned, catching her in his arms, his face solemn. "Sea water is pouring around a boulder that's blocking our way. We're really close as the waves are crashing against the rock on the other side. I'm going to dive under and see if we can get through. I'll be ten seconds."

Safiya clung to his shoulder, trying not to panic. "I'd rather take my chances and come with you. Don't leave me."

He grimaced then exhaled. "Okay. Josh, follow us through and grab onto anything you can then get out quickly but try not to be seen."

"I will."

Ryan wrapped Safiya's fingers around the cord at his waist. "Hold on tight and don't let go. The closer we are the better. You'll be under me when we dive, but it's safer then above."

"I'm ready." She gripped the cord and took a breath. Instantly her ears filled with a roar that obliterated everything. She kicked hard, fighting through foam, and battering waves, to finally daylight above the surface. Her heart raced. They'd escaped, but to what?

Ryan held her in one arm as they surfaced and were promptly thrown against a rock. He grunted at the impact but grasped her and the rock firmly. She clung to him, trying to breathe through the excruciating pain in her right knee.

As the wave receded, Ryan hauled her up out of the water and away from the incoming waves. Lashing rain made it hard to see, but she hobbled along beside him as best she could. They were on the far side of the large boulders under Morcago Ledge.

Josh staggered over to them, blood dripping from a cut on his arm. They'd made it. She'd never been so thankful in her life.

Indignation welled. She wasn't a violent person, yet right this minute, she could easily take a baseball bat to the Oliveira brothers and the Kilgours without losing a moment's sleep. How dare they bash an old man and an innocent boy. How dare they blow up sacred drawings by the original custodians of this island. How dare they knock her out, dislocate her shoulder and try to destroy her future. If there was ever an ideal time for karma to strike those bloody monsters, this was it.

She held on to Ryan's hand as he guided her onto a higher boulder. A series of nasty gashes down his back only fueled her anger.

Josh joined them as Ryan indicated they should crouch behind two vertical boulders and peep through to the rock ledge on the other side. She could see the trawler rolling with the waves, much more aggressively. As she watched, it smashed against the rocks.

"Damn." Ryan ran a hand over his head. "The rain is so thick I can't see if Bill got away."

"That's good. It means the Kilgours can't see him either," whispered Safiya.

"Where's Mr. and Mrs. Kilgour?" Josh crouched beside her, his gaze scouring the ledge.

She looked up to the crevice then along the rock ledge. "I don't know, but with luck, they've been washed out to sea."

"There!" Ryan pointed off the far end of the rocks, where a yacht listed on the waves. "It's the Oliveira's yacht and they're on board."

"Why didn't they blow up the cave?" Safiya looked up at the cliff face. "I see a yellow cord. Is that the fuse?"

"Detonating cord." Ryan scoffed. "It must have got wet, or the flame fizzled out."

A loud boom sent them lurching back. Thankfully, Ryan cushioned Safiya's fall. "Was that the cave?"

He shook his head. "The trawler."

She peered through the gap to see the trawler lurching to one side. Flames engulfed the interior.

"My God." Safiya clung to Ryan as she prayed Bill had escaped.

Several gun shots rang out then a long blast of what sounded like a machine gun. "Who is shooting?" yelled Josh.

"Could be my team." Ryan peeked over the boulder. "The rain is clearing a little. I can see a yacht motoring toward us, between Seal Rock and South Point.

A far-off horn blasted three times. Ryan squinted. "That came from a bigger yacht, further out."

Safiya rose slowly and stared across Shark Bite Bay. Her spirits lifted. The *Francine* surged across the bay. Help had arrived.

Tatatatatatatatatatatatatat.

She ducked down again at the blast of gun fire. "What are they shooting at?"

"Shit. Bill is rowing the tender one-handed. Paul and Joanne Kilgour are shooting at him. My team is shooting at them." Ryan leaped from rock to rock, making for the furthest point, Josh on his heels.

Safiya carefully followed, cringing at how low the trawler had sunk. Waves battered the portside of the hull, washing over the deck. As she watched, it sank out of sight.

Biting down on her lower lip, she clambered over the rocks, ducking behind a rock when more gunfire echoed round the bay.

Water washed over her feet. The tide was coming in. They needed to get off these treacherous rocks quickly. Another ten minutes and there'd be nowhere to go.

A cloud of churning white foam surge from the stern of the *Sea Sprite* as its engines powered up. They were escaping.

"It doesn't matter." Safiya looked for Bill, crying out when she found him floundering in the water. His inflatable had been shot. The *Francine* had almost reached him but would they be in time. She couldn't tear her gaze away, willing Bill to hang on for another minute. As she watched the Francine surged forward then a man dived into the water, ploughing through the waves to Bill. "Thank God." She sank to her knees, too relieved to worry about the blood seeping from a cut on her knee. A life buoy crashed into her hip.

"Safiya, get down." Ryan's shout snapped her attention to the *Sea Sprite*. She stared in horror at Joanne and Paul Kilgour holding rifles aimed at the rocks. There was nowhere to hide. They were sitting ducks. She flinched as several gunshots rang out. A bullet hit the rocks to Safiya's left, spurring her to action. She dropped to her chest and stayed as low as possible, holding the life buoy in front of her and flinching every time a shot rang out. She screamed when a bullet hit the buoy.

"Stay down, Safiya, I'm coming," yelled Ryan.

"No!" She peeped under the buoy. "I'm okay."

He kept coming then fell forward, grunting. An outgoing wave swept him off the rocks.

"No!" She screamed and jumped into the water, using the lifebuoy for balance as she kicked toward Ryan's lifeless body, floating face down in the water. "No, please don't die. I love you." Tears streamed down her face as she kicked and sobbed. More automatic fire rang out as the incoming swell washed over her. She choked on a mouthful of salty water.

"Ugh." She held onto the buoy with her injured arm, moaning through the pain to reach for Ryan. She wrapped her arm around his neck and rolled him as an outgoing wash swept them away from the rocks. Even with the waves smashing against the rocks, the howling wind, and drenching rain, she could hear her heart hammering in her ears.

With each kick, staggering pain shot through her knee. Sobbing and in agony, she hooked two of the lifebuoy's ropes over Ryan's arms, pulling them up to his shoulders then dragged down on another, pulling his head up on the buoy. It was the only thing she could think of to keep him afloat.

Fear and relief swamped her at the amount of blood trickling from a wound above Ryan's left ear. It wouldn't be flowing if his heart weren't pumping, yet all this blood in the water would attract the sharks this bay was famous for. Getting a grip on herself, Safiya clasped Ryan's jaw and pinch his nose then began blowing air into his mouth. He hadn't been face-down long, but she knew she had to get air into his lungs.

Seeing the *Francine* closing in gave her hope. She continued pushing breath into Ryan even when a fin with a white tip appeared several meters away. It was quickly followed by a much larger gray fin. The second shark cruised past, close enough for her to see a cold black eye before going under.

Cold dread almost overwhelmed her as the shark with a white tip circled again, so close she could have reached out and touched it. Her heart almost stopped. Before she could work herself into a full-blown panic, a dolphin popped up causing her to scream. The dolphin clicked loudly then plunged underwater. Within seconds a pod of dolphins had surrounded Safiya and Ryan, continually circling as they gracefully rose and dived.

Thankful for their presence, she went back to blowing air into Ryan's mouth. Out of her peripheral vision, Safiya saw several dolphins soar into the air before plunging into the water. She couldn't believe her eyes, yet they seemed intent on keeping the sharks away with their aerobatic display. One dolphin stayed close, gliding up to nudge Ryan with its nose several times.

Ryan suddenly spluttered, coughing up a heap of water. "Safiya?"

"I'm here." She held on to him as his torso and legs sank.

He focused on her then hauled in several breaths, coughed again then raised a hand to his head. "Safiya, I didn't think I'd ever see you again. Fuck. Are you okay?"

She clutched his hand, unable to hold back the tears. "Yes, but you've been shot."

He winced then looked around. "You saved my life."

"We saved each other's lives."

"Where's Bill?"

"I think one of your friends rescued him, but I'm not positive."

"What's behind my head?" asked Ryan.

"A lifebuoy. It's keeping you from sinking."

"My guardian angel." He kissed her forehead. "I'm so proud of you, Safiya-Ameerah. You really are one in a million."

"Yes, I am." She would have said more, except a loud clanging distracted her. Glancing behind, her soul soared as a huge anchor and chain plonked into the water. Safiya looked up to see Zoe, Madeline and most of Ryan's friends leaning over the railing. Three men dived into the water, reaching her and Ryan in seconds. She'd never been happier to hand Ryan into the capable hands of Talos and Nick, so they could get him out of the water, and still the dolphins kept circling.

Jarred's arms came around Safiya. "You have our gratitude, Safiya. Ryan would have drowned without you. If there's anything you ever want or need, you only have to ask."

"I'll think of something." She winced as he moved her right arm.

"Let's get you onboard and deal with that head wound. Are you hurt anywhere else?"

"Ryan fixed my dislocated shoulder, but it's on fire and my knee took a hammering when I got slammed into rocks."

"You're an amazing woman, Safiya. I'd be honored to have you join the Special Operations unit of Steele Security. Our team could do with a linguistic specialist. He turned her then drew her gently against his chest, swimming backward toward the yacht's step ladder.

Wow. Her heart swelled with happiness. Finally, people appreciated her. Valued her.

As they reached the back of the charter boat, Talos and Simon helped lift her as gently as they could from Jarred's arms. It still wrenched a scream from her throat.

Once on deck, she grimaced at the bloody gash in her knee. She appreciated Talos carrying her to a cushioned bench in the galley. "What about Josh?"

"Sam will pick him up in the tender," assured Talos. "There's an inlet on the other side of Morcago Ledge where it's safer to land."

By the powerful aroma wafting through the galley, Darius and Madeline were dabbing antiseptic cream onto Ryan's head and back as he leaned against the sink. She wished she could see his face.

Sergeant Hawthorne stood beside Bill at the other end of the bench, notebook in hand and scribbling like crazy as Bill sat back and told his story. His broken wrist had been placed in a sling, and a bandage taped around his head. He held up his precious diary and gave her a wink before continuing with his story.

The beautiful German Shepherd sat by Ryan's feet, staring up at him with adoration.

Jarred sank to his haunches in front of Safiya. "As our medic is otherwise occupied, I'll clean up your knee and head then put your arm in a sling."

"Are you sure Ryan's okay. They shot him in the head." Safiya struggled to get the words out without crying. Even though her head, shoulder, and knee pounded in agony, she had an overwhelming need to be certain. Her brain and body seemed to be shutting down, but she fought to stay focused. "He wasn't breathing." She clutched at Jarred's arm. "I thought he was dead."

"She's exhausted and going into shock." Ryan was suddenly sitting beside her, gently drawing her against his bare chest. He lifted her chin until she had no choice but to meet his eyes. "Listen to me, Safiya. The bullet barely grazed my skull. I'll have a headache for a day or two, but that's all."

"Your back?"

"What's a few stitches? You saved me from drowning, which would have been worse than a headache and stitches. I'm fine, sweetheart."

"Your heart was pumping, but I knew I had to make you breathe." A sob escaped Safiya. "Then the sharks arrived, and the *Francine* was so far away."

"Safiya, listen. Bill and I are okay." He stroked her cheek. "I need to check your injuries for myself."

"I hurt all over." She melted into him, so very, very tired.

"Lean back against the cushion and rest while I clean up your knee."

"Okay." She did as he asked, dozing as Ryan and Jarred tended to her injuries.

"That will do until we get you to the hospital." Ryan kissed her head. "I meant what I said, Saf. You're an amazing woman and ... I love you."

"Pardon?" Had he just said what she thought he'd said, or had she dreamed it?

"I love you, Safiya-Ameerah."

"I love you too." Tears welled, but she fought them back. It had finally happened. Ryan loved her, but what did that mean long term?

"Now that you've cleared your name, will you move back to Curra-wong Island?"

He hesitated. "I love working with these guys, Saf. We're a team, but we're also best friends. My life is in Sydney, but I'm open to a holiday house here." He took a deep breath. "If that doesn't appeal to you, I guess I could start up my charter business on Curra."

She could see his heart wasn't in it, but no one had ever offered to change their life for her. There was one more thing she needed to know. "Did Jarred send you to Currawong Island to spy on me?"

"No. I swear I didn't even know we'd been hired to watch you. When I found out, I didn't know how to tell you. I was terrified you wouldn't believe me. That you'd leave me."

She smiled. "I'll never leave you. Jarred offered me a job with Steele Security. Plus, I know your friends and their partners are your family, so it would be silly not to accept. We should stay in Sydney."

He smiled. "I'll build you a beautiful holiday house here. We can visit Bill and Zoe regularly and see how things pan out."

"After surviving treasure hunters, bullets and sharks, I think that's a grand idea."

"I've got more good news," announced Sergeant Hawthorne. "That fancy yacht out there has cut off the *Sea Sprite's* escape. I've had a report the Kilgours are wounded, but it's not life-threatening."

Ryan grunted. "They deserve to spend the rest of their lives in prison. What about the Oliveira brothers?"

"They're responsible for wounding the Kilgours." Jarred caught and held Safiya's gaze. "Simon has a program that identifies people if they have any form of documented identification. He discovered the Kilgours are wanted for stealing artifacts from a treasure hunting expedition off Morocco. He also discovered the Oliveira brothers were on the same expedition and work for a branch of the Spanish Government, fighting against looting of precious artefacts belonging to Spain. Your brother contacted their department and was told that Alejandro and Sebastian had tracked the Kilgours to this island after items they'd stolen from the Moroccan expedition were put up for sale. The Kilgours face a string of serious crimes. Where they serve their sentences is something the Federal Police will have to sort out with Spanish authorities."

Ryan raised an eyebrow. "That's why Alejandro talked the Kilgours into leaving us in the cave. I assume he did something to sabotage the dynamite too."

"Dynamite?" Jarred frowned.

"Yeah, the Kilgours were all for blowing up the cave and burying us inside it."

Safiya smiled. "The fuse didn't ignite. I'm glad Alejandro and Sebastian aren't bad guys, but if they were all on the original expedition, wouldn't the Kilgours recognize Alejandro and Sebastian?"

"Yes, that was the intention. They wanted the Kilgours to recognize them. Then they were to offer the Kilgours a deal to avoid extradition. It was done in hope of unearthing the rest of the items they stole from the Moroccan expedition. The Oliveira brothers hadn't counted on unearthing another Spanish treasure on Currawong, but decided if there was one, they'd claim it for their country. That will all have to be figured out with the Australian authorities."

"Where is the Sea Sprite now," asked Ryan.

Jarred's lips twitched. "It was boarded by the crew of the super yacht that intercepted it and is now on its way back to Dugong Marina. Senior Inspector Gibbs isn't taking any chances."

Safiya's pulse picked up. "Crew of what super yacht?"

"Your father's." Madeline pointed out the window opposite. "They were firing automatic weapons at the *Sea Sprite*, distracting the Kilgours from shooting at you."

Safiya stared at the sleek turquoise and white yacht, anchored off Shark Bite Bay. She had to admit, it was an impressive sight, sitting four levels above seawater with a helicopter perched on the top level, yet the life of a billionaire's daughter wasn't for her. She'd be happy in a pretty white cottage with a garden and a dog, as long as Ryan lived there too.

Everyone seemed to be holding their breath, waiting for her to react. She thought about the text from her mother, and what Madeline had discovered. It was time to forgive and move on. She smiled at

Ryan. "Once they know I'm safe, they'll probably cruise on to New Zealand, but I'd like them to stay for a few days to get to know you and Zoe and Bill and Frankie and your friends."

"I'd like that too." Ryan got down on one knee. "Safiya-Ameerah Farid, I know this is sudden and we haven't spent a lot of time together, but I love you. Will you do me the great honor of becoming my fiancée, then one day soon, my wife, my partner, and the mother of our children?"

"Oh, Ryan. Yes. I love you so much." She wanted to fall into his arms, but she couldn't take any more pain. Instead, she leaned forward and kissed him.

Ryan took her hand and raised it to his lips. "I don't want to rush you, but the sooner we're married the better."

"I agree, my love, but I suggest we wait until our injuries have healed."

"Whatever you want, sweetheart."

"I'll be watching my letterbox for the wedding invitation," called Bill. "Not every day a man's only son marries a brave and beautiful young lady."

Safiya looked across to Bill's tear-filled eyes. "Thank you, Bill."

Ryan got to his feet. He squeezed her fingers then released her to walk across to Bill. "I love you, Bill."

They hugged each other and held on for ages.

Tears ran down Safiya's face. She noticed Darius wiping her cheeks and several men cleared their throats. Madeline turned into Jarred's chest and after a slight hesitation he wrapped his arms around her. They looked so right together, Safiya couldn't help but wonder what their futures held.

Someone started clapping then cheers and laughter broke out. It melted Safiya's heart. She would start a new journal and fill it with the happiest moments of her life.

EPILOGUE

Cloaked in a contentment he couldn't hope to describe, Ryan jumped off the wharf and joined Simon. They strolled over the warm sand of Dutchies Beach in companionable silence. Their friends and loved ones were relaxing at the other end, appreciating the warm weather and each other's company. Even his adoptive parents and grandparents were enjoying themselves.

Safiya lay on a towel under a green striped umbrella where he'd left her. He chuckled. *Probably catching up on some well-earned sleep.*

Yesterday had been filled with rivalry, laughter, and happiness, starting with a beach workout then an impromptu game of soccer between the Steele Ops boys and the Sheikh's security team, all ex-Navy seals, aided by Garcia to even things up. It had been physical, rough, and intense. Luckily, the ladies and children had been otherwise occupied, splashing about in the yacht's pool, and getting ready for the wedding.

Sporting more than a few bruises, Ryan had returned to Aunty Frankie's House with his mates to clean up and dress, before they made their way to the turquoise and white yacht, so he could marry the woman who made every day brighter.

When Safiya had emerged from the yacht's saloon holding her

father's arm, Ryan's heart soared. She'd chosen a creamy, lace dress with tiny straps that hugged her curves, and she wore her hair up in soft curls. They'd married in front of friends, family, and the Sheikh's crew on the largest of the sundecks.

With a slight breeze and the sun's warmth that could only be found in the tropics of Northern Queensland this time of year, they'd made their vows to cherish, love, respect and honor each other. After the ceremony, they'd sat down in the formal dining room to a sumptuous feast, prepared by the yacht's chef and her assistant, who the seal crew referred to as the Black Rose. Discovering Rose Blackett had been a Night Stalker awed the Steele Ops boys, especially Ryan and Nick. The USA's Night Stalkers belonged to the Special Operations Aviation Regiment. These chopper pilots were the best of the best.

The rest of the day had been spent enjoying the Sheikh and Dana Farid's hospitality, and the yacht's amenities, dancing on the largest deck, and then another fabulous meal, before Ryan and Safiya sneaked off to her stateroom to spend their first night together as a married couple.

It was unreal to think nine weeks has passed since he'd returned to Currawong to check on Zoe and clear his name. He'd been full of apprehension stepping off the wharf, onto this same beach, expecting to be shunned or ignored. Then to discover Safiya here. He could only thank his lucky star fate had smiled on them. He still occasionally woke in a sweat, dreaming she'd blown up on the trawler or drowned. Safiya's warm body beside him mostly kept nightmares at bay.

Zac Gibbs and a team of Federal Police officers had taken custody of the Kilgours once they'd been treated at the medical center. They'd been reprimanded and would face a Brisbane court later in the year. The five other treasure hunters had been taken to the mainland, interviewed and deported. Alejandro and Sebastian Oliveira were escorting the Spanish treasure back to their homeland, although a handful of gold sovereigns and a chalice had been presented to Curra's museum. It wasn't proof the Spanish had discovered Australia first, but it was possible.

Curra's people had never experienced such excitement, although everyone seemed pleased when things returned to normal. Best of all, the saber had been returned to Bill by Sergeant Hawthorne, after he'd found it hidden in the Kilgours house. Bill's quick thinking had saved his great-grandfather's diary and would now be displayed in the museum, along with the saber.

The Island's council held a huge feast, inviting everyone to celebrate Bill's return and to thank those involved in the rescue. Safiya, Ryan's team and Garcia had all been made honorary citizens of Currawong, which meant they could legally own land on the island. The boys had talked about it and decided they'd each buy adjoining blocks at Whale Point. Garcia immediately bought the old church Zoe loved and planned to renovate it for her. The two were now engaged.

During the two weeks Ryan had stayed on the island with Aunty Frankie and Bill, Safiya had gone off with her parents to mend bridges and heal. Ryan spent the time renewing old friendships and repairing the relationship with his adoptive parents and grandparents.

Slowing to appreciate the laughter of his friend's children as they ran back and forth with buckets of water to fill their moat, Ryan grinned at their innocent delight, his heart swelled with anticipation of bringing his own children here one day.

He'd visited Zane's grave with Tommy. They'd shed a few tears for the friend who'd made their childhood such an adventure. Cammy was finally getting her dream. She'd taken over the Angler's Point Café, which was now known as Cammy's Café by the Sea.

"You okay, mate." Simon's question snapped Ryan back to the present.

"Yeah, just thanking my lucky star for all I have. It's mind boggling."

"I know. Who'd have thought all those weeks ago at that Gala, you and Safiya would end up married nine weeks later."

"Tell me about it. How's the plans coming along for your wedding?"

"Darius and our mothers have it under control. If I had my way, we'd elope, but both our families would be crushed. Mamma has convinced Darius to have a typical Italian wedding with all the bells and whistles in late September."

"September?" Ryan laughed. "I feel for you, mate."

"Thanks. Hey, I looked into those two guys who humiliated Safiya at Uni."

Ryan stopped walking altogether. "Go on."

"Ian Hudson hasn't work security since. He's been blacklisted by the AFP and can't apply for a security license. The blackmailer, Jason Clarke was never paid off by the Sheikh. However, he did end up in hospital after a severe beating around that time."

"Don't you love karma." Ryan's gaze wandered to Tommy, Sam, Nick and Talos, who had built a fabulous sand fort for the kids, although, who was getting more enjoyment out of it was a toss-up.

"Yeah, I do." Simon clapped him on the shoulder. "Gotta go help my girl out of the water. Enjoy your honeymoon." He walked into the shallow water and caught Darius as she staggered about, trying to get her flippers off without falling.

Ryan laughed. It reminded him of Safiya the first day she'd arrived on the island, falling about in her leopard skin bikini. He started forward again.

Under the shade of a portable gazebo, the Steele Ops ladies and Camilla chatted away, as they watched over a sleeping baby and the antics of the men and children.

Bill and Aunty Frankie lay snoozing on deck chairs under another umbrella, worn out from yesterday's excitement. Having a second chance with Bill meant the world to Ryan. They'd talked about his biological mother, and the hidden cave. One day down the track Ryan, Tommy and the boys would take a closer look.

Ryan glanced out over the ocean as the Sheikh's crew winched the speedboat into the hull of the spectacular yacht. Safiya's parents were headed to the Cook Islands to continue their world cruise. They'd appreciated the two weeks with their daughter, taking her round New Zealand and showering her in attention, before cruising back to Curra to collect Ryan.

On the trip to Sydney, he'd gotten to know them. Understanding the perils and threats they'd protected Safiya against went a long way to forgiving them for overlooking and undervaluing her. Hearing Jamal Al-Saad had returned to London and accepted an arranged marriage had been the icing on the cake.

A deep chuckle drew Ryan's attention to Jarred, sitting beside Madeline in the shallow water where she played with Jane's eight-month-old daughter. Jarred kept shooing flies away from little Ella. She kept trying to catch his fingers.

Madeline had written an enchanting article about Safiya for a popular magazine. There had been one photo of Safiya with her parents and another with Ryan, cleverly positioned to hide most of his face. In the article, Madeline described the lengths the Sheikh had gone to give Safiya a normal and safe life. She emphasized how proud the Sheikh and his wife were of their daughter. How happy they were to officially announce her engagement to a humble man who'd served his country as a Black Hawk pilot, with honor and heroism.

Ryan returned Madeline's wave and continued his course. Safiya hadn't moved. He had to smile. She'd hugged her parents then waved them off at the wharf, before succumbing to an afternoon siesta under an umbrella.

He reflected on the last few weeks. They'd been wonderful. No, sensational. Coming home to Safiya's stunning smile, kisses, and passionate hugs. She cooked like a professional chef yet had no problem stepping aside so he could do his share of the cooking. Sometimes they cooked together, which was often interrupted by a bout of lovemaking. He'd never been so happy or eaten so well in his life.

They made love most nights then cuddle until sleep claimed them. Ryan couldn't be happier for Safiya. She loved her job as a linguist and helping Darius in the robotics lab. Once a week, Madeline, and the Steele Ops ladies, as they liked to be known, met for lunch. Jarred had surprised Ryan and the boys by installing an indoor swimming pool, basketball court and gym at the new Steele Security headquarters, which they took full advantage of.

They'd made a pact to meet twice a month for a game of golf, or to go surfing, or a strenuous hike. It didn't matter what they did, as long as they got together for some male bonding.

The success of their last five major missions has set Steele Security up for a bright future. Jarred had tripled his security guard staff and hired two more office personnel. Their new headquarters could also house their van, the Blackhawk, and a small chopper.

The Steele Ops ladies insisted everyone get together once a month for family fun. It might be in a park, on a beach or at one of their homes. Ryan wasn't surprised, Jarred and Madeline had readily agreed to join them. It was always a good day.

"Whatcha doin', handsome." Safiya sat up and lowered her sunglass, peeping over them at him. "You're looking rather pensive for a man who got married yesterday."

He laughed and held out his hand. "I'm just appreciating how lucky I am, sweetheart." He pulled her up and into his arms then kissed her lightly, conscious they had an audience of grinning women close by. "I wondered if you'd like a nap."

She giggled. "If I look tired, it's because you kept me up all night."

"You look beautiful, as always, yet I'm sure you could do with a lie down." He wriggled his eyebrows. "With your husband."

"Ah, now that you mention it, I think a *rest* would do us both the world of good."

Holding hands, they ambled toward the steps leading up to their small cabin, ignoring the giggles and innuendos aimed at them.

Ryan raised their joined hands then kissed the back of Safiya's. "I love you, Safiya-Ameerah Dutch."

"And I love *you*, darling."

ABOUT THE STEELE OPS SERIES

Steele Ops is a romantic suspense series set in Australia, Vietnam, and Europe. The team of six ex-Special Force soldiers now work for Steele Security. Their job is to defend, protect and retrieve the vulnerable, with the odd covert mission thrown in. These brothers in arms are somewhat cynical and hardened by their experiences. Commitment is not on the agenda. At least it wasn't until one by one, they are captivated by attractive, courageous and enthralling women.

PREVIEW - STEELE JUSTICE

The last two days had been most enjoyable. Surprisingly warm for the middle of July, although they *were* in the tropics of Northern Queensland. Jarred leaned back on his hands, watching Madeline dip Ella's toes in the water as they played under a striped umbrella at the water's edge. She'd make a great mother, if her inconsiderate husband got his head out of his ass and gave her a child or two.

The baby babbled away in her own language, kicking at the water as she gripped the edge of Madeline's bikini bra in one chubby hand. It would be a miracle if she didn't expose the glorious bounty under her fingers.

Where the hell was Madeline's husband? He paid Jarred a fortune to keep her safe, while he lived in Vietnam, running his multi-million-dollar software company, and overseeing the rescue of vulnerable girls and children. It was a worthy cause, but damn it, what about his wife?

If she'd been single, Jarred would have made a move on her six months ago, when he'd walked in on her in *his* bathroom. Hell, he'd never forget the sight of her naked. She frustrated and unnerved him. She drove him crazy with a need to have her naked beneath him, over him, or on her hands and knees in front of him. His attraction to her was off the Richter scale, yet the one thing he'd sworn never to do, was seduce a married woman. He would not follow in his father's deceitful footsteps. The humiliation Jarred had suffered as a teenager, along with his mother and sister was never far from his mind. They'd lost their closest friends.

All that aside, Madeline drove him nuts, worrying about her safety and who wanted her dead. Over the last six months, she'd put her own life at risk to assist him and his team. When things had gone wrong, she'd turned to him for comfort. Each time they touched; it wore his resistance down another notch.

Madeline laughed and the soft, husky sound went straight to his groin. *I will not become my father.*

"Hey, boss." Simon waved Jarred over. "Got a minute?"

"Certainly." Jarred strode over to Simon, well away from Madeline's exceptional hearing.

"You asked me to keep digging into Madeline's family and friends. I've found a couple of things that are ringing alarms."

"I'm listening." Jarred gave Simon his full attention.

"First off, Elliott Shaw has a million-dollar life insurance policy on Madeline."

"You're kidding?"

"Nope. To be fair, she's got one for him as well. If they both die, it all goes to Trang Huynh, Elliott's business partner."

"Interesting. What about Madeline's family?"

"She seldom visits them or her in-laws. Phone calls are rare and short."

Jarred stared out over the ocean. He'd had no idea she spent so much time alone. "Has there been any suspicious activity at her apartment block, since we installed the cameras?"

"No, but I got a lead on the men who tried to kidnap Madeline and Safiya at the Gala."

Jarred clenched his fists. "About time."

"The car they used was found dumped near a dockyard at Botany. I checked the surveillance cameras for that morning onward and found them three days later. Once I had their mug shots, I ran them through my program. All three are German and came up on ASIO's watch list."

"Why?" Jarred dreaded the answer but it could be the lead they needed.

"They're known to work for a Chinese underworld syndicate."

"Fuck."

A phone began chiming from a bag hanging under the striped umbrellas.

Madeline passed Ella to Talos and reached into the bag. "Hi, what's up?" She frowned. "Sorry, can you repeat that, the line is crackling?"

Jarred narrowed his eyes as Madeline stiffened. "That wasn't part of the agreement." She stared out to sea. "We had a deal. You promised." She looked down at her feet, her stance almost defeated as she exhaled. "When and where?" Another moment passed as she listened intently. "You've got to be kidding. I am not doing this anymore." She ended the call and sank to her knees. "Damn."

"What is it, Maddie?" Jarred crouched beside her. Tell me."

She blinked at him then forced the phoniest smile he'd ever seen. "It's nothing. My ... editor has a job he wants me to do. It's overseas .... He's insisting I'm the only one who can do it." Her gaze darted away.

"Bullshit." Jarred grabbed her wrists and pulled her to her feet, so he could look her in the eyes. "You work freelance. You can refuse any job you don't want. It was Elliott, wasn't it?"

Madeline tried to pull free. "It's nothing I can't handle."

"Really? Then why do you look as though you want to scream or cry?" Jarred drew her against his chest. "You may as well tell me, Madeline, because I won't let you out of my sight until you do."

Her lips quivered against his bare skin. "Looks like I'll be seeing a lot of you then."

ACKNOWLEDGMENTS

As always, my appreciation and heartfelt thanks to the wonderful people who helped me deliver another book I am proud of.

My friend and critique partner, S.E Gilchrist, who inspires and encourages me. I love our brain storming sessions.

Special thanks to my brilliant editor and friend Juanita Kees. She really kicked my butt with this book. Her guidance and professionalism are always appreciated.

Patti from Paradox Book Designs. This wonderful lady always listens and delivers covers I adore.

ABOUT THE AUTHOR

Erin Moira O'Hara grew up in the Blue Mountains of Australia, with a garden backing onto native bushland, hidden caves and fabulous lookouts. Weekends were spent exploring, climbing trees and creating secret bases. Her love of reading began with visits to the local library as a child, where she became absorbed in a world of intrigue, fantasy and action-packed adventures.

The moment Erin read her first romance; she was hooked and dreamed of her own hero and writing romantic adventures. She now lives close to Lake Macquarie, the largest, coastal, saltwater lake in Australia. The family home overlooks bushland and is surrounded by birds and an acre of ever-growing gardens. She shares this paradise with her husband, three eccentric hens, two spoilt cats and one adorable dog called Murphy-girl.

Erin's writing encompasses everything she loves best—intrigue, suspense, passion and romance.

Reviews are appreciated, as they help readers find books and increase a writer's visibility.

If you would like to know more about Erin Moira O'Hara, please visit her website. https://erinmoiraohara.com

.

www.ingramcontent.com/pod-product-compliance
Lightning Source LLC
Chambersburg PA
CBHW020344120726
47904CB00002B/440